THE PEENEMÜNDE DECEPTIONS

Peenemünde: windswept corner of the Third Reich and birthplace of the space age. Otto Fischer, a severely wounded Luftwaffe officer and former criminal investigator, is summoned to solve a seemingly incomprehensible case: the murder of a leading rocket engineer during a devastating air-raid. With only days until the SS assume control of the production of a remarkable new weapon, Fischer must find a motive and perpetrator from among several thousand scientists, technicians, soldiers and forced labourers. As he struggles to get the measure of the secretive world in which imagination moves far beyond the limits of technology, a solitary crime draws him into a labyrinth of conspiracy and treason.

THE PEENEMÜNDE DECEPTIONS

The Peenemünde Deceptions

by

Jim McDermott

Magna Large Print Books
Long Preston, North Yorkshire,
BD23 4ND, England.

British Library Cataloguing in Publication Data.

McDermott, Jim
    The Peenemünde deceptions

    A catalogue record of this book is
    available from the British Library

    ISBN   978-0-7505-3889-3

First published in Great Britain in 2013 by Claymore Press,
an imprint of Pen & Sword Books Ltd.

Copyright © Jim McDermott, 2013

Cover illustration © Benjamin Harte by arrangement with
Arcangel Images

Published in Large Print 2014 by arrangement with
Pen & Sword Books Ltd.

Magna Large Print is an imprint of Library Magna Books Ltd.

Printed and bound in Great Britain by
T.J. (International) Ltd., Cornwall, PL28 8RW

Chapter One

Tired, he pressed his face against the window and stared into the flat, colourless sea, following it out until he couldn't be sure that it wasn't sky. A familiar horizon: playful, shy, almost always a matter of guessing where one thing became another, where breathing became drowning.

The Baltic: the road of seabirds' tears. To the boy it had been the world itself, a grey world, more shades of it than to be found in a Luftwaffe depot. A violent place, sometimes; painters chased its elusive light, sailors ran before the dark, immediate squalls, but his memory had calmed these extremities, faded them to safer mid-tones. He recalled the air and water only at their most guileless, the soundless calms that seemed to go on forever, soothing, deceiving. A small, still world of indistinct boundaries, marked only by the graves of those lost within it.

No dead reckonings today. He blinked himself awake, lit a cigarette and felt the pain returning as his face departed the cool glass. The young obergefreiter sitting opposite glanced enviously at the smoke but avoided looking directly at him (most men in uniform did, he'd observed). It seemed churlish to cough, but he drew too deeply into his damaged lung, more smoke where it wasn't needed. When his eyes cleared, he managed a shrug and leaned forward to offer the thing to a man who could use it. A slight nod for thanks: the economy of manly pity.

The train slowed, its ageing axles squealing hideously as they passed through Bansin-Herings-dorf-Ahlberg. Even across two decades, his young proletarian's prejudices held firm: a cold, self-conscious place, guaranteed its trade even in thin times, smugly secure in its reputation as the resort of Kaisers. Too scrubbed still, he decided: too *zimperlich*, obscenely out of its time. His bored mind's eye drifted across the quaint, stolid bäderarchitektur's whitened walls and regular red roofs, and imagined it atomized, all future histories truncated into the moments an eighty-eight millimetre would require to traverse its mounting and put one through the collective, rustically shuttered window.

A sin, even to think it, his mother would have said, but the towns had earned some ill will. She had been a drudge here, cleaning their hotels' high-ceilinged bedrooms and ornate water closets, bearing the condescension of under-managers, head maids, guests and even house-boys, earning half a pittance for hours that a clock would have jibed at, and still, not a single deposit of spite or resentment had stained her stoic soul. She'd been Old Germany: devout, hoping only for the balm of her covenanted portion, thinking no ill of her many judges. A wholly admirable woman, and whenever he was tempted to wish for more of her nature in himself he recalled her hands and knees. Cautionary tales in purple, they'd surrendered years before the rest.

His eyes stared at nothing, stinging yet refusing

to close. Since departing Berlin he had known it would be like this, the memories falling like old newspapers that a rotting cord had let slip. To make sense of the summons required that he question it, and questions had an inconvenient way of shaking out the past, of raising dust. He glanced down the length of the carriage, seeking distraction. It was at least as old as he, its nominal seating arrangements overburdened by a press of bodies, loaded according to the convex wall principle of military redeployment. His own space, staked out with luggage and rank before the majority joined the train at Swinemünde, was relatively generous, but his maudlin, self-indulgent mood saw it as a close confinement. The narrow sweep of his vista, the crowd of uniforms, the nicotine blur and shared weariness of war, all of it heightened a sense of passing into ... he strained to define it, but *it* eluded him once more, leaving only the faint peal of things mis-placed and lost. *The wrinkles which thy glass will truly show, of mouthèd graves will give thee memory...*

He shifted, dislodging dead Englishmen's unwelcome reveries. A stabbing nerve took their place, reminding him that he had sat still for too long, one of his new regime's most pronounced *Don'ts*. He began to move his right hand in small figures of eight, working the flexors and extensors of his forearm, trying not to engage the bicep and deltoid until their turn came. The motion was im-mediately painful, but he persisted, willing it to become an unthinking habit, concentrating upon the wholesome view through the windows and the stale smells around him, on not grimacing.

The obergefreiter, his fingers almost scorched, flicked the fragment to the floor. He reached into his tunic, glancing around to account for the other officers nearby, and offered a flask. It was a forbidden pleasure to men on duty, but to refuse was unthinkable. He took it, raised it to his lips and swallowed carefully, trying and failing to by-pass the burn tissue in his throat. Pear schnapps, a tart's drink; before the war he wouldn't have rubbed it into an angry boil, and now it was as welcome as a nurse's warmed hand.

'Nice.' He managed to gasp the word or something similar, and returned the flask. Another nod, the apparent limit of his new comrade's expressiveness.

More familiar names passed by – Ückeritz, Koserow – villages still, though translated from historic poverty to stolid prosperity at the blessing of the Prussian Northern Railway. Of Ückeritz he retained only a single, sublime memory, but to Koserow he owed a father, born and raised in a stinking net-repairer's cottage less than a hundred metres from the high tide mark. It was probably a villa by now, elevated upon bad taste and the profits from city dwellers' weak chests. It was the same all along this coastline; what God had forgotten or left to the Swedes, the Second Empire's taste for recreational flagellation had resurrected and even endowed. In Koserow's case, the trend had gone so far as to begat that defining artefact of bourgeois inactivity, a pier. *Good for it*, he thought, perversely pleased that at least one echo of his pedigree hadn't yet fallen into the shit pit.

The shadow of the Streckelsberg darkened the train briefly, and then they were in Zempin, where the new order became apparent. The town had begun its gentrification a few years earlier than Koserow, and he recalled its then-newness, the bright sense of anticipation its attractions had held for the boy at the edge of manhood: the cycling trips, boating weekends, the clumsy flirtations with girls from the south (*two-week temptations*, they'd called them, with all the seasoned insouciance of rural virgins). But Zempin was now the gateway to the secured area, and most of its citizens had been evacuated to make room for the technicians and their families. The setting was ideal: to the south of the town, the narrowest spit of land – no more than a sand-break between the Baltic and Achterwasser – connected what lay beyond to the rest of the peninsula. As it crossed this precarious foundation, the train passed through an archway cut through triple wired fences, the entrance to a latter-day Keep. Wonderfully defensible against eastern Usedom: not so much against the known enemy.

The first signs were visible soon after. Too much smoke hung lazily in the warm, dank morning as they approached Zinnowitz, though the town itself seemed untouched. Yet another spa, but a modest one in every sense: inclined, unlike the *drei Kaiserbäder*, to be grateful for its visitors. *Though perhaps not for today's*, he thought. The train slowed, giving a clear, leisurely view of a long rank of bodies, placed neatly outside the railway perimeter's fence: the late discoveries, only now recovered; those who had crawled into cellars that had fallen in after them; or fled along the long, white beach, imagining that bombs didn't belong in such a setting; or into the woods, where the irrationality of panic told them that where they couldn't be seen they couldn't be hurt. All of them disappointed in their expectations, and as decently covered as the available tarpaulin allowed: a torn honour guard, to welcome the war to this previously untouched sliver of the Reich.

'Jesus.'

The obergefreiter was staring out of the window. He seemed mildly outraged, as if the deaths of civilians could still be a novel enormity in the world. But he recalled himself, and raised the flask to his mouth; it slipped, and into a moment he packed a minute's frantic scramblings to keep it off the floor. The look on his face as he succeeded – like he had waved himself upright from a cliff edge – was comical, and the broken man who had watched the performance started to laugh. Yet even as his stomach contracted in that unfamiliar reflex, the bodies outside had begun their work: memories from the East, pouring out of their box, bright and immediate, reminding him of what could change a man more for the worse than burning aviation fuel. *The dead, reckoning.*

Chapter Two

Their journey ended at Zinnowitz station. From here to Peenemünde the railway was electrified, but its power lines had been down since the raid. The train's passengers, most of them from the same ersatz grenadier battalion brought in to help clear the rubble and rebuild the fences that kept people both out and in, disembarked and assembled on the sidings, waiting for someone to put them to use. The few Luftwaffe personnel, bound – with a single exception – for the west site, clustered self-consciously a little apart from the others, like swans lately obliged to board with chickens.

With only the one good hand for his kitbag and case, he was helped down to the tracks by the obergefreiter. The kindness was offered matter-of-factly, without a hint of pity; it was worth another cigarette, but before he could reach for the pack a polite cough required his attention. He turned to a pale, smartly dressed but slightly dishevelled civilian, a young man barely into his twenties. He seemed tense, or anxious: a small, intermittent tick ruffled his beardless face; his eyes, reddened by grief or tiredness squinted in the indifferent light; and hands bearing fresh marks of unfamiliar manual work flitted constantly, minding nothing. One of the junior smart fellows, probably, experiencing a hard awakening.

'Hauptmann Fischer?' A higher voice than the robust frame suggested, the pronunciation a little too precise, more delivered than spoken.

He nodded, smiled, realized – too late – how upsetting this might be to someone unprepared for it.

'I'm Kaspar Nagel, assistant to Dr von Braun, the Technical Director. Generalmajor Dornberger asked me to meet you...' he managed to drag his gaze from Fischer's face and nodded towards the still-smoking northern skyline, '...most of our staff are a bit busy this morning.'

'I assumed it to be the case.' Fischer had managed to look at preliminary Luftwaffe intelligence before he left the Air Ministry the previous evening. A minimum of five hundred heavy aircraft, unloading on to an area some five kilometres square: someone wanting to make a point.

The young man waved a hand towards the smoke. 'You'll think it isn't too bad, when you see. Their first wave missed the main sites and dropped everything on the foreign workers' camp at Trassenheide. But then the rest of them hammered us.'

His eyes widened; like most civilians caught beneath one, he was finding it difficult to leave the experience. 'The bastards ignored most of the technical zones and concentrated on the Settlement, our staff accommodation. It was barbaric.'

Of course they did: materiel can be replaced, but not such peculiar expertise. In a disinterested way Fischer approved the tactic, though to say so would hardly be politic.

'Yes, barbaric.'

'We're to meet the Generalmajor at the test stands; he's inspecting them for damage. I've brought his car.'

A few metres away, in a small parking area adjoining the sidings, an old but immaculately maintained two-tone Hanomag Rekord idled quietly, flaunting its immunity from fuel rationing. Nagel took the kitbag and attaché case, placed them on the rear seat, and moved swiftly to open and hold the passenger door. Carefully, ensuring his good arm had sufficient purchase upon its frame, Fischer eased himself into the car, feeling all the pains that his doctors had said would remain an intimate part of whatever life remained to him. Nagel half-extended a hand during this ordeal and let it hang, having no intention of making physical contact. When his passenger was safely inside, he closed the door with the careful, imbecilic reverence that the sound-bodied mistake for empathy – a gesture ruined moments later by the crashing jolt of his arse on to the driver's seat. Every tortured nerve in Fischer's body re-ignited.

'Sorry.'

The journey was short and unpleasant, though there was little to be done about that. It was interrupted at several points by checkpoints puncturing wire fences some three metres high. They were waved through all but one of these at little more than a flourish of Nagel's security card. Much of the landscape to their right was as wooded as in Fischer's youth, the view restricted for all but a short open stretch, south of Karlshagen. Yet in one sense he found it fascinating. Their route – even that part occupied by the local

15

army camp – was almost entirely undamaged by the RAF's recent visit, though the principal target areas were at most a few hundred metres to the east. The British were rarely this single-minded.

After some fifteen minutes, mercifully unpunctuated by polite conversation, Nagel stopped the Rekord in front of a high, grassed ridge. Beyond it stood a tall, squared tower, a gantry of some form, with a single line of windows in its upper storey. On the ridge stood a group of men, uniforms and civilians, deep in conversation or argument, apparently oblivious to the new arrivals. Again, the absence of bomb damage was notable: neither the observation tower nor a collection of service huts nearby exhibited more than the usual effects of the scouring, near-constant Baltic wind. Paint was about all that was missing here.

An equally pained reverse manoeuvre brought Fischer out of the car and to his feet while Nagel held the passenger door once more, the same hand extended unhelpfully. By the time he was upright, they'd been joined by one of the uniforms – no, *the* uniform: that of Generalmajor Doctor Walter Robert Dornberger, a name that had been entirely unfamiliar to Fischer until a (very brief) briefing the previous evening. First impressions were underwhelming: the German High Command flattered itself that it turned out a good figure, suitable to its elegant uniforms, but Dornberger was the runt from that litter. At most of average height, slightly built and with a greyish, indoor pallor, he seemed more a specimen of middle management in fancy dress, the type who disappears when standing still. But the

Generalmajor didn't give the impression that he stood still very often; in fact, he almost bounded at them, propelled by some inner electrical charge.

'Hauptmann Fischer? Wonderful!' Unusually for a senior officer, he used his eyes as well as his mouth to smile, and seemed pleased to be interrupted. Cleverly, he ignored the matter of salutes or handshakes entirely, lunged forward and clasped Fischer's good shoulder familiarly. Not the sort of thing that career soldiers did, usually, but the campaign decorations on his breast gave the lie to any assumption that yet another Party favourite had been uniformed into respectability.

'Nagel, you can bugger off!'

The younger man stifled a yawn, gave an amiable half-salute and slid back into the Rekord. Dornberger tapped the roof.

'Leave the Hauptmann's effects in the guest-house. And get my car home safely. Come on, Fischer, over here.'

They moved away from the others, still busily chattering on the ridge, towards the huts. Closer now, Fischer realized he'd unfairly slighted the buildings, which were in fact low blockhouses with slit openings. The door of the nearest was ajar, mocking the *Entry Forbidden!* scrawled prominently across it. The interior was bare: a table, a number of basic wooden chairs and a bench; in the corner, a small, plumbed sink presumably serviced whatever variety of ersatz swill was available to drink. It wasn't immediately apparent why anyone should either desire or be denied entry.

17

'Sit or stand, whatever's comfortable.'

One of a number of words that Fischer no longer overused. He refused a cigarette and leaned against a low ledge beneath the observation slit, while the Generalmajor perched himself on the edge of the table and lit one with the slow appreciation of a man who smoked only rarely.

'Hauptmann, I'm going to be frank with you, and I expect your discretion. You know what we do here?'

'No, sir. That is, very vaguely.' Of course Fischer knew the broad details of the work carried out at Peenemünde. One couldn't occupy a desk at the Lie Division without having some inkling of how and why resources needed so desperately elsewhere poured into this place. 'The new weapons?'

'Among other things, yes. We've conceived, designed and built an entirely new form of device, something that the enemy can't even begin to match. It requires no pilot, no fixed site from which to be launched. Almost every major technical problem has been overcome, every design flaw corrected, all standards carefully set down. The British have put a lot of time and effort into destroying what is incapable of being stopped – a futile, expensive gesture.'

Fischer sensed that meaningless noises were appropriate. 'A very great achievement, Herr Generalmajor.'

'The Führer believes that what we've done will change the face of the war.'

'And you agree?'

Dornberger laughed. 'I do, heartily, as I want to keep my job and my budgets. But really, as the

18

enemy's resources increase, our own will contract. That's a fact. Only new technologies will keep us in the fight, and the British have done nothing to slow us.'

'I hear the damage wasn't great.'

'The Technical Director and I flew over the entire site yesterday. There isn't much, the experimental and production areas took some minor damage, but if I were Churchill I'd be hanging my head in shame. Even our losses in personnel were relatively bearable, though cruel. Did you know that the majority of our dead – I mean the German dead, of course – were women? We have many War Service girls here, and one of their dormitories was hit several times. I'm told that some of the survivors fled along the beach, but were gunned down by British fighters. Pitiful. A terror raid.'

The General flicked his cigarette at the observation slit and missed it. He frowned. 'However...'

The point.

'...we have a problem.'

'Why I am here.'

'Yes. You were recommended to me.'

Fischer could think of no one who might propose him for anything that didn't involve deception.

'You were a detective, I believe?'

'I was with Criminal Investigations, at Stettin, sir. But not for some years now.' The department had been rather over-titled: Fischer's job had largely comprised pulling knifed sailors, dockers and whores out of the harbour and then trying to narrow it down to less than a hundred suspects.

19

Otherwise, it was drugs, racketeering and, of course, 'other duties' as necessary – all very rewarding work.

'Yes. But then you volunteered for the Luftwaffe, and joined Fallschirmjäger 1 Regiment. An unusual choice, if I may express an opinion?'

Fischer shrugged. 'Falling was a metaphor for what I was doing already. At least a faulty parachute delivers clean air on the way down.'

'But you kept your sense of humour. Uncommon in that line of work. I said you were recommended, by a mutual acquaintance, Felix Linnemann.'

'Soccer Felix', head of the German Football League, part-time kripo and professional Party hack, a man without discernible qualities. A testimonial from him seemed ... odd. Fischer could hardly kick a ball, and had never made an effort to be remembered, even by his few superiors who cared about the work. And Linnemann hadn't been one of those. When he could be bothered to drag himself to Stettin from Berlin he had been interested in little more than patting heads, spouting slogans and holding news briefings to announce rare victories against anti-social elements.

The Generalmajor seemed amused, as if a prank was working as planned. 'Don't be too flattered. What I wanted was someone whose discretion I could trust absolutely. Felix told me that you were a good policeman but your own worst enemy, to the point of being investigated. You had an issue with the Racial Laws, I understand?'

'I managed to persuade them of my indifference.'

But not before being gifted a mild concussion, and a left ear that never quite worked properly thereafter, and then effective demotion. A re-assignment to the Squealer Squad, where innuendo, rumour and petty neighbourly grudges were moulded into something more by a team of time-serving sociopaths, charged with following real and imagined dissent across the hearth, into the bedroom and even the mind itself.

'Reeds should bend, Fischer, not poke.' Pleased, Dornberger savoured the observation and delicately picked a sliver of tobacco from his tongue. 'Still, I'm sure I needn't worry about you being a conduit to old friends.'

If it was a question of loyalties, Fischer had none. He didn't answer, relying upon the venerable tactic of uncomfortable silence to tease out something more.

The Generalmajor coughed and checked his watch. 'The raid, then. One hundred and seventy one members of staff and their families killed, as well as some six or seven *fremdarbeiter*.' He leaned on the term – *foreign workers* – too obviously, reassuring Fischer that they were both men of culture, obliged by a regrettable reality to deal in sophistries. 'In absolute terms it's an inconvenience, as I say, but almost nothing that can't be replaced. Unfortunately...' he stood and closed the door, '... we did lose one very valuable member of our senior staff. Dr Walther Thiel, our deputy Technical Director, was found some hours after the raid with his wife and children in a collapsed trench. All quite dead.'

'Tragic.'

'More than that, I'm afraid. He was one of our very best engine designers. He may be truly irreplaceable.'

'So in fact the British didn't waste their time?'

'I thought not, initially. Thiel and his family were dug out yesterday morning. Their bodies were placed with the other casualties in our site's schoolhouse – covered decently, of course. It seems that no one noticed, initially, but a number of the other casualties had been misidentified, and I stressed to my staff that mistakes in that respect were unacceptable. So everyone was checked once more.

'Suffocation must be a terrible way to die. But rarely, I think, does it involve a prior bullet to the forehead.' Dornberger pulled open the block-house door and waved Fischer out into the sun-light. This time, the eyes didn't smile with the mouth.

'We have a little mystery, and you will resolve it. Quickly.'

Chapter Three

Insofar as any adjective could do justice to the setting, *druidical* seemed most appropriate to Fischer, who loathed Wagner and could call upon no other Aryan exemplars. Backlit by a troubled horizon, a vast oval space, like an amphitheatre

22

pillaged centuries earlier for its stone facings, closed to a central, blast-darkened point. From there, if his meagre understanding was correct, vast energies hurled a huge metal phallus into the skies at phenomenal speed, to a height beyond that at which a man could breathe, beyond that at which any other device could intercept it. At its present stage of development the object was coming almost straight back down again, with slight but very necessary adjustments to carry it out into the nearby sea, rather than on to the heads of the men who launched it. But in its perfected state it would cross the seas in a matter of minutes, to fall soundlessly upon an enemy for whom death would come utterly unannounced. The future of war, prosecuted at a dispassionate, inhuman remove.

'Test stand seven, our busiest launch site.' They stood on the grass ridge, looking down upon the Generalmajor's subordinates, scuttering across the amphitheatre, checking for debris with the peevish preoccupation of misers who had picked up a coin and dropped two. It had been a short but steep climb, and both men breathed heavily.

'Herr Generalmajor, I'm fairly certain I'm not the person for this.'

Dornberger's hand clasped his shoulder once more – the wrong one this time. Fischer winced.

'I disagree. I mean, you *are*, and that's that. A good job, a quick job – you return to your Berlin office as if you'd merely been on home leave, and we can forget these unfortunate days.'

'I don't understand. Why isn't your own security dealing with this?'

'As you'll see, *our* security is effective only in a mechanical sense. We've taken great pains to segregate the various processes and keep each of them well-scrutinized, but we have no real intelligence function in place here.' Dornberger laughed. 'Ironic, really, given the amount of intelligence in place here. In any case, having our own investigated by the same would make for difficulties – we're all a little too close here.'

'Then why not bring in the GFP? This is a military installation.'

'Understaffed and over-committed, very likely to conclude that the first face they don't like is that of the perpetrator. A face belonging, probably, to someone upon whom they already had a file. Besides, they'd almost certainly insist upon slapping my technicians to warm up their answers, and I get upset about that sort of thing. You know the GFP's techniques, I'm sure.'

'SiPo, then? If it's a saboteur...'

'Absolutely not, for many reasons with which you needn't be burdened. But please accept that they're genuine. I'm sorry, Hauptmann, we need a dispassionate, unaffiliated eye, and it *will* be yours.'

Inwardly Fischer surrendered. There really was no utility in arguing further. On the strength of a two-minute telephone call, unburdened by any of the necessary paperwork or authorizations, his commanding officer had almost carried him to Stettiner Bahnhof and thrust him on to the Swinemünde train. 'Bring me anything we can use, Otto!' he had boomed, enslaved by his instinct for a splashy, sensational story, even one he

24

couldn't print. '*Wonder weapons ready to launch! Fire over England!* Anything!' That was Karl to the tip: his one remaining eye never missed the stuff that sold newspapers.

The Generalmajor was waiting expectantly. Fischer shrugged. 'You understand I haven't done this kind of thing for years?'

'Who has? Our age offers so much larger opportunities. Christ, an individual crime, it's almost bespoke.'

As Dornberger's staff moved towards the tower its massive scale became more apparent. A single railway line penetrated the amphitheatre's circumference from the east and terminated just beneath a slightly smaller tower, another gantry. Clearly, the structure also functioned as some sort of support for whatever was brought to it. Fischer had seen a few imprecise diagrams of the new weapons, but paper couldn't give an accurate impression of their size and potential power.

The Generalmajor mistook his silence for awe and commenced the tour. 'Look at it, Fischer. We're *years* ahead of anyone else. We've actually punctured Space itself, the Void, with the devices we launch from here. You're a soldier of course, so you'll see it with a soldier's eyes, but the fact that these are weapons is a mere detail, believe me.'

'Not to the Wehrmacht, surely?'

Dornberger smiled. 'Their support's been useful, I can't deny it. Truly, though, we have a way of looking beyond the coming victory, and even war itself. This will be very hard to take in,

25

I expect, but we've been here a long time, slowly building something memorable. Many years ago a film, an entertainment named *Frau im Mond*, drew a remarkable future for Germans. Did you see it?'

It was a film that couldn't be made in the new Germany, certainly. At the time, Fischer had thought it fantastical. He'd been dragged to the cinema only by a girlfriend's promise of a grope in the dark, but what he saw had been strangely inspiring, if the romantic sub-plot could be discounted. He nodded slightly, led by Dornberger, who needed it for the anecdote.

'If I tell you that, not two kilometres from here, the man who designed Herr Lang's space vessel works as one of the founding principals of our project, you'll appreciate the continuity of his – of *our* – vision.'

'Tomorrow, the stars?'

'Not tomorrow, no. Not in either of our lifetimes, however long they last. But whatever may come, it will have come, ultimately, from *here*.'

Fischer took some pride in his cynicism – it had grown stronger as his nation had become enslaved to hyperbole – but he found it difficult to remain entirely detached. If Dornberger's vision was only partly clouded by obsession, if even a part of it could be realized, the project would be epochal. He thought of his parents, of the quality of lives barely removed from the medieval, and then of his own expectations. If time remained still for him to have children, what wonders would they see? That a species could advance from that to *this* in just three generations was both terrifying and stirring.

'How long do I have?'

'Days, at most. Reichsmmister Speer will be speaking with the Führer today or tomorrow. No doubt he'll attempt to keep our projects within the ministry's purview ... but as I say, this may be difficult, given our present vulnerability. The longer you take the more visible our problem becomes and, unfortunately, scrutiny of what we're doing is intense and becoming more so.'

'Why so?'

'Because finally, and precisely at the wrong moment, all of our failures have become successes. Reichsführer Himmler attended a perfect launch and has since praised us to the skies. The Führer himself saw the film record of two launches, and was very enthusiastic – *very* enthusiastic. When I next spoke to him he actually begged my pardon for having disbelieved in the potential of our work. He told me that I was only the second man to whom he had ever felt it necessary to apologize. You can imagine how that made me feel.'

'Honoured?'

'Quite wretched. For years, we've laid down our own priorities and timetables, addressed the many unexpected problems and found proper, tested solutions. But now? Now, we'll never again work unhindered by just about anyone in Berlin who wants to kiss the Führer's ... hand. Already, we've been inundated by demands to know why *this* is taking so long, why *that* has been done the way it has, why we allow mere physics to prevent us strapping ten tonnes of explosives to a device that can reach the eastern American seaboard.

Having raised no expectations to date, we now sink beneath them.'

Dornberger recollected himself. 'I'm sorry. This facility, for your information, has been re-classified as Heimat Artillery Park 11, Karlshagen, a rather feeble ploy intended to encourage potential spies and saboteurs to look elsewhere. The facility at Peenemünde West remains what it is. The division of authority between the zones is an historical oddity. I am, of course, director of all activities here, but the western complex operates under Luftwaffe auspices. For the moment, all experimental facilities at Peenemünde East remain under direct control of Army Ordnance, though as I indicated, Speer's Armaments Ministry has responsibility for the production phase. Confusing, isn't it? But none of this will affect you. What *will* affect you is my need for you to investigate without anyone knowing why.'

'Because...?'

'Only five persons, other than you and me, are aware that Walter did not die in the raid. That is, in addition to the person who killed him – if, indeed, he was *additional*. I've told you that the need for discretion is paramount, so clearly it would be disastrous if everyone were to find out about it.'

Fischer nodded. 'Who are the five?'

'Wehrner von Braun – the Technical Director and my second-in-command, so to speak; Werner Magirius, my adjutant; Arthur Rudolph, Head of Production Engineering; Professor Hans Wierer of the Projections Department, whom I put in charge of collecting the corpses; and Kaspar

28

Nagel, your chauffeur today, who discovered the crime – that is, he pulled back the shroud from Thiel's dead face and saw the wound. Fortunately, he knew to be discreet. Now, for the purpose of giving you plausibility you are seconded to the *Heereswaffenamt* as from this moment. You are here, officially, at my request, to review our security procedures. You will report directly to me, of course. You will, I expect, be efficient and conscious of the urgency with which this matter needs to be resolved. Naturally, you will need access to areas and information for which you have no official clearance. All such necessary permissions will be waived upon my authority. You will be issued with a security badge to that effect. This has been made clear to station staff at every level, so if you meet with any difficulties, use my name, very loudly.'

'Where do I start?'

'Well, today we have our colleagues and workers to bury.'

'But not Herr Thiel, surely?'

'If not, I advertise the fact that something is not right.'

'Then I should see him now.'

Chapter Four

Now was less than an hour later, in a small, single-storey building within a maze of similar structures designated loosely as the Experimental Works, a pre-production area lying just to the south of the Development Zone. The corpse lay on two tables pushed together, covered by a tarpaulin sheet. Dornberger and Nagel were present, the latter as far from the item as he could be without standing outside. He had one arm wrapped tightly around his body and was drawing deeply upon a cigarette, which Fischer didn't consider to be at all disrespectful. The smell pervading the room was very familiar.

Dornberger nodded him towards the corpse. 'Our chief medical officer is a good man, but too garrulous for me to have involved him in this business. I think the visible evidence speaks for itself.'

Blond, handsome, wiry, dead: a ragged hole in the forehead. Fischer looked up. 'You've removed the bullet?'

'With some difficulty, yes. It wasn't too deep. Seven-point-six-five millimetre.'

Still, a mess. 'Well, the back of his head remains connected to the rest, so almost certainly it wasn't a Walther. I see no other, unexpected trauma.'

Thiel's face was widely bruised, but the force of the trench impacting upon him would account for that. His face was in repose: loss of consciousness or death itself would have been instantaneous. With Nagel's reluctant assistance, Fischer turned and examined the naked body. There were no further marks or obvious indications of internal injury, not even broken fingernails – because, of course, the victim had been in no condition to attempt to dig himself out of the trench.

'Where are his wife and children?'

'Already boxed. We checked them, briefly. The only signs of injury were those to be expected.'

'Such as?'

Dornberger and Nagel looked at each other. 'Bruising, some damage to the woman's hands. Both she and the two children had much soil in their mouths and throats.'

Thiel's mouth was clean. Fischer covered the body. 'Is there somewhere I can wash my hand?'

In a shower-block adjacent to the room Dornberger stood with a towel, almost hopping with impatience while Fischer rinsed away the ambience of Walter Thiel.

'What can I tell you, Herr Generalmajor? There's no coroner's report, so we can't say how much damage the bullet did internally. In any case, your rummaging would make that assessment very difficult. But the lack of an exit wound suggests a semi-automatic hand weapon with low stopping power. I'd say something like a Beretta, a Ruby or an FN.'

'But it killed him?'

'Something did.'

'You think a foreigner?'

'Why should I? We've used as many FNs as

31

Walthers since 1940, and Christ knows how many Rubys came home from Spain the year before that.' Fischer wiped his hand by clutching the towel, and briefly rubbed the undamaged part of his face. 'An obvious question, but did Thiel own a gun?'

'I don't know, possibly. All weapons here should be service-issue and, therefore, recorded. But you know how it is...'

'My point is that most crimes are domestic, as any police room on a Saturday night attests. The place to begin the search for a killer is within the family.'

'So, in an air raid trench, Frau Thiel shot her husband in a jealous rage while the RAF pounded them from above. She then expired and, post-mortem, expertly disposed of the weapon?'

'Slightly unfeasible, I agree. Who found the body? I mean, who dug out Thiel and his family from the trench?'

'We haven't been able to determine that. There was a lot of confusion. The German staff and foreign workers were doing what they could, quite frantically, to help those who were trapped in buildings that were burning or had collapsed. We've asked but no one has yet come forward.'

If it had been one or more of the foreigners here it was hardly surprising that they preferred anonymity.

'What about grudges? Did he offend anyone, professionally?'

'Definitely not. Walter was very well liked.'

'At least one person would disagree, I think.'

'You must find him, then. Or her.'

Next door, Thiel's shrouded body was being transferred to a plain casket. Three foreign workers – chattering Poles wearing the mandatory security badges for this area – did the dirty work briskly, nailed down the lid and carried him away. Nagel followed, loudly directing the cortege.

'If I can't discuss the crime, it will be very difficult.'

'Nevertheless, this *cannot* become generally known.'

A delicate matter. Fischer felt his hackles rise as he recalled his only prior professional experience of *delicacy*. On a winter's morning in 1936, Stettin's deputy mayor, a prominent local Party official, had reported himself to the kripos. His position brought substantial perquisites, including the right to relax outside the conventional moralities. During the previous evening he had enjoyed a drunken bout with two very young girls, who almost certainly hadn't. They were disadvantaged in every sense: both were orphans, personable and vulnerable, and available therefore to men who were neither. The encounter, in a room in Stettin's most prestigious hotel, the venue for all local Party conferences, had degenerated into what was circumspectly described as a 'regrettable incident'. The gentleman, once sober, had realized that the disposal of one dead and one critically injured child was beyond his own resources, not least because management, though obliging, had a strict no murder policy and was unlikely to agree to the use of their laundry trolleys. So he decided to call the police: not to throw himself upon the mercy of German justice,

33

but to arrange for professional cleaning services.

Fischer, the recording officer that morning, had told Soccer Felix's predecessor that the only part he'd play in the business would be to arrest the deputy mayor. For that, he'd serve six months' night duty covering the docks, the town's colon, during which time he was knifed, had a testicle relocated to his chest cavity by the boot of a drunken stevedore and was informed upon by at least one good German who objected to his drinking relationship with a Jewish gang-master. In the meantime, the deputy mayor had resigned after a decent interval and the Party emerged unsoiled by any association with the crime – which, of course, had become no crime at all. The hotel made no complaint about its sheets, the almost-dead girl disappeared as definitively as her very dead friend, and, astonishingly in a German bureaucracy, no paperwork referring to the incident was logged, ever. If the deputy mayor had departed the hotel with one of their bath towels there would have been more said about it.

That was the trouble: *delicate* investigations almost always concluded with the fiction that no crime had been committed. Clearly, this one wouldn't.

'I'll need an assistant who knows this place.'

Dornberger shrugged. 'Wehrner can spare Nagel. He's a good boy, but we've tested his discretion to breaking point already. So don't confide in him more than is sensible.'

Chapter Five

From the Experimental Works office, one of Dornberger's uniformed subordinates, a morose fellow named Schubert, walked Fischer to the guesthouse, where his few effects had been dropped off. It was suitably furnished for a Generalmajor's occasional use, though a near-miss during the recent raid had badly scorched one of its two bedrooms, rearranged the garden and emptied most of the window frames. Emergency repairs had been put in hand, but a layer of glass and brick-dust remained over the furniture and carpets. The bathroom, an inner, windowless room, was undamaged.

Alone, Fischer unpacked his spare uniform and slowly undressed. Regrettably, a half-length mirror attached to the bathroom door was intact also, giving him the opportunity to make yet another audit of what his doctors insisted upon calling his remarkably good fortune.

It was a curiously wilful interpretation. *Remarkably good fortune* surely would have placed him somewhat further from the impact point of a plummeting PoI-16 and the Bf 109 it had rammed in mid-air. Even merely good fortune would then have tried a little less assiduously to keep him alive on the tortuous journey to the dressing station, where, lacking facilities to treat major burns injuries, medics had pushed a rubber tube down his throat, immersed him in a tin bath of freezing water and more or less abandoned him to work on more hopeful causes. Fortune of any positive sort might have relented sufficiently to opiate the memory of the excruciating operations he had undergone at Potsdam to cleanse and stabilize his extensive injuries and begin the long process of making him remotely presentable to polite society. But fortune it was, and *remarkably good* at that, according to the white coats.

But I have half a face.

Yet both your eyes and your palate survived almost unharmed. Quite astonishing.

And a useless arm.

The tendons will stretch once more, with appropriate exercise. Be optimistic.

It hurts to breathe, to eat, to drink. And you tell me that it always will.

But you can do all of these things still. Remarkable!

Fischer regarded their handiwork in the mirror. He was – he had been – a fairly tall man, of medium build and reasonably good, upright posture, with adequately pleasing features – if not exactly handsome, at least he'd never frightened the ladies. But Bolshevik peevishness and National Socialist surgery had collaborated to produce a rather different aesthetic. It wasn't pretty, though certainly, it was going to be increasingly fashionable – a *mode*, in fact, given time and the very many available opportunities.

Much of the right side of his face was an anatomist's classroom model, its musculature exposed as if the epidermis had been flayed surgically for the edification of those who found such things instructive. New tendons, salvaged from still-warm human corpses (Aryan ones, obviously), connected the exposed tissue of his forehead, cheek and chin to the good skin on the left side, keeping what remained of his features in something like their proper place. His nose squatted uncomfortably between the new and old states and bore something of both, which, if it were possible, made the whole less pleasant than being entirely one or the other. Beneath his jaw-line, an area of damaged skin – hideously darkened and puckered but his own skin still – extended to his right shoulder, where the real damage recommenced. Part of the front deltoid was missing, and a fair proportion of his right bicep, though he had been assured that the remainder, if reinforced by further tendon work, would learn to compensate for what he had lost. His right hand was little more than a bird's claw. That, too, he was told, would regain some function in time. Apart from a further area of burn tissue descending from the nape of his neck to his lower back, that was it. Really, he hardly had reason to complain.

It all looked, and was, a remarkable improvisation, undertaken by men who'd been making up the science as the days and weeks passed. Four times his body had rejected most of their bright ideas, and they had been obliged to return to first principles. It had been an agonizing, dehumanizing experience, but only for Fischer. For his doctors it was a process of endless fascination and challenge, generating material for a series of career-enhancing medical papers. They told him that he was their favourite patient; they had wanted to keep him forever.

And they had not yet begun to discuss grafts. This would be stage two, he had been informed (surgeons liked *stages* much as actors did, he'd discovered): another six months of careful, controlled assessment, of constant exercise and adjustment, before a decision could be made as to what sort of monster they would regard as their minimum success. The day they told him this he had discharged himself, ignoring both orders and frantic warnings of the consequences, and reported half-fit for duty.

Late 1942's military job market was somewhat broader than the one he recalled. Large wars lower standards, but even so, he was surprised at his prodigal's welcome. His acting commander, overriding the doctors but wary of taking responsibility for what still looked like a dying man, offered him a selection of postings, any of which would release a fitter man to risk what Fischer had endured. There was the Wehrmacht's 'information centre', WASt, whose duty to notify the unsuspecting wives and parents of the military dead required ever more, and more industrious, employees. He considered that one only briefly. There were also vacancies within Luftwaffe Ground Support, whose role in ensuring that the tyres, flying suits and fuel got through was undeniably important, and as attractive to him as a summary execution. But then he had been pointed at the Berlin liaison and training office of the *Kriegsberichter der Luftwaffe*, the war reporters' unit (the

Lie Division, as his new colleagues more correctly named it), an institution devoted to devising ever less plausible misinterpretations of actual events. Fischer's new boss, Oberstleutnant Karl Krohne (a former newspaperman), had welcomed him with a drink, a hearty pat on the back, an immediate apology for the same and a thin departmental manual, which, it was suggested, was best employed to keep the glass from marking his desk. The interview, as he recalled, had been one-sided: some four minutes' reminiscences about the crime desk at the *Stettiner Zeitung*, where Krohne had learned his lamentable trade during the early Twenties.

He fell, less into a job than a calling. When no falsehood is too ridiculous to contemplate, making it half-believable, even to a populace conditioned to absurdities, is an expression of artistry. The news releases he had helped to write had conceived entire squadrons, equipped them and flung them at the Ivans – who, obligingly, had struggled as much as the German public not to believe in the phantoms. Cadres of black-coated eavesdroppers had been invented and inferred singly into bars and railway stations across the Reich, scaring a generation of civilians into fearful, prudent silence regarding matters about which they knew nothing anyway. Churchill had venereal issues, Stalin epilepsy; the Americans loved their comforts far too vehemently ever to risk becoming competent soldiers, and what seemed like the occasional battlefield reverse (such as losing an entire army at Stalingrad) was always shown to be a shrewd tactical adjustment to confound an imminent initiative on the enemy's part. Upon the Lie Division's pallet, black was palpably a shade of white, alpha a cleverly mooted omega, yin a yang by any other name. Like his colleagues, Fischer came to understand that *facts* were to be judged solely upon the weight of belief that attached to them. If something that went through their hands remained untrue, it was only because they hadn't tried hard enough to make its truth evident. Everything could be moulded, manipulated, re-fashioned: everything except the inconvenient tokens of other men's truths that Fischer and his colleagues bore upon their bodies. Perhaps, he had sometimes speculated, their excellence at creating new realities derived from an urge to escape the old, really real one.

But at least looking at it – the image of the new, improved Otto Fischer – no longer sickened him. What becomes habitual can be accepted, to a degree, even as a part of identity: *this is what I am, and will remain* (to be repeated twice daily, avoiding alcohol). So, the daily Prontosil dosages, the obsessively vigilant hygiene, the gentle repetitive exercises to stretch his many shortened tendons, and the constant anointing with glycerol had joined the mundane, minor groomings of the un-mutilated adult male, to the point at which they were no more onerous, though certainly more painful. They consumed time, but that didn't matter to him; finding a reason for them was more problematic.

A showerhead was fixed above the iron bath, a wonderful luxury. He stood in the warm down-pour far longer than he needed to swill off his traveller's coating of sweat and dust, enjoying the mild stinging sensation of water playing across his wounds. The soap – a grey, pitted concoction of near-industrial strength – was far too harsh to apply everywhere, and his left armpit, as always, was just a little too far from his right hand; but his nose reassured him that what remained couldn't offend. In any case, it wasn't likely to be the odour that people noticed.

He was dried and dressed within the half-hour, which he timed as always. At Potsdam he had enjoyed the services of a personal orderly, a man with one arm, lost in the First War, who had taught him the art of adept compromises. He had learned to knot a tie one-handed, though he often cheated and anchored the short end against his chest with his bad hand; he could also tie shoe-laces, load a machine pistol, cook a powdered egg omelette (as well as anyone could) and make a fair job of opening a tin without savaging the table surface beneath. He had – without requiring any instruction – learned to masturbate adequately with his left hand, though God knew he had little enough desire remaining to require the skill. The one necessary motor function that remained entirely beyond him was shuffling a deck of cards, though his orderly had demonstrated the technique quite expertly. But then, his psyche had always inclined more towards roulette.

When he was sure that he might represent the Luftwaffe without disgracing the institution, Fischer waited in the hallway, carefully avoiding dust and his reflection in yet another mirror. It was time enough to reflect upon the absurd task

41

he'd been given. *Days at most*: the logistics were daunting. To become sufficiently familiar with an enclosed society of scientists, technicians, their families, support staff and 'guest' workers to understand what might constitute a motive, to even begin to scrape through the instinctive reticence of strangers, to find and tease out the petty ill-will that feeds any investigation, would require more time and resources than he had any likelihood of acquiring.

Is that why he was here? Did Dornberger ask Soccer Felix for a man who could be guaranteed to fail abjectly and depart quietly thereafter? He could conceive of no positive recommendation that would have placed Otto Fischer at the top of a list of men to do the job required. Hundreds of former Bulls were better qualified, more motivated; probably would be delighted to be dragged back from the Front and see to the business without a nod or a squeak to SiPo, the SD or anyone else that the Generalmajor wanted to keep it from. Surely, he asked the silent, dusty hallway, this wasn't a choice in which any hope has been invested?

But failure didn't seem a useful outcome in any conceivable circumstance. Almost certainly, whoever had killed Thiel was *at large*, as the newspapers invariably put it, and perhaps not yet done. So what reason would the Generalmajor have to appoint an ineffective investigation – particularly when, reputation-wise, Fischer hardly had a head to roll? There was none that made sense.

Without knocking, Nagel entered. He had

changed into a dark blue suit, and looked appropriately, solemn – except for his face, which wore a broad, friendly smile. Impulsively, Fischer almost diagnosed a case of innocence and was forced to remind himself that he wasn't in the business of establishing who *hadn't* shot Walter Thiel. As the German judicial system itself determined (and who was Fischer to argue?), everyone must remain a guilty party until the evidence said otherwise or a Party card was produced. Still, even to an unpractised eye, Nagel seemed an unlikely assassin. The boy was as open as a French flank.

Obviously determined not to allow Fischer's face to upset him further, Nagel stared unerringly at it, and rubbed his hands briskly. 'You look very smart, Hauptmann. Ready?'

He turned on his heel, and collided heavily with a woman in the doorway. A mop and two filled buckets clattered loudly across the hallway's slate floor, and water splashed widely, spattering Fischer's uniform. Closer to the damage, Nagel's trousers were soaked. The woman backed away, terrified.

Nagel was mortified. 'Zofia! I'm so clumsy! Here, let me...'

He scrambled for the scattered buckets. She remained in the doorway, motionless, and Fischer saw that her apprehension had nothing to do with her part in the collision. It was himself: not the face, she hadn't yet glanced at his ravaged loveliness; it was the uniform she was staring at, paralyzed with fear of what *it* would do.

Ashamed, he raised his good hand, palm outward, to reassure her that a little water was not a capital offence, and noticed three things. Firstly, that her rough, poorly made clothes marked her out as a 'guest' worker – a Pole or Czech, probably, brought here to undertake the domestic tasks that any German might have done equally well, were it not necessary for the conquered peoples to understand their place in the new *Europa*. Secondly, unavoidably, Fischer realized that he was staring at quite the most attractive woman he had ever encountered: a beauty, impervious to the ravages of utilitarian clothing and forced service. Thirdly, his memory jarringly revisited the moment, perhaps twenty years past, a shore near the tree-line, a summer's day that moved from sunlight to rain and back again, heat and moisture weathering his pale, adolescent skin, when he had lain upon her.

Finally, she raised her eyes, and took in the new, extremely fortunate Otto Fischer, the wonder of modern, half-crazed restorative techniques. He saw, of course, the familiar effort not to react to an unexpected horror: to give an impression that burns victims were a mundane sight in those parts. As usual, the effort failed. He saw a little revulsion, quickly stifled; also pity, even for a member of an organization that had bestowed so much similar punishment upon her own race (a Pole, not a Czech: he could be definite upon that point, at least). What he did not see in those large, almond eyes – and for this he looked most carefully – was the slightest sign of recognition.

Chapter Six

In a clearing in the woods just south of Karlshagen, the first consignment of victims – almost four hundred souls – was laid to rest in a series of large pits. The bodies of the German dead were interred in hastily assembled caskets. The guest workers from Trassenheide made do with their tarpaulin shrouds.

It occurred to Fischer – a reluctant witness to more than one – that a mass funeral was the worst method of extracting a large number of dead from the living. There was no focus for the attendant pain, no single experience of mourning: only blanket platitudes, bewilderment and a brutally industrial process that mocked and then trampled upon any sense of personal loss. There wasn't even a party afterwards, to help drown the humiliation of it. Better, he thought, to wait until dark, bulldoze the dead into a decently deep pit, plant a monument over it and let the bereaved make their own arrangements to grieve. The monument was optional, of course.

As he and Nagel arrived, an unpleasant confrontation was taking place between Dornberger and an ugly bastard in the uniform of an Obergruppenführer SS. A naval officer and a pair of surplices – one Lutheran, the other a Catholic – flanked the Generalmajor. At one or all of them, the ugly bastard was wagging a sausage-sized finger in fashionable imitation of the Führer's haranguing technique during major speeches. But this was definitely an argument. Standing at a respectful distance, cordoned from the fracas by the pits, the families, friends and colleagues of the German dead silently awaited orders to grieve.

Nagel snorted. '"Nero" Schwede, our beloved Gauleiter. A pig, if that doesn't insult pork. Here for the photographs, no doubt.'

Fischer knew Schwede perfectly well by reputation. He had been an early and enthusiastic persecutor of Jews, gypsies, homosexuals, the handicapped, the mentally diseased and anyone else who failed to conform precisely to the ever-narrowing definition of what constituted a German. It was alleged that one of his particular quirks was a sense of duty so rigorous that he insisted upon attending 'interrogations', usually with a small coterie of admirers, during which he drunkenly urged on subordinates who seemed less than enthusiastic about doing real damage. His high rank in the Party was upon a point of precedence: he had been the first National Socialist to win an election, in 1924. This was nothing more exalted than a seat on Coburg's town's council, but it had broken the political impasse and earned the eternal gratitude of his future Führer. Schwede had since fattened up nicely, grown an Adolf moustache to go with his absurd little goatee, and appended the honorific 'von Coburg' to his surname: a doomed attempt to convince posterity that his veins carried blue blood rather than slurry. A pity his affectations had stopped there, thought Fischer; true low-comedy required props – a

46

monocle and a duelling scar, perhaps, or a whip, like his old friend Streicher.

'Who's the sailor?'

The 'sailor' wore the uniform of an admiral of the Kreigsmarine, with a string of ribbons adorning his chest, and the Obergruppenführer's harangue was having very little effect upon him. At one point, he laughed and waved a hand that, for all the slightness of the gesture, spoke volumes of contempt. Nagel squinted, a hand shielding his eyes from the strong sunlight.

'Hubert Schmundt, I think.'

Schwede launched into another bawl, but this time the admiral cut him short and pointed him back to his place in the rank of SS personnel that stood at right-angles to the grey uniforms: one flank of the 'U' enveloping a field altar. For a moment, the Gauleiter hesitated. His fists clenched as if to settle business in the venerable Freikorps manner; but the presence of witnesses – something he and his kind had always avoided back then – made this impractical. He turned and stomped away, leaving two black-clad minions to retreat awkwardly under the gaze of their large, desolate audience.

Red-faced, Dornberger turned to the priests and nodded, and the crowd bowed its collective head. Fischer hardly needed his kripo training to guess what it had all been about – the representatives of two deities, coming to the party wearing the same frock. There were priests at the service – and, by inference, God – which was anathema, naturally, to Schwede and his sort. For them, the promise of a life after National Socialism con-

47

stituted treasonable heresy – a new, super offence – and Admiral Schmundt had placed himself squarely among the fallen. Fischer discovered a warmth for the man, as he might for any imminently extinct species.

The service began; he and Nagel moved forward to join the second rank of senior site officers standing directly behind the field altar. It was some decades since Fischer had attended any sort of church, having trodden a reverse damascene road from his parents' graveside. A mother dead at fifty, a father at fifty-three: both worn down in the service of a God who, apparently, loved best those whom He called earliest. Amid coffins once more, he couldn't avoid recollections of his personal pietà: the Pastor's earnest, practised sincerity; the two, near anonymous plots in a windswept Swinemünde graveyard, filled in with dispatch and indifference; handshakes offered by the few relatives and fewer friends, their half-meant promises not to let slip ties that had never bound tightly; the sound of sea-birds, carrying desolately over the town's Ostbatterie; the tally of lives, counted in pennies.

But here was a more complex calculation of loss. Hundreds of souls had been expunged in minutes, by one of the countless acts of considered savagery currently staining what was misrepresented as the civilized world. The Trassenheide victims were blameless, but the staff and families of Peenemünde were not. Fathers earned their daily bread here by devising means to extend the world's barbarities; mothers raised their children to be proud of it, and uncritical of the

48

science that laid waste to other families. The whole was a corrupted display of healthy German domesticity transplanted into a neatly landscaped Hephaestus's forge, and what had the British done to it, other than what it strained to do to them? Yet each of the dead, standing individually before the tribunal, remained innocent of any crime that had demanded this collective punishment. Fischer failed to understand what he should feel about any of it. Moral equations required constants that had long been discarded, perhaps abolished.

Ignoring the prayers, he tried to cast his eye over every mourner, member of staff, soldier and local official at the service. Everything he expected was there: numbed grief, indifference, impatience and even boredom among those attending for form's sake. A few of the women, too distraught to care, wept loudly, uncomforted by the earnest ministrations of their friends. The children's coffins were the most harrowing aspect of it, naturally; some methodical idiot had decided to place them together, in the front, rather than among those of their families, and this amplified the horror of the spectacle considerably. The two priests separated to bless the deceased, beginning with the pathetically small ones, and Fischer wondered how they knew which corpse was Protestant, which a Catholic, which unbaptised. Perhaps the scale of the world's bereavements had reached such a pitch that the mere forms and requirements of salvation had ceased to be consequential. In their separate Heavens, Luther and Tetzel would be equally outraged.

49

The final blessings were being enacted when Dornberger's rather forced display of paternal grief was interrupted by two civilian gentlemen, who had rushed across to the altar with no apparent sense of occasion. After a brief exchange, the Generalmajor turned and waved a hand: six men immediately detached from the senior rank and hurried away with him.

'Excuse me.' Nagel made to follow them, but was waved back, curtly, by one of the six. Chastened, he returned to Fischer's side.

'Who are they? Other than Schubert, I mean.'

'Senior staff. My immediate boss, Wehrner von Braun. Detmar Stahlknecht, he's Director of Production Planning. Eberhard Rees, the Pilot Production Plant Director. Arthur Rudolph, Production Engineering. The other one isn't a Peenemünder. Herr Degenkolb is head of a special committee overseeing production at all ... special sites.'

'He's bothering to attend a funeral?'

'I'm not sure that's why he's here.' Nervously, Nagel glanced around. 'We should get back to Peenemünde. It's only the interments to follow.'

'You have no one here?'

'A tennis partner. One of the junior engineers, I didn't really know him, off-court.'

The officers and scientists were whisked away in three cars, leaving everyone else to find their own way back to Peenemünde East. There wasn't nearly enough transportation for the hundreds who had come to pay their respects, so Fischer promptly used his uniform and face to secure a place for Nagel and himself in one of the Ford

50

troop trucks that lined the track. Crowded between field greys, they sat in silence during the brief journey. Nagel was preoccupied, twitching occasionally as if in silent conversation and not liking what he was hearing. Fischer twitched also, given ample cause by the lurching truck and jostling shoulders of his neighbours.

At the gateway to the barracks – a former Strength Through Joy holiday camp at which, during the Peace, joyless *überismus* had been instilled into the progeny of the Party faithful – they were dropped off to walk the kilometre or so to the principal facility. This part of the site was curiously empty of the detritus of war. The road was flanked and cordoned by a high wire fence on each side, but the sparse scrubland beyond was neglected in the best sense. It had become, or remained, a preserve for insects, small mammals and birds: possibly the only unforested land in this part of Pomerania not given over to sugar-beets, potatoes, coastal erosion or military man-oeuvres. Its pre-war innocence touched upon a hundred minor recollections of Fischer's youth, and the call of a solitary peewit momentarily swept him back to the best of them. The familiar childhood fantasy returned: to trespass, wilfully, upon a secret, unsoiled place; to lie warmed by the sun and cooled by the grass beneath him; to watch small clouds scud silently from and to the peripheries of his unmoving vision; to know that as long as he preserved a state of perfect stillness he could not be seen, or blamed, or punished.

I didn't even ask her name. Unforgivable.

'...tomorrow?'

51

Nagel was looking at him, expecting a response, and Fischer decided that here was where he might make a start.

'Is this a happy place?'

'*Happy?*'

'Are there tensions?'

Nagel's face suggested that the question was an odd one. He shrugged. 'There are personalities. Sometimes the pressure of what's required can create a little atmosphere, if you see what I mean, when things don't go quite as well as they might. But nothing to be remarked upon.'

'No clashes worth mentioning?'

'Technical ones, certainly. And, of course, there's production.'

'Someone always wants more?'

'Requirements press.'

'But nothing that might encourage irrational behaviour?'

Nagel stopped. 'I can't think what you mean. In what way, irrational?'

'Excessive individualism, perhaps. A lack of commonality, confrontations to no useful purpose?'

'No, nothing like that.'

'And no ... *ideological* issues?'

The answers had been getting more abrupt, but now Nagel laughed. 'What ideological issues could there be?'

'No, of course not. You're right.' It was all sounding a little unlikely, and Fischer felt a familiar, warming sense of something not said. 'If I'm to investigate this matter I really will need to look at the security here. I'll need to speak to the

Army Commander.'

Nagel stopped. 'Generalmajor Dornberger *is* the commander.'

'But that's unusual, isn't it? I should have thought he'd have enough responsibilities already.'

'The arrangement wasn't planned, but the former commander had to leave suddenly, and the Generalmajor was obliged to...'

'Why? What happened?'

'Colonel Zanssen was in charge here until April this year. But accusations were made about him, and Reichsführer Himmler insisted that he be removed.'

'What accusations?'

'That he was a devout Catholic, and an alcoholic, that he had made slanderous remarks about the Party.'

'Who accused him?'

'I really don't think that I...'

'Please.'

'His subordinate, Lieutenant Colonel Stegmaier.'

'Did he have reason?'

'Well, Zanssen made no secret of his Catholicism. He went to church very publicly, at least once every week and sometimes more – you know what knee-scrapers Catholics can be. And certainly, he liked a drink, but then so do we all. I don't know anything about the things he's supposed to have said. It was a strange business.'

Fischer nodded sympathetically. 'But still, one might call it a confrontation to no purpose, with something of an ideological element?'

Nagel flushed. 'It was Army business. I didn't

think you'd want to know about that sort of thing.'

Fischer knew about Zanssen already. For the past two months the story had been making waves all around Berlin. General Fromm, Head of Army Ordnance, had objected to the Reichsführer's interference in Army matters and defended Zanssen very noisily, to the point at which Himmler had decided to drop the matter. It was Fischer's only solid piece of information on anything that had happened in this place.

He stopped in the road. 'Herr Nagel, I have only half a nose, but what there is of it serves pretty well. Please don't try that again.'

The young man was mortified. Of course he'd tell the Hauptmann anything he wanted to know. He hadn't meant to mislead; it was just that the nature of what they were doing made everything a matter for discretion. He had long since decided not to have ears, or opinions, or to involve himself in matters that weren't his business, which was only to be Dr von Braun's personal assistant – a wonderful job of course, he wasn't complaining – and certainly not to involve himself in man-oeuvrings, gossip, accusations, betrayals or any other dangerous game. In fact, he wanted to reassure the Hauptmann that he really wasn't the best person to talk to about such things, being, as he said, entirely outside the hierarchy. But, of course, he'd be completely forthright about the things he *could* speak of. He hoped the Hauptmann would understand his position.

They walked on in silence for a few moments, giving Nagel a chance to convince himself that this troubling conversation was concluded.

'Does Schubert have a problem?'

'What?'

'Herr Godomar Schubert. In the ten minutes I spent in his company he had a face as long as a damp Monday. I assume that isn't his habitual mood?'

'He's been disappointed recently.'

'Not in love?'

'Of course not. He *was* Director of the Pilot Production Plant, but they gave his job to Rees.'

'Why?'

'Numbers, always numbers. Everything we do at this site involves making ideas work. Sometimes it happens, sometimes not. That's the nature of research. There are always far more ideas than solutions, I'm sure you see that.'

'But you said *numbers?*'

Nagel shrugged. 'We're at war. An idea that works becomes a weapon. From that moment, *Can it be done?* becomes *How many, how quickly?* We've had great success in taking the unlikely and making it possible. It's been more difficult to meet expectations once *possible* needs to be made flesh, or metal. Schubert's efforts weren't considered ... adequate.'

'By Dornberger?'

'Herr Degenkolb.'

'So he has ultimate authority here?'

'No, he has overall charge of the allocation of certain resources, but he doesn't outrank individual site commanders. Schubert's removal was part of a deal that he and the Generalmajor agreed in order to resolve a number of outstanding issues. But no one here welcomed it.'

'Nagel!'

They had reached the entrance to the Experimental Works section where a large, handsome man waited: the sort that alpine pursuits or fashion journals featured on their covers during the Peace. If Nagel had named the staff in the order in which they followed Dornberger from the funeral, this was von Braun. He was wearing his funeral suit still; it looked expensive, a perfect fit.

'Pack all of the last quarter's future production estimates and an overnight bag. We're going to Berlin.'

'Yes, sir. May I ask…'

'No.' He glanced at Fischer. 'I wish you well with this business. Walter was a very close friend. I understand you've been told you have very little time?'

'Yes.'

'That may be an exaggeration. The Reichsführer wrote to Reichsminister Speer this morning, on the authority of Adolf Hitler. As of now, production at this facility is no longer under the administration of the Armaments Ministry.'

Nagel paled. 'Oh, God.'

Von Braun shrugged. 'We make do with what we have. What we have is the SS.'

Chapter Seven

In the late afternoon, accompanied by an ober-gefreiter appointed as his guide (or guard), Fischer walked through the experimental and development zones, meeting with very few more restrictions than if he had been taking a turn in the Tiergarten. It hadn't yet been made clear whether his alleged expertise would be required still: the Generalmajor and the entire Peene-münde hierarchy had rushed off to Berlin to determine their fate under the new order, leaving him feeling a little like a jilted correspondence bride. Until he knew more, it seemed a pity to waste the hours staring at walls.

He spoke informally to a few members of staff in the Development Shops, expressing his regrets at the death of their colleague. Insofar as he could pierce their entirely justifiable reserve without revealing his purpose, he gained the impression that Thiel had not been a controversial figure. Those who said that they had respected him did so unguardedly, without apparent reservations; he had been a brilliant engineer who lived for his work and his family, a core element of the team that created new science here. For the rest, well, Fischer had better talk to the Doctor's friends; as to his character, the most they were willing to say was that they really couldn't say. Fischer came away with no further sense of Thiel the man than he might have derived from a personnel file.

The tour of the site, in contrast, was a revelation. The test stand had evoked a sense of latent power, but, isolated from everything else (for very good reasons), it had given only a first, inadequate impression of what Dornberger and his people had laboured to build here. From his childhood, Fischer knew the topography of the area intimately, yet in the years since it might have been that trolls had climbed to the surface, swept away the scattered human imprint and laid a grounding from which eternal war might be waged.

Initially, the prospect was modest: a relatively human-scale clutch of experimental workshops, no doubt raised according to an original plan and added to, haphazardly, as needs dictated. That modesty made the dislocation all the more pronounced when he walked on and, in a very few metres, encountered the other-worldliness of the supersonic wind-tunnel housing, a structure that might have graced a World Fair yet to be imagined. Similarly, the power plant – an enormous modernist structure not unlike its famous counterpart at Battersea – was a striking anomaly, having no aesthetic connection to the low woods that surrounded it. After that, the guidance and control laboratory seemed almost blandly functional, yet the purpose of its instrumentation astounded Fischer: from here, men deciphered the radio signals sent by missiles in flight, the words of the living weapon, relaying its progress to its creators.

But each of these individual impressions, though striking, was eclipsed by the whole. Fischer was wandering through a sprawling, utterly utilitarian prospect of hive-busyness: a thousand processes converging simultaneously towards a single end. Had it been a town, one would have called its planners deranged; what was purpose here would be considered dementia in a world in which order and neatness were synonymous. But that was only because the purpose defeated conventional understanding. Like an adult human mind, Peenemünde had accumulated and reflected stimuli, its form adjusting fluidly to accommodate each new necessity. The meaning of some of these could be deciphered only by an adept, while others were mundanely practical: a cluster of oil pipes, added dangerously to the side of a building that had never been meant to support them; a temporary lean-to, larger than a house, servicing a process unanticipated until some new challenge declared itself; and, almost everywhere, a gordian confusion of rail lines of varying gauges, surrounding and even thrusting through the buildings, making the tour a fraught, interrupted series of hops between its many wonders.

Fischer's polite spirit of enquiry had failed him within minutes, leaving a growing, near-juvenile sense of enthusiasm for an unexpected German miracle. But it was only upon the final stage of his inspection that he encountered the revelation: the thing that brought him close to Believing.

British bombs had smashed the roof of the massive assembly hall, but most of what lay far beneath had suffered only light damage from the

59

rubble that fell on to it. Standing precariously upon a ledge above a half-collapsed wall, four tremendous missile housings recalled the monumental guards at an excavated Middle Kingdom temple. Their shape was determined by aerodynamic necessities, yet for Fischer, a member of a propaganda unit, it was easy to discern the same power-as-beauty aesthetic that marked so much of the Reich's symbolism. Hell, it was working on him, so what would the British think? The hollow, inhuman sleekness, awe-inspiring even beneath a heavy layer of brick dust, trampled upon rationality. He had seen nothing like them; there was nothing like them. The power of the new, the alien, was overwhelming; it demanded his conviction of their power to alter the odds, to make redundant every calculation of what was possible, to carry war far beyond the stretch of a man's imagination.

A small, cold voice interrupted and then stifled his excitement. He had been seized by the same old illusion: that a *miracle* could redeem the errors of human ambition. No doubt it would seem possible for a while: the unnerving shock of invisible, unheard death, the civic disruptions, the fears of politicians for the mood of their people – all of that would cause dancing in the Reich Chancellery, a place where men *wanted* to be convinced. But the British and Americans would counter with weapons or measures that redressed any advantage, in the process relocating war to a new, higher plane of devastation. That was the way it had always worked, the greatest leaps backwards: from bronze to iron, bow to harquebus, musket to machine pistol, demi-culverin to self-propelled missile; why should he imagine that what was being fashioned in this place marked an end-point of annihilation?

Reason, as always, was an uncomfortable corrective. One merely had to measure resources, make the calculation and let the result stamp upon longing. A nation could excel in the martial disciplines, yet the basic principle endured: that an enemy calling upon greater means had to be beaten quickly, and certainly before further enemies were acquired. But, seduced by 1940s fatal victories, they had allowed that understanding to fall away; had believed that the impossible could be repeated indefinitely. And now that something of the truth was bludgeoning its way back into their leaders' consciousness, what was their response? To chase a new wraith, a new illusion of invulnerable might. And Dornberger and his men had fashioned one for them: a beautiful, terrifying thing, a shield to deflect the late onset of sanity.

'Seen enough, Herr Hauptmann?' The obergefreiter wanted to leave; for almost two hours he'd been talking to himself.

'I have, thank you.'

At the boundary of the production area, Fischer showed his security badge to a guard and passed through the checkpoint. At the opposite side of the road, he paused, lit a cigarette and sat on a bench beneath a young beech tree.

The end of the working day was approaching. The trickle of persons passing through the gate became a small stream and then a brief, good-natured flood. Fischer noticed a definite gradation of attention paid to those exiting the sector,

61

determined by the type of security badge they displayed. Two highly ranking civilians passed through with nothing more than a salute from one of the guards. At the other end of the scale, three foreign workers were made to stand back as a number of female secretaries had their own badges briefly checked, and then they were subjected to a minute's fairly close questioning before being allowed to pass through and climb onto a waiting flatbed truck, where several of their fellow ausländers were waiting already: smoking or chatting with what appeared to Fischer to be fairly good humour. No one was searched physically in the twenty minutes or so that he observed the procedures.

He threw the cigarette, untasted, into the road, and stood up before the checkpoint guards decided he was behaving strangely. He was hot, and wearied by the volume of information that, despite appearances, he had almost fully absorbed during the past few hours. He walked slowly back to the guesthouse. A few civilians overtook him on their brisk, short journey from office to Settlement, and two of them took the time to nod politely – though not, fortunately, to notice his face as they hurried by. Three soldiers, loudly debating the merits or otherwise of pickling asparagus, broke off momentarily to salute, almost surprised that the slow rhythm of their day had been punctured by military conformities. Most incongruously amid the technological superabundance of Peenemünde, a grey-nosed mule stared impassively at him as several foreign workers loaded its cart with air raid detritus. Perversely, this pageant of impressions, of an almost parochial community minding its several businesses, raised his mood slightly. A world that encompassed commuters, livestock and pickles argued, however falsely, against a coming German extinction.

With the day's last light hardly illuminating the now-spotless guesthouse, Fischer slowly removed his tunic and shirt. On the kitchen table was a covered plate with utensils neatly flanking it, and a flask of water to one side. He was hungry, and the temptation to sit and eat immediately was strong. But he knew that if he did so his neglected routine would ruin every mouthful, so he went first to the bathroom, to wash his body and two faces. Slowly, gently, he cleaned and dried each, and then with his good hand applied glycerol, methodically describing circles from the old to the new and back again, willing their fusion into something that was neither that Otto Fischer nor this: a thing innocent, uninformed by fates or consequences.

Later, when he had finished his meal (of what appeared to be real meat sausages, and only slightly grey potatoes), he dragged an armchair closer to the fireplace, and covered his legs with a blanket stripped from the bed. After a day of novelties crowding in, one immediately after the other, he didn't expect to sleep. But the clamour of thoughts subsided gradually to a state of outright unconsciousness, and then to a series of fragmentary dreams, of which only two he recalled clearly at dawn. The first was the usual mess of unpleasant memories and fears that daylight tends to defer until the vulnerable hours. The second was simply a literal memory of a day, a beach and a girl who didn't think to offer her name.

Chapter Eight

She returned with his breakfast at 7.30am. He was dressed except for his tunic, which hung in the bathroom, the previous day's creases loosening in the condensation from his morning shower (hot water at dawn: a remarkable achievement). He had shaved in the hope that she would be coming, and allowed neither the pain nor pointlessness of the gesture to dampen his unusually good mood.

She made no eye contact; a tray was placed upon the kitchen table, the previous evening's plate swept up, and she was almost out of the door before he could think of something – anything – to say to keep her there.

'Good morning.'

She half-turned and performed a slight dip, somewhere between a shrug and a curtsey, and made another attempt to get out of the house.

'Zofia...'

She stopped and remained motionless, like a dog waiting for its daily whipping.

'Your name. Zofia? I think it means "wise", doesn't it?'

'Wisdom, sir.' She barely whispered it.

64

'Yes. Yes, well, thank you, Zofia. And for my supper, too. Did you prepare it yourself?'

Jesus. I sound like an importuning goat.

'I ... keep the house. Cook, clean.'

'But not here. Cooking, I mean?'

His persistence was distressing her; both of her hands, gripping the plate and cutlery, had become quite bloodless.

'There is no oven here.'

The kitchen's chimney space almost flaunted its emptiness, and he felt some warmth on the side of his face that could still manage a flush.

'No, of course not. Sorry.'

A pause grew into something mildly excruciating. Not yet dismissed, she waited, eyes firmly upon the linoleum-covered floor. Her clothes, her demeanour, suggested a firm effort to deflect attention from her otherwise obvious attributes: the peasant shift and skirt removed any hint of curves beneath; her rough, over-large shoes made the visible span of legs above them seem too thin; a cheap woollen cap entirely hid her hair and covered half her forehead, heightening an overall impression of proletarian lumpenness. But none of it distracted his memory from what lay beneath: her slenderness, small breasts and long nape, a rear that God must have wept upon as he moulded it. And her posture – the disguise was further betrayed by her inability to move in the manner of someone crushed by a sense of inferior worth, by a life of servitude. As to that, she might usefully have understudied his mother.

His age, perhaps a little younger: *well preserved*, as the patronizing, pseudo-compliment observed.

He knew nothing of her background (they had coupled almost without conversation), though she was certainly not of the world she affected. This woman was – had been – of reasonably comfortable circumstances, and probably well educated. She had holidayed abroad, after all, when such things as holidays happened in the world, and had possessed the self-confidence, the awareness of what she was, to approach a foreign boy and steal his heart for a day. Cool promiscuity requires a degree of sophistication in a teenage girl – he'd sensed something of it at the time, of his being the gauche, unprepared party to a practiced seduction. Even twenty years on, a memorable experience; yet she hadn't recognized him. Was there so little left of the boy she'd screwed in that other age?

He really should think of something more to say.

'You'd better go. If it isn't too much trouble, you might find some writing paper for me. It isn't urgent, but if I could have it waiting for me when I return this evening, I'd be grateful.'

She nodded quickly, already backing out of the kitchen door, and Fischer cursed his stupidity. Too polite. He was a conqueror, a strutting specimen of the *vorlagenrennen*, bound by fate, biology and standing orders to place his boot upon the throat of lesser human species. How could she interpret a pleasant manner, an attempt to be courteous, other than as a clumsy prelude to rape?

He lifted the cloth from the tray, and groaned. Her revenge: oatmeal, and ersatz coffee. He thought of oatmeal as he would anything that had the consistency of something digested twice already, and it was doubtful that there would be another chance to eat before evening. He picked up the cup and took a first sip with a pre-emptive wince of disgust. At least he had no cause to compliment Zofia on her breakfasts; in fact, to do so would only offer further proof of depraved intentions.

There was also a sealed envelope on the tray. A note, from Dornberger: he would be returning to Peenemünde by mid-morning, at which time, he suggested, Fischer and he should meet to discuss fruitful lines of approach to this investigation. Once more, he emphasized a need for speed, or 'alacrity', as he put it.

Fischer sighed. The envelope had opened easily – too easily. There was a trace of moisture still on the seam, to which, undoubtedly, a kettle's spout had been applied some minutes earlier. It was absurd: why would a foreign worker be trusted to carry official correspondence? There was nothing in it that incriminated – Dornberger had been carefully oblique – but this was Germany, where anything not marked *everyone* meant *no one*. Secrecy had become the nation's spinal fluid, and she was a Pole, the beaten enemy: cleaning, cooking and authorized to carry dispatches with the oatmeal. He wondered if it were merely egotism: an unthinking assumption that the vanquished had already accepted the Reich's self-awarded thousand-year tariff as an immutable truth. Or was it the usual German synthesis of a Prussian model of rigid, all-pervasive efficiency administered with Bavarian unconcern? Perhaps the

Wehrmacht, feeling itself too successful in all theatres at the moment, was merely adjusting its security protocols to give the enemy a sporting chance. It would hardly be more preposterous than the likely truth: that the minds of brilliant men floated above mere practicalities.

A shooting offence for an *ostarbeiter*, of course, but he had no wish to see her tied to a post – tied, because the prior interrogation would leave her unable to stand unaided, he could be sure of that. Only he and she would know about this, if he chose not to speak of it. It was having the choice that made him uncomfortable.

To confront her, he told himself, would be counterproductive. If she had acted on her initiative alone the deed was inconsequential; if she had accomplices they would know that he knew, and be warned off. For the moment, it was better to do nothing. He almost convinced himself that this was a rational decision, a clever, well-judged strategy; but an unreliable half-memory of a smile, of her hand twisting his hair as she pulled him down on to her, killed the logical argument.

He refolded the note, slipped it into his tunic pocket and considered its content. *Fruitful lines of approach*: Dornberger was perhaps a fan of trash detective fiction, where brilliant observation, ludicrous serendipity and preternatural deduction solved the case every time. If so, he was going to be disappointed. Fischer knew only a single methodology: to ask questions until someone said something stupid. And that, unerringly, was the one he intended to employ.

It was almost twenty-four hours since his return

to Peenemünde, and he had yet to commence anything that resembled an investigation. But some things seemed to him reasonably clear already. Walter Thiel – apparently a near-perfect human being – had at least one enemy; an air raid was almost certainly the very best means not only of disguising a crime but its method, motive and opportunity also; and Generalmajor Dornberger – apparently a remarkably frank, open and accessible employer – was not being wholly truthful about something. That *something*, unfortunately, seemed to involve Otto Fischer being regarded as the best man for the job. He sighed once more, enjoying the sensation.

The front door crashed open as though the business end of a Ferdinand had tapped upon it. Utilizing his preternatural powers of deduction, Fischer identified the cause without bothering to turn around.

'How do you feel about oatmeal, Nagel?'

Chapter Nine

'It's our, fault. All of it.'

Bleary of eye and slump-shouldered, Nagel sat at the kitchen table, stirring cold oatmeal with the wrong end of a spoon, trying to expunge Berlin by talking about it.

'The Generalmajor tried to defer the decision, but it was too late. The raid was just what Himmler needed to argue that things had to change.

Better security, more resources, a tighter grip on the process. Everything the Führer wanted to hear, he heard. It was devious, without courage, just the way the Reichsführer likes to do things. Afterwards, he sent a polite note to Speer telling him that he was taking control.'

'So what will change?'

'I don't know. Very little with regard to staffing, I should imagine. All the hierarchy here are utterly irreplaceable, no matter what the Reichsführer intends. A new top man in Production, I expect, and the Generalmajor will have to accept that. But I think he knows it's been a possibility ever since the Führer became enthusiastic about what we do. Otherwise, some of the uniforms hereabouts will change, but definitely, the main alterations will be to ... production.'

There it was again: the catch in the voice, the hesitation. And yet it was such an innocent word.

'You said *our fault*. Define *our*, and then tell me what it is that you did.'

'I mean the bosses here. Well, it was Arthur Rudolph's idea – he's the real Party man. But no one objected to it or came up with anything more sensible. Hell, who'd dare to?'

'And the problem?'

Nagel sighed, and scratched his blond head. 'The space between what can be done and what is required. Do you really need to know this?'

'I think so, yes.'

'You visited the assembly hall yesterday, and saw them?'

'The missiles? I did. Very impressive.'

'The Aggregat type four, or A4. It will deliver a

70

warhead at greater speed than that at which
sound travels – a *super-sonic* device. Imagine,
death approaching too quickly for the victims to
appreciate, it's almost futuristic. Ignoring the
possibility of malfunction, there is no technology
that will prevent an A4 from reaching its target,
once launched. It's our premier project, so to
speak.'

'A wonder weapon?'

'It's hard to say. The Generalmajor has worked
hard to convince our masters that it could be a
war-winning device, but there are ... difficulties.'

'Technical difficulties?'

'Yes. The science is unusually complex, and
there are always limitations. At the moment, the
guidance system remains rudimentary, and the
operational missiles will have to be dispersed
widely to prevent the enemy destroying them
before they can be used. Also, the fuel that lifts
them from the ground is problematic.'

'A new formulation?'

'Quite the contrary. The combustion process
mixes liquid oxygen with ethanol, for which, of
course, we shall need to take many, many potatoes
from German mouths. Bad harvests may create
problems.'

Fischer preferred information to be ladled, not
dripped, and felt his patience waning. 'But it will
work? So, again, the problem?'

'*Production*. For the past few months the Armaments Ministry has been at our throats, urging a
vast expansion of the rate at which we produce
the A4.'

'What *is* present production? A rough estimate,

71

of course.'

Nagel laughed. 'Oh, I can give you a rough estimate, all right. It's zero, or thereabouts. Not a single unit has been delivered to the Army as of today.'

'Ah.'

'The issue isn't *present* production, but what we'll be able to produce in future. We used to have rational goals, but since the Führer became convinced of the A4's value, everyone's lost their sense of reality. Reichsminister Speer was insisting that we accept a production target of nine hundred units per month by December. That was fanciful enough, but for a while his idiot deputy Sauer tried to push for double that number. And the most that the Generalmajor can promise is three hundred and fifty units per month by the end of the year, with an unspecified increase over the course of 1944. On *present* resources, that is.'

'So this is a matter of expectation. But where does *fault* lie, and why?'

For a few moments Nagel said nothing. He stared into the oatmeal, by now a near-solid mass supporting a captive spoon.

'Two weeks ago, there was a meeting between Dornberger and Degenkolb to try to agree future targets. It was the one at which Godomar Schubert was replaced: I mentioned that, I think? But he wasn't the main item on their agenda. They were there to talk about manpower.'

'In what sense?'

'Skilled labour. Enough to meet Speer's required production level. You know that we use foreign workers here?'

72

'It's difficult to miss when your meals are prepared by one.'

'Well, there aren't nearly enough of them. *Everyone* wants foreign workers. They staff the Reich's factories and public works, and release our own men to fight. But the resource is finite, and unless we declare war on yet another country the limit's been reached. We've tried desperately to increase our own allocation. It hasn't happened. So the Generalmajor and Herr Degenkolb agreed an alternative.'

Of course: a cheap, plentiful, uncomplaining and infinitely pliable alternative, always ready at a moment's notice to work overtime.

Nagel didn't attempt to disguise his distaste. 'I saw Wehrner's copy of the minutes. They couldn't even admit to it on paper. They stated *sträflinge* – convict labour – when what they mean is *häflinge*. We have a number of them here already, in a sort of trial project, but now they're talking about thousands.'

'So, the wonder weapons are to be built by pacifists, communists, homosexuals, priests, gypsies and Jews?'

'It's our *fault*, you see? After all, who controls all such labour? Who decides that it's labour at all?'

Fischer nodded. Wirtschafts-Verwalthungs-hauptamt: the SS's economic and administrative department had sole control of the disposition of all 'resources' in their possession.

'We might as well have hung out a fucking invitation.'

As any businessman knew perfectly well, if you want to expand you need new shareholders. The

73

trouble was that it was extremely unlikely the Reichsführer SS would be a silent partner. The new, forward-marching Germany was uncannily similar to any *ancien regime*: each department of government guarded its borders and vied bitterly with the rest to seize an ascendancy that would establish its boss as their Leader's favourite. They were all, in effect, courtiers, queuing to kiss their monarch's perfumed rump. By taking control of production of the new weapons, Himmler was associating himself with the war-winning project of the moment. Far more importantly, he was cheese-paring the authority of the Führer's long-term darling Albert Speer. To witness the real war it was only necessary to wander down Wilhelm-strasse on a working day.

Fischer scratched his chin, as he'd been expressly forbidden to do by his doctors. It was a habit from his kripo days, an unthinking gesture denoting the absence of any idea how to proceed. He'd scratched it a lot, back then.

'Assume that I'm not dismissed this morning, and tell me about Walter Thiel.'

With some reluctance it seemed, Nagel obliged him. Thiel had been with Dornberger almost from the start. He joined the fledgling solid fuel research group at Kummersdorf in 1932, when he was just twenty-two years old. He was a chemical engineer by training, but his specialism was propulsion design. He had transferred to Peenemünde in 1940 when he was appointed Deputy Technical Director under von Braun. It was predominantly his work that had resulted in the development of motors producing far greater thrust per volume than had previously been thought possible, so his loss was a major blow, the one incontrovertible success of the British raid. His replacement had been appointed already: his former assistant, Martin Schilling.

As to Thiel's character, he had been well respected for his intellect and as an unselfish collaborator, but he was not gregarious. Dornberger and von Braun had known him for more than a decade, but perhaps the man closest to him in a personal sense was Klaus Riedel, chief of Ground Support at Peenemünde. Their respective families were neighbours at the Settlement; their children played and attended school together. Riedel had been extremely upset, quite overcome by grief, in fact, since the raid, and those who knew him best assumed that Thiel's death was the cause of this.

Nagel could conceive of no motive for murder. He knew of no one at Peenemünde with the slightest grudge against Thiel, professionally or personally; nor of any circumstance or event that might have earned him a deadly enemy. Perhaps, he suggested, this had been a crime in error – the wrong victim?

Not so precisely-in-the-middle-of-the-forehead wrong, it hadn't. Fischer's experience of homicides didn't encourage faith in mishappenstance.

'Was Thiel's home damaged during the raid?'

'It was almost untouched. A window was blown in, I think.'

'I'll need to look at it, obviously.'

'We did so, the morning after. No bloodstains, or anything else that needed an explanation.'

'Still, an ex-Bull's eye, eh?'

Nagel nodded, distracted by the mess in front of him, or the one all around.

A soldier's fist hammered on the door: Fischer's appointment with the Generalmajor.

Chapter Ten

The senior offices occupied a neat corridor on the second floor of House 4, the Army Administration building: white walls, a tastefully neutral carpet and several views of the Rhine Valley all encouraged a sense of comfortable, quiet purpose that, Fischer imagined, reflected the top-tier corporate environments from which the facility had poached its staff. And in a sense that was precisely what was represented here: technical excellence devoted to realizing a superior product, the foundation of modern German industrial success: an occasion of pride, notwithstanding the end to which the facility's efforts were directed.

Stripped to his vest, Dornberger was shaving in a small sink in his office's toilet annex. He nodded to the heavy sideboard behind the desk. 'Get yourself a coffee. It's real.'

Fischer's badly damaged nose had confirmed it the moment he entered the room. He could hardly believe the Reich possessed stocks of the precious commodity still.

'Greek booty, from a little shop in Akazienstrasse. Not for sale to the public, of course.'

'A Party emporium?' The hot, black liquid burned Fischer's tender throat, but he bore it manfully.

'Actually, no. The proprietor was a comrade in my Fußartillerie regiment. We downed arms together in 1918, just south of Guise. He was brighter than me, went into the dried goods business and prospered, while I'm here, deprived of sleep, shaving in a Pomeranian shit-closet and feeling all of my forty-eight years this morning. Go on, have some more. He gave me two kilos, a late repayment for saving his balls.'

Attempting a show of reluctance, Fischer refilled his cup to the brim. 'At the Front?'

'At a whorehouse in Busigny. I wouldn't loan him the price of entry, so to speak. He and I were the only patrons that evening not to get a dose.'

'May I sit?'

'Please. Now, you should know what's happening. It will almost certainly affect your duties here. As I'm sure you've heard from Kaspar, the Reichsführer has taken responsibility for production of the Aggregat A4 rocket. That wasn't what I'd hoped for, of course, but it could have been worse. All experimental and design work remains within the purview of Army Ordnance and the Armaments Ministry, and I continue, as before, to report directly to General Fromm and Reichsminister Speer. To that extent, things have not changed. However, the project will get a new Head of Production. Brigadeführer Dr Hans Kammler is, as the rank suggests, of the SS, and will be inclined to have different loyalties from our own.'

77

'You've met Kammler?'

'Yes. Yet another architect, I'm afraid. It's hard to move around Berlin these days without colliding with one. But his special talents lie elsewhere.'

'And they are?'

Dornberger helped himself to coffee. Fischer sensed that he was using the pause to search for a discreet way to put it.

'Logistics, I would say. He's had responsibility for setting up SS labour camps in the new territories.'

Or the fine art of getting the most for the least calories. Fischer had no experience of these facilities, but he'd heard enough from those who had to get a sense of the kind of man Kammler was.

'I assume that the Brigadeführer doesn't know about Thiel, or my presence here?'

'Not yet, no. I don't intend to tell him, unless circumstances make it unavoidable.'

'I don't understand. Surely the SS will be assuming responsibility for security over production?'

'Of course. But not here, not at Peenemünde. What we'd hoped was safely hidden is, unfortunately, in plain and tempting view. God knows, if the British hadn't mistaken their targets it could have been catastrophic. So, it's been decided that dispersal of the processes is mandatory. We'll continue to do the research and development work at Peenemünde, as I say, but all production will move elsewhere. Where, we don't know yet, but probably quite far from here.'

Dornberger laughed. 'It's ironic. A week ago I'd

have bartered my soul to prevent this, but now I see it as a sort of gift. What we have is a very rare confluence of intention. I want the SS somewhere other than here, and the Reichsführer is pretty much of the same mind. So, a little of my Empire has been annexed, but I retain full control over the heartland. Perhaps you hoped to be relieved of this burden, Fischer? I'm afraid I must disappoint you. In fact, I'm eager to hear your thoughts on how you intend to resolve our problem.'

There were muffled sounds in the corridor outside Dornberger's room. The working day had commenced, a normal day in what might almost pass for a normal environment. But Fischer knew all about how an office's formal protocols and structured hours could deceive. His sole personal experience of office life, at Stettins Police Praesidium, had removed any illusions on that point. At Augustastrasse 47 there had been no deep carpets to muffle the tread, and the morning shift arrived not to a hushed corporate ambience but the scent of the previous night's business: vomit, cigarette smoke and the cheap perfume that working girls used to disguise the odour of their previous tricks, the 'fresh' adding to the patina clinging to every piece of furniture in the building. His colleagues – men who, with few exceptions, had long since forgotten the better days they'd allegedly seen – would shuffle in singly or in pairs, remove their jackets, light cheap cigarettes and slowly re-animate to the bare level required to get through a month's deferred paperwork. There wouldn't be too much noise at first: chairs being kicked back or re-arranged; files dropped or tripped over; new variations upon interminable football sagas, diagnosed by self-anointed experts across two or three desks. Eventually, the scattered intrusions would rise to a sustained crescendo of clacking typewriters, extemporary interrogations in the corridors and the enveloping bustle of kids, taking or delivering orders for coffee and *blechkuchen* from the café at the corner of Grabower Strasse: the cogs beginning to turn freely, the Kriminalpolizei engine picking up steam after a cold start.

Downstairs, more quietly, the human backlog would be marking its time in the cells: the sobering drunk, brooding on what he'd done to his children's mother the previous night; the tart who'd tired of coughing up a percentage and donated a blade instead; the well-dressed fairy who'd tried it on with a plain-clothed Bull in the Helios (home to cinematic wonders and queenly assignations since 1909) and offered too little by way of apology: all of them waiting patiently, hopelessly, to be processed by a cadre of inured placemen.

At the other side of the vast stairwell bisecting their neo-Gothic pile, the truly undesirable elements had their own, discreet world, where they strenuously uncovered what no one had previously thought to be crimes. In 1934, Stettin Gestapo had been deprived of their boss, 'Butcher' Hoffman, a creature so deranged that he remained one of the very few National Socialists to have achieved a criminal conviction for excessive brutality in office. After a respectful pause to mark that loss, his protégés had redoubled their patriotic efforts and, in time, exceeded his inspiring record. The rest of Augustastrasse 47 knew exactly when their good work began each morning, because that was when the other noises commenced: the scrapes, the thuds, the cries of those in grotesquely mis-named 'protective custody' whom decent German society had most to fear: communists, non-importuning homosexuals, evangelists and the few remaining Rosengarten Jews who hadn't yet taken the hint and fucked off to America. So many different lives, homogenized by the same misfortune: to be indoors when the knock came.

Office life didn't really do justice to what Fischer had known there. It had been the pulse of Stettin's daily enema, just two blocks too far from the Oder to be ejected hygienically: Fischer's pulse also, for thirteen years too many. And now? Now, he was required to step off the kerb once more, and he doubted that his foot would find a carpet beneath it.

'My thoughts are quite uncomplicated, Herr Generalmajor. I need to speak to Thiel's neigh-bours and his colleagues, his family also, if any survive. I shall have to retrace his movements for at least the day prior to his death, and possibly for the week before that. I will certainly need to look at any and all information you have gathered on him as part of site security and I would app-reciate it if you could determine whether he was under any form of wider surveillance, no matter how routine. As to resolution, it won't occur as a result of intuitive genius on my part, or by the discovery of a microscopic fibre in someone's lapel. If I'm to resolve this to your satisfaction it will be by persistently, even obtrusively, bothering people you'd rather I didn't involve.'

Dornberger had been nodding since the first item on the list. 'But you won't tell anyone why you're asking these questions?'

Fischer sighed. 'No. As you say, it will be a security matter. Certain unspecified accusations have been made that may or may not have involved information from Dr Thiel's office. Clearly, Thiel himself is no longer able to exonerate himself and, as our lead comes from a source or sources whose reliability is uncertain, we must fully investigate all potential exposures. In a sense, the air raid will assist the deception. Without my having to prompt it, the natural assumption will be that I'm investigating whether some form of security failure encouraged or permitted the British to make their assault. Of course, there is a further advantage to this approach.'

'Which is?'

'Part or all of it may turn out to be true. I doubt that Thiel was murdered because of his taste in socks.'

'Quite.' Dornberger spread his hands. 'Anything else you need?'

'Luck, inspiration, a little more of that coffee, if possible.'

Chapter Eleven

Nagel took him to the Settlement. The damage here was far greater than at the Production and Experimental zones. Its entrance was – had been – a vast gate with substantial wings: the *Brandenburg Tor*, Nagel explained, without apparent irony. It had housed most of the site's senior unmarried male staff, each of them in a small but well-provided apartment. One entire wing of this accommodation had been obliterated by British ordnance, though the three monumental archways remained intact. Through and beyond the structure, rows of neat white houses were interrupted by swathes of destruction, as if a giant fist had swept across a toy village. As with all bomb damage it was entirely arbitrary: Fischer noticed several buildings bearing no visible injury, surrounded by craters in which only a mass of splinters hinted at what had been family homes. Foreign workers, clustered in small groups, were gathering rubble and removing it in handcarts. In several places small fires were burning still at ground level: deposits of domestic fuel oil, probably, trapped beneath soil that had folded in over collapsed houses. It should have smelled much worse than it did, but fresh Baltic air, blowing off water less than five hundred metres away, scoured the site.

Nagel sighed. 'As bad as it was, there could

have been far more casualties. But most of those who wanted a shelter managed to find one before the British second wave came in. Thank God they hit Trassenheide first.'

Fischer had to agree; he would have assumed at least a thousand dead on the visible evidence.

'But I'll show you something amusing.' Nagel led him around a corner now comprising a single house, flanked by recently manufactured match-wood. A small, low sign identifying *Hindenburg Strasse* stood at a slight angle. And that was it, the damage; the street itself, built up on one side only, showed no more evidence of hurt than if it had been caressed by a slightly playful breeze.

'The senior staff quarters – almost all the married heads of department that the British came to decapitate live here, in this one row. There's hardly a window pane blown out from one end to the other.'

Fischer couldn't say that he felt *amused* about it. Only a short distance away stood, or rather lay, the remnants of the Peenemünde community club, converted a few months earlier to provide a dormitory for War Service girls. Many of them, thinking a substantial building would be safer than a makeshift trench, had stayed and died in their beds, badly. Between there and here, too many other tokens of fate's sense of humour blunted Fischer's own. Still, it would have been pleasant to send Churchill a *before and after* picture postcard of Hindenburg Strasse, and have the old drunk choke on one of his Cuban cigars.

They came to one of the middle houses in the undamaged row. 'This is Walter's house. Next door is the Riedels' home.'

One was twin to the other: white, substantial, detached, gables face-on to the road, each with an unfenced, lawned garden to the front; two windows to each of the first two storeys and a single one to the upper, flanked by the steeply sloping roof – an attic room that a kid would sell his or her soul for, probably. All of it quite pretty, in a bland, suburban way; perhaps two or three years old, if that. The clean, modern interpretation of traditional hanseatic architecture reminded Fischer of a 'lifestyle of the future' article in one of the Sundays, of the sort that almost always got it slightly wrong.

A young man in civilian clothes emerged from the side of the left-hand house and walked unsteadily towards them. He was quite stocky, with a thick shock of dark hair, quite unfashionably long, that gave his face a romantically debauched look.

'Hello, Kaspar,' he said, quite formally, and held out his hand.

'Hauptmann Fischer, this is Klaus Riedel. Klaus, I told you that the Hauptmann was going to be looking at security here? He's speaking to all senior staff.'

Riedel tried to smile, but his heart didn't seem to be in it. What Fischer had imagined as nervousness appeared rather to be just nerves: very badly frayed nerves. He glanced back to his house and swallowed, visibly. 'Do you mind if we speak out here? I'm afraid my wife is ... well, the raid, you know...'

'Yes, of course, Herr Riedel. You appear to have

been spared, though?'

'We were very lucky, but...' He waved his arm, encompassing most of the row of undamaged homes, and said nothing more, as if the gesture were eloquent enough.

Nagel punctured the pause. 'Klaus does the moving business here. He makes sure that what we build gets from the assembly line to the launch site, and then up into the air from one of his test stands. He treats them like babies. I always say I wish I had a car as comfortable as one of his transporters.'

Riedel smiled bleakly. 'You wish you had *any* sort of car, Kaspar.

Fischer calculated that subtlety would be entirely wasted upon a man as distracted as this. 'I wonder if I might ask you about your neighbour, Dr Thiel?'

He hadn't even decided what to ask, precisely, but Riedel's reaction made any further effort pointless. Tears welled up in his eyes, and for a moment his legs twitched as if about to give way. Nagel caught hold of his elbow, and held him tightly.

'It's my fault! My God, I killed them!'

The sort of confession that Fischer used to dream of, but it was tainted with a distressing sincerity. He meant something else.

'Please explain that.'

'I ... when the raid began, I saw Walter carrying his little girl into the house. I shouted at him, told him he was being stupid, that he should get them all to the trenches where it was safer. I persuaded him! If he and his family had stayed where they wanted to be, they'd be alive, not in a mass grave!'

He started to cry, the sort of stifled, lip biting half-weep that's difficult to carry off disingenuously, unlike that mainstay of the interrogation room, the full-blown, theatrical sob. Nagel's attempts to console him were both clumsy and futile: this was a man carrying soul-sized guilt.

'I'm sorry, Herr Riedel. You say you saw Dr Thiel at his home. Do you know anything else of his movements that day? Please try to remember.'

With an effort, Riedel recollected himself. 'Yes, I do. I was with Walter for most of it. I believe he had a meeting with Dr von Braun and Martin Schilling to discuss something about the scheduled A4 test launch that day. Anyway, the test was cancelled because of a technical issue. Because of this, both Walter and I had time on our hands, so we played tennis before lunch – we always bring our racquets in case there's an unexpected break. It was a fine day, though the wind blew too strongly for us to have more than a knock-around. We had lunch together at House 4's dining room, and then the Generalmajor called an extraordinary meeting of senior staff to discuss the new production targets from the Ministry.'

Riedel glanced at Nagel to reassure himself that he wasn't telling tales.

'It was the usual sort of thing. The Generalmajor was insisting that the A4 was now ready to go into full production, and Walter insisted equally firmly that it wasn't. We've heard a lot of

87

that lately, but voices weren't raised. The meeting finished about four o'clock. A question had been put during the meeting that specifically addressed my own and Walter's areas of expertise, so he and I remained in the Experimental Works offices until about six, when I returned to my home. I think Walter went back to the engine test-bed for a little while before he finished for the day. The next time I saw him was after midnight, when...'

'Yes, of course.' Fischer didn't want to set him off once more. 'Would you tell me the nature of this particular business that you and Dr Thiel needed to discuss alone?'

'It's very technical...'

'Please do your best.'

'We've had a number of problems with the fuel injection system for the A4. We considered a potential issue to be vibration created within the mechanism when the missile is being moved. I had a few ideas about reinforcing and increasing the padding material on the test stays, and also perhaps improving the suspension system for our transporters. But as I say, this was one of a number of possible causes, and Walter and I spoke only in broad terms about it. May I ask why you're asking these questions?'

Curious that it had taken Riedel so long to *become* curious; perhaps the innate German deference to authority afflicted even the virtuosi.

With slight modifications, Fischer rehearsed the version he had offered to Dornberger. Gratifyingly, Riedel nodded distractedly and seemed to lose interest halfway through the explanation – the word *security* had such broad, discouraging implications. It was fairly clear that he wanted to get back inside, so Fischer thanked him for his time and, for want of a good hand with which to shake another, gave a short, rather Prussian bow.

Thiel's home could be examined at another time, when Riedel was elsewhere. Fischer and Nagel walked back to the Brandenburg Tor, where workers were raising scaffolding to shore up the glacis exposed by the abrupt disappearance of its north wing.

'You seem to be on good terms with Herr Riedel.'

'Klaus? Yes, he's a good fellow. We all like him.'

'And yet, you're – forgive me – a secretary. Do the various professions here mix easily?'

Nagel shrugged. 'As with everything, this place is unusual. When we're working you'll never see more rigid segregation, not even in the army. But socially it's not so formal. Men like von Braun don't drink with labourers, naturally, but we've been here for years, cut off from the rest of Germany, so it isn't just a workplace. There are families who socialize outside their natural rank, there are technical staff – bachelors – who take every opportunity to mix with the War Service girls, and some of them get married.' He grinned. 'I mean, some of them are *obliged* to get married. It's very informal, and very much encouraged. We have a lot of social nights that bring people together, you should come and see.'

'I doubt whether anyone would thank me for doing so.'

Nagel paused, and the silence acquired a very

familiar frisson. 'May I ask...?'

Fischer winced. The stages of reaction to his wounds could be plotted like a campaign that had already run its course: horror, stifled revulsion, a brief period of pretending that there was nothing to look at, and then, inevitably, the questions. *Tell me all about it. Does it hurt? Did you suffer much? I suppose that girls are out of the question ...* vicarious toes, dipping into what they feared the very most, courtesy of the hideous yet obliging Otto Fischer, hero and cautionary tale. As to what would be an appropriate response, he had yet to stumble upon it. The truth was literally indescribable, so something else was required. He might downplay his ordeal as a certain sort of British officer might dismiss a threatened decapitation, but that would make him more, not less, of an oddity. A sincere Attend To Your Own Business would be simpler, but he had no intention of setting himself even further from human company than his wounds had taken him. Silence, the kindest response, was useless: it attracted all the more attention from those who felt they needed to understand the pain of others. The problem, always, was expectation: his would-be audience deluded itself that what they wanted to hear was an honest – in fact, an analytical – description of his experience. But how it was, how he *felt* about it, required him to address so much more than the incident and what followed. The only frank response would involve an admission that he was living the consequences of something uncomfortably close to a protracted suicide attempt: one that had been maturing since 1937. And that was in every way an inconceivable admission.

He glanced at the patient Nagel. 'Better not to. Is there somewhere we might eat?'

Chapter Twelve

The site's main dining room at House 4 was the obvious choice. The electric railway was functioning again, and they took a train at the Settlement 'station', a low, island platform, without an office, fence or other support structure. Within a minute of their arrival the north-bound train pulled in; its two small carriages – small in every sense, almost like mine-stock – were obviously old and fairly dilapidated, but more than half-full. As Nagel explained, rail transport was free within the Peenemünde facility, so it was the preferred mode of travel, even among senior staff. The result was unnervingly democratic: they sat among a few volunteer workers, a sociable gaggle of technicians' wives and a crowd of off-duty soldiers, all maintaining their own discreet company as people did on trains. It could have been a pre-war outing, though their journey was over so quickly that Fischer was reminded more of a fairground ride.

Security at the administration building required him to sign a visitor's book and surrender his gloves to an ageing steward. To spare stomachs, he parted with one only. There was a small bar adjacent to the dining room, but Nagel led him swiftly past it. Consumption of alcohol was discouraged until evening: part of Peenemünde's near-invisible concessions to the mood and necessity for sacrifice elsewhere.

Lunch was adequate, at best: bland and filling, but at least someone among the kitchen staff knew how to make a proper dumpling. They sat with about two hundred others in a large room, lit by floor to ceiling windows, several of which were held together by tape. Most of the neighbouring diners were chattering away obliviously, and again Fischer was reminded strongly of a quite ordinary peacetime setting. Apart from the number of uniforms and the quality of the food being served, they might have been lunching at one of the Reich's great industrial combines, surrounded by idle chatter about a coming weekend, or the cheerily poisoned barbs of office gossip. Even the same boundaries of corporate privilege distinguished Peenemünde's top military and technical staff from the other ranks. The table at which he and Nagel sat was laid with a white tablecloth, whereas most of the others were bare; their own cutlery was bespoke and polished, the rest merely generic and burnished to a pewtered gloss; their meals were served by white-coated staff, while other ranks had to queue for their (identical) portions. It was important, presumably, that everyone be reminded of his or her place.

A number of the nearer diners glanced across at them, and the effect of his visible wounds on their appetites was difficult to ignore. Nagel flushed, still conscious of his own recent trespasses.

'I'm afraid that I use you as a Trojan horse,

Hauptmann. I usually sit over there, with the other senior secretaries, but the Generalmajor insisted that you were to be treated as one of the plates, so here we are, top table.'

'Plates?'

'As in name plates, upon office doors. Still, it's the same food, isn't it?'

For a while they ate silently. The fork in his good hand, Fischer moved several pieces of grey, nondescript animal product a decent distance from the more edible content, while his lunch companion determinedly ate everything on his plate. Both declined the pudding: a dense, suet-like mass swamped by a white sauce that almost certainly had never met a cow. As their plates were cleared, Nagel frowned. 'It really isn't this bad, usually. But our chef was injured during the air raid, and since then...'

Fischer didn't need the apology; the rest of Germany had been frowning for the same reason for the past five years or more. He took out a cigarette, changed his mind, offered it to the young man. 'Apart from Riedel, who are the people who knew Thiel best?'

Nagel laughed. 'Ah, a straightforward question.' He lit up, drew deeply and gave a brief, dis-heartening analysis of the human Peenemünde.

The hierarchy of engine development was clear enough: von Braun, Thiel, Schilling, and these men were in each other's company a great deal, naturally. But the site's wider research and development relationships were complicated. There was also the Design Bureau under Walther Riedel (at this point, Nagel explained the confusing abundance of Riedels at the site: Walther Riedel, surreally, had replaced Walter 'Papa' Riedel as head of the Bureau; they continued to work together, and were related neither to each other nor to Klaus Riedel), which co-operated closely with the engineers, and many other disciplines were similarly drawn into professional proximity. But the question of who worked with whom on any working day didn't begin to address the reality of their relationships.

Men who toiled in entirely different disciplines at Peenemünde often shared a close history, Fischer was told. Klaus Riedel, for example, had been a friend of Thiel's not only because they were neighbours at the Settlement but also fellow engine designers from the early days. Both had been among the founders of the famous *Raketenflugplatz* at Berlin where, in 1931, Riedel had been responsible for a groundbreaking rocket design, the *Mirak II*. Staff who emerged from this group and from the rocket experimental programmes at Siemens and Heylandt-Werke comprised most of the facility's senior technical staff, so connections bordered upon the incestuous. Dornberger, von Braun, Walter Riedel, Arthur Rudolph, Thiel and Klaus Riedel were all graduates of one or more of these practical academies, and had collaborated at Kummersdorf and elsewhere before Peenemünde was ever founded. And even before any of *that*, an inordinate number of the facility's staff had come out of just two universities, Darmstadt and Dresden, with personal ties that fell back into prehistory.

Nagel smiled almost apologetically, though none

of this was his doing. 'Examining connections here is a bit like surveying mist, unfortunately.'

Christ. Fischer wouldn't have believed that his expectations could be lowered further. 'What about the foreigners?'

'We have about three or four thousand. The figure's been rising all the time as we approach a production phase. For the moment that number will fall. We've had to send away about a thousand of them so we can accommodate Germans who've lost their homes at the Settlement. That may or may not be temporary, depending upon how loss of production to the SS affects us.'

'And those that remain? How are they supervised?'

'All ausländers are confined at Trassenheide, Karlshagen or Wolgast at night, but when they're here they tend to be supervised by civilian staff, or soldiers who are really civilians.'

'What does that mean?'

'About half the military ranks at this site are held by men who aren't really part of the Wehrmacht. The Generalmajor and Army Ordnance prefer at least the illusion that the technical and engineering staff are subject to military discipline, so most of them get some sort of rank. I haven't, though.' Nagel didn't seem too displeased at the oversight.

'So without enough real soldiers to guard them, the guest workers can wander around their badged zones almost at will during daylight hours?'

'Not quite, but ... the trouble is, we use so many of them that strict supervision would require a lot more security than we can requisition. Most

95

resources are put into the perimeters – that is, either keeping people out or in, not watching those within it.'

'But foreigners aren't allowed near the technical areas, surely?'

Nagel shifted uncomfortably. 'We have a group of Russians, anti-Bolsheviks, who *are* technical staff. They work in the blueprints office of the Design Bureau, and contribute a great deal to the process. Really, they're quite a Godsend. More Russian volunteers assist in manufacturing graphite parts for the warheads, and there are a couple of Poles who assist senior staff.'

'You have extensive security files on all foreigners working here, of course?'

Nagel didn't even bother to answer that one, and Fischer felt a little more of the ground beneath him disappear.

'So, to summarize, there are just two external points of security, one at Zempin, the other at...?'

'Wolgast, the bridge.'

'Thank you. The southern bottlenecks are secured, then. To the east, north and west lies the sea, but no further perimeter security?'

Nagel smiled, ruefully. 'No, though there *is* a sign on the beach at Zinnowitz: *No Poles or dogs*. I shouldn't imagine it deters either. And there are regular patrols, of course, though only at night.'

'Thank God the destiny of the Reich is being taken seriously.'

He sat in probably the most sensitive research facility in Germany, and its internal security arrangements were only slightly more rigorous than those at a Berlin club on ladies' evening. The

Führer's person – all one of it – was guarded by the equivalent of up to two regiments of highly trained SS personnel. This entire peninsula, home to almost as many enemy nationals as Eastbourne, was protected by two border checkpoints, a disparate group of Army regulars, reservists and rank-appointed civilians, a cluster of flak batteries (employed only reluctantly, in case attacking pilots guessed the importance of what it was they were bombing the hell out of) and a stretch of fine, unspoiled beaches.

Nagel shrugged. 'What can we do? It's all about resources.'

No, it was about taking a serious business more seriously than at present – a frozen, unreal present that the long expected air-attack had failed to disturb. Fischer was beginning to find this air of semi-detachment more than a little irritating. He understood well enough the attractions of preserving the quality of the life they had – it was one that was almost without parallel elsewhere in Germany. They enjoyed sports and social facilities that most ordinary people hadn't seen for years, a decent diet, excellent housing and, until three days ago, a level of personal security – however illusory – that the Reich's urban population would have sacrificed their collective first-born to recover. It was as if *here* and *the rest* were entirely different worlds, and the balance lay entirely to the advantage of Peenemünders. Who would want to lose that?

But this wasn't a vacuum; it wasn't a society set apart, absolved of responsibility to understand what was happening elsewhere, what was happening *now*. All around them, reality pressed with fearsome force: at Hamburg, where forty thousand citizens had died recently, flattened or burned during terror raids; in Sicily, part of an allied nation six weeks ago and now a vast Anglo-American base, poised to launch God alone knew what into the soft underbelly of the Reich; above all, in the east, where a remorseless tide of vengeance was pressing furiously, trying to bury Europe in a new, darker Dark Age. The nation stood upon a cusp of catastrophe whose implications were beyond imagination, and Peenemünde basked comfortably in its pre-war insouciance still, collectively wondering whether anyone was for tennis.

'Well, it isn't my business, of course.' He stood abruptly. New diners were replacing the previous sitting, and he was tiring of the fresh wave of disturbed glances. 'It would be useful if we could speak to Dr von Braun and Herr Schilling about their relationship with Thiel. I assume it's possible?'

'Schilling, certainly. He's probably at the Development Shops. I'm not so sure about Werhner. He may be in Berlin still, briefing the Reichsminister.'

In fact they encountered Martin Schilling immediately outside the dining room, about to join his colleagues for lunch. Nagel introduced Fischer, and the scientist nodded unenthusiastically. Like von Braun, he was a rather sleek, well-nourished young gentleman. The brown laboratory coat he wore gave a first impression of routine dreariness, but the dark blue silk tie beneath was held nicely in place by a gold pin, and his shoes were of a quality that a more frugal man would not have risked in a working environment.

The request wasn't welcome, obviously, but Schilling agreed to postpone his lunch. They sat on a bench in the building's foyer, where the passing bustle made their conversation a discreet one.

It was a straightforward, unproductive interview. Schilling repeated the seemingly universal opinion of Walter Thiel as an excellent scientist and valued colleague, respected by many and resented by none: a paragon, almost. He took mild offence, however, at being described as the dead man's assistant.

'I was a *colleague*, though necessarily a subordinate also. Walter worked upon increasing the propulsive power of motors. I've been concerned with guidance.'

'Gyroscopes?'

'No. My problem had been how to enable the A4 to accelerate on a constant trajectory until sufficient velocity has been achieved to allow the external fins to guide the missile. Do you understand?'

Fischer assured him that the explanation was wonderfully precise.

'I only ask,' continued Schilling, 'because the process of building this missile has been the most complex of any scientific endeavour yet undertaken. May I also ask why you're interested in his work, Hauptmann?'

Fischer pointed out that, as the only senior technician killed in the recent raid, Thiel was also the only man unable to answer questions regarding security in his work place.

'There's no issue about security in Development, is there? We've never had one before.' Schilling glanced at Nagel, who examined his own shoes with great interest.

Still irritated, Fischer spoke severely. 'In any facility designing secret weapons there must be security issues, Herr Schilling, particularly one in which a great number of non-Germans are employed. I think perhaps your attitude is shared by others here, hence the Generalmajor's enthusiasm for a fundamental review of the present procedures.'

To his credit, Schilling backed down gracefully. 'Of course. Since the bombing we can hardly expect things to carry on in the same way. It's a new world now, I suppose.'

'You'll be surprised to know that *that* is a relatively perceptive opinion, sir,' said Fischer, dryly. 'There appears to be something of a holiday atmosphere about this place.'

The scientist shrugged in a manner that simultaneously conveyed polite regret and the fact that he really couldn't care less. 'We are a product of our work, Hauptmann. For years we've eaten, slept and drank our disciplines, and if we ever discuss anything that happens outside, it's with colleagues who are equally unworldly. Our perspective must be a skewed one.'

'On that I couldn't comment. Tell me, how many foreign workers are employed in your department?'

Schilling frowned. 'As technicians? Six, I think,

on a permanent basis. Other, non-skilled workers fetch and carry materials as needed.'

'So, a technical worker will understand something of the processes here? I mean, I assume that he sees them being undertaken over a long period?'

'Well yes, but only to a point. No ausländer is allowed to work in more than one technical area. Nor is he allowed access to any written data – excepting the Russians in the Design Bureau, of course. So, the opportunity to understand more than a very, very little of what goes on here is entirely denied to him.'

'And Dr Thiel's personal areas of expertise? How many foreigners are familiar with that?'

'Just one.'

'Would someone be able to point him out to me?'

'Certainly, upon the Great Day that comes to us all. He died at Trassenheide, during the raid. Now, if you'll excuse me, the final lunch-sitting finishes in a few minutes, and I'd appreciate a little nourishment, however vile.'

Fischer stood up with him and practised the formal nod once more. 'Thank you, Herr Schilling. You'll understand that all this is very new to me. I'm still trying to grasp the detail of how your weapons are constructed.'

Schilling smiled thinly. 'We don't create weapons here, Hauptmann, merely the means to accommodate and deliver them. What we do is to make things go further and faster than anything that was ever conceived by man.'

When he'd gone in, Fischer turned to Nagel.

'You said that Dr von Braun is in Berlin today? I'll speak to him tomorrow, perhaps. In the meantime, I need to go there myself. Can something be arranged that won't require me to be away for more than a day?'

Nagel shrugged. 'The airfield. If you think it necessary, the Generalmajor will authorize transport.'

Chapter Thirteen

The Fieseler Storch banked steeply as it approached Berlin-Tempelhof, and Fischer reached instinctively to check a non-existent parachute harness. It was his first flight since the Crete campaign – a long grounding, though it hadn't blunted his distaste for travelling in machines only slightly less prone to buffeting than a Chinese kite. For a former member of an elite airborne force, he was a remarkably bad flier.

With the Generalmajor's somewhat bemused blessing he had hitched a ride on the 'medical supplies' flight from the Luftwaffe experimental airfield at Peenemünde West: or, more accurately (as Nagel explained), the twice-monthly shopping trip to maintain the facility's strategic reserves of alcohol and tobacco.

The pilot, a loud, cheery fellow, was delighted to discover that his sole passenger was ex-Fallschirmjäger. He'd often, he declared, carried the heroes of the parachute regiments into battle, and a great honour it had been, too. Fischer had hoped that this was a pleasantry, something to get out of the way before he took a nap; unfortunately, it had proved merely to be an introduction. For the entire ninety minutes of the flight to Berlin, the man hardly drew breath while recounting, in minute detail, his exploits before and during the Norway campaign, which had ended abruptly when his BV142 went down outside Hønefoss, killing the co-pilot and all seventeen troops on board.

'Fucking lucky, eh? I'd have walked away from it, except for the knee.' He had insisted that Fischer tap its metal replacement to corroborate the event, and then offered an obscenely technical analysis of the things he was obliged to do more carefully these days.

'Herr Douglas von fucking Bader, that's me!'

So Fischer was feeling unusually tired by the time he prised himself away from his new comrade and walked into the vast, curved terminal. Waved through the services' checkpoint, he descended to the u-bahn and caught a crowded train to Potsdamer Platz. He emerged into light rain and the organized frenzy of trams, automobiles, double-decked buses, bicycles, the occasional horse-drawn cart and seven converging streams of preoccupied pedestrians. Grabbing a packet of cigarettes and a newspaper at the first booth out of the station, he pointed himself towards Wilhelm-strasse and the Air Ministry.

He'd been away for just forty-eight hours, yet a faint sense of unfamiliarity dogged his footsteps the length of Leipziger Strasse. Physically, the city remained almost untouched by the war, but a pervasive *ennui* dulled its citizens, fed – if that was the correct term – by too few kilocalories, vanishing basic commodities and far too much news of 'stabilized' fronts that moved closer to Germany at each successive stabilization. This wasn't new, of course; the loud, opinionated, iconoclastic buzz of pre-war Berlin had long since faded to the grudging murmur of a city determined not to be bothered. Individualism had become self-absorption: no one caught anyone's eye any more (he was grateful for that, at least), or measured themselves against the increasing shabbiness of their neighbours. One wit – there were those still, at least – had suggested that the city's changed circumstances necessitated a new civic coat of arms, its main device to be a human back, three-quarters turned away, slightly hunched.

This should all have seemed like coming home to Fischer, an adopted son, yet he felt otherwise, and it occurred to him that it must be the fault of Peenemünde. He'd spent two days among people for whom it was mid-1940 still, a time when the cost of conflict was not yet perceptible, much less experienced. There, Germany was on the march still, not reeling; it wasn't redeploying hastily to counter the consequences of yet another strategic blunder; it wasn't watching forlornly as the ration allowance shortened and queues lengthened almost daily. There, even the air raid, for all its deadliness, had been an aberration: an intrusion into the relative idyll of a lifestyle recalled mostly in memory by other Germans. Back in Berlin, the contrast – the atmosphere of tense expectation – struck him with renewed force. It couldn't quite be called fear, not yet: more a sullen conviction that worse was in the way of better.

The relative emptiness of Wilhelmstrasse, the hub of government; hardly dampened the perception. Its monumental façades, like that of the terminal building at Tempelhof, chilled the spirit. If any sense of permanence was conveyed here it was a cold, inhuman strain, unmindful of the merely biological elements that soiled a noble setting. *This* Germany was on the march, too; it was just the people who'd been left behind.

The Air Ministry was the worst of them, the inaugural blunder in the phased comedy of *Germania*. One had only to glance at and pity the guards at its entrance, vainly trying to meet the expectations of the cliff behind them, to wonder at the hubris that conceived it. As he entered the building on any working day, Fischer felt that he owed an apology to a thing unseeing and indifferent: a regret, for his mere mortality. The acoustic was equally alienating; already distant, the on-going removal of vital staff to the underground facilities at Zossen-Wünsdorf had gradually created a sound-space reminiscent of the fled grandeur of a mediaeval cathedral. It wasn't an entirely adequate simile: cathedrals were much smaller, and served more modest causes; but as in them, it was becoming possible to hear the distant, crisp percussion of heel against stone floor without seeing a single face.

However, it was a Sunday, and Fischer's office was almost busy. Dissemblance recognized neither God nor family life – particularly the latter, and even more particularly on Sundays, when the wife and kids had far more time to reflect upon what the Tommies, the Frenchies or the Ivans had done to Father. In any case, the Lie Division had just inherited that entire section of their floor (the obviously more valuable Luftwaffe film unit had been evacuated during the previous week), and the expendables were enjoying the luxury of sufficient room to stretch out their various prosthetic discomforts. Detmar Reincke, a young Saxon whose rugged farming face had been enhanced considerably by a detonating ammunition dump outside Minsk, greeted Fischer with a wave of the only hand he'd thought to keep.

'Otto! I thought I smelled something old and ugly. You can't have caught a dose already?'

It took a while to dispense with the pleasantries, thanks to Karl Krohne, who had spilled the details of Fischer's supposedly confidential assignment even before the first polite enquiry was made. No, he assured them, it was not a place of fantastical buildings rising like a Baltic Manhattan from the forests. Yes, there was an inordinate number of attractive, single young women there, but most of them neglected to walk around in shorts and halter-tops, though yes, it was very close to the beach. And no, he hadn't managed to get *any* in the past forty-eight hours.

Reincke closed his eyes rapturously. 'All that *muschi*, just begging for it. Jesus!'

Fischer looked around. 'Where's Uncle Fred?'

Oberleutnant Friedrich Melancthon Holleman: shot down over Utrecht in 1940, losing half a leg and about a metre of colon; considerably older than most of his workmates and therefore con-

106

demned to being inconvenienced by a bunch of damp-arsed infants, as he reminded them often; prone to taking early lunch-breaks with former Luftflotte 2 cronies that sometimes continued until 'the light stopped bothering him', or *dusk*, in the vernacular; a former member of the Berlin Ordnungpolizei who'd had the bad judgement to join a flying club back when climbing into a cockpit counted as a hobby and not a farewell.

'He's trying to beg that week's leave from Karl.'

Holleman had no intention of waiting for Berlin to go the way of Hamburg, or his sons the way of their friends in the Hitler Jugend. For weeks now, he'd been on his telephone, pestering friends in the suburbs to take his family for the duration. When those friends had turned out to be mere acquaintances, he'd hurriedly built Plan B around a decaying lake-house in the Spreewald, inherited from his parents almost a quarter of a century earlier. It needed some windows and a water supply, and his presence to affect them, and it was the opinion around the office that he'd be lucky. But Holleman's native optimism had somehow survived a long career on Berlin's streets and a disastrously brief relationship with altitude, so no one thought to try to talk him down.

'Otto Fischer!' Holleman beamed from the door, confounding universal expectations. 'What a fucking eye-sore!'

'Hello, Freddie. Fancy a drink?'

Their usual dive was *The Silver Birch*, just off Potsdamer Platz: a pit most recently spruced up to welcome the Huguenots (the fall of plaster from its walls could be tracked by the incidence of new posters pinned to what remained). The venue's undeniable charms were irresistible. Its resolute and carefully nurtured shabbiness deterred the ministerial hordes who infested that part of Berlin; its flagrant disregard of licensing laws managed to give the elbow both to the National Socialist fetish for time-keeping and the work ethic in general; most attractively, its owner, either through startlingly effective contacts or a network of blackmailed vintners, had managed to maintain a supply of reasonably cheap, shockingly strong beverages in a time of ever-shrinking resources. It was also comfortable, as only truly shabby places can be, and the establishment was proud of the fact that a notable number of its more faithful patrons had chosen to die on the premises. This was not so much testimony to the bar's standards as to the preferences of the honoured dead who, once settled with a glass in their hands, had never really wanted to go home. The two tiny rooms that comprised the *Birch* had become the unofficial mess of the Lie Division's walking wounded, most of whom respected tradition and intended at some point to add to it.

They sat at a small, age-blackened table beneath a tattered panorama of Hohenschwangau-Neuschwanstein. It had been Fischer's invitation, but Holleman, still slightly delirious at the unexpected windfall of a week's leave, insisted on buying the drinks. His price was a detailed dialogue, delivered without pause, upon the necessary renovations at Spreewald and a tactical appraisal of how the hell he was going to get up and down a ladder. It took a while (and seemed to take longer), but eventually he flagged sufficiently for Fischer to ask the question.

Holleman frowned. 'At the Alex? A few, more now than a couple of years ago. Some of the retired Bulls have been brought back to replace the ones who've gone East. Why?'

'I was hoping you'd know someone who won't be too curious about why I'm curious.'

Holleman mulled it over. 'Gerd Branssler. Straight bloke, had a few problems after 9 March.'

Any Bull, serving or retired, understood the reference. At some point prior to 9 March 1937, the Reichsführer SS, allegedly suffering from severe menstrual pains, had decided that anyone with two or more time-served convictions could – actually, *should* – be re-arrested. On that whim, thousands of petty repeat-offenders and perverts had been off'd to camps that had been built and therefore needed to be filled. Fischer had been on sick leave at the time, trying to coax down a testicle, and wasn't directly involved. But it had been the moment at which the Kriminalpolizei got a first clear view of the future of German law enforcement. Some of them, even a few of the harder cases, had found it difficult to take – no one, after all, likes to lose an entire cadre of snitches at a stroke. The incident had been one of the many shoves in the back that pushed Fischer out of the door; if Branssler had decided to stick it out, he probably had kids to feed.

Holleman drained his glass and wiped the froth from his mouth. 'He won't put his arse on a shovel for you, but he won't tell tales either. His brother married a *mischling*, so he's not ... dogmatic. And you don't know any of that, by the way.'

'Can you call him? Say that there's a bottle of Courvoisier in it for him?'

'As soon as we get back. Another?'

Chapter Fourteen

Three hours later, Fischer sat at a window table in the *Final Instance*, waiting for Branssler. It was too close to the Alex for him to feel entirely at ease, but it was also one of the few such places thereabouts still open, and as a restaurant with booze – as opposed to a bar with food – it didn't attract too many Bulls.

He was sipping yet another weak beer he hadn't paid for, courtesy of a proprietor with a boy somewhere north-west of Kiev. The place was almost empty in the sunlit early evening. An old woman moved slowly between tables, brushing away crumbs and laying out cutlery, while their host, leaning on the counter, minutely checked his copy of *Der Angriff* for fragments of good news. Fischer apart, his custom comprised a lone couple, huddled at a corner table at the other side of the room, giving each other their full attention. Their hands were entwined tightly, offering the meagre audience testimony of their love, and they didn't care who knew it. A last stop before the Schlesischer Bahnhof and the Front: his kit bag and her red eyes said it all.

110

A little after six, a thick-set man with Beef stamped all over him entered the restaurant, glanced around and came straight over to Fischer's table.

He grinned. 'Hard to miss.'

Fischer nodded. 'I don't get much undercover work any more.'

They shook hands, left to left, and Branssler asked for a glass of wine. From the look on the proprietor's face when he brought it, nothing else was going to be free that evening.

The Bull was relaxed. 'What's the problem?' he asked confidently, with the air of a practiced fixer.

'Is there anyone upstairs at the Alex who'd be willing to talk?'

'Gestapo? No chance. Those boys don't do that, not with us or anyone else, not if it's business. You were kripo – you must know what it's like.'

Fischer nodded. It had been a faint hope, at most. 'Why would you want to?'

'I need to know if they've investigated some-one, recently or otherwise.'

'It may be a few names. I'm not sure.'

Branssler laughed. 'No problem, then. Just walk in, ask for the key to the file room, and shout up for a coffee when you feel like one.'

Fischer told him to forget it, and for a while they talked about the old days, chasing honest career pimps and straight-up murderers. A menu arrived, and after mature consideration they both ordered its only item: the day's 'special', *gaisburger marsch*. It came too quickly, with potatoes but no *spätzle* ('that'll be what's special about it'). Branssler was good company. He laughed a lot at his own crap jokes and didn't seem to give a damn about anything except his pension, so it was easy to see why he was one of Freddie Holleman's cronies. They both finished with an imitation cognac ('if this is the *eaux-de-vie* I'm a rent-boy') and an even more imitation coffee; Branssler allowed Fischer to spend his coupons on the bill, politely refused the bottle of real brandy he'd brought, and waved away an apology for having had so much of his time stolen.

'For once I was the prettiest guy in the room. It's been a pleasure.' He picked up his hat and rose to leave. But then he paused, and put out a large hand.

'Did you bring the names?'

Fischer handed over the list, and Branssler scanned it briefly.

'Don't hope for much. I'll back off quicker than a frog from a fart if I get noticed.'

Fischer watched him leave, knowing before he saw it that both ends of the street would get a practised glance as the hat went on. He remained at the restaurant for a further ten minutes, finishing his disgusting coffee, and decided to walk home: five kilometres that felt like three in the balmy August evening. As a wounded Luftwaffe officer in Berlin, he was based officially at the Reinickendorf lazarett, but the severity of his wounds, and the unlikelihood of his ever being fit to return to active service, had made him semi-visible to his superiors. It had taken very little pleading to be allowed to reside outside quarters, and he had quickly found rooms in Moabit,

112

conveniently close to the Krankenhaus, should one of his injuries relapse the rest. It was also an easy, walking commute to Wilhelmstrasse, half of which cut through the Tiergarten. Better still, and like most accommodation in that area, it was cheap, and spacious enough for all of his possessions (but then, so was his kit bag). His landlady, Frau Traugott, a septuagenarian epileptic who seemed grateful for the company of his more obvious afflictions, handled his laundry, cooked for him occasionally but otherwise took the view, unfashionable among her profession, that his business was not hers. She hadn't even insisted that lady friends not be entertained, though after seeing him for the first time she'd probably thought the prohibition otiose. They got on well, as deliberate strangers do.

In the near-darkness, on the Lord's Day, she was punishing her doorstep with a pumice stone when he arrived home (her family was old-time religious, except when it came to cleaning). During daylight she preferred to stay in her apartment, inventing chores or listening to the BBC (she didn't bother to keep the volume low) while conversing almost incessantly with her three semi-feral cats. When evening came she usually staked a claim to the near-outdoors, Mediterranean fashion, where she performed all the duties of a *blockhelfer* without actually reporting to anyone. A long widowhood and her medical condition had done no favours for her social life, but she seemed content enough to Fischer – at least, he had never heard her complain, a quality that placed her in a sub-species of one. She had just two other, long-

113

term tenants, sisters who had both lost husbands in the First War and who kept their own company in a manner that even St Jerome might have thought abrupt. In the five months since Fischer had moved in they had acknowledged his existence, as Frau Traugott had confided to him, to the extent of a single reference to 'the poor military gentleman upstairs'. This was very much his idea of how neighbours should conduct themselves.

'You're back, Herr Fischer.' She climbed painfully to her feet and dropped the stone in the bucket. 'I have some cold pressed tongue...'

Hurriedly, he assured her that he had eaten already, quite magnificently, and after a moment of inner struggle, he offered up the bottle of Courvoisier. Her unaffected joy at receiving the gift – *any* gift – gave him a rare stab of guilt. At Tempelhof he'd quietly lifted the item from Dornberger's shopping pallet while Douglas von Bader haggled with a feldwebel from a transport unit, so she was now officially sabotaging the Reich. His protests were useless: she insisted that he come in and toast Better Days with her, which they did from cracked crystal goblets. The moment it was down he excused himself, but with a single finger she detained him while she found his post for the past two days, a pause that gave his legs time to become fully reacquainted with her cats.

Forty minutes later, stripped, washed, re-moisturized with glycerol and perched on the edge of his bed to avoid mess, he managed to stop sneezing.

Chapter Fifteen

Waking at first light, he left the house before Frau Traugott could threaten a breakfast of cold tongue, and filled his stomach at a workers' canteen on Alt-Moabit. Another glorious day was spreading its wings, and his walk through the Tiergarten, shared with hundreds of other early-rising Berliners, was as restorative as a dawn dip in the Baltic. Even the right side of his face – a notoriously unforgiving barometer – felt more good than bad in the warm breeze. Entirely out of character (and ability), he made a go at a verse or two of *The Alabama Song* as he strolled around Potsdamer Platz, until his throat gave a warning stab on behalf of innocent passers-by.

He arrived at the Air Ministry before 7.30am. The Lie Division office was as yet unoccupied, as he had hoped and expected. It was commonly understood in the profession that effective deception required bright eyes and keen minds, neither of which were likely to be manifested until mid-morning at the earliest. This was not something likely to endear the department to the rest of the Luftwaffe, but no one was going to alter things. The high proportion of cripples who manned (or, as Freddie Holleman had observed, partially-manned) the Division gave it a vaguely piratical air, which tended to unnerve the occasional uniform who sought to impose a more conventional, military schedule. Threats of sanctions, effective elsewhere, could hardly be so against men whose experience of pain so visibly exceeded the most sadistic fantasy, so no one bothered to make them. In return, Fischer and his colleagues set their backs to the millstone for at least five hours each day, turning raw field-data into misinformation, disproving stark realities and making light of mere catastrophes, to the point at which Up and Down became no more than the self-forged chains of pedants. And then they lunched. It was hell, as they'd reminded each other more than once; but the truth couldn't be left to fend for itself.

Fischer was 'on leave' still, so an early arrival couldn't be regarded as disloyalty to prevailing policy. In any case, the telephone call he needed to make – to an organization that ran very different office hours – wasn't one that he wished to be overheard. He checked the corridor, closed the door and dialled. When he reached the switchboard he asked for the man rather than the department, and was put through immediately.

'Horst? It's Otto Fischer. How are you?'

There was a considerable pause, the sort that suggests a bad or reluctant memory.

'Christ, I thought you were dead.'

'I tried, believe me. But you? I thought Intelligence required brains?'

'A common error. Forgive me, Otto, but what do you want?'

At least it was going to be a frank exchange, one way or the other.

'I have a problem, and I don't know quite how

116

big it is. I can't even say what sort of problem, to be truthful. I'm groping everywhere at the moment, and my hand keeps landing in the shit. So I'd be grateful if I could just ask you a question, one that needs no more than a yes or a no. May I do that, Horst?'

Again, a pause: not surprising, given Horst's line of business.

'Ask.'

'I have some names. I want to know whether they've ever been of interest to your people, whether any enquiries have ever been made, for any reason.'

'German names?'

'Yes, every one.'

'We don't investigate Germans. We leave that to Gestapo and the SD.' He almost spat out the names. Something else that was hardly surprising.

'I understand that, yes. But if one of them were involved in betraying ... confidences? That would be something you'd chase, wouldn't it?'

'Only if foreigners were involved, and outside the Reich, you know that.'

'That's the thing, Horst. I don't know, one way or another. I don't even know whether any of these men have done anything wrong, ever. I'm just looking for a way through the woods, and espionage is one possibility. May I give you the names? Believe me, I wouldn't ask if it weren't too sensitive to leave to ... others.'

On the whole, Fischer considered this his least worst approach. Horst Ganz was a stickler, always had been, even in his Stettin days, and they had never been close enough for one to ask the other to risk anything. But the question-about-a-question was irresistible. If he said no he was walking away from something that had the potential to do harm to Abwehr, to the benefit of the greater enemy. If he said yes, then Fischer might take a further small hop towards an indefinable goal.

Still nothing. 'Look, Horst, if you do this and it comes up blank, then there's no harm in it. But if one or more of the names have files, then you'll need to know what I know, and why I'm asking. Either way, I'll give you everything I have. That's fair, surely?'

An even longer pause. He could hear Ganz breathing rather heavily, exercising his paranoia, calculating the number of directions from which he might be buggered.

'Otto, if I may ask ... who *are* you, these days?'

A very good question. 'I'm ... non-affiliated, Horst. As close as might be Feldpolizei, but not that either. You can speak to a Generalmajor Dornberger at Heimat Artillery Park 11, Karlshagen, if you want reassurance. But please don't go into the detail of what I'm asking, it would defeat the purpose. You can say that I'm just making general enquiries.'

He could hear Ganz scribbling a note. 'You can give me your names, but it won't be more than a yes or no, I promise you that.'

'That's good enough, Horst, thank you. So, how's the family?'

The small talk turned out to be miniscule. Ganz's wife had gone, years earlier; she'd taken the children with her and it could have been messy, except he didn't mind and was now seeing a woman he used to arrest quite regularly, usually on Saturday nights. He mentioned the name, familiar to anyone who'd worked at Augustastrass: most of his former colleagues had arrested her at one time or another, or imposed an ad hoc fine against an alley wall. That was about it. Ganz was obviously desperate to get off the telephone, as Fischer had hoped. He replaced the receiver, knowing that he'd now stepped out a little further than common sense dictated.

Anxiety was an unfamiliar sensation, and he regarded it as slightly preferable to hopelessness. At least it was positive: that is, he positively hoped not to reap the consequences of his actions, in the same way as if he were wading through stagnant, drowning-deep water, with the algae he'd disturbed threatening to pull him down. He thought of the universal comforter of men in this position, the chain of command, and realized that there wasn't one as such. In effect, he was charging around Berlin, asking questions, making himself known to the sort of people who very much believed that it was *their* job to ask questions, on the authority of a telephone conversation and a potentially fatal commitment made on his behalf.

'Oh God.'

Fischer leapt almost clear of his desk. It had come from the floor, somewhere in the office. He kicked back his chair and walked down the aisle between the two lines of desks until a single boot disturbed the view. Lying full-length on a greatcoat, his artificial leg for a pillow, Freddie

Holleman held his head with great tenderness.

'I've just become a party to something, haven't I?'

Chapter Sixteen

Without considering the very many consequences, Fischer told Holleman everything. He
even included the part about Zofia (it was the
only revelation that his colleague visibly enjoyed,
that he had to be led away from). And as he
unburdened himself, the anxieties faded a little.
Certainly, it took no great intellect to appreciate
that a problem shared in National Socialist Germany was a problem doubled; but as much as he
enjoyed his own counsel, being the sole instrument and probable scapegoat in this matter felt
like the wrong end of solitude: the shit-covered
end.

His new confidant was impressed, in a way.

'Christ, Otto. Couldn't you have volunteered
for bomb-disposal? Worn a menorah for a hat? I
mean, *Christ!*'

'You're right, Freddie, of course. I couldn't see
a way to refuse.'

It was fortunate that only one member of the Lie
Division – *this* one – habitually slept in the office.
He and Holleman weren't quite close friends –
they'd known each other for little more than six
months – but the man was discreet and tough, too:
one of that breed of Berliner that even the Party

remained wary of offending; who cared hardly at all about procedures, chains of command or what the current policy was on anything. The day they'd met, Fischer had instinctively disliked him: the sort, he'd decided, who made trouble for the sake of proving some self-serving point. But Holleman wasn't really so much a troublemaker as a trouble-magnet, and his habit of blundering through and out of it suggested that some aide to the Deity, perhaps the patron saint of endearing arseholes, had cast a paternal eye upon him. So Fischer had revised his first opinion and found some kindred virtues instead. The two men were older than their colleagues, both of them ex-police, and this gave them a first excuse to form a perimeter whenever anyone in the office said anything bad about Bulls, or old farts generally. They kept company on the bad days and talked too much when drunk about things they should have avoided; so they'd each gained a measure of how far the other would go, and it was pretty far. Dangerous talk cost lives, but it also built the only trust worth the name. Fischer didn't want a partner in this business, and he didn't want to be alone; with Holleman, there was at least a chance of avoiding.

He helped to steady the patient while the ex-temporary pillow was re-attached: a comradely gesture that the strong smell of alcohol-charged vomit made him regret immediately. Hastily, he volunteered himself for coffee detail while his colleague sorted himself in the office washroom. This involved further, loud evacuations, audible from a considerable distance down the corridor, which made the Alt-Moabit breakfast shift

121

uneasily. Holleman had a troubled relationship with drink: he couldn't resist it, but his constitution could take surprisingly little before the consequences were made drastically apparent. It was an affliction he was obliged to suffer often, but he did it with such cheerful fortitude that commenting upon it, or suggesting that he might consider drinking a little less, seemed somehow mean-spirited. It couldn't be denied that anyone who could buy his round from the floor was a *mensch*.

'Jesus.' As Fischer returned with the coffee, the other half of their fledgling cabal was holding himself upright with the help of the washroom's doorframe. Everything from his sparse hairline downwards had been sluiced, including the uniform. Mindful of his weakness, Holleman usually kept his only spare in the office, but foresight didn't always work as efficiently as the ravages of excessive bonhomie.

He was resting his head on one hand, as if to sleep it off further. 'You know what I want?'

'Much aspirin?'

'I want it explained to me how the gentleman took one in the head and was then placed in the trench without his family making any fuss about it.'

'It's curious.'

'Was his wife an abettor who got unlucky? No, because why the hell would she have had him brought to the trench after the event? Did she try to fight off the assassin? There's damage to the hands, but that most probably happened as she tried to dig herself out. In any case, what were her children doing while she was struggling?'

'They were all drugged?'

'But then, a person or persons would have had to carry the entire family from their home to the trench. And even if they could have done it without being discovered, *why* do it? They had no idea that it was going to be just about the only trench that collapsed that night. Are you going to give me any of that fucking coffee?'

Holleman took a hurried sip and struggled visibly to keep it down. 'And why...' he belched, '...are you the only uniform who can solve it?'

Fischer considered this. 'My first thought was that I was being fitted for a suit. But it may be that my startling reputation's preceded me.'

'Well, I think this Dornberger fellow's pulled the pin and shoved the egg up your arse. Where the hell will you start? How many staff and workers are there?'

'About five to six thousand.'

'A small town, then. It has a security apparatus?'

'None. That is, a military presence to guard the site itself and, supposedly, the foreign workers. Some SS guards for the camp workers.'

'No detailed files on staff?'

'That's why I'm here in Berlin.'

'It's like they've asked a blind fucking stone-mason to solve Gethsemane.'

Fischer's desk telephone rang. As he went to answer it he glanced at the wall clock: nine o'clock precisely.

It was Ganz: short, sweet and relieved. The Abwehr had no information on the names Fischer had given him; nor, failing further evidence that

123

one or more of them were in contact with the enemy, any plans to gather any. Of course, if Fischer discovered anything that was of concern to Military Intelligence, he'd remember his promise?

It had been a phenomenally swift response and told Fischer at least something. He wondered whether it was Ganz lying to him, or Ganz innocently passing on someone else's lie.

The remainder of the office was filing in, singly or in pairs. Those who had major combat injuries tended to do so more quietly than the fully ambulant ones, as chatter distracts from the tricky business of balancing; but few of them were as solemn as the workers trudging into a thousand similar offices across Berlin that morning. This was a fairly contented place, because the business of deception – despicable, morally unconscionable – was also perversely enjoyable. It had become unofficial staff policy (unofficial in the sense that it had been formulated in a bar, one long, drunken Friday evening) to exceed the Luftwaffe's expectations of the department by exploring the bounds of what was credible, and then crossing them, wilfully. This had turned out to be a challenge, because the bounds, if they existed, lay somewhat further out than anyone had expected. Krohne hadn't used every deception they'd placed into his Pending tray, but nothing had been sent back with *preposterous!* scrawled upon it. In fact, nothing had been sent back, ever. Holleman's theory was that a file room existed somewhere deep within the Air Ministry, stuffed with bizarre lies about more or less everything. As the world itself became ever more demented, secret protocols would release this reserve gradually, with each new slice of dissemblance achieving a sort of verity by being slightly less deranged than the reality it joined. In the meantime, it was the Lie Division's job to keep stocks up to strength. So, at least once every office day, even through the enervation imposed by almost universally bad news, there was a momentary release of laughter as a new idea, raised by one of their own or a bright fellow in a field unit, was kicked around and further excessed.

'And to think they're paying us for this!' Detmar Reincke had once marvelled – in error, given that most of them had already paid heavy deposits for the privilege of tenure. Still, no one claimed that it wasn't preferable to rotting in a lazarett, and infinitely so to a pained, pitied retirement.

Fischer remained in the office for most of that morning. His work – if that was the correct term – was at Peenemünde, but one further conversation was needed in Berlin. So he shuffled papers around his desk, took another look at a fiction he had been working on two days earlier (a discourse on the German soldier's cheery response to the requirements of service on the Steppes) and watched his colleagues murder information as it arrived. Their routine began in the usual manner, with a coffee break; but this important work was interrupted almost immediately by nudges and furtive laughter, which escalated into the occasional launch of a crumpled piece of office paper, its trajectory carrying it from desk to desk. Fischer asked what it was about, but no one answered. Finally, Reincke sniggered and threw it at him.

It was a bulletin, the news of the morning: the death in combat of Standartenführer Kurt Eggers, head of the SS's counterpart *Kriegsberichter Kompanie*: Number Two in the field of professional lying, a man surpassed only by Goebbels himself, and even Joey didn't possess quite the gold-standard qualifications of Eggers: a priest *and* a newspaper editor in civilian life.

Once Holleman got hold of it, their mourning became less discreet. 'My spiritual father,' he wept, as close to dancing as his hangover and single leg permitted. 'How could he have been killed? Wasn't his tank understood to be a hospital?'

Hurriedly, he organized a literary competition. The event needed a proper eulogy, a valediction: so the most ludicrous, pandering, implausible hagiography that managed to pass for publication or broadcast would win its author a full evening's drinks at *The Silver Birch*. It was either a depressing or uplifting comment upon the human spirit that not a single member of the Division didn't immediately drop everything else and set himself to the challenge.

It was a calmer Holleman who took the call just after eleven, when everyone had settled down to thinking about an early lunch. He placed a hand over the receiver.

'Gerd Branssler's coming in. He doesn't sound happy.'

'Not here. Tell him Bernie's. When?'

'As soon as he can.'

Bernhardt's Café on Potsdamer Platz was a little more upmarket than either Fischer or

Holleman preferred (it had been decorated in the present century), but it was large and the tables were well spaced, offering a degree of privacy. That was all it had going for it. Even before the real stuff disappeared, the establishment's coffee had been a poor, thin brew; the *muckefuck* that replaced it was a peculiarly execrable blend of barley, acorns and, possibly, dung, drunk more as a badge of suffering than for pleasure. At 11.30am, the place was still hoping for the lunch rush, so there were few stomachs being tortured when they entered. They took a table at the end of the bar, separated from the others by the bulk of the cashier's desk, and ordered nothing.

Branssler arrived about fifteen minutes later. His Bull's traverse swiftly took in and dismissed the other customers. Satisfied, he came over and sat down without removing his hat.

'What a fucking mess!'

Neither Fischer nor Holleman said anything. Branssler didn't look like he wanted a conversation.

'Right. I have – *I had* – one reliable contact. Owed me for some stuff I forgot back when it still could have hurt him. Well, I burned that chit this morning. Wait.' He waved down Fischer's apology. 'So, I said I had a list, and were his people interested in any of them? Why, he asks. Just a little fraternal back scratching, I tell him, nothing below the table. So he asks to see the names, and then pisses off for an hour. Comes back with three friends, fucking *three*. I'm asking myself, Gerd, is everything in order, affairs-wise? Are the wife, the kids and the dog properly provided for? Because

127

when four Gestapo crowd into the same room as yourself, it isn't an interfuckingdepartmental social.

'My by-now-former mate says, Gerd, we don't mind doing favours for kripo, we being all one and the same family. But would you mind telling us a bit more about what it is with these blokes?' Branssler shrugged at Fischer. 'Sorry. They wouldn't take bullshit for an answer. I had to give them your name.'

'I expected it. Don't worry.'

'*You're* the one who should worry. Anyway, I said you were looking at security and had to check everyone, it was just a routine thing. Told them they could contact the Generalmajor and check you out. But I get the feeling they aren't going to do it that way.'

'I don't suppose they answered the question I asked?'

Branssler winked. 'Not as such. But I told you I was owed. When his mates had gone, my man pushed your list back to me. Told me to fuck off with it, so I did. Here.'

Fischer opened the crumpled paper. One name had a cross, pencilled against it, and a word: just the one. He showed it to Holleman.

'Well, it's *something*.'

Yet very little, for all the risks that had been taken. Fischer was now marked, lit like an airfield, for the sake of a single word next to a single name that might mean nothing at all.

'Thanks, Gerd.'

'These names, they're all up at that place on the Baltic, aren't they? The secret weapons place?'

'Yes.' The list spoke for itself. Fischer had known perfectly well what he'd been giving away.

Branssler nodded. 'I went there years ago, a holiday with Greta, before the kids came. It has lots of trees still?'

'It's one big forest, almost.'

'Good. If any jobs in security come up, let me know. There's nothing like a forest for hiding in.'

Chapter Seventeen

Getting to Berlin had been easy, thanks to von Bader and the Cognac Express. Getting out proved much more difficult. At noon, word went around the office that train timetables were being suspended, but it was mid-afternoon before they found out why, and after that the bad news poured in like the dam walls had cracked. Like spiteful, cynical children, they'd all had a laugh at the late Kurt Eggers's expense without thought for the wider circumstances. It seemed that a lot more, better Germans had died, and a lot more had fled, as Kharkov, the city that Hitler had sworn would be defended to the last man, was abandoned to the Ivans. More than a fortnight earlier, Goebbels had stopped boasting that the *Citadel* offensive was going to be Stalin's Sedan, so everyone had been expecting more bad news from the East. But not this: this was enough to clamp the mouths of even the loudest clowns in the Division. Everyone sat silently at their desks, taking in the worst of it, or whispering in the corridors, trying to hear a new version that wasn't quite as bad as the old. No one cared about Kharkov itself: the city had changed hands so often that there wasn't anything worth holding on to. But this time the Soviets hadn't taken it sneakily while the Wehrmacht was busy elsewhere: this time the city had been defended with everything they had, and still it had fallen. *Citadel* hadn't just failed: they had pushed almost a million men and three thousand tanks into a set, 250 kilometre deep trap, and the jaws had been sprung. There had been the newsreels proclaiming the lightning German advances, the encouraging talk of consolidations that somehow shaded imperceptibly into brilliant holding actions and failed encirclements, and today the search had begun for a sanguine vocabulary to describe a pasting. Ten months ago they had stretched out an armoured fist and touched the Caucasus; now, their heels slid backwards in the mud as a juggernaut pressed westwards across Belorussia and Ukraine, the Reich's putative thousand-year breadbasket.

Even Holleman's humour failed him; he stopped being beer-hall loud, forgot about his literary competition and wandered morosely across to Fischer's desk, pretending there was a purpose to it.

'How miraculous are these miracle weapons, Otto?'

'Not loaves, nor fishes.' A child, a blindly optimistic child knew what was needed: about a hundred fresh, well-trained divisions and a surgical removal of unreality from the Leadership, neither of which was remotely in prospect. Holleman, decades both from childhood and any sense of optimism, nodded and stared at the floor. Even with the hangover, he was probably thinking of several drinks, all broaching the brims of their glasses.

Until the scale of the Soviet breakthrough could be assessed, much of the rolling stock in the city had been put under an emergency halt order; but as with all temporary measures, there was no possible measure of *temporary*. Nothing was leaving Berlin for the north that afternoon (although trains were still coming into the city). Nothing, as far as he could determine from several calls, was flying to Peenemünde airfield from Tempelhof or Gatow until the following day at least. Finally, at 4pm, he heard about an LBA flight from Staaken to Swinemünde. Having worn down a station orderly by refusing to get off the telephone, he was told that he could travel as cargo in the JU52, if he really needed to: if it was *important*.

The flight was scheduled to depart at 5.30pm, so there was hardly time enough. He was able to beg yet another ride, this time from the Air Ministry's service post van. He knew the driver vaguely: an elderly ex-Luftschutzamt ground-staffer who occasionally wandered the Ministry offices, chatting to old comrades while he waited for the dispatch bags to fill. The old man was happy for the company, but there was a familiar price: a droning, minute recapitulation of the August 1918 retreat that made the twenty kilometres from Wilhelmstrasse to Staaken seem more like the homeward commute from Troy to Ithaca. Fischer began to suspect that the Reich's entire military transportation cadre was devoted to moving memories, not things.

They arrived at the airfield with twenty minutes to spare, and found that the flight had been delayed for lack of part of its cargo. For the next two hours, Fischer sat in the airfield office, drinking beer, swapping stories with the duty controller and fighting off offers for his Fallschirmjäger plunging-eagle badge. In the meantime, a quartermaster's clerk frantically attempted to track a consignment of flying suits that had disappeared in the short journey from the warehouses of Ernst Rihm Uniformfabrik. Eventually, the merchandise turned up (it had been misdirected to Gatow), a strip was torn off the blameless driver (probably for having dared to show initiative) and the JU52 was hurriedly loaded. A further half-hour passed on the concrete before they were given permission to depart, so the light was fading fast as the plane levelled off somewhere above Oranienburg.

The flight was as noisy as bones engaged in the proverbial, but Fischer, too tired even to explore his habitual queasiness, let the tension of the past hours drain away as he was rocked in his makeshift cradle. The co-pilot, warned of his uniform and wounds, had rigged the accommodation expertly: a harness, strapped to the bulkhead, relieved most of his weight and allowed him to favour his bad shoulder and arm without effort. His seat was a box, cushioned by a blanket and wedged between two crates; vitally, this allowed his legs to firmly cradle his kitbag and its precious contents: three bottles of Scotch whisky, a commodity he hadn't thought survived anywhere in Germany or its many new territories. But Staaken's duty controller was a popular man, able to do favours for many important people, and he kept his eye upon the very many objects of desire that passed through his domain. Eventually, he had proved too persuasive; every few minutes Fischer fingered the bare patch on his tunic and wondered how it was that he felt not the slightest regret for parting with it. Worse, now that he knew the going rate for other men's heroisms, he was almost certain he'd be open to offers for his gold wounds medal also.

They were just south of Prenzlau when, without warning, the plane banked sharply and plummeted from its allocated altitude. The pilot was shouting something, but Fischer didn't need to hear it. A flash of bright light, a reflection, through one of the window ports seized his attention before it rose steeply out of sight. Without thinking (later, he wished he'd taken the time), he uncoupled himself and stumbled wildly across the narrow span of the fuselage, striking first his head and then his bad arm, agonizingly, against the opposite bulkhead. That took care of any sense of orientation, and instinct alone threw out his good hand to grasp one of the holding rails that traversed the length of the plane. As the JU52 levelled off he pulled himself tightly to the window and tried to assess damage he'd inflicted upon his broken body; but when he opened his eyes once more and looked out into the void, a larger point of life or death seized all of his attention.

In the very last of a beautiful evening, high

above them, hundreds of vapour trails painted the darkening sky in elegant, clustered parallels, all of them pointing one way: east-south-east, to Berlin.

Chapter Eighteen

A little good came of it, at least for Fischer. Like the town itself, Swinemünde airfield was blacked out, and refusing incoming air traffic. After a fraught half-hour in which he feared they would be re-routed far to the east or west, the JU52 was directed to the small airfield at Heringsdorf, no more than twenty kilometres from Peenemünde. The trains here were running normally, and after an uncomfortable few hours' doze on a bench at Heringsdorf station he caught the earliest service to Zinnowitz and, via the electrified line, to Peenemünde East. At the guesthouse he placed his kitbag carefully upon the hall floor, expecting but not hearing breakages. Berlin had got it from the British, but his small, precious part of their Celtic fringe was safe.

He telephoned the Air Ministry immediately. Freddie Holleman had stayed all night, there and at *The Silver Birch*, and gave him the statistics the Lie Division had managed to gather. At least 750 aircraft, more than a thousand dead: civilians mainly, most of them in the southern suburbs of Lankwitz, Lichterfelde and Mariendorf. Also, for once, the bureaucrats had been underneath it.

134

Though most of the centre of the city was almost untouched, a small stretch of Wilhelmstrasse had taken a pounding, with hardly a government building entirely untouched. Eight windows in the Air Ministry had been blown in, one of them belonging to the Lie Division. Holleman, returning unsteadily to his desk at the time, was proudly convinced that the British had targeted him in particular.

'Four thousand fucking windows in this building, and the *viermots* go for mine. Who's going to tell me it was an accident?'

Neither man said it, but this was something else that everyone had known was coming: the moment that Berlin finally lost a sense of future days. Hammer-blows were striking in rapid succession – Hamburg, Sicily, Peenemünde, Kursk-Kharkov and now this; it didn't take a pessimist to spot the portents being loaded onto a conveyor belt, nor a visionary to see what the end of it would be. Fischer recalled a moment, in the JU52, an expression on the co-pilot's face as the plane stopped tumbling and he came aft to check on their passenger: as if he was seeing for the first time a version of his own, coming fate. By the same token, Fischer wondered how many of those Berliners who had glanced distastefully at his wounds on the u-bahn, in restaurants or passing by him in the streets, were thinking of him this morning: were wondering what was it was going to be like, to be like him?

Holleman said goodbye without attempting a joke, which underlined the strangeness of the day. Fischer listened to the hum of the disconnected line for a few moments, replaced the receiver and sensed her, behind him. Curious, that a lack of anything tangible – a noise, or odour – should lead him to so definite a conclusion, but with a teenager's certainty he turned around.

She had forgotten or discarded the preposterous cap, and her hair – thick, short, blonde, precisely the colour he recalled or had invented in memory – framed her face in the manner that had gripped his attention on the beach at Ückeritz all those years before. A goddess in a peasant's shift; or as close to one as a country boy could imagine.

She coughed politely, though he was already drinking in the view.

'Would the officer like some breakfast?'

'Thank, you, yes. I'm very hungry. Is there any chance that oatmeal is unavailable?'

She nodded forlornly, deaf to the feeble witticism, and he had to remind himself once more that he was part of the cause of her misery, not its relief.

'You might also mention to Herr Nagel that I've returned, if you see him.'

She dipped a knee, and left. Calculating the distance between the kitchens and guesthouse, and the time required to spoil whatever he was going to eat, Fischer decided that he needed a shower. It was two days since that awkward necessity had last been discharged, and he almost looked forward to it. But he misjudged his new skills; by the time he had stripped, showered, massaged his wounds and dressed, she had returned and gone again. He stared at the breakfast on the kitchen table and, like the same teenager,

136

embraced a self-indulgent regret at having lost something that hadn't ever been an opportunity. So the fresh bread rolls pleased him only a little, and even the real fake coffee – Reiner's malt – failed to rekindle the pleasure he'd felt earlier for an imagined frisson.

As he ate the matter of Dr Walter Thiel intruded upon his whimsical mood, and he found himself questioning more than the facts. Here was a murdered man in a universe of murder, a victim of perhaps the only truly targeted act that night, a conundrum. Yet really, what did it matter who had shot him, or why? What did a single act signify in an age in which violence was the acknowledged norm? More pertinently, why had he, Fischer, so supinely accepted a task that seemed to mock common sense?

There was something about this that offended him. He was used to taking orders as soldiers should: to receiving, obeying and not interpreting their doubtful utility. He could recall a period of only two to three years between leaving the family home and joining the police when his life hadn't been a matter of doing what he was told. It was a rather sad record, other than for a dog. True, he hadn't needed to stifle any great nihilistic urges upon that path, or fight off the siren-call of the barricades; but a life lived less at the initiative of others might be something to recall with greater satisfaction than he could admit to. Perhaps it was the capricious nature of his present task that goaded the inner spartacist; perhaps it was the weather, the times, Zofia.

Perhaps acquiescence was the wrong response.

137

He couldn't argue with a Generalmajor's epaulettes, but having been given a task and a timetable, and no resources with which to achieve either, it was as if he were expected to knot the noose they were going to dangle him from. That wasn't, to employ a term much out of fashion in recent years, reasonable.

Nagel walked into the kitchen and sat without an invitation. 'You're back, then.'

Fischer considered him for a moment: his guide, his conduit to the rest of Peenemünde and its many discretions – his only hierophant, in fact, of the mores of a society that was utterly unfamiliar to him. This, also, didn't seem quite right. And another thing nagged at him: here was a young, presumably healthy man, the sort who could handle a *panzerbüchse* quite expertly with a little basic training: the sort they were crying out for right now, to put in the way of any number of freshly triumphant Soviet shock armies.

'Nagel, why aren't you in uniform?'

The young man blanched visibly.

'I mean, *how* are you not in uniform? Is Eva Braun a relative?'

It was none of Fischer's business, of course; but as *he* wore a uniform, several medals and a number of quite hideous tokens of active service, his moral ascendancy was unassailable.

Nagel's explanation was ragged, tortuous, and didn't disguise the predictable fact of his having enjoyed the right sort of patronage at the most felicitous moment. Fischer was quite sure that claims for his technical and secretarial abilities, his irreplaceable value to Doctor von Braun, were accurate enough. But more and more women, many of them at Peenemünde, were discovering that they too could master the masculine arts of office management. Indispensability was relative: Fischer himself knew of a man, a highly regarded physicist in civilian life, whose job at the Front was the repair and re-fitting of thrown tank tracks. Talent in itself meant little; having the right people to appreciate it was everything. The way the odds fell was hugely unjust, but then so was life, and he didn't begrudge Nagel his good fortune. In fact, he intended to hang him with it.

The young man finished reprising his many qualities, and was by now reduced to the state of nervous contrition familiar to recruiting sergeants in bathhouses. For a few moments Fischer continued to stare, allowing guilt and the ravages of aviation fuel to work their magic.

'I don't think I'll be requiring your assistance further, Nagel. But please thank Dr von Braun for sparing you. It was very kind.'

'Oh! But I'm sure he wouldn't...'

'You see, I don't feel that I'm being helped at all. By you, I mean, or anyone else for that matter, so I doubt that I can help with the Generalmajor's problem. I know, I've only been here for a very short time, and there's much I've forgotten about police work. Still, I sense that I'm being played, that I'm being given a near-impossible job and the run-around.

'So how do I do this? Trying to find a motive seems pointless. Everyone tells me that there are no tensions between the staff, no occasions of friction, nothing less than adulation for the late

Dr Thiel. Of course, you're all under pressure to produce these weapons. There are technical difficulties also, because these are entirely new ideas, and this too is a concern. But on the whole I'm offered the impression that this is a place where people are clenching their jaws, giving the salute and pulling together, shoulder to shoulder, like in a bad newsreel.

'I don't believe it, Nagel. I don't believe that thousands of scientists and support staff, working under constant scrutiny from Army Ordnance, the Armaments Ministry, RSHA and the Chancellery, tasked with saving the Reich with a series of new wonder weapons in the face of, frankly, not entirely satisfactory news from the Eastern Front and Italy, aren't shitting themselves for their careers. I don't believe that there aren't temperaments clashing as a matter of course, let alone a matter of life and death. I don't believe that some of the people here aren't quite capable of sliding a – let's say rhetorical – six-inch blade between the shoulders of their professional colleagues and taking delight in the fact that they've done so. In short, Nagel, it's all very unconvincing.

'People react *badly* when pressured. Of course, I haven't seen much evidence of it yet, because I'm an outsider, and ranks tend to close. Since I arrived, everyone – *everyone* – has told me that Walter Thiel was a tremendous fellow, without fault and loved by all – an absolute prince, in fact. Well, he may have been all of that. But someone didn't get on with him. This being the case, either Thiel was keeping secrets from all of you, or all of you are keeping them from me. I don't find that helpful, as I may have to tell Generalmajor Dorn-berger.'

Nagel winced. 'I promise...'

'Or shall we begin again, Nagel? Go back to that moment when I didn't assume that everything you told me was half-credible? What do you say?'

The young man said nothing at all. Fischer wasn't surprised: he'd thrown out shirking, deception and conspiracy in the space it took to drain a lukewarm cup of pretend coffee. A certain deflation was to be expected.

'Well, let me start, then. Dr Walter Thiel: what was your opinion of him?'

'I respected his work very much.'

'I'm pleased. So, my question?'

'He could be ... difficult, sometimes. He didn't like poor work, or what he considered to be shoddiness. If he thought colleagues weren't up to his own standards, he'd say so.'

'A perfectionist, then. And was his own work beyond reproach?'

'Definitely. When he joined Dr von Braun at Kummersdorf, the engine development pro-gramme was heading firmly in the wrong direc-tion. It was Thiel's work that turned it around, that made a reality of the concept of a relatively small engine producing unthinkable thrust. Without him, I hardly know what we'd have done. What we *will* do.'

'Let me ask this in a different way. Was there any aspect to his methods that anyone – *anyone* – might have found objectionable? Beyond him impugning their competence, that is?'

'He sometimes thought too quickly.'

'A heinous fault.'

'No, it's … he was a genius, and that isn't an easy quality to live with. If there was a problem – and there are *always* problems – he became a little single-minded. We've seen him make a dozen modifications to an assembly in the space of a single morning, tirelessly thinking, pursuing a solution. He rarely paused, and that was the trouble.'

'In what way?'

'He often wouldn't find the time to document the changes he made. It made "Papa" Riedel bite the furniture, because it was *his* job to set down the designs, and one can't devise or rationalize procedures and standards without a paper trail of what's been done. *I'll get round to it* he used to say, and wave Riedel away as though the man was a fly on the pie. It was his principal fault. That, and his intolerance of imperfections.'

'It seems to me that there was a real potential for clashes.'

'Of course there was. It's ironic – most of the writing that Dr Thiel found time for took the form of critical marginalia on other people's papers. No one ever came to blows about it, they're scientists, not pugilists. But what made it worse, usually, was that Walter turned out to be correct about whatever it was he took exception to. Unfortunately, his way of being in the right sometimes made it worse.'

'So a temperamental man too?'

'Not aggressively so. It was more a weakness, I'd say. He tended to react badly to setbacks, to become quite depressed, rather than angry. In fact, he took a brief holiday earlier this year, a sort of rest cure, to get over a particularly frustrating period in his work. But God knows, we've had enough setbacks, and you must understand what we owe him.'

Fischer considered the two remaining fingernails on his right hand. 'Not an entirely perfect human being, then?'

Nagel shrugged. 'Who is? But nothing that was less than perfect about him could have been the slightest cause for murder, I'd be willing to swear to that. The colleagues who most disliked Walter's methods had the greatest respect for his work. The fact that they didn't all drink together doesn't mean anything.'

'I'd heard he wasn't gregarious. A loner?'

'In what sense? He didn't socialize much outside of work, but he had a family. In a way, he was *too* gregarious. He and the Generalmajor used to argue about bringing in expertise from German industry. Walter wanted it but the Army likes to keep its projects under tarpaulin. He was probably right, though.'

'And the other thing, the argument they had about whether the A4 was ready for production?'

'That was Walter's perfectionism in full flow. He sometimes forgot that we're at war.' Nagel smiled. 'But he wasn't the only guilty party in that respect.'

Indeed. 'Well, now a delicate question. Was Dr Thiel fond of the ladies?'

The belly laugh scattered flecks of sputum across the table. 'Hauptmann, if Lida Baarova

143

herself had squatted naked on his face, he'd have prised her off with a slide rule! Dr von Braun sometimes referred to Walter's children as proof of the triumph of duty over will.'

'Did he have any views on the use of forced labour?'

'I doubt it, for the same reason he wouldn't have had a use for Baarova. It wasn't engine development, so it wasn't his business.'

'Did he have *any* social contact with the foreign workers?'

'Christ, no! I doubt if he ever said a word to one of them, outside the Development Shops.'

Fischer inspected the pattern at the bottom of his coffee cup. Nagel being honest was hardly more enlightening than old, evasive Nagel. It was clear that Walter Thiel himself wasn't going to offer up any revelations regarding his death. The answers, if any, lay at the other end of the perpetrator/victim relationship. Not that he had hoped for much; had Nagel not been an innocent in matters of criminal investigation he would have recognized the questions for what they were: clumsy gropes in a very large and foggy darkness.

Thiel, unfortunately, had been shot in the head. This suggested much, though none of it good. It was a clinical, disinterested method of human disposal: a method that anyone with a grudge would hardly consider sufficient to the purpose. Therefore, Fischer could hope for no assistance from a tortured, lonely conscience, or the remorse of a decent man or woman made temporarily evil by desperate circumstance. The person who put a

144

bullet into Walter Thiel was a professional: calmly, comfortably camouflaged amid several million others with similar qualifications in this disordered age.

So why did he – or she – do it?

'Right.' Fischer levered himself to his feet. 'Let us then speak with the blessed circle.'

Nagel frowned. 'Who...?'

'Those who know, Nagel. Those who *know!*'

Chapter Nineteen

Six people were aware that Walter Thiel had been holed at some point during the dark hours of 17/18 August. Everyone else – with one possible exception – believed him to have gone to his eternal rest in more or less the same manner as hundreds of others who had died at Peenemünde and Trassenheide the same night. Fischer was willing to assume that Dr Walter Robert Dornberger had not requested an investigation into a crime committed by himself; therefore, there were a further five memories that had the potential to cast light upon the life and strange exit of Dr Thiel. One of these could be excused further punishment for the present; the remainder comprised three scientists and an adjutant, none of whom, from the non-evidence of Abwehr, Gestapo and kripo files, appeared to possess known sociopathic tendencies.

Of the four, Werner Magirius – Dornberger's

adjutant – was the man most likely to have been closest to his boss throughout that night, and therefore least likely to have enjoyed an opportunity either to do, or to see, mischief. On the other hand, his military training made him the most likely to have discharged the said mischief effectively. The remaining three formed an odd set. Dr von Braun was, according to more or less everyone at Peenemünde, the big cheese: *il stupor mundi*. Perhaps not as brilliant technically as the late Thiel in matters of engine design, but an excellent example of modern minor nobility, the fulcrum of the machine that created the wonder weapons. Of Hans Wierer, Fischer knew little. Nagel said that he was Head of the Projections Department (whatever that was), and likely to have had very little day-to-day contact with Thiel. The only coincidence of fates here appeared to be his entirely arbitrary appointment as the man charged with gathering bodies after the raid. However, he knew of the matter and so could not be dismissed. Of the three scientists, Fischer liked Arthur Rudolph the best because, on a subjective level, he liked him the least. He might be a perfectly fine fellow, but he was also a faithful Party man, keen to introduce slave labour into the production process and not, therefore, someone who might lose sleep over a matter of human suffering.

Obediently, Nagel telephoned Rudolph's office from the guesthouse. Yes, he was available at the moment to speak to the Hauptmann. In fact, he'd expected a visit for the past three days. Fischer then dismissed his assistant. He had no intention of hearing the testimony of one of the six witnesses in the presence of another.

Rudolph lived two doors down the corridor from Dornberger in the administration building; but whereas the Generalmajor's office was a very comfortable affair, decorated with fresh flowers, a picture of the Führer and several photographic portraits of its occupant, the Chief Production Engineer worked in a spartan room, devoid of any decoration other than a number of schedules pinned crudely to one wall. The man himself, who rose from his desk as Fischer entered, was a tall, well built figure in a tweed jacket, with what the British would call a rugby player's face (this seemed the work of God, rather than an opposing team). He had a shock of wavy, unkempt hair, and a cheerful expression that didn't appear to have been tacked on.

'The phantom investigator!' Rudolph's handshake (hurriedly transferred to Fischer's left hand) was firm but not competitive, and his survey of his guest's face managed somehow to probe without being offensive.

'It is *astonishing* how surgical reconstruction is advancing. Forgive me, but are you in any pain?'

'Very little. I feel it when the weather turns, of course.' This was not a good start. Fischer was being interrogated amiably.

Rudolph nodded enthusiastically. 'Yes, you would, and always will, I expect. I *do* wish I could show you to my little girl. She has a perfectly innocent child's interest in wounds.'

'Well I'm glad I can spare her that ordeal. I understand that you saw Dr Thiel's body after it had been placed in the schoolhouse?'

'I did. He'd been shot, in the head. Quite horrifying, even among all the other deaths that night. I was very upset. Walter and I have been colleagues for many years now.'

'You didn't meet at Peenemünde?'

'At Kummersdorf, in 1934, I believe. He replaced poor Kurt Wahmke that year.'

'I'm sorry...?'

'Kurt died with two others in an explosion. They were testing an experimental fuel mixture in a rocket assembly. Obviously, it didn't work too well. It's curious...' Rudolph's eyebrows rose. 'Do you know, I hadn't thought of it until now, but Walter's has been the first fatality of any member of the technical staff connected with this programme since that day. And he replaced Kurt.'

'But they were very different deaths.'

'I wasn't suggesting that fate took a hand, Hauptmann.'

'When, exactly, did you see the wound in Dr Thiel's head?'

'I don't know, it was all very confusing. I was helping to check nametags on the bodies in the schoolhouse when the Generalmajor called me over. I don't know whether he did so immediately upon discovering it or a minute later. Either way, it was a shock. All I recall is that he told me not to speak of it. And...'

'Yes?'

'Well, if it was something not to be spoken of, I did wonder why he'd bothered to call me over and have yet another person know about it. I suppose I was flattered. The confidence spoke to my seniority, in a terrible way.'

'Were you here on the site during the raid, or at the Settlement?'

'I was here, in my office. There was too much work, and I'd decided to carry on, perhaps taking the following morning to sleep late if necessary. I don't live at the Settlement, by the way. Like Dr von Braun, I have a requisitioned house in Zinnowitz. It's very pleasant, though until now I'd considered its remoteness from Peenemünde an inconvenience. Not any more, eh?'

Rudolph laughed again. Fischer was struck by his apparent good humour: it seemed at odds both with what had been said of the man's convictions and the general mood around the site.

'If I may, Herr Rudolph? I believe that you were involved recently in discussions on how to resolve production issues?'

'Yes, I was. Is this relevant?'

'I'm not yet sure. Please bear with me. There have been suggestions that *häflinge* labour be utilized here?'

'It was *my* suggestion. At least, I urged the Generalmajor and Dr von Braun to consider it strongly.'

Rudolph made the admission easily. No defiance, nothing apologetic; perhaps a hint of puzzlement that the question had been put at all.

Fischer flanked the point. 'I'm only a soldier, of course, but surely the work that needs to be done is too *technical* for such labour?'

The engineer leaned forward, enthusiastically. 'No, that's exactly wrong! Assembly of the

149

weapons is a precision process, and needs well-trained staff. At the moment we have a core of technical personnel who supervise the assembly processes, but the very little production that's taken place so far has mainly utilized contracted foreign workers, *gastarbeitnehmer*. Not only do we not have enough of them, they're also the wrong people for the job.'

'Would you explain that?'

'Yes. You understand that their contracts are fixed-term, negotiated with their governments, at the conclusion of which they return home? While they're here, we can train them, but when they leave we start over again. In any case, it isn't really satisfactory that they go off with all that valuable information in their heads, is it? So, we thought of replacing them with *zivilarbeiter*, hostage labour, rounded up at random from the streets of the occupied territories. You probably know that we have substantially more of this type at Peenemünde. But this would be a *very* unsatisfactory arrangement, because gathering sufficient numbers with the education to acquire the necessary skills would be very much a matter of flinging dice. Now, look at camp labour – it's readily available, reliable, and we can take our pick of them. From your perspective – security – they're subject to much more rigorous supervision, which will be mandatory once we're in full production. Really, there's no disadvantage to using them.'

It was logical. 'But isn't the standard of such labour unsatisfactory? I mean, their *physical* standard?'

Rudolph smiled. 'Ah. You think I'm callous. An endless supply of cheap, ill-used labour that we can replace as it drops? No, again, you're wrong, Hauptmann. The workers will be treated very well, I assure you, far better than where they are at present. For two months now we've had a small number of them here at Peenemünde, as you probably know. We ensure that their SS guards deal gently with them, because broken bones can't build missiles. I think you flew to Berlin two days ago on the supply aircraft?'

'I did, yes.'

'No doubt you're aware of its purpose generally. Would you be surprised to learn that an element of that cargo is cognac, with which the General-major bribes the SS commander? Specifically, to keep his men in check, and their charges un-abused? A bottle each week, as regular as the tide.

'Of course, we're not saints, merely prag-matists. The *häflinge* exist, an uncomfortable fact. You may regret it and you may be surprised to hear that *I* regret it. I have no doubt about our nation's path or its purpose, but it may be that some elements within the Party have made a vice out of necessity, and we must deal with that. The *häflinge* exist, as I say, and they will continue to be used for the Reich's benefit. Perhaps things will change, after victory. But until then, I think it's much better that *we* use them, reasonably.'

It was this sort of argument, made by decent men for whom the last moral boundary lay some-where to their rear, that wearied Fischer. He nodded, as though the point were now obvious. 'Yes, I understand. But now, production will take

151

place somewhere other than Peenemünde, won't it?'

'That's true. But we'll still be needed to supervise it. Can you imagine the SS having the expertise to build the weapons, to maintain the necessary technical tolerances? No, wherever it happens, Peenemünders will be in charge.'

Fischer stood. 'Doctor, was Walter Thiel a happy man, do you think?'

A shrug. 'Walter was too highly strung ever to be *happy*, but he was always happiest at his work. And no, I have no idea why anyone might want to hurt him. Except the British, that is. Now, if I may...?'

Fischer thanked him. As he opened the door he glanced back. Rudolph was already poring over his paperwork, immersing himself in the next problem of production, making the necessary technical adjustments to accommodate the fates of others.

Chapter Twenty

To Fischer's eye, the wounds of Peenemünde appeared to be healing quickly. Most of the gangs removing debris had disappeared, and long-term repairs were beginning to replace the stopgap measures of the previous days. Scars were becoming weals, holes levelling out into patches, bereavements passing into numbed memory amid the thoughtless noise of luckier fates. He had seen it all over those parts of Europe he'd helped to deface: the resurrection imperative.

The facility's non-production areas were to be fully active once more within three weeks. This was not an estimate but a decree from General-major Dornberger, and so had assumed an embryonic inevitability. In the meantime, Fischer noticed that someone had come around to the controversial idea of making the site less inviting to an aerial enemy. Untouched buildings were being repainted in camouflage patterns to blend in with the surrounding trees; those that had suffered bomb damage and were not considered necessary for future use were being abandoned and left as prominent ruins to mislead enemy reconnaissance into believing that Peenemünde had gone else-where; sandbags had begun to appear in fashionable quantities; and Fischer noticed a new urgency in the movements of uniformed staff other than at mealtimes. He approved: with a little imagination and a degree of squinting, one might almost have thought the Reich was at war.

He was wandering through the single storey blocks that flanked the eastern side of the Development area, a maze in which Professor Hans Wierer and his Projections Department had their home. He had called from House 4 to request an interview, but he was only partly convinced he had spoken to the right man, the response having been something between a grunt and a sigh.

He discovered Wierer at his desk in a small, dark office, in an area that seemed to contain a number of disparate processes, and guessed that this was a makeshift arrangement. The man him-

153

self was a tall, almost cadaverous Austrian with a face that a smile wouldn't fit, and greeted Fischer as a leper might a new missing part. To each question he replied in the same dogged, impatient tone while scratching a patch of his neck that was rapidly becoming inflamed. A hydrogen peroxide splash, he explained, sourly; they occurred sometimes, when one's attention was distracted for some reason or another. No, he hadn't known Dr Thiel very well, though they had spoken occasionally when he, accompanying Dornberger or von Braun, needed to discuss internal wiring or control panels – which, despite his title, was Wierer's real expertise. Yes, it had been his responsibility for gathering and identifying the bodies of all Germans killed in the early hours of 18 August, an honour for which he hadn't yet offered the necessary thanks to the Generalmajor. He didn't really know why; perhaps because he had an orderly mind and could be trusted not to prevaricate when identification was problematic. No, of course he hadn't personally identified each corpse: that would have been impossible. A number of the administrative staff had assisted, given that it was they who had the most day-to-day contact with residents of the Settlement. Yes, it was indeed unfortunate that a number of the corpses had been misidentified originally. But perhaps the Hauptmann had some understanding of what bombs do to human tissue, being as he was a member of the Luftwaffe? No, he had not been present when Nagel pulled the tarpaulin from Thiel's face and the wound first became apparent; only the Generalmajor had witnessed it. He had been called over by the latter some moments later, and asked to clear the hall. Would it now be possible for him to return to some useful employment, as he found that he had more than enough of his own business to attend to? Yes, it had been his pleasure also.

Leaving the Projections Department, Fischer permitted himself an impulsive liking for Professor Wierer. Miserable bastards weren't constrained by unspoken issues, because there were few they weren't prepared to air wantonly, and at length. As far as they were concerned, they *spoke their minds*, they were *forthright*, or they *said as they found*. None of them admitted to being merely boorish (much less graceless), but you knew at least where you were with the type. Police work would have been much more pleasant had the criminal psyche inclined to such brutal honesty, instead of tiresome, shallow obfuscation.

Wierer gave a strong impression of being a paragon of honesty, a much overrated virtue. He was bereft of charm, palpable humanity or patience, but of artifice also – and, unfortunately, breathtakingly unhelpful. Of the scientists who had seen the wound in Thiel's forehead, only Dr Wehmer von Braun offered any possibility of further – of *any*, Fischer corrected himself – enlightenment.

But von Braun, as Nagel had told him earlier that morning, was in Berlin once more, meeting Reichsminister Speer and certain others to report on why (Nagel's words) the latest production targets couldn't be met, with or without shiny new

155

facilities. Dornberger had sent von Braun alone because (again, Nagel) the Generalmajor was sick of repeating himself to Speer, and having one golden boy explain it to another might be more effective.

Nagel, apparently, had more sense of the odds than his masters. 'Naturally, it won't work. If you tell Speer that he can't have a thousand missiles a month he'll immediately demand fifteen hundred. That's why he's the Führer's favourite. He gets impossible things done.'

This had confused Fischer a little. 'I understood that the Reichsführer SS now has his hands on production?'

'On the physical process, yes. But I doubt that Speer's going to let go that easily. As things stand, as long as he can keep the programme itself, the Reichsführer's going to be his employee – in effect, meeting the targets that the Armaments Ministry sets.'

So the war between the ministries continued, and Fischer would have to wait, perhaps even until the following day, until von Braun returned. Unfortunate, but he was not to be unoccupied, as Nagel had promised him something extremely *interesting* at three o'clock. Given his experience to date, he hoped that it wasn't going to be a late luncheon.

They were to meet at the rear of the assembly hall. As Fischer approached, it became clear that this was not going to be a private meeting. Civilian and military personnel stood around one of the bays, several forming small groups that appeared to be working parties. Nagel waved from the edge of one of them.

'Perfectly timed, Hauptmann. Now you'll see something to tell your kids.'

That would be quite a feat, given Fischer's much reduced chances of conceiving them. 'What is it we're seeing?'

'There's going to be a mock test-launch. The Generalmajor thinks it might resolve a couple of minor technical problems and also give everyone a little *boost* after what's happened recently. See, they're bringing it out now.'

From the bay, a Hanomag tractor emerged slowly, pulling a long wheeled platform with a sloping rig lying almost prone on a latticed bed. Upon it, secured by two massive cradles, sat one of the fearsome weapons that had so impressed Fischer three days earlier. It seemed outsized, even for its substantial carrier, and it occurred to him that perhaps the missile was too fast in flight. Surely its psychological impact would be so much more intense if its intended victims could actually see and hear it approach?

'Don't worry, Hauptmann, the warhead's a dummy.' Nagel was fairly swelling with vicarious pride.

'The thing that carries the missile, I've seen nothing like it before.'

'*That* is the Meillerwagen. All the work of Klaus Riedel. It transports the weapon to its launch site and then erects it, as tenderly as a mother cradles her baby.'

'As in Meiller-Kipper, I assume? But why not use a tracked vehicle?'

'Less reliable, too harsh a ride. In any case it

157

would be redundant. Believe me, no one would dare transport one of these sweethearts over broken ground, not with a live warhead. Yes, it was made by Meiller-werk, but to Klaus's design.'

'A useful man?'

'Invaluable would be more accurate. You can't imagine how many failures we've had due to the delicate nature of the weapon's electronics and fuel systems. Any one of those many goblins can be wakened by the slightest rough treatment of the casing. What Riedel does is to keep them deeply asleep. He makes mattresses, as he puts it.'

The tractor and rig were moving very slowly, perhaps five kilometres per hour, allowing those in its path to scatter casually. Fischer found this aspect of its performance a little underwhelming.

'I should think that one of these in transit is very vulnerable to attack.'

'No, this is for our benefit. We've timed a fully loaded assembly moving at almost forty kilometres per hour – though, of course, one wouldn't want to attempt that unless absolutely necessary.' Nagel laughed. 'Otherwise it might reach the skies sooner than intended.'

With his war reporter's eye, Fischer imagined a military parade comprising several ranks of such vehicles, all carrying Aggregat missiles, their deadly tips pointing threateningly to the skies. It would be a prospect to deter the ambitions of the most adventurous would-be enemy – assuming, of course, that a time might come when Germany was not at war with all the nations she wished to impress. Power as overarching spectacle – one art

158

in which the Reich led the world. He only wished the underlying logic had been better understood, that a threat remains a threat only for as long as it is merely threatened.

Clear now of the crowd and the loading platform, the tractor accelerated smoothly. Several observers clambered into a Ford truck. Nagel turned to Fischer. 'They're going to Test Stand One to see it raised and fuelled. I can't of course, with my authorization. But if you...?'

'Thank you. I've been impressed enough.'

Nagel nodded absently, clearly wanting to be a part of the group that was departing. But then something occurred to him. He started, and flushed.

'My God, Hauptmann, I'm sorry! There's a message for you, from an Oberleutnant Holleman. Will you telephone him, please?'

House 4 was closest. Furiously wondering if certain young men at Peenemünde had empty barns for minds, Fischer ran across and begged the use of an empty office from one of the female secretaries.

The connection, fighting its way through Berlin's damaged exchanges, took a few minutes, and the line was very poor. He was too late: Holleman had left the Air Ministry an hour earlier to begin his Spreewald leave. But he had left word – in fact, a very precise form of words – for Detmar Reincke to deliver in his absence.

'No idea what this means, Otto, but Freddie told me to tell you that Gerd Branssler says to find the trees, quickly.'

Chapter Twenty-One

Fischer had no intention of hiding. The office in which he took the call seemed as comfortable a waiting room as any other, so he sat at the desk – to give him a very small authoritative edge – and passed the time browsing once-familiar passages from a copy of *Die Xenien,* a solitary indication of intelligent life in an otherwise depressingly technical bookcase.

He waited for almost half-an-hour. Probably, they had been directed first to the guesthouse, which wouldn't improve their mood. He hadn't given his name to the secretary, but there was little doubt she would recognize any physical description they offered.

There was no knock on the door; and he assumed their training hadn't extended to formalities.

'You're not von Braun.'

Fischer hadn't noticed the name plate. 'In this uniform?'

Only two of them: the usual, slightly-too-large suits, grubby collars and tired, knowing expressions on their simian faces. They hadn't yet thought to remove their hats.

'Jesus. The Ivans really fucked you up.' One of them found the view faintly amusing; the other stared – appalled, probably, that decent society hadn't been spared it.

Fischer smiled widely, to make a point. 'One or the other did, that's for certain.'

Abruptly, the amused one tried a scowl instead, and sat on the edge of the desk, within slapping distance. 'So, Otto Fischer, a hard case who sends someone – *sends* them, mind, like a fucking valet – to find out what we keep in our files. Unbelievable! Is that how it works, George?'

George, a lugubrious soul, shook his head, said nothing.

'The only time anyone gets to know what *we* know is when *we* tell them. No good comes of it, mind, because it's what we know about *them*, and usually, it's a sort of goodbye gift. But not you, Otto. *You* walk straight in and bang on the front desk, and ask what the fuck we know about Maier, and Schmidt, and the Kaiser, and not so much as a formal fucking introduction. Is that polite, George?'

George shook his head again. He was very upset, or hurt.

'What really itches is that when someone mentions names we don't know, our bosses wonder why we don't know them, and why don't we? And then we get schlagstocks stuffed up our arses and wriggled about until we jump. You've made us jump, Otto, so now we're entitled to ask what *you* know, and why it is you're wanting to know it.'

George was nodding now. The routine was tiresomely predictable, but at least they were talking rather than walking him down the corridor. Fischer shrugged.

'You were told what I've been doing here.

Security checks, that's all.'

The one who wasn't George had another chuckle. 'Hear that, George? Security checks. Here's a fellow who does them properly. None of your polite interviews and glancing over the staff references. This one comes down to the Alex and rolls up his sleeves.' He glanced at Fischer's right arm. 'Well, sleeve. And then fucks off again, cool as you like, once he's sure we can't be of assistance.'

Chandler appeared to be required reading at Alexanderplatz. Fischer gave them what they wanted.

'I'd have thought that even Gestapo might have worked out that this place isn't a debating society. Everything here's classified, only they've got thousands of foreigners wandering around, helping themselves to the Reich's secrets like it's bratwurst night in a health spa. So the *Generalmajor* (he stressed the word preposterously) told me to do a proper job. The thing is, they don't have files on the foreigners, they don't have many files on their own people, and no one seems to think that it's a bad idea to have Russians working on blueprints. All in all, I've known tighter security in a Greek shithouse. So, the first thing I think I need to find out is if any of the staff here have histories. And seeing as how no one *here* can tell me, one way or the other, I decided to check whether anyone else ever asked the same questions that I'm asking.'

'Who's *anyone?*'

'You. Kripo. Abwehr. Not the GFP yet, but I'll get around to it.'

162

That got Not-George's attention. 'And?'

'Don't get excited. It was a waste of time. They're a set of National Socialist heroes, loving fathers and devoted husbands. Until I hear differently, which, unless there's a security service I haven't yet met, isn't likely.'

'So it's the Elysian fucking Fields out there?'

'Well no, Herr...?'

'Don't be silly.'

'What I mean is that no one's got a past. Is that surprising? Most of the technical staff came to Peenemünde from Kummersdorf or one of the big industrial laboratories, to which they went straight from university. They're close to innocents, most of them. They don't eat, breathe or shit what isn't their particular speciality.'

'Fucking intelligentsia. Pansy fucking degenerate fuckers.' George, a little recovered from his previous dolour, rolled every syllable between his tongue, teeth and fat lips before spitting it out.

The other one scowled for a few moments, loath to give up the bone; but he had done the comedy and there were no other non-violent options. He announced the newer, kinder Not-George with a theatrical sigh.

'Look, Fischer, we don't want this shit. Me and George, we don't sleep any more, not since Prinz-Albrecht-Strasse decided that doubts about the final victory are officially Naughty. We're stretched, we're tired and we're fucking peevish, so listen. We *know* you were asking for a reason, and that bothers us. But you just carry on with what you're doing, and when you've finished, you do a thing. You do it, or we'll make you uglier than you

163

are already. Do you know what that thing is?'

'I tell you what I find.'

'You tell us *everything* you find. Who's not putting the lid back on the pickle jar, who likes to wear his wife's frocks, who thinks the Ivans have got a point – *everything*. Written reports, signed and motored around to Alexanderplatz as soon as the ink's dry. Clear enough?'

Fischer assumed an answer wasn't required. The trade-off was one he had been willing to make since being dragged into this business. Better – just – to have a scorpion on the shoulder than under the eiderdown. At least you knew when and where you were going to get it. And there was one definite advantage to the arrangement.

'Then I need something from you.'

Not-George's eyebrows rose, trying to kiss his hairline.

Fischer returned the name they had provided inadvertently. '*Everything* you have, and quickly, please.'

Chapter Twenty-Two

At the guesthouse, where he intended to shower away his soiling ordeal and toast its departure with a whisky, Zofia was waiting for him with an envelope.

Even as his fingers confirmed that she'd opened and re-sealed it, he managed a smile – the good version, the one that utilized only the left, undamaged side of his mouth. She, in turn, offered a quick nod. It struck him at that moment that they had all the ingredients for a full-blown relationship: deceit, awareness, acceptance and a mutual uncertainty, all enacted in an awkward space across which nothing was ever really going to be said. From his own experience, it was almost a definition of marriage.

She was delivering an invitation: a formal one, to dine with the Generalmajor that evening. A bath, then: no scotch.

'Zofia, is it possible for my uniform to be laundered promptly?' It should have been an order; it emerged almost as an apology.

She assured him that it would be returned within the hour if she could take it immediately. He liked the way she said it, and read far more kindness into it than had been offered. He stripped in the bathroom and passed each item to her around the door, acutely aware of a growing sense of vulnerability as the layers between world and flesh peeled away. At any other time he would have paid for her company, but it was a profound relief to close the door and turn the key.

Searching for what remained of the soap, he found a small jar of Dresdner Essenz bath salts in the bathroom cupboard, and without hesitating emptied half its contents into the bath. There was a momentary agony as the minerals ate at the burned areas, and then a warm, beautiful numbness replaced the nagging discomfort that was more familiar to him than weals to a persistent flagellant. For a great while, marvelling at the absence of sensation, the feeling of being disconnected entirely from pain, he lay still and contemplated nothing more than his toes.

He was almost late for his dinner appointment. His clothes; immaculately cleaned and pressed, were laid out for him by the time he'd woken, climbed out of the lukewarm bath and dried himself. Even his boots were shining blackly for the first time in days. He dressed quickly (by his standards) and, as this was a formal affair, wore his Knight's Cross at the throat. That was trickier, and wasted more time than he had, but he was moving in a society in which appearances and achievement counted greatly.

The five-minute walk to House 4, interrupted by not a single member of staff or foreign worker, was almost unnervingly peaceful. He became acutely aware of the sound of trees moving in the wind, of his heels upon the metalled surface and the monumental muteness of unlit buildings, gliding past like discarded theatre sets, or biblical ruins. But as he entered the administrative headquarters and ascended to the senior dining room his sense of sharing the world returned as if registered upon a dial. At the threshold to the party a steward in white took his cap and left glove; loud laughter and the musical clash of bottle against glass led him like the Ghost of Christmas Past into a warm glow of male conviviality. The waiters aside, there were about a dozen men present, only two of whom, Dornberger and Godomar Schubert (the one sour face in the room), wore uniform. Fischer recognized Rudolph, Rees, Riedel, Stahlknecht and von Braun, who must have escaped early from Berlin. The others he didn't know, but all had that

166

air of easy confidence that comes from knowing exactly how good one is at one's business.

Politely, the various conversations paused as he entered, and Dornberger made introductions. Two of those whose hands he avoided seemed uncomfortable with such a graphic reminder of the real world, but the others were blithely, even enthusiastically, dismissive of his wounds, and glanced knowingly at his Knight's Cross. Anecdotes would be expected: a little vicarious heroism to spice the cuisine.

Dornberger lifted a glass of gin from a passing tray and pressed it into Fischer's hand. It was a drink he disliked normally, but the smell of it was so reminiscent of his recent bath that, with a squirt of soda, it sparked his appetite finely. Around him, small-talk graciously avoided the everyday intricacies of their work and concentrated upon being truly small: enquiries about Berlin's remaining nightclubs and the availability of luxury items; an informed discussion on varieties of port; an amiable argument about whether *Germania* could ever be built, given the world's known reserves of marble. It all encouraged an air of pre-war ease that Fischer, by now halfway into his second gin, found quite charming. He could hardly lay claim to the experience, but he felt as if he might have been a guest in the sort of old-fashioned gentlemen's club to which German nobility used to pester their English cousins to propose them.

Clearly, some effort was being made to welcome him into the fraternity. At one point he was led by Dr von Braun to a seat midway down the length of the large dining table and asked to sit.

167

As he did so, the others gathered around, winking or giving the nudge to their neighbours.

'How does it fit?' asked Dornberger, solicitously.

Perplexed, Fischer told him that it was quite comfortable: a response that hardly merited the gale of laughter that engulfed the company.

Von Braun had to shout the punch line: 'The Führer thought so, too!'

The greatest living arse had warmed the same piece of furniture only four months earlier: at a dinner to celebrate the half-successful launch of two A4s (or rather, the entirely successful launch of one of them). Debate had raged mildly since about whether the seat so honoured should be given a brass plate to commemorate the event. In the meantime, Kaspar Nagel had used his initiative and penknife to notch the rim of its backrest. House 4 catering staff haphazardly rotated the eighteen chairs around the dining table, and this might have given rise to schism and controversy as to which of them had been the True Receptacle.

They were still discussing that fateful visit when a dining bell sounded. Fischer was urged to remain where he was, and the others moved so easily to their own chairs that he suspected an immutable order of seating. Dornberger, naturally, occupied one end of the table, and Arthur Rudolph the other; von Braun sat to the Generalmajor's right hand and assumed the job of directing the wine waiters.

'I'm afraid we can expect only simple fare, Hauptmann.'

Fischer's neighbour, a man introduced as Ernst

Steinhoff (something in Guidance and Control), smiled regretfully and poured a little water into their glasses. He was correct, in a superficial sense: they were served a soup, a meat course and a pudding; but the small printed menu in front of each diner identified the first as *Consommé Niçoise*, the second *Poularde du Mons au Champagne*, and the last *Corbeille de Fruits*. Fischer tried to recall when he had last eaten so well, but a brief, depressing audit of his life to date confirmed that this was probably a new peak. He wasn't alone: the air of satisfaction that greeted each course seemed a little overdone, until he recalled the meal he had eaten here the day he flew to Berlin. The discrepancy was startling, and under steady, grateful prompting Dornberger explained the mystery: a guest chef, brought in from Anklam for the night, paid in provisions for his own restaurant.

Fischer listened to nearby conversations for a while, saying nothing. Predictably, there were too many amateurish observations upon military strategy: too many opportunities, given and taken, to use words like *necessary* and *regrettable*. But after the platitudes had been exhausted, the shirts unstuffed, Fischer's neighbour to the left (Hermann Kurtzweg, an aerodynamicist) prompted the shy Steinhoff to admit that he and Fischer shared both the rank of Hauptmann and an interest. The first was an honorific, recognizing his record for the world's longest glider-flight to date. This was Kurtzweg's cue to hold forth enthusiastically on the form of the device, but Steinhoff seemed slightly embarrassed by his achievement, as though events had retrospectively thrown a dilettantish light upon it. Fischer nodded often, agreed where necessary, and resisted the urge to mention his feelings whenever he'd survived a 'flight' in one of those infernal devices.

Then formal toasts: the Führer, Success To Our Endeavours, Victory. Also Happier Days, which struck Fischer both as daring and somewhat insolent in light of the overall quality of life here. And small cigars – surprisingly, given what had preceded them, the ordinary ten-centimetre ration items. But Dornberger had also authorized a release of more of his precious stock of real coffee, which brought a fresh murmur of contentment from his guests.

When the last of it had been drained, the Generalmajor broke the spell. He stood, rapped the table with his knuckles and waited until the discussions died away.

'Gentlemen, don't worry. This is not another toast. I don't ask you to drink more than you wish!'

Feeble, but most of them grinned politely. Fischer noticed that von Braun was performing the second-in-command's traditional role of leading the response.

'A most enjoyable evening for me. I hope you found it so, too. I'd no particular occasion in mind when I invited you at such short notice, but it seems to me that certain apposite things may be said nevertheless. We have found, have we not, that we are at war? The British failed in their intention of killing you all, but the fact of the raid has brought necessary changes that will affect each of us. For that I feel a certain regret. We are a family here, and no family relishes separation, particularly one that is forced upon it. But we change, and we adapt. We bow to circumstance, but even so, we maintain our loyalties, our cohesion, even when we are apart! I think we've forged a bond here that will survive any challenge. What do you say, Klaus?'

Riedel had taken a mouthful of wine while Dornberger was speaking, and its violent ejection reduced most of the table to helpless laughter. The Generalmajor moved around the table to a point directly behind him, and placed a hand on his shoulder.

'I'm sorry, Klaus, I couldn't resist. I should say to all of you grinning monkeys that Dr Riedel has today, I believe, solved one of the most pressing of our problems – that of *consistently* raising the A4 to a launch position without placing catastrophic pressure upon the fuel manifolds. If his solution works – and his solutions usually do – then we're a big step closer to full production.'

There was generous applause around the table, and Fischer joined in as best he could, slapping the table with his left hand. Riedel flushed deeply. He seemed embarrassed by the attention, and squirmed slightly beneath Dornberger's grip.

'So, we have a special occasion after all. Now, gentlemen, that's all I'm going to bore you with, but I suggest you don't rush away. We have cognac and kümmel to come.'

The table rose. Dornberger leaned down to Riedel to make a last, discreet comment, then waved Fischer over to the fireplace, where von Braun was pouring himself a small *digestif*. Many of the others congregated around Riedel, pressing him for the details of his triumph. All of them gravitated gently away from their boss. Fischer recognized the widening zone of discretion for what it was: a curtain falling upon a very enjoyable evening.

'Hauptmann, you had visitors today. Did we not agree that you'd be discreet?'

Dornberger seemed irritated, but coldly so; von Braun, edgier, almost threw back his brandy. Fischer felt no inclination to apologize.

'Sir, this investigation can bear no more circumspection. If I'm to find a motive, I need to know what the victim knew, and what his assassin knows. I can't do that without asking questions.'

'But *Gestapo*, for God's sake?'

Fischer shrugged. 'Who better? If anyone should be concerned with the character of those who work here, wouldn't it be them? Or would you prefer the SD? All they've been told is what we've agreed I should say, so it's my neck, not yours.'

'You've told them...?'

'That I'm looking at security, nothing else. That I made enquiries because I need to know if anyone here has ever been investigated, for whatever reason. It's perfectly plausible. It's what they would expect to hear. But in return for not beating the hell out of me they've insisted they be informed of anything I find.'

'And you'll do that?'

'Yes, willingly, because I'll find nothing. At the conclusion of this business, you'll get a typed report stating the very obvious things that are wrong with security here, with my recommendations on what needs to be done to put them right. And I'll present a copy to Gestapo, with a ribbon tied around it. I might even add something to their copy, to the effect that you need shaking up a bit, just to give it – to give *me* – credibility. Because, of course, I intend, if possible, to survive this assignment.'

Dornberger and von Braun glanced at each other. Fischer sensed that neither man was used to placing his sensitive parts in the calloused hands of strangers. The soldier pursed his lips, the scientist shook his head slightly, but it wasn't as if there were other options available to them. They had opened the bag, removed the cat and placed it in the crook of his arm. One had to expect a scratch or two.

He took a sip of the cognac that von Braun had pressed upon him. 'Gentlemen, look. I was treated gently by their standards, so it's likely that with the Reichsführer's move into production here, Gestapo and SD are already being pushed to work out who it is they're going to be dealing with. Now, I've started to do their job for them, and it's in their interest to let me continue for as long as they believe I'm doing it properly – with enthusiasm, as it were. You, you control the scope of that investigation and get to see exactly what they're going to get, before they get it. It seems to me you might almost have planned it this way.' Fischer smiled. 'If you could have known how events would turn out, that is.'

'Please don't be impertinent, Hauptmann.' Sourly, Dornberger glanced once more at von Braun, but they were persuaded. They had to be:

they could hardly call the Alex and claim there'd been a misunderstanding: that the nice men in ugly suits needn't worry themselves further about whatever it was that had brought them to Peenemünde. Nor could they just dispense with Fischer's services, now that the same nice men were using him as their surrogate nose. The corpse of Walter Thiel, shamelessly misrepresented to posterity, was growing heavier as its nutrients bled into Usedom's needy soil.

There was something vaguely satisfying about his little victory, and Fischer savoured it. The meal had been good, the conversation unexpectedly entertaining, the irritation of his temporary masters pleasing. For the first time he felt that he'd grasped a small initiative: nothing to be too sanguine about, but at least a step away from the sense of helplessness that had chased him during the past few days. The fact that he had Gestapo to thank for it made it all the more worthwhile.

Only the growing certainty that brandy and wine shouldn't have been poured on to gin cast any sort of shadow on his mood – a shadow that seemed to be lengthening. He hadn't really meant to say it, of course, because he wondered if it might be true. Normally, he'd have been more discreet, more willing to let the thing reveal itself. In fact, the slip was so out of character that he wondered if he were actually intoxicated – an unforgivable lapse.

Dornberger, quelling his irritation, had turned away and was saying something more. Fischer didn't catch it the first time. He begged the Generalmajor's pardon, but the man continued as if he hadn't heard. It was something about a doctor, though there were so many of them in the room that he'd have to be a little more specific, thought Fischer, hugely amused by his own acuity, as the shadow darkened and became complete.

Chapter Twenty-Three

As upon every morning, Zofia arrived at Peenemünde at 6.30am, in one of the trucks that ferried the domestic workers from Trassenheide. She had kept her head down throughout the short journey, discouraging conversation from the other unwilling commuters, even the Poles among them. The time spent in the truck, like every other slice of the day, was carefully mapped out in her head, in the hope of anticipating and deflecting any attention that was avoidable, that demanded a response. To those who were not Germans, Zofia said as little as possible; to the Germans, she said only what was necessary. No doubt she was considered rude, or possibly shy. She didn't care, if it was the price of preserving as much anonymity as their collective existence allowed.

But not being noticed had never been one of her talents. Her family, her many boyfriends, even other girls had told that she was blessed: a real beauty, a Polish rose. It was hardly a surprise then (though no less a humiliation), that almost immediately following her arrival she had been picked out to serve the bosses. It wasn't put so crudely, of course, but they liked pretty things to be seen: their suits, shoes, motor cars, servants and every other sort of dainty that reminded them of the well-padded futures they'd anticipated before the war. She knew of two other girls who'd been chosen similarly, and now they were gone. One had returned home to Lille, unscathed, at the termination of her 'contract'; the other had gone to God, helped along by an abortionist attempting to deal with what might otherwise have been an embarrassment for her employers. A lesson was learned, and they hadn't been replaced; only Zofia remained, the sole domestic servant trusted to provide for visiting Quality. She was, in a debased way, highly valued. The Germans expected their forced labourers to be under-motivated, yet her work was faultless, her manner respectful, and she had declined to become pregnant by either of the men who had raped her since she arrived at Peenemünde.

This life-apart-from-life had endured for almost four years now, and there was no prospect of it ending. Her services, unlike those of foreign volunteers here, were not time-limited: she was one of the *zivilarbeiter* rounded up and sent to Germany late in 1939 in reprisal for the sabotage upon a railway junction in Torun, her home town. One moment she had been walking home from her job at a fabrication plant office; the next, she was squeezed into a prison cell with eighteen others, stripped, slapped and starved for two days before being transported like livestock to Swinemünde, where she had first sight of her new opportunities. Since that day, she had managed to

176

smuggle just two notes out to her parents: the first to tell them that she was living, the second about the other most necessary thing.

The work was degrading enough, but the arbitrary manner in which she had been brought to it could hardly be borne by a sane mind. Memories of life before her abduction were too painful to allow – the men she had chosen willingly; the three-room apartment overlooking the river that she had shared with her best friend and her dog; a time when there had been such a thing as will, and the means to express it. Recollections of her parents were the worst, because theirs had been the greatest loss: their innocence the most brutally torn away. The truth was that before she could ever see them again they would be dead, and nothing then could be re-paid: the laughter at solemnity, the easing of small adversities, the forgiveness of brief, adolescent rebellions against their love. For all of the debts she carried, the thoughtless slights she had given them, absolution in memory alone remained.

So Zofia felt her hatreds to be righteous, and this was a small comfort. With down-turned eyes, a respectful demeanour and quiet, reliable industry, she damned to eternal torments the important visitors to Peenemünde for whom she cooked, cleaned and, occasionally, bled. On bad days (and most of them were), she wished cancer into their marrows and other, scrofulous men into their marital beds to pollute not only their own loins but their legacies also. She hoped, when she could not think of anything more subtle, that Germans might be removed from the world entirely.

For most of the time, this mute torrent of imprecation was directed at the person of the Generalmajor, who remained unaware of the poisonous burden he carried. He had no permanent accommodation at Peenemünde and used the guesthouse as his occasional home away from Berlin, so he was, for want of variety, her customary means of release. But when visitors displaced him temporarily, Zofia re-directed her loathing accordingly, whether the subject treated her with courtesy, indifference or as a vessel in which to express his inadequacies. It was enough that they were who they were, and drawing breath still.

She was in no sense partial, but the new one, the gargoyle, troubled her most of all. He was hideous: a wound in a uniform, something that a more merciful God would have allowed to die in the field; yet not quite a monster – like Kaspar Nagel, he tried his best to persuade that he was otherwise, despite the evidence. But she wasn't deceived. His scars were manifestly the mark of a natural justice, and she had little doubt that his soul was mutilated. Germans were universally culpable, even if some were able to hide their deformities better than others.

It vexed her more that he spoke and acted as if they were both human beings, when the Racial Laws said she was only part of one, a very small, inferior part. He did it clumsily enough, sometimes; but he had a habit, a vice, of assuming an equality between them, and that provoked her more than anything else. When she brought him a breakfast so bad that she herself would have refused it, he thanked her. When he wanted her to do something for him he asked, rather than told her, and he said *please*, for God's sake. When he had trouble doing what other men did without thinking, he looked almost apologetically at her, as if he were imposing upon her patience. He was mocking her, with a vision of what the world should be, not what it was.

Worst of all, she found herself responding to it. The previous day, she had made a better breakfast for him, and cleaned and pressed his clothes more than adequately – carefully, even. She was beginning to answer his questions with more than a grunt, which both exposed her and weakened the resolve that allowed her to survive here. Whatever his purpose at Peenemünde, she hoped that it would be done soon. It was better to know and live with the worst, than fear the uncertainty of something less.

Providing for the guesthouse was only one of her duties, despite her reserved role as comfort for the eye. At the start of each day she worked the kitchens with other women, scrubbing floors and utensils, polishing chrome and brass and, if it was her turn, feeding the chickens in the small kitchen garden. Their own breakfast of dark rye bread and barley coffee so weak that it was, in effect, heated water, was taken as they did their chores, because a woman who stopped working could expect a slap at the very least, and often a kicking from one of the reservists who delighted in expressing their very little authority.

At seven-thirty, Zofia delivered breakfast to the guesthouse. She always entered carefully, listening for evidence of movement from the bedroom.

179

A year earlier, one of the visitors, a civilian purchasing agent from the Armaments Ministry, had wakened early and been in the mood for games: first a little light rough stuff, then forced penetration as he pressed her face hard into the table, and finally a good-natured reminder that, by allowing herself to be raped, she had contravened the laws against miscegenation and might be executed, or at least sent to a camp, should she think of speaking of it. The threat had hardly been necessary.

With only one good arm, the present occupant wasn't likely to attempt anything similar, but still she preferred to avoid contact. She moved very quietly when in the guesthouse, always taking care to position the porcelain and cutlery upon the tray so that it wouldn't rattle when she put it down. She ensured that fresh towels or other laundry were delivered each evening, and she removed any household waste at the same time, so as to be in and out quickly the following morning. Men, she had found, tended to be more playful after a night's rest.

But this morning was unusual. Down the short corridor from the kitchen, the bedroom door was open, and she could hear voices. The officer was seated on the edge of the bed, stripped to the waist, and what she saw was terrible. The tray almost fell from her hands, which would have been a pity, because she had opened the door so quietly that he hadn't yet noticed her. It was difficult to look, and almost impossible not to stare. The wreckage of his face continued down the right side of his body; she had noticed his hand already,

180

but it hardly seemed possible that everything between the visible wounds could be so damaged and he lived still. He should have died, she thought: a mercy that even a dog should expect.

Peenemünde's chief medical officer was with him, checking his temperature. The parts of him that weren't wounds looked pale, haggard; he listened, shook his head wearily, and refused something offered with a gesture of his good hand.

'Really, it was a reaction. I should have realized, but the taste was disguised by the liqueur.'

The medical officer shook his head. 'Are you sure? I've never heard of a similar effect.'

The Horror smiled: an awful sight. 'I was about four, and my mother left me to play in the kitchen while she hung laundry out to dry. There was a dish placed on a low shelf, she used them to flavour spirits that my father brewed illegally in our outhouse. I put a few in my mouth, enjoyed the tartness, and took another handful. She found me on the floor, convulsing and unable to breathe. Fortunately, a doctor lived very close by, and he induced vomiting so severe that my belly hurt for days afterwards – it probably saved me. I've avoided them since, of course. Last night was the first time in my adult life that I ... one would have expected the thing to have worn off by now.'

'Elderberries! Well, I shouldn't have thought of it, so I'm glad to have your empirical diagnosis. At least let me give you some antacid to calm your poor stomach.'

Zofia backed out of the kitchen door silently, unnoticed by either of them. It was better not to

181

be thought an eavesdropper. She waited with the tray at the corner of the Development Shops compound until the medical officer emerged, and then returned as if she were only now bringing breakfast. The coffee would be lukewarm, and were it for anyone else this might have worried her.

Again, she entered without knocking. The bedroom door was open still; he was sat on the bed rubbing an ointment into his wounds. The uninjured part of his face showed no emotion or pain as he worked the burned flesh, making gentle, circular motions until it was absorbed. At one point he paused, picked up a cigarette that balanced on the rim of an ashtray on the bedside table, took a single shallow drag and replaced it. Then a further scoop of ointment, and the ritual recommenced: round and around, caressing the half-shoulder, the half bicep, the claw that had been a hand, with no more apparent connection than if he'd been the medical officer administering it to a patient. Zofia felt an uncomfortable sensation, one that went against heart and instinct; it was something like a wish, for better than he had.

She had remained motionless, but he glanced up, sideways, and all of that detachment, that *poise*, disappeared. He grabbed at a shirt that lay beside him and tried frantically with one hand to pull it around his body, and the part of his face that wasn't deformed became as red as the rest. It was a moment of shared, obscene intimacy, something both of them would have paid to avoid. She felt his shame as much as her own revulsion: the pleading stare, begging her not to be there, like a slap, but not delivered in anger. She turned away, much too late, threw the tray on to the kitchen table, and ran from the guesthouse.

On the way back to the main kitchens, she tried to think, to measure the damage. *There'll be punishment*, she told herself, but the fear that should have gone with the thought was absent. Expecting the worst was the wisest course, but really, what had she done? A stupid question: it was enough to be where one shouldn't be, to catch one of them in the wrong mood, at the wrong moment; but *this* one didn't seem the type to take out on her what fate had placed upon him. He could report her, of course, and let those who enjoyed inflicting punishment do their job. No, not this one, Zofia told herself; and usually, she could measure men.

Absurdly, the thought occurred that he might even apologize. It would be the decent, gentle-manly thing to do and therefore ludicrous: a mockery of them both. Yet the thought wouldn't go away. It would be best to go back, she decided: after allowing a decent interval for him to eat his breakfast and calm down, she'd go back rather than wait until evening. At least then she'd know what to expect.

Chapter Twenty-Four

Doctors who dabbled in the embryonic field of trauma management had warned Fischer that some things might hurt more than the wounds: that there would be occasions when eyes couldn't hide the reactions behind them, and he should prepare himself. It was only natural, he'd been told. Expectations of norms were strong in people as they were in animals, and it was important that he adjust his own expectations accordingly. He was going to be regarded with revulsion: as a thing that should have died decently rather than inflict itself upon the sensibilities of a community from which it was now, irrevocably, set apart.

This would be difficult to bear at first, they said. At worst, it might – as they had seen often – do to the mind what aviation fuel had done to the body. But they assured him that, with time and proper mental discipline, it need not continue to burn with the same intensity. He might even become indifferent to the stares, the half-steps backwards, the faces turning away from the prospect of his ravaged own. He might, eventually, recognize these reactions as being little more than fear for the self. He would be astonished, they told him, to find that he could re-fashion his own normality, in time.

But he'd been warned that progress would not be a consistent, rising path. The mind's armour

was fragile, prone to being pierced by the unexpected, the untimely and even the too-familiar.
There were no rules to this, nothing to be done
that might deflect or anticipate the moment.
Something, sooner or later, would get through
and hurt: perhaps send him backwards, for a
while at least.

He had accepted all of it, resigning himself to
what he knew would be the least pleasant part of
his new, unpleasant life. For almost two years
now he had known exactly where the point
between acceptance and desperation lay, and had
managed his own expectations accordingly. He
knew that it couldn't last, that some sort of loss
of self was coming; he just wished, desperately,
that it hadn't been her. And that it had been a
matter only of his wounds.

Thank God she doesn't remember me.

He stood at the water's edge, only some five
hundred metres from the guesthouse. For a while,
lost in the moment's melodrama, he'd thought of
not stopping when he reached it (there was that
about native Usedomers: they knew most of the
uses to which a sea could be put). It had been a
delusion, of course: if he'd possessed any measure
of that sort of courage, the fish would have had
him long ago, before the Ivans ever thought to
remodel the outer Fischer. So long ago, in fact,
that he could hardly recall the order of events
through which his small expectations of himself
had been sifted and reduced to a core of near-
vacancy.

There were several objects in the water, just
north of where he stood. One of them in parti-

cular, rising too high from the calm surface, took his eye and he walked towards it. He recognized it long before he reached it: knew, even as he drew closer, that he should have turned around and walked away. It seemed a day for doing that.

The tan, rubberized canvas was burned down one side, its fabric parted entirely, and Fischer could see the sequence of events as clearly as if he'd been watching a newsreel. If the man had been conscious still when he hit the water, he would have held on with the other arm, trying desperately to keep it in the vest, to stay afloat. It had been a warm night, and the water's temperature would have been high enough for him to survive until light came. But the burned area was large, and Fischer didn't think that he had been in a condition to hold on, not for long. He hoped, earnestly, that it hadn't been for long. The RAF issue number stencilled on the breast was intact, and so he was obliged to lift the thing out of the water. If there were parents still, a wife, they'd want to know for sure.

He found it difficult to move away. The breeze, the odours of the boundary between water and sand, added their weight to that of the *Mae West*, holding him there: home, almost. Deliberately, he kept his face to the north, away from the land, trying to shield from his mind's eye almost everything behind him, and re-create this place at another time, a time before he began the journey from a kind of life to emptiness.

But that was impossible, because the one re-called the other. Imagined states of innocence are defined by their loss, not tenure – his memory

186

was acute on that point at least. For the rest, he had only a sense of creeping descent, with no markers to register how far he had gone or what was to come. Within that seamless passage, only guilt provided a form of clarity.

He began, as he usually did, with the sin of complicity: to have been a fully functioning element of the moral crisis of this age. He might have – he had – argued to himself that it had engulfed them all indiscriminately, blamelessly; but too many of his compatriots had floated, adapting to their new verities. No doubt some had merely acquiesced to what they hoped was a finite ordeal, until the easy victories persuaded them of their error. For a little while Fischer had convinced himself that detachment was possible, that he could be simultaneously amused, revolted and absolved by the distance between what he saw and what he understood himself to be. To a man whose engagement with society was at best intermittent, it was comforting, for a very little while, to see that detachment as another proof of identity. But to maintain the fiction it would have been necessary not to stand in the shit that he wished to ignore. And Fischer had been a policeman, an instrument.

He recalled the way his initial dismay had metastasised to the same cold indifference to human pain that marked all of his colleagues. When his department was subsumed into the RSHA, a rationale for self-disgust had merely been codified: his work, never very notable, suffered further: sick leave became more of a support than last resort; his excuses a currency, buying time to avoid the choices that a new order determined necessary. Eventually, he stopped chasing compromises and accepted them as blows instead, to the point at which he hadn't known where the canvas was, much less whether he was lying on it. From there, regaining a degree of self-respect had required a socratic gesture: the knock on Soccer Felix's door; the note, begging to be excused; the search for a clear, unhindered way out.

He emerged into 1937, when a man seeking a new start could have closed his eyes, thrown a stick and hit something promising. Every part of society that was not accelerating into war production was hurtling towards war itself, convinced that it yearned for anything but. Opportunities abounded for reincarnation: for dropping present disappointments in favour of a nicely fitting uniform, loud camaraderie and a *lebensraum* prospectus. In that mêlée, Fischer had been spoiled for choice, but he had taken his time, looked carefully, chosen wisely. He had applied and been accepted the same week, leaving an already-departed wife to mourn the man she hadn't ever known or really tried to know.

After the minimum required period, careful always to excel at what was merely required (he was described by his CO, a wit, as *adeptly competent*), he had volunteered for that honourable, mad role. Six times he hurled himself from an aircraft, the requirement for the coveted badge, and as he did so the binds of his troubled anima had progressively unravelled. Elite societies tie themselves to simple truths, and theirs had been the simplest of all: the regiment's motto, inherited from their old Prussian Landespolizei days, was *For Glory and Fatherland,* but it might more aptly have been *Tomorrow Isn't Coming.* They were intended as an extended suicide squad, the vanguard of reckless military operations and their last-ditch recovery when it all went wrong: they trained for it, they looked forward to it; they even drank to poor odds in their well-provided mess, and pitied the ordinary soldier for his survival anxieties. So, when peace turned to fighting, there were few of the qualms that usually tormented the moral being: Fischer knew he wouldn't be around long enough to care.

But like his leaders he found that nothing falls as planned. In 1940 he glided, air-sick to his stomach, into Fort Eben-Emael and won his Iron Cross at the cost of no more than a torn-out fingernail. Later that year he was dropped on Sola air station and survived unharmed the massacre of sixty men of his unit by a single Norwegian machine-gunner. Maleme in 1941 was the worst: Fischer was one of just fourteen men in his company to be pulled out at the end, the rest shot like pigeons as they drifted down towards well-prepared New Zealander positions. Not a scratch on him: only the bloody memorials of comrades' deaths, splashed across his camouflage tunic as if to taunt his unspoken ambition, and then the Knight's Cross to rub it in. It was at about this time, roughly when he was trying to rationalize his unit's second reprisal against civilians who had momentarily forgotten to be civilians, that Fischer discovered his sense of moral clarity had quite worn off.

Even the grounding of the Fallschirmjäger left him untouched initially. The Führer, over-whelming military genius of the age, gazed down upon the slaughterhouse of his finest troops and went about-face. Cunningly, the majority of his airborne troops were redeployed to the mud, to be squandered like mere infantry. As a small compensation for this professional disappoint-ment, the ground war on the Eastern Front proved to be incomparably deadlier than Bel-gium, Norway or even Crete – deadlier, and far dirtier, even between front-line troops. In that existential struggle, men ceased even to imitate men, and inhumanity became common. What Fischer saw, and did, was the stuff of millenarian ravings: the custom and usage of a new, entirely unhinged world.

Perhaps fate had been waiting only for him to accumulate a necessary sense of what he could become, given the opportunity. After that, he hadn't needed even to be careless, much less suicidal; the most blessed luck could survive only so many of the not-a-step-backward defences that the Führer deemed the future of German tactics after Moscow. He recalled the day vaguely, though its traumas blurred the detail. It had been just another shift at Satan's coal-face: a brief bombardment, the Ivans throwing them-selves prematurely at a virtually undamaged line, a massacre, a withdrawal, reinforcements, a bet-ter prepared and executed bombardment, a new assault – this time with aerial support – and then everything had descended into familiar, abattoir confusion. Tactics dissolved, became gruesome hand-to-hand struggles along the entire line, German L56 batteries depressing fire almost at point-blank range into a mass of advancing T34s and KV-1Cs, the skies above torn by competing attempts to seize and hold a brief moment of air superiority. It was this latter conflict, mostly unnoticed by those beneath, that intruded catastrophically into Fischer's little hectare of Hell.

He'd known at some conscious level that he was burning, yet there was little physical sense of it. All around him his unit lay scattered, dismembered by the direct impact of two aircraft upon their emplacement. Someone behind him was screaming, and the smell of fuel, overpowering at first, remained strangely persistent even as the stuff ate into the tissue of his nose. But the speed with which one thing had become another was so removed from expectation that its horror was entirely muted, detached in the manner of a half-composed report upon a distant event; he was dying, probably very badly, and yet it really wasn't so hideous. Insofar as he had felt anything at all, it was a sort of readiness.

It's strange, he'd often thought since, how good fortune waits until a man goes right down before it really unloads upon him. Still, he could hardly fault its implacable sense of humour. A self-indulgent moral crisis, an extended death wish unfulfilled, a hideous re-birth. And now? Now he was right back where he'd been in 1937, searching out other men's dark corners, but without the distraction of a salary and all that skin.

The breeze played across his face, refreshing the old and soothing the new. The tide, such as it

191

was, had turned, and he was obliged to take a step back. It occurred to him suddenly that what he had thought of as innocence was rather a state of unknowing: that whatever he imagined to be a resolution lay somewhere else, somewhere yet to be discovered. It made him feel a little better, that at least he needn't add the squander of years to his sum of regrets.

He looked down at the life vest he'd been clutching in his good hand for almost an hour now. An apt term: it had held a life, a sum of parts, come to its uttermost moment and then released. He opened his fingers, let it drop into the surf. They should hope: for a while longer at least, they should have hope. It's what he would have wanted for himself.

Chapter Twenty-Five

Achym Mazur was, to his own mind, a renaissance man, or as close to one as Trassenheide had any reason to expect. Among other qualities too numerous and subtle to list, he could lay claim to being a labourer, physicist, trombonist, thief, liar, hypocrite and fool; a man also beloved of animals, particularly very small ones that considered him a universe of warmth and unstinting nutrition. So he itched, more or less always.

Labouring was his compulsory occupation, the one for which he was handsomely recompensed with a fine home and all the swill he could eat. Or perhaps not *all* he could eat. Achym often felt that he could devour three villages and have room still for a hamlet, but that was because he'd been put into training for eating on a special diet of, to tell the truth, not enough swill. This made his job more difficult, as anyone that does heavy lifting on very few calories can attest; but, like his colleagues in the labouring business, he compensated by doing what he was obliged to do very slowly, and fairly incompetently also.

The physicist was no longer required for duties, the play of eternal truths being spread preciously thinly in a world of wood, wire, mud, lice and swill. In contrast, the trombonist Achym Mazur was very much in demand, particularly on Saturday evenings when, as one of a group of musicians from his hut that was popular in all the other huts too, he helped take minds briefly from the world as it presently was. Always sensitive to the Führer's tastes, the Hut Twelve Big Band (drums, bass, trombone, trumpet, clarinet and zither) played only the Negro jazz compositions of white American Jews: Artie Shaw, Benny Goodman and – until they discovered that he retained a foreskin – Woody Herman were particular favourites, much requested and danced to by camp inmates. Indeed, to employ what Achym knew to be the appropriate vernacular, Wigs were, generally, Blown during their concerts. Most of the guards enjoyed the noise too (they pretended not to, naturally) and, although they'd closed down the band a year earlier, a paternally blind eye had been turned to its prompt resurrection. They'd just wanted it to be known that they could do it whenever the mood took them.

Achym Mazur the thief was his most lucrative incarnation, though his talents had developed late. He had arrived at the camp in a state of wet-nosed innocence, imagining that if the Hermans were consummate bastards to a man, at least his own folk would compensate by their innate fraternalism. Once that illusion had shattered, he'd perforce become adept at making things disappear much as bad magicians did – that is, once disappeared, they didn't reappear (as far as any German could tell). Hardly a day passed when he couldn't manage to extract at least one item – a tool, a piece of rope, wood – from the research site and bring it back to the camp. Whether a use could be found for any particular item he disappeared hadn't been in point, at the start: it had been enough to demonstrate that it could be done. It was a way of reassuring himself that he still exercised will. But practicalities had asserted themselves quickly as the noises from his stomach increased. He focused his efforts, thieved as the market dictated, and gradually his business had become as healthy as any that counted also as a rolling capital offence. He stole on his own account and also ran three or four other inmates (the number varied according to individual need), who stole to order and allowed him to take the risks of fencing for a small commission, which, on a fairly substantial turnaround, made a reasonable profit most months. It was a business that couldn't provide formal statements of capital and operating results, but he felt he had modest reason to be satisfied with the way things had gone. Compared, that is, to the very obvious ways they might have.

The liar was in business with the thief, obviously; but the hypocrite was an unwelcome (though uncontested) circumstance. He was coming to realize that, too often, his mouth stood upon principles that the rest of him dropped whenever expedient, which was more or less always. He found that he despised his countrymen for their efforts in 1939, but recalled that he hadn't even considered joining the struggle when he might have done something worthwhile. Back then, not curtailing an academic career had seemed much more important than the academic question of whether surrender would come sooner or much sooner. He had since come to loathe Poles' acquiescence in the brutal face of defeat, even as he refined a whole dictionary of personal sophistries to rationalize his continuing failure to attempt anything remotely heroic. Working for the Germans he ate, a little, while many Poles who didn't starved. And, like many of his countrymen, he had too little to think or say about the plight of their Jewish countrymen, though few of them were ignorant of what was going on. Indeed, and also like many of his compatriots, he often didn't think of Jews as his countrymen at all. To this he couldn't, or wouldn't, give a name.

He had arrived on the peninsula two years earlier, having been caught in possession still of his proscribed university texts (Poles, it had been made amply clear, weren't going to need an education in the new Poland). This was his first wartime visit to Usedom, but as a boy he had been here several times when, like many other wealthier

Polish families, the Mazurs had discovered a taste for German spa towns that the locals' obvious coldness towards ausländers hadn't discouraged. In fact, it seemed to encourage the Poles to return. As his mother used to say, they can dislike us as much as they want, but if they take our money, they can shut up about it.

The racial awkwardness that piqued the adults hadn't stopped their children playing football and other beach games with Germans of their own age, or even groping their sisters, when the chance arose (as it did most days). Ironic, Achym had pondered sometimes, lying in his Trassenheide suite, how so many Aryans had marched eastwards to lord it unknowingly over their own blood kin. Since his arrival he'd recognized two of his former holiday acquaintances, local boys with medical conditions keeping them from active service, who now guarded the fences. They'd declined to recall him, and he hadn't pressed the matter.

This striking descent in his fortunes, from bourgeois tourist and future scientist to slave labourer and lice-farm, had tormented him at first. But slowly, the new Achym had, with all his other accomplishments, learned to accept a fate, an event, which he'd had the power neither to prevent nor rectify. The fact of his humiliation became just that: it was one he shared with his entire nation, and it would continue until the moment that circumstances changed, a moment he couldn't, in the least degree, anticipate or influence. He was no longer obliged to bear responsibility for his failures or successes (other than with his neck), to measure his life against the expectations of his parents or colleagues, or even to fight off his mother's plaintive demands for a grandchild. And all of it, ironically, was the liberating consequence of his confinement. Had it not been for the food and the constant reminders of who regarded themselves as the winners in this arrangement, Achym could have been almost content to sit back, so to speak, and enjoy the war while it lasted.

So it was difficult for Achym to really despise the Germans. For what they'd done to Poland he burned with a fierce nationalistic outrage, obviously; but many of the ones he knew personally were (their overweening arrogance aside) almost human. Not the technical fellows, of course: they seemed to occupy a state of aloof, other-worldliness that he regretted the more because, in a different milieu, he might have been there himself. But most of the others were much like ordinary Poles: self-absorbed, pliable, extremely receptive to bribes and increasingly preoccupied with news from whichever Front was moving at a particular moment. A few were to be avoided: the ones who'd been broken long before the war started and had found a captive audience upon which to relieve their inner deformities. But most of the other Germans avoided that sort too, he'd found.

Achym had acquired two tame Hermans at Trassenheide, willing, at a price, to contemplate almost any infraction that wouldn't get them sent East. One was a reservist in his mid-forties, a former welder with occupationally bad eyes, whose appetite for strong drink was satisfied by a steady supply of the inmates' home-brewed ethanol. The other had a club-foot, strong feelings for one of his fellow guards and a misplaced impression that Poles, a romantic nation, were less likely than his compatriots to despise his inclinations. Both turned blind eyes, left certain locks unlocked, and acted as middlemen for commodities that weren't readily available to sub-humans.

Naturally, Achym didn't buy their compliance with his own money or goods, because he possessed none. This was where the thief excelled: he took orders from his guards, went to Peenemünde on the daily transports, worked, stole and returned either with the items ordered or something acceptably similar. Most of the stuff was mundane: cigarette lighters, the occasional silver spoon, a length of linen long forgotten in an airing cupboard. But sometimes the unusual was required, and Achym seized such opportunities to become indispensable. A few months earlier, the reservist's wife, a woman of large, kitsch tastes, had watched an otherwise forgettable cinematic romance in which, at the penultimate moment of consummation, the blond, uniformed protagonist had pressed his nose against an even blonder woman's cheek and murmured 'Chanel?' Thereafter, her husband's waking existence had imitated art (the darker parts of Judgement triptychs) until Achym returned from a building shift at the Settlement with a mostly-full bottle of Kölnisch Wasser tucked under his jacket. The day after that, Hut Twelve acquired two music stands, disappeared from a school at Heringsdorf and delivered by a near-fraternal German guard.

So, as far as anyone on the losing end of circumstance could find his situation tolerable, Achym did so. He was careful not to offend, and definitely not to participate. He didn't join the official escape committee, or the Red Front (a group of Poles, very unpopular among the rest, who thought it was good and proper that Russia rule Poland once more), or any of the shifting groups of his countrymen who regularly tried to goad the guards into taking a shot at them from across the fence. On the other hand, the fact that he managed to obtain things for his hut, either by theft or the fencing of others' thefts, deflected messy suspicions that he was either a collaborator or a coward. Achym had reached the ideal state of being thought of quite favourably, but not very often.

That state was invaded on 14 August 1943, when Achym the Bloody Fool clocked in. The most volatile of his sub-contracting thieves was a young Pole of almost startling beauty named Rajmund, who preferred to be paid in cigarettes. These he used to bribe German guards, for reasons he kept to himself. Achym didn't mind secrecy in principle; it was the boy's business and reticence was a virtue, after all. But for a while now he'd had an uneasy feeling – an itch, in his highly sensitive nose – about where things were going. Rajmund had graduated from mere sullenness (about his situation) to pointless insolence (to the softer guards) and then, without giving notice, to declaring Principles. He was becoming a standard Polish nationalist: the sort who thought that anyone not suffering for the cause was pissing on his ancestors. Their nation was cursed with like-minded souls, having had ample opportunities to garner injustices over the centuries, and Achym respected the philosophy, if not its practical application, which usually involved cavalry charging at tank formations, and similar. But it was the sort of thing that one left at the door at Trassenheide, or stored up for when it could be usefully expressed. Rajmund, he was almost certain, wasn't storing it up. Something was going on and it involved what was happening up the road at Peenemünde.

Like Achym, Rajmund's sub-humanity extended to holding a degree in applied sciences: in his case, aerodynamic engineering. Both of them, wandering around the various security zones, saw things that their training couldn't help but partly decipher. Unlike Achym, however, Rajmund worked with the Hermans, and not merely as a human mule. Having volunteered under the *Fremdarbeiter* programme, he was one of the few Poles who had been posted rather than dragged to Peenemünde, and assigned as a technical assistant in the Development Shops. Again unlike Achym, who firmly shut his mind to the siren call of awareness, Rajmund began to go out of his way not only to observe but to take notes of his observations, many of which he wrote while on, and then hid beneath, his bunk in Hut Twelve. This structure was immediately below Achym's (the reason he'd been recruited in the first place – business was always done most effectively in whispers, and in the dark), so if the *schwabs* decided on a hut search, Achym would be guilty by proximity. That

200

was bad; what was far worse, Rajmund had managed to get his hands on a gun.

When he discovered this, Achym began to suspect that the boy had moved entirely out of radio contact. Being found with a weapon invited a bullet from another one, or at least a ticket to a camp, a real camp where you were fed every fourth Tuesday and beaten on the days between when your stomach rumbled. What the fuck, he asked Rajmund politely, was he thinking? Of shooting his way back to Poland?

Rajmund wouldn't talk about it. The little bastard let Achym see the thing, knowing that by doing so he was placing his neighbour's cock in the mangle; but he wouldn't talk about it. He just put on a jaw-jutting, ready-to-do-what's-right look that Achym was willing to swear had been practised in a hut-window reflection, and then hid the thing under his bunk with the growing dissertation on Things To Do In Beautiful Usedom.

This posed so many potential problems that Achym was foxed. He liked Rajmund, had a genuinely soft spot for the kid, but his other employees (three of them, all from Hut Seven) thought that some sort of emphatic point should be made. It was easy to say, of course, but what? He couldn't just take Rajmund off the payroll and cast him loose, or disappear the deadly items, because the young hero knew enough to bury their import-export trade ten times over, and Achym with it. He couldn't be threatened into sanity because he wasn't the sort to take it the right way, and besides, it wasn't sensible to threaten people who owned one more gun than you. But neither could Achym just ignore the situation and carry on as before, because his nerves were not-so-gradually shredding at the prospect of starting over in an *arbeitserziehungsläger*.

He'd almost reached the extremity of asking Club-Foot to deal with the business (Club-Foot would have welcomed *any* chance to deal with Rajmund), when the boy did the only remaining thing that could have surprised: he disappeared. One morning he started his shift at the Development Shops but then he forgot to return to the camp that evening. For almost three days, not a sign of him; Achym, torn between throwing himself on his pet guards' mercy and following the idiot's example, desperately played for time until a sensible course suggested itself. The first thing he did was to check under Rajmund's bunk, but he found nothing. That felt good in an immediate, superficial way, but filled him with a more measured sense of dread about where and why the items had gone. Then there was the problem of Rajmund himself. The inmates were counted twice each day, at 6am and then again exactly twelve hours later. It wouldn't have been too difficult to get a heavy smoker to risk shuffling himself around during the tally in return for a couple of packs, but that was a dangerous, expensive and very short-term solution. In any case, it couldn't cover Rajmund's absence from his bench at the Development Shops. Fortunately, there was a minor food-poisoning epidemic scything through the camp at that moment, something in the swill that briefly but intensely ravaged intestines, and Achym bribed one of the trustee medics to sign off

202

Rajmund for two days' shifting practice. But that was the trouble: the thing invariably worked its way through *within* two days, leaving Achym with a looming problem of what to do then. At this point, much too late, he realized that he shouldn't have done anything at all, because now there was a paper-trail with his name printed neatly all over it.

His remaining employees handed in their notice. They were upset at corporate policy towards Rajmund, who, they believed firmly, would have been better smothered as soon as he started exhibiting semi-heroic tendencies. They also worried that Achym might soon be questioned rather forcibly about what was going on, and they preferred to sever their professional links with Hut Twelve before that happened. Besides, they'd been nurturing their own guards and had been planning to go into competition for some time, so the problem gave them an exit that wouldn't play too much on their consciences.

Achym was beginning to sense that Fate's arse was casting its vast shadow overhead, bays opening, when Rajmund re-appeared, casually waiting in the back of one of the transports at Peenemünde as the shift ended. It was the third day of his truancy; for the previous ten hours, Achym had been helping to build a shower block in such a distracted mood that he hadn't disappeared a single tool, nail or length of copper, though construction (and demolition) always provided the best chance of risk-free acquisitions. As he and his co-serfs shuffled out of the security gate that evening, he was wondering just what it would take to bribe the trustee medic into permanent silence *and* convince the Hermans that he hadn't noticed Rajmund had been missing for days, when there the offending item was, sitting at the tail-board, somehow managing to look both sternly serious and as cocky as fuck.

He wouldn't explain himself; all Achym heard was that, as a Pole, he'd be proud if he knew what had happened, but nothing was going to be said. What was done was done, he was told. Fortunately, Achym knew Rajmund's ego couldn't leave it at that, and he wormed out a few of the more important details. No, Rajmund didn't have his notes, but they'd been put to good use; yes, he still had the gun, but he was going to need it; of course the Germans knew nothing of what he'd been doing, so Achym needn't worry for his own skin.

But Achym found that he couldn't stop worrying about that most precious commodity. What did Rajmund mean, he'd be needing the gun? What use was a gun to an inmate of Hut Twelve? Most of the Wehrmacht's three hundred and fifty divisions were fairly busy at that moment, but didn't Rajmund know that they could spare enough men to close down any Front he was planning to open up? And how could he be certain they didn't know what he was up to? Germans were shifty: they let you weave enough rope for a nice drop and then kicked away the chair: everyone knew that. To all these earnest remonstrations, Rajmund just shrugged and pretended to find the view on the road back from Peenemünde to Trassenheide interesting. It wasn't until they were back in the camp that he came awake and dropped the really shifty bit of news.

'*When?*' shouted Achym, forgetting that discretion was both his watchword and business card.

'Tonight. As soon as it's dark enough. Don't ask me why, Achym.'

'*Why*, for Christ's sake?'

'I just have to. Really, you mustn't ask.'

An infinity of infinitely bad possibilities occurred to Achym in the space of several heartbeats, every one of which he felt thumping furiously in his chest cavity. This was it, the end; most likely he'd be placed outside of his trombone before being summarily executed against the rear wall of Hut Twelve. Or perhaps they'd arrange a transfer, to a place where his weight in fertilizer product would be gauged at the front gate to save time later that day. Either way, he'd almost certainly see some use as a football while a decision was being made.

He put it to Rajmund that he was being selfish: that if he did what he was threatening, Achym would be standing in the deepest pile imaginable, and so would everyone else in Hut Twelve who didn't have an alibi for the past week. But even as he made the case, he knew that an appeal to a fanatic's sense of proportion was futile. Casualties were expected – even hoped for – in any heroic struggle, and that was definitely what Rajmund believed he was part of.

For three hours Achym paced the hut, trying to construct a combination of circumstances from which he might emerge intact, and failed by several kilometres. All the while it grew darker, and nearer, and everyone else, oblivious to what was going to happen, went on with their lives as if tomorrow would turn up as usual. He considered violence (upon Rajmund), ratting (to the others in the hut) and even betrayal (to the *schwabs*), but he kept coming up against the rather pathetic truth that he wasn't courageous enough to seek confrontations of that sort. In any case, he really *was* quite fond of Rajmund.

This dour review of his prospects occupied Achym so completely that he didn't notice when it happened. At some point, Rajmund must have wandered away from his bunk with what he thought was an appropriate nonchalance. When Achym turned to try a final plea to whatever sanity remained to him, he was gone: he'd disappeared himself.

Not breathing, Achym waited for the shot, or a dog's furious barking, or the howls of delight as half a dozen guards kicked Rajmund into a better place. When he heard none of it, he realized that he'd been given a full night to contemplate what the Germans were going to do by way of reprisal.

Lying on his bunk in the dark, Achym was profoundly moved by the looming tragedy of his blameless fate. He even prayed, making his peace with a deity he'd last bothered about the matter of a righteous parental beating, a decade and a half earlier. With that last extremity discharged, he almost experienced a sense of calm: of knowing that his affairs had been arranged by an unknowable fate to some indefinable purpose, and that he was expected to contribute nothing. For a little while, he was almost proud of the composure he managed to scrape together, until he realized that it was just Nature's chemistry, anaesthetizing the looming shit-slide.

But when all seemed bleakest, the ancestral Mazur luck re-surfaced magnificently. About an hour after Zinnowitz's distant church bells struck twelve and ceased for the night, when dark introspections gave way to even darker ones, a small, irritating hum became a growing, terrible roar that swept the entire span of skies above them, and Achym was unchained by the one circumstance he couldn't have anticipated. The idiot British had come to Peenemünde, to make up to just one of their Polish allies for what they'd utterly failed to do in 1939.

It was difficult to recall quite what happened, or when. More or less everyone screamed at first, as explosions ripped apart the huts, burying some inmates and dismembering others. But astonishingly, there was no panic: people just helped each other to move fallen spars off bodies, or to beat out the fires that ignited in the hot, dry night. It must have lasted a very short time, but no one could really say whether it was ten minutes or an hour. Vaguely, Achym recalled straining at an entire wall of wood that had fallen upon a line of bunks, and, with the help of a dozen others, lifting it clear again. He pulled a fellow inmate from beneath a quantity of rubble that should have crushed him utterly, but the man grasped his arm, got up and thanked him. Someone else lifted Achym when *he* fell and with ludicrous consideration tried to brush him down, even as more of the hut fell around them. And then, while their ears were still ringing and their eyes blinded by dust and ash, the Germans were among them, shouting, herding them into what, suddenly, had become the safe outdoors once more.

At that point no one was counted, or missed. Work details were organized, and lines of those of the dead who could be re-assembled were laid out carefully as dawn arrived. The survivors were allowed to rest; Achym queued, took a cup of something warm from a hastily organized mobile canteen and sat on the stoop of what had been Hut Twelve. He took a sip, and another; his lip twitched, he smiled, and then he laughed, a snigger that quickly became something uncontrollable. Other inmates, passing by with their own cups, recognized the usual signs of what this sort of thing did to minds, and pitied him. One of them, an old man who'd probably been about thirty a couple of years earlier, stopped and patted his shoulder solicitously. But Achym just couldn't stop laughing.

Brave Rajmund, the archetypal Polish hero: got a Cause, then risked his life and those of everyone else in his hut, the first inmate of Trassenheide ever to scale the wire fence. And barely an hour later, the fucking thing wasn't there anymore.

No one was allowed to sleep. The bodies had to be identified to mark them off the roll, and Achym made sure he was one of the volunteers who did it. There was no good reason why he should; the *schwabs* would assume that the selfish bastard had taken advantage of the raid and just walked away, so the rest of Hut Twelve (those who'd survived the night, that is) were safe now, and what the hell did Achym owe him anyway? All the same, he searched until he found a really mutilated one and told them that it was Rajmund Ulatowski, no doubt about it.

He tried to convince himself that it was a noble act, a contribution to the struggle. But really, he knew he'd done it only that Rajmund's equally beautiful sister might think of him as less of a worm.

Chapter Twenty-Six

In a quietly tasteful office, a hundred years or more from present barbarisms, Fischer considered the prettiness of Dr Wehrner Magnus Maximilian, Freiherr von Braun: a sleek, well fed, beautifully balanced young man, a credit to his finely tailored clothes. An unfailingly charming man too, even to the very many of his colleagues who couldn't approach his level if they stood on two boxes: the sort who glides, rather than climbs, into authority. When he tired of exercising his scientific brilliance he was said to play the cello and piano equally brilliantly, and even composed in the avant-garde style (or *did*, before the Führer's opinions on proper music became generally known). His mother was actual royalty, or a descendant of it at least, so her marriage to a mere freiherr had been seen in some quarters – some very glittering, gated quarters – as a bit of a come-down, socially. Still, in their son's presence, Fischer felt as much a part of the same species as a slug might of the Dresden vase it slid down.

Not even Otto Fischer thought that Otto Fischer was pretty, but no one would have suspected von Braun of sharing the opinion. The smile that greeted him as he entered the Director's office was little short of dazzling: the sort of job that the old Kaiser's personal dentist might have taken credit for. A hand shot across the desk, revealing a gold link on an English doubled cuff. Fischer, certain that von Braun was the type to use a hearty; crushing grip, pulled back his right shoulder slightly.

'Of course. Forgive me, Hauptmann. How stupid of me.' There: he'd made Fischer feel guilty about his withered arm, and they hadn't even sat down yet. 'I'm surprised that we haven't managed to speak until now. Walter was a close friend, and a valued colleague.'

'I tried to find you on a couple of occasions. I believe you were in Berlin.' Somehow, it came out like an apology.

A shrug, a *moue*: the elegant spread of hands that more or less explained everything. It was like watching a Maybach describing a circle, on glass. 'I'm afraid that my time belongs to Reichsminister Speer at the moment. You must understand how it is?'

Of course; a terrible bore. 'Yes. Could you tell me the circumstances of how you came to see Dr Thiel's wound?'

'Certainly. It had all been very confusing, as you'd imagine. My secretary and I were obliged to rescue a great deal of vital paperwork from the safe in this office, even as the bombs fell around us. I don't have your experience of warfare, so I'm afraid that I was somewhat scared, and out of sorts.'

They might have compared notes, with Fischer perhaps mentioning how *out of sorts* he'd felt on his final day on the Eastern Front, when half the burning sky dropped on to him in the middle of a continent-sized slaughterhouse. But one didn't wish to seem truculent.

'We'd managed to get everything safely to one of the cellars, and then I went to find the Generalmajor. He was supervising the fire-truck crews, making sure that they weren't giving their attention to the wrong buildings. And the flak batteries wanted permission to fire at the British aircraft, so he had to attend to that also – his authority alone could do it.'

Jesus.

'When I saw him again it was almost daylight. Bodies were being brought into the schoolhouse, mainly from the Settlement, and there was a lot of confusion – I mean, a great deal of noise, as relatives discovered their loved ones, or failed to. That was harrowing. I'm not ashamed to say that I may have cried at some point. But it was the Generalmajor's hour. He organized everyone as if we were on a field exercise, and each of us accepted a duty. My first responsibility, with more or less everyone else, was to assist with the fire-fighting. But then I was asked to ensure that shelter was arranged for all the bombed-out families, so I was kept very busy on one of the few telephone lines that survived the bombing.'

'You arranged for the foreign workers to be

moved from Trassenheide to Swinemünde?'

'It seemed the only sensible solution. Obviously, the site wasn't going to be functioning as usual in the short term, so it was far more important that vital staff and their families be rehoused than the ancillary workers.'

'And the decision was made *that* morning?'

Von Braun looked blankly at Fischer. 'Yes, of course it was. There wasn't time to debate the merits of other, possible options. Clearly, we couldn't allow the raid to interfere with our work more than was absolutely necessary.'

A thousand *fremdarbeiter* extracted within a few hours of the raid, plus about six hundred who died during it. Fischer had attended a few compromised crime scenes (he'd compromised a number of them himself, he recalled), but nothing on such a herculean scale.

'With this responsibility I was busy for more than an hour, and the bodies were being collected in the meantime under Hans Wierer's supervision. It wasn't until about eight o'clock that I'd finished all that could be done for the moment. Then, I was called to the schoolhouse.'

'You'd been making the telephone calls from here?'

'Yes, this is where the undamaged lines were. Robert didn't give a reason for my summons but then, Generals don't *ask*, do they? When I arrived there it was obvious that a certain discretion was being exercised. The hall had been cleared, and only five others were present among hundreds of corpses, many of them men and women I'd known personally. It wasn't a pleasant experience.'

'Please think carefully about exactly what you saw there.'

'I was met at the entrance by Kaspar Nagel. He seemed very upset, but so did we all, I expect. He took me over to where the others were stood – kneeling, I should say – around one of the covered bodies.'

'I'm sorry. Were *all* the bodies covered at this stage?'

'Yes. The depots here contain massive quantities of canvas, for obvious reasons. There was more than enough to do the decent thing. Well, Nagel and I approached. The Generalmajor said something like "Look at this Werner, my God!" and then he pulled back the sheet from Walter's face. It was a terrible sight – I mean, to see Walter dead. Actually, he looked quite peaceful. One might have assumed that he was asleep, but for that awful wound to his forehead. I was quite overcome. I believe that Kaspar had to support me for a moment.'

'Was the cover removed completely from Dr Thiel's body?'

'No. Just from his head.'

'And did you see anything of the bodies of his wife and children?'

'They had already been examined and re-covered.'

'What happened then?'

Von Braun shrugged. 'You probably know this. The Generalmajor told Wierer to have the body taken to one of the Development Shops – discreetly, he insisted. Then, he told us that this must be investigated and we should treat it as a most secret matter.'

'Were there any subsequent discussions between yourself and any of the other five men regarding the incident?'

'Naturally, the Generalmajor and I needed to discuss a replacement for Walter, but no, I haven't since spoken about the murder itself, to anyone. It isn't a topic that recommends itself.'

For some minutes von Braun had been punctuating his testimony with glances at his wall clock, a hint that any ex-Bull would cheerfully decline to take.

'This may seem an obvious question, doctor, but clearly I have to ask it. Can you think, of any reason – *any* reason – why someone might want to shoot Dr Thiel?'

'It's a perfectly reasonable thing to ask. I've asked it myself constantly over the past four days. But I can think of only one purpose to be advanced by his death.'

'And that is?'

'The sabotaging of the work we do here. There are perhaps a dozen truly indispensable men at Peenemünde. Walter was one of them.'

Chapter Twenty-Seven

Rajmund was alive, and gone, and for the first time that she could recall she felt a vague sense of hope – or at least, of a slackening of the despair that seemed as much a part of life as sleep. Of all people it had been the repellent Athym Mazur who told her about it, about his miraculous, absurd deliverance. For days she'd assumed that he'd died under a British bomb, and even that had been a small, bitter comfort, to know that they couldn't reach and hurt him. But a true miracle had saved him, from the bombs *and* the Germans, and they didn't even know it. Mazur had been very careful to tell her of his part in that, and she had no doubt what sort of reward he hoped for.

Pig-headed, self-confident Rajmund had listened to her, finally, and done the right thing. *You can't stay here*, she'd told him: *just get out, and run.* It was only fair: he'd come here to protect her (so he imagined), and she'd done the same for him; and now he had the gift of non-existence, accidentally bestowed by a faulty flight-path. It made her stronger, having only the care of herself, and God knew, she needed strength. The event that saved her brother, that gifted to her such intense joy, had cost the lives of hundreds of her countrymen. It was difficult to know how to bear such remorse: to find a place for it with all that she bore already.

But there was comfort to be had from small things. Here, no one hoped for anything of tomorrow, or felt any longing for the near past; no one had any expectations to be dashed, or tormented. So the easing of one part of her pain – Rajmund's stupid, pointless, loving presence here – was a sip of water to a swollen mouth, or balm upon a wound. It was something she held tightly to herself because comfort, like pain, wasn't to be shared. Here, Zofia was obliged to give the same face to the world, and the world treated her as before.

With four other women she was peeling potatoes for the lunchtime sitting at the administration building. Three of them were Polish, one a Frenchwoman, and the talk was necessarily trivial, though full of bravado. The Poles were becoming, to their dawning and quite insufferable self-satisfaction, patriots. None of them knew her national anthem, nor Stefan Batory from Stefan Stec; only one had finished her elementary schooling before being dragged off to drudgery on her family's pig farm: the others had been merely the progeny of a thousand-year peasant mentality that measured worldly wealth in how little a belly hurt when night fell. But it was salutary what an invasion, a savage occupation and the carefully planned erasure of national consciousness could achieve. To hear them now, they might have been marching with Hetman Zolkiewski (though none of them had heard of him, either); what the Germans had confidently consigned to oblivion was flourishing beneath the boot.

At last Alenka, Malwina and Ola, still loudly arguing the superiority of more or less anything Polish, carried their bowls of potatoes to the sinks to be washed, and Zofia braced herself for what was coming. The Frenchwoman, Élodie, had a conspirator's habit of waiting until they were alone before making her latest demand. It would be framed as a request, of course, for information, or an item, or that Zofia carry a message to someone else. Until a week ago this could

216

have been done at Trassenheide; now, they were on different sides of a new internal fence, raised for the benefit of the refugee German families, and they could meet only at Peenemünde itself, the most dangerous place to do anything courageous.

Zofia took the note reluctantly, as she always did. From the moment she'd arrived at the camp others had been urging her to help *the cause*, but she feared their reckless courage almost as much as she did German brutality. They had schemes for escapes, of course, which she'd expected, and she had no problem helping with necessary information and the occasional supplies that could be removed discreetly from the kitchens or the guesthouse. She was Polish after all, and had to do her bit. But they weren't satisfied; they had much bigger plans. Some of them intended to wage war from within Trassenheide, acting as a sort of unofficial intelligence arm of the Allied effort. They were compiling charts of Peenemünde, of what was done where, and how. They were stealing components and trying to devise the means to get them out of Germany. They were even talking – though thank God it was as yet only talk – of an uprising that would first secure certain areas of the research station and allow them to sabotage its most vital functions before any reaction could slaughter them, gloriously.

Between herself and all of this, Zofia quietly placed some distance. She refused to try to enter areas for which she was not badged, because her discovery would mean transportation or even death for no good purpose, and she believed that life wasn't to be squandered on a point of aimless heroism. Nor, particularly, would she do what even they were too embarrassed to ask outright but merely hinted at, which was to use her obvious advantages to make herself agreeable to useful Germans. In fact, she expressed her opinion of the implicit suggestion so forcibly that no one repeated it. They had since allowed her to contribute only to the extent to which she felt comfortable, though she suspected that further requests would be made if and when one of their mad schemes was actually implemented.

But Élodie was different. She didn't seem to possess the capacity to take no for an answer, and waved away Zofia's objections impatiently, as if she'd been talking to someone who wasn't quite bright enough to understand what was required but would just have to do what she was told anyway. She had a power, a quality of leadership perhaps, to make others go against their inclinations. And being French, there was a certain glamorous distance to Élodie that intimidated Zofia in a way no Pole could emulate. There was a rumour that her group – of a number of fellow French workers, most of whom kept well away from the Poles – had already managed to smuggle some documents out of Peenemünde and get them to Paris. If it was true, and most of the *fremdarbeiter* wanted it to be, it gave their leader a moral authority that made refusal to assist her all the more difficult. So Zofia tried to help when she could, and occasionally agreed to do the sort of thing that she had firmly refused to her own kind.

It was difficult; Zofia wished that she could be

more like Élodie, in whose veins ran ice, or something colder; who gave the impression that she could read a book, build a wall or castrate a goat with equal detachment, a quality that was both comforting and unnerving. But then she had the strength to be strong, being entitled, as a *gastarbeitnehmer*, a contracted worker, to double the daily kilocalories permitted to Zofia. Nevertheless, it was a strength poorly used: it raged at what neither noticed nor cared; it planned great schemes in a place where only tiny insurgencies were possible. The French and Poles were too similar in that way; the gesture was everything, the glorious failure infinitely more valued than the mean victory. Zofia had never understood the imperative. It invited trouble because it actively sought it, and there was trouble enough in the world already.

But Rajmund was free, and Zofia could rejoice at his bravery because he had not paid the price of it. It gave her a little more inner iron, made her willing to go a little further when Élodie asked reckless things. Unfortunately, this newly discovered courage coincided with something else – a problem, and Zofia wasn't sure what it was. Since the raid the Germans had become more *German;* the lax, almost languid air of academic detachment was fading, and the casually revealing conversations had almost ceased. A few of the more negligent technicians were still to be overheard in the dining rooms, breezily discussing matters for which they'd be shot elsewhere; but generally, they were finally getting a sense of what war required of them. Zofia was no longer a mute ghost, reliably invisible, at their exchanges; when she approached now, their eyes turned and *saw* rather than saw through her, and their voices fell, or rose, to chase her away. They were becoming nervous, and about more, she sensed, than British bombers.

Élodie tapped her knee with a knife. Faint Polish gabble could be heard from the kitchens. The others were returning with more potatoes.

'Can you find out what they're going to do about the bombing?'

Zofia's school French slowly construed. It was her luck to have to deal with just about the only Frenchwoman whose great-grandfather didn't screw a Polish woman and take her home with him. She would have been much more at ease speaking German, but Élodie couldn't (or wouldn't), so their conversations were stilted, and this emphasized the distance between them. But it wasn't language itself that was the problem today.

'I don't understand.'

'They're repairing everything as fast as they can, except the assembly hall. Why is that?'

Zofia shrugged. 'How would I know?'

'*That's* why I want you to find out, of course. They trust you. You can get into the administration building. There must be some piece of paper that discusses what's happening. You know how the *Boches* are about writing down everything. We need to know if they're going to do anything different because of the raid.'

For a moment Zofia was dumbfounded. It was so far beyond anything she'd been asked to do previously that she thought she'd misunderstood:

that she was being required merely to assist the fanatical, stupidly brave person who'd do the thing. But Élodie was looking at her, dispassionately, like she'd asked no more than that Zofia pick up a loaf of bread on her way home to Trassenheide that evening.

'But *how?* I'm just...'

'You read German like it's your own language. You know most of the men who work in the building by sight. And you'll draw the least attention by being there. I would not ask if I could do it myself, or send someone who knows precisely what to look for.'

'If they catch me I'll be shot.'

Astonishingly, Élodie shrugged. 'It's a war, people die; but you'd have to be stupid to be caught. I've done this myself, in the Experimental Works: I walked in, I swept the floor, and when no one was looking I took some papers from a desk. Those papers are now in Paris, or London. It's war: we have to do these things.'

If Zofia had been slapped it couldn't have shocked her more. She was being asked to join them: to become a partisan for a country other than her own. And for what? The slender chance that whatever she found and handed over before the Germans came for her just might be of use to someone in a laboratory in England or America? And it wasn't just a matter of her own life. If she was successful, she would be abetting another firestorm upon Trassenheide, probably, that would kill a few hundred more Poles so that English civilians wouldn't have to suffer the same. Perhaps this was the small incentive Élodie

221

was holding out to her: that she wouldn't see the consequences of it if the Germans had shot her already.

'But I'll have to find an excuse to go there, a reason. You'll have to let me try to arrange something.'

Élodie nodded, satisfied that yet another of her strands was now vibrating, and Zofia felt a stab of anger. The Frenchwoman would be returning to her country at some point, and doubtless she'd pass on her accomplices' names to someone else whose loyalties couldn't be judged, or relied upon. That was the only advantage of being a Pole here: the continuity of things. The chances of returning home, ever, were entirely dependent on what was happening outside, beyond the wire, the one place that Zofia couldn't go. In the meantime, she played the foot soldier for someone who cared as much for her safety as any general might.

'Where are those fucking potatoes?'

This was the 'under-chef', Gerhardt: a tramp-steamer's cook from Danzig whose cross-eyes moved constantly and malevolently; who liked to maintain *a tight ship* by shouting for things that he knew perfectly well were in hand. The potatoes were there, and just about ready, as they were at precisely this time each morning, but still, a profane shout and sometimes a slap was necessary. He was a strange, unreadable creature. After shifts were done he often stood at the canteen block's rear door, smoking a cigarette, allowing the women to remove scraps before they fed the bins. He didn't, to Zofia's knowledge, ever ask for favours in return. She used to think that Gerhardt

222

was merely foul-tempered: that there was a very small amount of good within him, tainting the plentiful bad; but eventually she realized that, as with other small acts of seeming kindness here, it was merely whimsy. He was treating them according to the dictates of a coin flipped in his head, as a lout might treat a dog. Élodie said (at least, it was how Zofia translated it) that her last act at this place was going to be to stab Gerhardt in the mouth with her potato peeler and watch him bleed to death. It was likely she'd have to take her place in a queue.

'They're just coming in, sir.'

Zofia nodded at the Three Fates. Obediently they emptied their shares into the large copper pot and carried it, almost effortlessly, into the kitchens. Élodie stood up, dropped the peeler into the tin to be counted, and walked away without a word, her usual mode of departure. She'd already hidden a very small package that Zofia had passed to her, one that she'd been carrying around for two days without once wishing to open it. Almost certainly it contained some electrical or mechanical component necessary to make one of the German weapons fly – a failed component, obviously, discarded during testing, picked up by a Pole and, in the spirit of co-operation, handed over to the only people who knew how to get things out of the site and out of Germany. A tiny contribution to Final Victory, that's how they'd think of it. Or perhaps they were collecting components to build their own weapon, and launch a war upon Peenemünde from Trassenheide. If it didn't fly, well, it would be little different from most of the ones the Germans had lit the fuse beneath so far.

If Zofia hadn't felt so miserable at the prospect of her coming valour, she might have smiled at the thought.

Chapter Twenty-Eight

Of the men who knew of Thiel's shooting, only Werner Magirius had yet to be interviewed. Fischer went to the administration building's reception and was told that Dornberger was in Berlin that day. However, his adjutant remained on site and was probably in the Generalmajor's office, if the Hauptmann cared to look.

That was indeed where Magirius was, knee-deep in papers, carefully replacing a hastily evacuated filing system. He was distracted but greeted Fischer cordially – a pleasant-faced young man, about thirty years old, with a healthy crop of medals pinned to his breast. There followed one of the most frustrating discussions Fischer could recall. Yes, the adjutant understood why he was at Peenemünde, and that the Generalmajor had given him permission to speak to whomsoever he wished. Yes, the necessity of finding whoever had shot Walter Thiel was obvious. Magirius, though no scientist himself, considered Thiel to be one of the most gifted men he had ever met, and was horrified by what had happened on the night of 17/18 August. No, he couldn't possibly say more until the Generalmajor was present. No, these were not the Generalmajor's orders; merely Magirius's wish not to say anything that might be misinterpreted or in any way considered outside the scope of what could, in propriety, be said. As a military man himself, he was sure that Fischer would understand. He apologized, but couldn't really say more for the moment.

No, Fischer didn't understand at all, but he left it there. Nonplussed, he wandered down to the secretarial pool on the ground floor and watched them for a while, busily transforming technical notes and requisitions into foolscap. It was an easy prospect, admittedly, and he wondered whether Dornberger and his senior staff had a deliberate policy of hiring personable, blonde young women. There wasn't a girl or woman present who couldn't provide the visuals for a magazine article on the Reich's eugenics policies, or how to fill a sweater. Their response to his presence was interesting. A few glanced up at him for a few moments too many, and one girl involuntarily placed a hand over her open mouth. But on the whole it seemed that reactions to his injuries were slightly less pronounced now, more of an ordeal to be borne than a traumatic, unexpected confront-ation. Perhaps he was becoming a familiar sight at Peenemünde. Perhaps he was getting prettier.

The pool manageress, a handsome woman in early middle-age, came over and asked if she could be of assistance. She had a clipped, precise delivery, an air of quiet assurance and a way of holding herself that told a man he'd better not even think about it.

'Thank you, yes. Could you tell me who pre-pared work for Dr Thiel?'

Her eyes narrowed sympathetically. 'Poor Walter, it was so terrible. And the children! But no one here is allocated to any single member of staff. Naturally, the Generalmajor and Dr von Braun have their private secretaries, but everyone else submits their work to the in-tray and we hand it out as girls become available. Unless...' she smiled and lowered her voice, confidentially, '...the handwriting's particularly awful. Then we give it to the one who's most familiar with that hand.'

'And Dr Thiel's hand was legible?'

'As far as any scientist can write legibly, Walter could. But of course, we didn't receive everything that he wrote directly. If it was something he was doing for Dr Riedel's office, it was handed to them and incorporated into the Design Bureau's notes, which we typed up when delivered to us.'

'This would be Walter Riedel?'

'Both of them: "Papa" Walter and his successor, Walther.'

'Did anyone else receive Dr Thiel's work?'

'No. That is, I don't believe so. They don't always tell us what they're doing, of course.'

'Of course not. Well, thank you for your time.'

It was a *waste* of time, clearly. Whatever Thiel was working on would have been perfectly trans-parent to the scientific minds around him, so there was no motive to be found in his scrib-blings, much less in what a secretary may have made of them, if anything. He told himself that he was water-treading without a shore in prospect: going through pointless procedural motions that

226

led to the sort of report one placed upon the boss's desk on its way to the *unsolved* bin. Only this time there was no one to absolve him of indifference, to say never mind Otto, we'll wait for something to turn up.

An exquisite feeling of helplessness struck him, and he helped it along by summarizing his progress. There was no plausible motive, no apparent opportunity, an infinity of suspects (for any number of reasons he couldn't begin to determine) and a looming obligation to identify the perpetrator to a Generalmajor. With what he had at present that interview would be as comfortable as briefing the Führer on why Stalingrad still didn't have a decent liverwurst shop.

As he left House 4 a small plane flew low over the site. Two of the flak emplacements that guarded the building trained their guns upon it and tracked it towards the nearby airfield. *Better.* He was even saluted, smartly, by the sentry guarding the entrance, whose weapon was presented correctly, not slung casually over the shoulder.

'Hauptmann!'

Kaspar Nagel caught up with him at the wind tunnel building. He was almost out of breath, so this wasn't an accidental encounter, yet he simply fell into step without another word, as though proximity alone was the goal.

Am I being monitored?

Fischer stopped, forcing Nagel to do the same. 'Was that the Generalmajor's aeroplane I saw?'

'Yes. He's been in Berlin again. Another appointment with the Reichsführer, I think.'

'Will he return here directly? Or should we try to find him?'

'He's meeting with Arthur Rudolph and Dr von Braun...' Nagel checked his watch, a battered Omega 30mm, '...in about an hour.'

'Then let us waylay him, shall we?'

Vehicles coming from the Luftwaffe airfield entered Peenemünde East at the Development area's north gate, so it was a matter of waiting there in the company of two suddenly alert reservists. Within five minutes the familiar two-tone Rekord pulled up. A Generalmajor's braided arm handed an ID card to one of the reservists, and Dornberger's face, framed by the dirt that his windscreen wiper couldn't reach, fell slightly as he noticed Fischer and Nagel. He parked just inside the gate and got out of the car.

'What is it? Wait...' he took his briefcase from the rear seat and handed to Nagel a file, sealed with a tied ribbon and prominently marked *Most Secret!*

'Take the car. Give this to Wehrner and tell him to read it immediately. Let Arthur Rudolph see it also, but no one else.

'Now...' Dornberger came to Fischer's left side, took his arm and started walking, 'what do you want?'

'Divine inspiration, ideally, Herr Generalmajor. Otherwise, I have to report that your adjutant won't speak to me unless you're present. The other matter is resources.'

'He will. What sort of resources?'

'I mean, what are you going to give me, sir?'

'I gave Nagel to you.'

'As you say, a nice boy. And unable to provide the slightest expertise or practical assistance to an investigation. *And* he's one of my principal witnesses, so his continuing *help* is a problem for me. Now, unless someone comes forward to throw himself upon our mercy, it will be necessary to speak to quite a number of people here. I'd hoped otherwise, but now that I understand the potential scale of what needs to be done I must have *useful* help.'

Dornberger was looking across at the assembly hall, looming above the nearer Development Shops. 'We really should get rid of it. My pride and joy. It almost invites attention.' He glanced back at Fischer. 'Well, what do you want? Someone to question witnesses? A secretary?'

'I'd like to bring in an assistant. From Berlin, a colleague. He'll know what needs to be done, and he's very discreet.'

'That isn't something I can offer. Security here is…'

'Severely lacking, if I may say so, Herr Generalmajor. You give a good impression that bears very little scrutiny. I'm asking to bring in one man – a former policeman – who understands how to do things. Given the vast number of foreign workers you employ in almost every sensitive area, and the absence of rigorous protocols to monitor them, I would hardly consider my request for a single further German a strain upon the system.'

Dornberger reddened. 'That's uncommonly forthright, Hauptmann.'

'Sir, I only point out what seems obvious. From what I've seen by way of improvements over the past few days, I think you're of the same mind. I can have him here tomorrow, perhaps the day after, if you agree.'

For a while they walked in silence, punctuated by the rhythmic slap of Dornberger's briefcase against his breeches, and Fischer had a sense that further objections were being tested and discarded.

'You can absolutely vouch for this man?'

'He was a Berlin uniform. Discretion was like oxygen to him. He'd have taken a nod, a wink or a bribe equally well.'

'What a world, Fischer! Bring him in then, but quietly this time. Your boss appears to be a very talking man.'

'Oberstleutnant Krohne was a newspaper editor during the Peace.'

'I assumed something of the sort.'

Fischer excused himself at House 4 and found a telephone. Detmar Reincke was on sick leave that day and Fischer's request to be put through to someone else got him Salomon Weiss, a former pioneer and the Lie Division's only broken neck, whose impeccably Aryan antecedents and thick blond hair made him the butt of unending office japes. Weiss told him that Holleman had no telephone at the lake house, but that he'd given a contact number for a nearby hotel in Köthen, with instructions that it be used only *in case of a real fucking emergency, not for any stupid shit that Karl thinks up.*

Fischer took the number, telephoned the hotel and spoke to the owner. Herr Holleman, she said, came to wash and dine at the hotel at about seven each evening, there being no hot water at his home at present. He gave his name and told her that he'd call later. In a way he was glad. It gave him a few hours to think of a convincing reason why Freddie should oblige a comradely request rather than tell him where he might place it.

'Fischer!' Dornberger stood in the doorway, almost trembling with pent-up busyness. 'A thought. You might wish to join us in my office. What I'm going to say affects you too, in a way.'

They took the single flight of stairs very quickly, at the Generalmajor's pace. He pushed open the corridor door at the top of the stairs and then, immediately to his right, that of his office – another security lapse, to be added to the list that Fischer was pretending to compile.

She hadn't heard them approach. Politely, Dornberger coughed, though she'd already come to a sort of frozen, terrified attention.

'Hello, Zofia. What are you doing?'

Chapter Twenty-Nine

Marcin Konopka. Marcin Konopka. Marcin Konopka.

Silently, Achym practised his new name. He did it most of the time he wasn't thinking about everyday matters, because he was going to have to answer to it for the rest of what was probably going to be a very short life. He didn't like it; in his opinion, it didn't scan nearly so well as *Achym Mazur*. But then, he was probably biased. His name, after all, was the only heirloom the *schwabs* hadn't been able to steal from him, and he felt strangely sentimental about letting it go. Still, he wasn't ungrateful; Marcin Konopka had very decently died without causing any fuss, and bequeathed a thoughtful consideration: an identity.

But it had cost the former Achym Mazur heavily. He had almost certainly lost one of his pet guards, for whom the illicit transmutation of one person into another went far beyond anything that contraband should be capable of buying. It had required an ugly reminder from Achym that homosexuality was a far greater crime in the new Germany than mere identity-theft (even when committed by an *ostarbeiter*), plus a consoling offer of every cigarette he possessed or was likely to acquire in the near future. But the thing was done; now, Achym Mazur was officially two metres south of the forest floor in a clearing near Karlshagen, while Marcin Konopka had risen like Lazarus, though not to anything nearly so comfortable as a pied-à-terre in Bethany.

Apart from his grounding in acoustical engineering and a deadly trombonist's technique, the dear-departed Achym had possessed only one real talent: a nose for trouble. It had been the nose that sniffed out the difference between a risk and a suicide attempt in his daily dealings with guards and inmates, back when he still had hopes of a comfortable war. It was the same nose that drove him half-mad during the disappearance, resurrection and apotheosis of Rajmund Ulatowski, when every permutation of potential disaster had presented itself more or less as a likelihood. It was, most recently, the nose that had twitched on the morning of 18 August, as its owner sat exhausted on the stoop of what remained of Hut Twelve, drinking weak, hot coffee and wondering at his miraculous deliverance, when the guards came.

Taking a leaf from the senior Apostle, he had denied Hut Twelve. Yes, his arse was warming its ruins, but so what? He'd queued, picked up a coffee and planted himself on the first comfortable surface he'd found, if that was all right, sir? No, Hut Twenty-Seven, over there, sir. Of course he'd move on, right now, if that's what sir wanted. No, he definitely wasn't trying to be cheeky, wouldn't think of it; and would sir like a cigarette?

In the annals of fucking off tidily, Achym scratched himself an entry that morning. By the time an officer came to take the roll call of survivors, he was at the back of a group of inmates from huts nineteen and twenty, and dodged from the second to the first as the tally was completed on the latter. He'd then searched frantically for Club-Foot, who wasn't usually on duty until midday but who almost certainly would have been called in early to help cover those bits of the perimeter the British had dismantled. The limp wasn't difficult to spot; the request was harder to put into words.

'You want to die?' Club-Foot had sounded a little wistful as he repeated it.

'Right away, Boss.'

'Can't be done.'

Achym had expected it, and he had both the

233

threat and the promise ready. But before he opened his mouth he made sure that other Germans were close by, so that Club-Foot would be obliged to explain himself and fill in a form if he shot his pressing problem. Even so, there followed a few moments of palpable tension before he stopped staring, shrugged and told Achym to make himself invisible for a few hours.

That wasn't easy. About mid-morning, the Hermans started to round up some of the inmates for no apparent reason, and Achym, his nose twitching once more, hurriedly found himself a work gang and spent the rest of the day helping to clear rubble and reconstruct the fence. Fortunately, the disaster's scale had made security very lax; no one asked his name or checked him off a list for the first time since his arrival, and none of his co-workers was anyone he knew. So, when evening fell and he found Club-Foot once more, Achym Mazur remained, as far as anyone could say, either dead, missing or neither.

His former pet guard smirked by way of greeting and for a moment Achym feared he'd found him a dead girl's identity (which would have been a brilliant joke under other, less trying circumstances). But it was all right; Club-Foot had taken care to lift the badge and papers of someone of Achym's age and general appearance. He was smirking, probably, because this was a definite, irrevocable goodbye. When he handed over the goods and took Achym's papers to place in the Dead pile, he gained more shit on Achym Mazur and Marcin Konopka than either of them would ever have on him – and fifty cigarettes too, to be provided as acquired.

Marcin Konopka had been back in the world for almost a week now, and much of his attention had been devoted to avoiding inmates from Hut Eleven, his home in a previous life. Fortunately (if that was the right word, and even Achym wasn't sure), most of Konopka's former neighbours were dead or being patched up in a makeshift szpital outside Zinnowitz, so the chances of discovery were less than they might have been. Still, whenever a workmate asked his name, he always said Tadeusz and left it at that. He also avoided the forlorn queue that formed each day outside the guards' office, of inmates seeking allocation to a repaired hut as each became available. Living under canvas, he'd found, was far more anonymous, if only slightly more comfortable than attempting the same in a woodshed.

The rest of his attention focused upon rebuilding his lost empire. This would necessarily be a one-man business. He had no intention of employing staff, now that his identity was a magnet for would-be snitches and blackmailers, and as stealing was his only option he had to be at Peenemünde as often as possible. This involved a dangerous degree of voluntarism, something the guards always, and rightly, suspected. He'd had to re-invent Marcin Konopka (a former librarian, apparently) as a general handyman and carpet-fitter, and spread around as much of his meagre cigarette wealth as he wouldn't make Club-Foot think he was, well, foot-dragging on his payments. So far the investment hadn't seen much of a return: about enough to break even and supplement his diet by a potato or two. But at least he was beginning to think that his new life might continue beyond the next checkpoint.

He'd risked himself and his fresh identity only once in the previous days when, stupidly, he'd tried to find out whether his trombone had survived the raid. How he could possibly make a claim to it was something he hadn't stopped to consider. The inventory clerk had been so curious about the question that he'd followed him out of the door and halfway to the latrine. *Stupid, Marcin*, he'd told himself: *fucking stupid; good old Achym would never have done it.*

It wasn't just a case of exercising his old caution, because there was something else now: something he couldn't begin to figure out, even with his nose working double shifts. He'd had a hint of it the day he went to look for his trombone. Naturally the inventory clerk had been a last, very stupid resort. His first idea was to find one of his former bandmates, though even this was a madly dangerous thing to do, given that the strength of the bonds of jazz had never been tested under National Socialist servitude. But about that at least, he needn't have worried. He couldn't find *any* of his six co-swingers, nor anyone who could tell him where they might be. They'd been disappeared, just as surely, as effectively, as Rajmund Ulatowski had disappeared himself.

He didn't know what to make of this or how to cover himself. There was no question of him wandering around the camp trying to find out what had happened – he might as sensibly have scaled one of the fences and waved a *yarmulke* at the nearest observation tower. But the absence of everyone he knew definitely meant something, and not knowing things made the new Marcin every bit as nervous as it had the old Achym. So, as he couldn't do anything to resolve it, he decided to become a mystery himself. All that he was, all he comprised, was an identity card, a thin file somewhere in the orderly office and a selection of security badges. The fact that he inhabited flesh, bone and an unattractive set of clothes was immaterial: the bureaucratic state didn't recognize the personal, only the record of it. As long as he conformed in every way to what the Reich knew him to be, but in such a way as not to encourage it to think too much about what it knew, he should – he *might* – be safe. In his own estimation, Achym Mazur had enjoyed many fine qualities. Marcin Konopka would possess just one, the gift of being entirely unremarkable.

But still, he needed work. It wasn't enough that he keep himself in the odd potato; he needed as many opportunities as possible to re-build his business and re-gain a quality of life that would count as living. For a while at least every job at Peenemünde was going to be construction work, with boundless occasions for clearing, lifting and disappearing objects that no one realized they'd yet lost. So Achym had to get on to the work details, and right away; that ate into resolutions about getting anonymous. You put yourself forward, someone always notices.

There was one job, a peach, that there wasn't any way of resisting. In their otherwise trium- phant miss, the British had somehow managed to bomb a single storey block attached to the east wall of the administration building. The block was now mostly gone but in going it had taken with it a section of the outer brickwork of the larger structure. Achym heard about this from one of the more talkative trustees, and immediately bribed himself on to the work detail as a master bricklayer. It cost him five cigarettes, a fortune, but it wasn't every day that a man had the chance of an entrée into the world of unsecured office furnishings.

That was how he came to be at the corner of House 4, ladling mortar on to what he was fairly sure was a brick, when it happened. It was so unusual that he spent several minutes considering it, which was foolish because everyone was being watched more closely since the raid. The guards now behaved as though their former indolence could be redeemed by a display of ruthless Aryan efficiency: hardly any of them went off for a cigarette or a swift piss any more and they didn't even slouch, which Achym previously had thought a physiological imperative of the race. Instead they stayed alert and watched their workers very closely, as if searching keenly for an excuse to do something typically German. The unpaid Help, if it was wise, did its best to look as though it understood the new rules.

But there were some things, startling things, that couldn't just be ignored. And there she was, walking right past him, straight into House 4 like it was the local swimming baths, or tea-rooms. To his knowledge – and he made a particular effort to know things, even to the point of paying for enlightenment – she had never before been permitted entry at the front of this building: her badge, he was fairly sure, didn't authorize it. His own was the correct one, but he had three, two of which had cost him more cigarettes than anything else he'd bought here. He couldn't believe that she had the means to do the same, but there it was: the guards had just glanced at her and waved her through.

Admittedly, there was a lot about her he didn't know. She would hardly speak to him, and Rajmund had had a brother's cold indifference to the intentionally casual queries he'd tried to raise. The *thing* had been mentioned, of course; Rajmund had been too outraged at the time to keep it to himself as a brother should, and it had been Achym, already fearful about the boy's lack of discretion, who had persuaded him for his own sake, and for that of his sister, not to make more of it. There were also vague rumours that she might belong to one of those groups in the camp that planned for a world other than this one, though he hoped there was nothing to them: it was better by far that she didn't test her already-shifty luck. So what *was* she doing, he wondered, as he tried to look busy with his brick.

Occasionally the members of the work gang who knew how to lay bricks glanced curiously at him, but he had made each of them two cigarettes wealthier, so he wasn't going to have problems. He ladled a little more mortar, shoving off what he'd already piled on. Half-an-hour she'd been in there, or a little more: much too long merely to be delivering something. Staring at the entrance, willing her to emerge, he pushed his brick on to the previously laid course, and reached for another while his neighbour hurriedly tried to re-lay it correctly. A guard glanced at them, frowned, and turned away. *Too close, Marcin*, he told himself. *Look busier.*

As the minutes passed he felt more and more strongly that he should do something, but it wasn't easy when everything was forbidden. If he said he needed a crap they'd laugh at him and say go on then, crap; if he became ill suddenly, they'd kick him until he was cured; and it just wouldn't do to ask if he might break off for luncheon. There was no conceivable reason why he should go into the administration building, even if today's badge said that he could. Unless, of course, the structural damage went deeper than they thought.

Quietly, he put it to one of his fellow bricklayers.

'Eh?'

He assumed a purse-lipped, expert look, and fondled the damaged area. 'Mm. See, it's like I said.'

Bewildered, the bricklayer stopped mixing mortar and stared blankly at the wall. The other one looked at him as though he were half-witted, so he turned to the nearest guard instead. In his fluent, Hamburg-accented German, he explained the problem.

'Sorry, sir, but the rear brickwork isn't holding the mortar properly – the bomb must have powdered it. If we try to replace the outer face without stabilizing it first, the new stuff's just going to fall off, probably within a day or two.' He smiled,

240

confidently, to emphasize the expert nature of the diagnosis.

'Shut up.'

He shrugged. 'Ok, boss. We'll just cross our fingers, then.'

The guard stared at him for a moment, and turned to his mate. 'Hans, go inside and kick the other side of the wall. See if anything happens.'

The other *schwab* shook his head. 'That's a secure room, telegraph office or something like it. No one's going in there, not without some braid's permission.'

Shit.

The guard turned back to him and shrugged. 'Do your best. And make it fucking excellent, or else.'

It was just about the worst thing he could have tried, and he'd got himself noticed. If he said anything more it would be a rifle-stock to the head and the finishing touch from a Knobelbecher. He picked up another brick, looked at it hopelessly, and applied a trowel-full of mortar.

Some minutes later, head bowed, Zofia walked out of House 4. She was accompanied by just one of the civilians who worked there, and he wasn't even holding her arm. Achym took this as a good sign: she always kept her head low, so that didn't signify much, and the fact that she could still walk was a pleasant relief to him; in fact, it was so pleasant that he forgot to move, and received a kick from Hans, who'd been longing for an excuse since he'd opened his mouth. He returned, hurriedly, to his adopted trade.

They had almost finished the work when a

uniform exited the building. Despite his recent salutary experience, Achym stopped and stared, horrified. He'd heard about this one from some of the other Polish workers, but it was the first time he'd seen him in the flesh. What made it worse was that the officer seemed very angry, which made the damage even more lurid. Achym recalled himself in time to avoid another kick, but even so, even as he pretended to lay a brick, he couldn't tear his eyes from this manifest lesson on what war did to things.

The creature glanced around, saw him staring and walked straight over. *Oh no.* He stopped no more than a few inches away and thrust his face forward. Even the two guards recoiled perceptibly.

'Seen enough?'

Achym nodded dumbly, knowing that it didn't matter how he reacted, this was going to be very bad.

'Want to look like me?'

He shook his head, equally dumbly.

The officer glanced down at the work they'd been doing, and laughed, and Achym couldn't say that this wasn't worse than his being angry. It just didn't look *right*.

'Then learn a different trade, quickly.'

Chapter Thirty

The call seemed far more urgent now and Fischer willed Freddie to be there. The hotelier took an age to return to the telephone, only to say that Herr Holleman presently had his leg off in the shower, had shouted some quite unnecessary, *soldierly* things at her by way of explaining this, and could she take his number, please?

He waited almost half-an-hour, sitting by the guesthouse telephone, playing with an unlit cigarette and the corner of the doily that covered the hall table, trying to make sense of what he'd seen earlier. But he could think of nothing that explained both the situation and its aftermath, not in this time and place. It made him nervous, and when the telephone rang he almost grabbed at the receiver.

'Otto, what the hell's going on?'

Holleman was as irritable as two days' renovations to an inheritance could have made a one-legged man with bowel trouble. In the background Fischer heard the polite clatter of crockery and discreet conversations and wondered if the lady who owned the hotel yet appreciated the full extent of her predicament.

'Freddie, I'm sorry to say that I need a big favour.'

Silence, as he'd expected. Voluntarism, the step forward, was alien to both men's philosophies.

'I need help. I know, I know, I shouldn't be doing this at all, but there it is. I need someone who understands how to dig for things quickly, who isn't too bothered about offending his betters. Anyone come to mind?'

Fischer heard heavy breathing. To pre-empt a decisive refusal, he ploughed on, detailing what he had done and what remained to do. He was careful to paint an even bleaker picture than necessary: Holleman had to come, but not in any doubt as to what to expect. He even mentioned the interview with Gestapo, and what he'd promised them.

'Thanks for the warning, Freddie.'

'Bastards. You owe Gerd Branssler for that.'

'I know. I'll make him take the brandy next time.'

That might have been the opening, but Holleman said nothing more. He was probably thinking, trying to figure out the number of ways that saying yes would be a bad idea. For a moment Fischer considered mentioning that day's events, but he wasn't ready to offer his interpretation of what he'd seen. It wasn't inconceivable that if Holleman formed one of his own, he'd just hop back to his lake house and nail himself in.

'Karl Krohne would never agree, not having two of his best men go missing.'

Thank God.

'Freddie, be honest. We aren't the best at what we do. In any case, lying isn't a living.'

A dangerous bluff: Holleman took great satisfaction from working short hours, sleeping late and sharpening mere untruths to tips of

244

brazen distortion.

'Are you mad? It's quiet, it's safe and it pays.'

The strong points, definitely. 'But it isn't work, Freddie. It's where men like us hide. Don't you miss what you used to do, even a little? No, don't tell me, because I know already. You were puking up your arsehole when I first told you about this business, and still you went right to the nub of it.'

'Well, I was good once. Not good enough for a hat and coat, maybe, but I used to smell out stuff.'

In Berlin's underbelly it would have been impossible not to, but Fischer didn't say so. 'Freddie, I badly need that nose now. How's your house coming along?'

'Done, more or less. The water supply's reconnected, and we'll never get electricity out here. The window frames could use a coat or two.'

'Leave that to the kids – it's better than them going off with the *pimpfen*. Listen, I'll deal with Karl, you just get back to Berlin, sort things out and come up to the seaside.'

Holleman made a noise in his throat and hung up.

Fischer went out on to the guesthouse porch. It was early evening and the sun shone strongly still, but an approaching storm was darkening the north-western skies above the now-redundant assembly hall. It complemented his mood perfectly. For the first time his sense of helplessness was tinged with something intangibly threatening: an itch that skin experiences immediately before being penetrated. Something seemed to be happening, something wide and deep, and as with a

245

storm front, things caught out in the open needed a form of cover.

He was standing there still, savouring the quality of his luck in the glow of that startling light, when she hurried across the road towards him, bringing the evening meal. This time he didn't attempt conversation. He stood aside, followed her and watched silently as she laid it out on the kitchen table. This might have been intimidating (he hoped so), but nothing about her manner hinted at what had happened earlier. There were no furtive glances, no hint of expectation or fear of consequences: just quiet, matter-of-fact backbone. When it was done she gave him a half-nod, half-bow and stopped, because he was blocking the doorway, her only way out. He didn't have a plan, or even an intention – it was the only thing he could think of to draw out some sort of reaction. But she just waited, eyes down, hands folded together, unmoving. Having brought about the impasse he could think of no way to further or emerge from it, and that was why she was going to win. It was necessary to do nothing until it became unbearable for one of them, or until he did something bad, which was impossible. Checkmate, therefore.

As he moved aside she nodded, as though they both understood the play, and left. He turned and watched her go, refusing to run as the first of the rain came down, hard.

When he had washed and oiled himself, Fischer ate his supper slowly, staring at the kitchen wall, contemplating the nature and power of impotence.

Chapter Thirty-One

She had no recollection of ever being so angry, not even with the Germans. The way they'd looked at her, *knowing*, and then just turned away, almost as if they were amused but too polite to let it show, to move on to more pressing matters. *Go on*, they seemed to be saying, *see if it makes the slightest difference...*

She deserved it, and much more. A half-wit would at least have left both the corridor and office doors ajar, to allow the modest cacophony of two booted soldiers, hurrying up an echoing stairwell, to give a hint of what was coming. A moderately prudent slave-worker, confined in a place where ruthless men worked to sustain an inhuman regime, might have recalled her situation sufficiently not to mistake the Generalmajor's office for a lending library, a place to browse at leisure. But there it was: stupidity of the sort that even her brother wouldn't have risked, because she'd allowed herself to forget that it was always safest to be frightened.

For a moment she'd seen the noose as clear as a promise before her. The law was precise, unequivocal: for everything that doesn't deserve a beating or transportation, death. But the moment stretched into a pause, and she began to think again. The Horror looked shocked – at least *he* reacted to type – but the boss and the big scientist were *odd*, though she couldn't say how or why. She wouldn't have believed it herself, the pathetic lie about cleaning a desk that was never to be cleaned. But they pretended to, like in a bad film about spies, and then had her escorted away as if she were a visiting Hat.

Kaspar Nagel actually told her not to worry about it. He patted her shoulder like a sympathetic friend and told her not to *worry*. It passed all strangeness; was this a new pastime, to play with the mind of someone they'd chosen to destroy? It had happened elsewhere, before her eyes. It was what Germans did when they felt playful. She recalled an afternoon only weeks after Poland surrendered, when she'd been sitting in a café in Torun, quietly talking to a girlfriend and avoiding the admiring glances of their new overlords, when they'd had their first go at the local Jews. Out on the street, right in front of the café, the cheerful slapping and kicking, the actual *beating*, of ordinary men and women whose only crime was to be there, who'd gathered as ordered. She'd covered her mouth and watched games being played with them while they stood almost to attention, their answers recorded carefully upon official-looking paper as if they were obliged to apply for mitigation from the new order, anxious not to offend further but bewildered as to what it was they'd done already to deserve this. And then the poor man who had argued when one of them casually kicked that woman: Zofia was sure he hadn't even known her, but he was an old gentleman, well dressed, and wouldn't take that sort of behaviour from anyone, not even a

248

uniform. So they told him to go: told him loudly in Polish to *fuck off home* while they winked at each other. He turned away, disgusted, he shouldn't have done that. And the pretty young officer, she would never be able to understand why, pulled out his pistol and shot the old man in the back of his head, casually, as if despatching a runt game-bird. No one, she recalled thinking at the time, should have had to see such a thing happen, for any reason.

The people here didn't seem to be like that, but who knew what Germans could do? The fact that the bosses spoke well and dressed respectably meant nothing; their smiles deceived and their fine manners hid a cold, nerveless opinion of everything that wasn't them. That was a fact, Zofia told herself, not an opinion. So however miraculous her escape from that building had been, however inexplicable their behaviour toward her, she feared – she knew – that it wasn't done with: that there'd be some form of retribution

And in the meantime she continued to serve the men who were arguing how best to torment her. While the Horror was elsewhere she cleaned every room in the guesthouse, furiously trying to calm herself, and all the while her hands trembled violently, her heart pounded and her head spun with the constant re-counting of the stupid, suicidal thing she'd done. Élodie can go to Hell, she told herself, and take the Struggle with her. Rajmund was safe now: why should she commit suicide, help kill her own parents with grief, for the sake of a damned Frenchwoman and her ridiculous sense of self-importance? At one point, lost in these silent remonstrations, she found herself polishing the dress-buckle on his dress uniform, and decided she might as well shine his best boots too. The shirt he'd worn to the boss's dinner, that would need to be laundered. He hadn't asked, of course. Even so, she picked it up from the floor and placed it in her basket with the bed sheet and comforted herself with the thought that it couldn't hurt to placate an animal that might be thinking of biting her.

It was the crowd of these matters, pressing remorselessly, that held it away for so long, the thing that had bothered her until the moment she'd been caught: why, when she'd been trying and failing to find a good reason to go to House 4 without attracting attention, had she been sent there? And upon whose order?

Chapter Thirty-Two

It was difficult to persuade Holleman to depart the platform.

'A toy train! Fantastic!'

He had come up from Zinnowitz to the Settlement station on the electric line and when the train came to a halt Fischer had been obliged to bang on the window. Holleman, entranced still, was looking everywhere but outside, staring at those passengers who stared at him, particularly the children, who each got a wink or a knowing tap of the nose. Then, of course, the driver had been made to wait while a large, clumsy, one-legged man grappled his kitbag and extra suitcase down from the rack and out on to the platform, jostling more or less everyone between himself and the door. It took a while because no one tried to help him.

He watched the train until it was almost out of sight and sighed. 'The twins would kill for one of those.'

Franz and Ulrich: unfashionably unobjection-able twelve-year-olds, full of snot and curiosity, the only thing Holleman had ever done that he couldn't joke about. He had brought them to the Air Ministry a couple of times. They had stood silently by his desk watching him work, or wan-dered around the office gathering a crop of sweets, model aircraft desk ornaments and unsewn insignia: the memorabilia of hard men made sud-denly mawkish in the presence of innocence. When Karl Krohne asked, Holleman told him they'd come to see what their dad did; when any-one else asked, he said they'd been brought to where the Deutsches Jungvolk people couldn't follow.

'How are they?'

Holleman lit a cigarette, shrugged. 'All right. It's been four medicals now, so Kristin's nearly biting the walls. I've done my best to get them to bed-wet, but they're cleared for evacuation each time. We've had four official requests that they be sent off to the KLV, and they've had four replies from me, asking sincerely that they fuck off. If the lads are going to be trained up for an SS

251

division, Adolf s going to have to collect them himself. I told them, there's no way we'll let it happen, and they haven't denounced their dad yet, so it could be worse. They're looking forward to the lake like mad things.'

Fischer imagined Freddie *en famille*: he wouldn't be discreet. The Spreewald was probably a good place to hide a brood with detailed recollections of what their father thought of the Leadership, war strategy, the price and availability of cheese.

Holleman dropped the almost-whole cigarette onto the concrete, crushed it and rubbed his hands together. 'So, Hopalong Holleman and Fischer the Face take on the bad guys. Where do we start? What about a drink?'

Fischer laughed, allowing himself a lightness of spirit for no good reason. 'Sorry, Freddie: that comes later. Alcohol isn't sold or consumed here – officially – until night falls, by order of the management.'

'Jesus! I've fallen into Hell!'

They walked slowly to the guesthouse. Fischer gave Holleman more details of the conversations of the past few days, and what he'd heard that morning at Dornberger's meeting.

'They've known that production of the missiles would be going somewhere else since the raid, but Speer told Dornberger yesterday that it'll be underground.'

'All of it? How?'

'Caves, I think. They'll have to enlarge and equip them, obviously, but the advantage – other than being bomb-proof – is that the workforce they have in mind won't be objecting to the conditions.'

252

'Where?'

'I don't know. They're looking at some sites in the Saar, but no one knows for sure. All that Dornberger's certain of is that he'll lose some of his men to it, those working in production already.' Fischer unlocked the door to the guest-house. 'So Arthur Rudolph will be going, and Eberhard Rees, possibly Stahlknecht too. God knows how many of the junior technicians and *fremdarbeiter*, any one of whom may have shot Thiel.'

'This thing,' said Holleman with great satisfaction, dropping his bags in the hallway, 'is a large, steaming midden.'

'You don't quite know all of it yet, Freddie. Yesterday, something…'

He paused, thinking to tell it as he experienced it, to describe his impressions, fleeting as they were. 'I walked into the Generalmajor's office with him. We were talking, so I wasn't entirely taking in the room. But there was Zofia, the girl I told you about, and I swear to God, Freddie, she was searching his desk. She said that she wasn't, of course. Hell, she's got nerves of glass, told him – us – that she'd been sent to clean the place. Had a chit that said so, and the proper badge too. But I *know* she was rifling his papers, and I can't see how Dornberger couldn't see it too. Yet he just told her to go, to get out and come back later.'

'Fuck off!'

'Mad, isn't it? By this time von Braun and Arthur Rudolph were in the room too. I don't think Rudolph had any idea what was going on, but von Braun was looking at Dornberger like …

253

you know what I mean?'

'Like they're talking with their mouths shut?'

'That's right. And then they *both* looked at Nagel, who's waiting at the door, and von Braun says, "See that she gets safely back to the kitchens, would you, Kaspar?", as if her ladyship's car's got a flat tyre and Nagel's a passing ADAC man. And *then* they get straight down to business, about where production's going and how it's going to affect manpower. Not a single word about what just happened.'

'She's *that* pretty?'

Fischer snorted. 'Helen of Troy couldn't have pulled it off. I've been going back over the thing all day, trying to see it differently, like I missed a detail that would make it innocent. She *might* have dropped something the moment before we walked in and she was simply picking it up. But I didn't see any *it*. She *may* only have been about to stack some papers prior to polishing the desk, but I'm guessing that she knows perfectly well that even to touch them would be absolutely forbidden unless the building was on fire. She might, even, have been looking for an innocent piece of paper that she had every right to see, but a foreign worker has no rights, much less *every*. And anyway, what papers on the desk of a Generalmajor are likely to be innocent? The only way I can see it is that she was snooping, a capital offence. And both the Head of Army here and the chief scientist did their best to make it look less than trivial.'

'I'm glad you waited until now to tell me this.'

'Sorry, Freddie, but I needed you here. God

254

knows, there's too much work for fifty Bulls if we do it Alex-style. But let me ease the pain of it a little. Get two glasses from that cupboard.'

With a magician's flourish Fischer pulled a bottle of whisky from the sideboard, and Holleman's face lit up like a dawn offensive.

Early afternoon, drinking hard liquor: police work as it was done in the good old days. How many kommissars were hopeless drunks by the time they handed in their badges and then found it was a habit they couldn't afford to take into retirement? They died young, and it wasn't the job they missed. As Fischer and Holleman took their first taste they glanced at each other, amused, recognizing the procedure: *just the one, or maybe two. That's definitely it. Well, if you're pouring a third and a fourth, Franz, I'll keep you company. It'd be a shame to let that bottle die of loneliness.* And then it's four o'clock, and what's the point of going back to the station now? The only good part of the good old days, and even that stole your liver, eventually.

'Who was Johnny Walker?' Holleman, spread luxuriously on the sofa, his metal half-leg propped up on the cushions, peered affectionately at the label.

'I have no idea. He looks a happy, polite fellow.'

'I don't like whisky.'

'No?'

'I adore it, heart and soul. The English are a wonderful people, when they're not being utter shits.'

'The Scots, I think. Hence the name.'

'Skirts aside, it's the same thing. You know that,

failing a confession or a betrayal, there's no possibility of resolving this?'

'Of course not.'

'So I'm to lend credibility to a failure?'

'To be a witness to the fact that I'll fail correctly.'

Holleman considered his amber reflection. 'Do you remember the Wedding murders?'

'Vaguely. They weren't such big news in Stettin as Berlin, I recall.

'It was a grand name to give to just two killings but they happened the same night, to similar girls, so everyone panicked – this was only a year after the Kürten business, remember? The next morning they turned us all out on to the streets – schupos, kripos, even cadets – and told us not to come back until we'd interrogated every two-legged thing from Schönholz to the Tiergarten that wasn't a budgerigar. And I mean *everyone*: I don't think I slept or ate sitting down for three days. And what did we get?'

'Nothing, wasn't it?'

'That's right. By the end of the week there'd been no more killings, and the Oberregierungsrat was beginning to think he might just keep his job. So everything starts winding down, but quietly, you know? A month later the investigation was more or less dead on its feet. The girls' families were clean, boyfriends likewise, the thousands of interviews we'd done provided no useful information, and finally, someone points out that the only connections between the two killings were approximate time, *very* approximate place, and gender – a hell of a coincidence, but then, that's what make a coincidence, isn't it? The thing is, the effort was reckoned a success even though it failed, because we'd thrown everything at it and done lots of good, solid police work. Once a panic dies down, once people stop thinking it's going to be their daughters next, everyone can accept that some cases can't be solved.'

Holleman poured himself another, this time entirely to the brim. 'Anyway, what was the point of putting a rope around Wedding? Couldn't the killer have crossed town for the night? It didn't make sense, other than to show that someone was going through the motions.'

Fischer held out his glass. 'And that's what I'm doing?'

'What else? We're running a two-man investigation of a town-sized population, half of them ausländers, a place where you can't spot the snitches, where there are no pimps, whores or known pansies we can work on. Easy enough knowing where to start, but what then? You've spoken to just about everyone it's possible to say knows *something* about Thiel's death, but the next step's like pissing into the fog. Do we knock on doors, like we did in Wedding? How long's that going to take? And what chance is there that the fellow with the gun's still here? I don't know. Do you?'

'You never solved Wedding?'

Holleman sighed. 'A kid confessed to both, about two years later. He'd been pulled in for rape and battery, so I can't really say that the Bulls who worked on him didn't just tack on unfinished business. I heard they messed him so

257

badly he'd have held up his hands to Franz Ferdinand.

'But you know what, Otto? I'm beginning to like your friend Zofia. Even if she's not the man with the gun, there's something badly out of place, and in a *place* where important secrets should remain so. Let's just suppose for a moment that what happened to Thiel wasn't about sex, or money, or revenge, but who he was. If that's the case, motives jump up like s-mines. We can assume that the foreigners here don't want the work to be successful. So, is she part of a sabotage effort?'

'If she is her timing is terrible. The development work here's just about finished. Thiel was involved in perfecting the propulsion system, but if anyone wanted to cripple the programme they should have shot him a year ago, and six or seven others with him.'

Holleman lay back on the sofa, holding the glass to his forehead. 'All right, she's stealing secrets. Thiel caught her in the act and threatened to tell Dornberger, so he had to go.'

'On today's evidence, Dornberger doesn't give a damn about secrecy. And anyway, the only foreigner with access to Thiel's department died on the night, at Trassenheide. Sorry, Freddie. This has all been bouncing around between my ears for hours now. Zofia's being a naughty girl, but I don't know why and I can't see the connection.'

'Well, if everything goes nowhere at least you can hand her over to Gestapo. I assume that we're going to watch her, at least?'

'Can't hurt, can it? Pass the bottle.'

A fourth followed the third, and Fischer's entire

worldly estate was reduced to just two bottles of Scotch, his Knight's Cross and his gold wounds medal. Tacitly, the conversation was allowed to drift away from business to the main preoccupations of war: the Front, food, air raids and Holleman's attempts to act as a one-man evacuation committee for his family.

'How bad is Berlin?'

'It isn't, for now. You'll hardly notice the damage, north of Mariendorf – I can't believe the British got that close and didn't see Tempelhof. Wilhelmstrasse, of course, a prime hit, entirely by accident. But that's not the point, Otto. It isn't what they did but how they did it. They sent a fucking armada! We couldn't put anything like that into the air any more. And the ring of steel that's supposed to make Berlin a slaughterhouse for enemy aircraft? The flak towers pointed their guns, opened up and that was it. The British just plotted a course around them. We managed to bring down just fifty of them, sixty at most. And this was their first real attempt, an unfamiliar target, badly plotted, when they were most vulnerable to the defences. What's it going to be like when the Amis finally climb off their arses and join in? Berlin's going to get it like Hamburg; it's a question of timing, that's all. I want Kristin and the boys far away before then.'

'I can't see the Allies being interested in the Spreewald.'

'No? Well, if the Tommies aim for Lübeck again they might hit the lake. They're both in Germany. You don't mind if I take off this damn leg?'

It was still off, sitting upright on a chair at the

kitchen table, when Zofia brought their evening meal three hours later. Fischer was dozing in the armchair, but one of his eyes opened and blearily tracked her as she laid out the food. She didn't take any interest in the new arrival, though she removed his leg from the chair and placed it more properly on the floor beside the kitchen sink. She wiped the spot where it had been, glanced once more at the set table, and left. A moment later, Fischer shifted.

'What do you think?'

Holleman made a low, obscene noise in his throat. 'A real peach. Are you sure you...?'

'A long time ago, when I was a beauty myself.'

'In your mother's glass eye, you were. But I can see how she might make a man not think straight. Perhaps Dornberger's smitten?'

'I doubt *he's* got eyes for anything but rockets. And von Braun would have to be smitten also. I don't see the young Baron risking his reputation and neck for domestic staff, not even the pretty ones.'

'World-class arse, though.'

They ate much later, when they'd sobered sufficiently to recall the penalty for sleeping on empty stomachs. Holleman excused himself politely before they sat down, and Fischer was certain he discreetly vomited in the bathroom while donning his 'dress leg' for dinner. Impressively, he then returned, ploughed through his cold meat and potatoes and even managed half a suet pudding, while Fischer just pushed most of his around the plate.

'Tomorrow...'

Holleman breathed deeply and burst into loud, tuneless English song. 'When the world is free-e-e!'

Tomorrow surrendered to the inconsequential Now, whose embers were stoked just before midnight when Fischer, losing his thread in an argument about whether Polish girls were more, less or just as inventive as their German sisters, felt it absolutely necessary to take a second bottle from the sideboard.

Chapter Thirty-Three

Day one of the investigation proper, all previous fumblings to be discarded.

'Start again, Freddie.'

'Really? I thought I'd done you ample justice.'

'In fact, let's start by agreeing not to write anything more than we need to.'

Holleman shrugged and crushed the paper into a ball. 'Fine. Exactly how we street-shufflers do it. I just assumed that Bulls preferred paperwork.'

'We preferred being in nice, warm offices. Paperwork was the excuse.'

'So where do we start?'

The guesthouse kitchen, or Peenemünde Special Investigations Kommandatur as Holleman had referred to it twice already that morning, waited for breakfast. Time, which flowed like a swollen river during the hours of their inebriation (wisely, they'd decided not to close their eyes and risk sleep), had come to a stagnant halt at about first light. By seven o'clock their stomachs and wits were crying out for something more nourishing than fermented enemy barley mash. Work was the only way to avoid thinking about it.

'We start where we can, Freddie.'

'Me threatening folk at one end of the Settlement and you at the other. We meet in the middle?'

Fischer rubbed his head, which at that moment hurt considerably more than his face. 'A waste of time we don't have. Half the population leaves for the office in about an hour, the other half for one of the wives' clubs, or the beach, or whatever will keep the children quiet for a few hours. In any case, what do we ask? *Excuse me, madam. Did you by any chance happen to see someone put a hole in Herr Doctor Walter Thiel's forehead as you dived under the bed in the early hours of 18 August last?*'

'Not a fruitful approach.'

'We're going to have to be clever, Freddie. Find the options with the fewest variables and try to make our own good luck, because God knows, it isn't going to be thrown at us.'

'Three legs and one and a half faces between us, and you talk about luck?'

'Think about what the Generalmajor and others have told me. In the immediate aftermath of the raid, bodies in and around the Settlement were recovered both by Germans and foreign workers, yes?'

Holleman nodded.

'It only occurred last night, when I'd given up thinking straight, or soon after. What were the

262

foreigners doing here?'

'Helping to dig out bodies.'

'No, I mean what were they doing here *at all?* It was about two o'clock in the morning. Obviously there'd been no time to bring up workers from Trassenheide and besides, there'd have been far too much to do there to spare guards to accompany them to Peenemünde. They were here already, long beyond their curfew.'

'Why?'

Fischer shrugged. 'Exactly. A special job? Night work? There'll be some good reason, I mean, no one would allow *fremdarbeiter* to just wander around in the dark, not even with the poor quality of security here. That's not my point. The thing is, there couldn't have been *that* many of them, surely? Ten? Fifty?'

'So?'

'So, where would you prefer to start hunting for a witness? Among two to three thousand Germans, all of whom you'll have to treat tenderly? Or do we go after a handful of foreigners who we can intimidate to hell...?'

The last word died away. The door was pushed open and Zofia backed in with a breakfast tray. Eyes carefully averted she placed it between them on the table and began to collect the detritus of the previous evening's bacchanalia. Without the slightest effort to hide his curiosity, Holleman followed every move intensely, as if willing a confession to ... something. Fischer watched them through a pounding headache and a longing to make a start on the bread rolls.

As always she was done within a minute and

keen to leave. He waited until her hand was on the door.

'Thank you very much, Zofia.'

Her knuckles whitened, she gave a curt nod and was gone.

'Otto, you tease!' Holleman tore off a large chunk of bread with some gusto and waved it. 'If you carry on like that she'll find a reason to remember you. Well, your cock, anyway. How do we...?'

He stuffed the entire piece in his mouth, so Fischer had to wait for the rest while the hands made pointless gestures to indicate that talk wasn't possible.

'...find out which foreigners were here on the night?'

'I'll ask Nagel what the procedures are. The choices wouldn't have been made entirely at random.'

Fischer went straight to Wehrner von Braun's office and asked his secretary for Kaspar Nagel. She glanced briefly at his face, shuddered delicately, and directed him to the engine test-bed block. He found both Nagel and his boss with a group of technicians in the low building, clustered around the largest motor – or cluster of motors – that he had ever seen, and he was Luftwaffe.

The Technical Director waved him over. 'Your timing's awful, Hauptmann. Can it wait?'

'Of course, sir. May I watch this?'

Von Braun shrugged, already giving his attention to the monster. Nagel went to a nearby table, returned with an extra pair of ear-mufflers and beckoned him back to the safe-point with the others.

Everyone leaned on a sandbag barrier like on-lookers at a racetrack bend. At the end of the line Fischer had the best view of the rear of the device, on which he counted fully eighteen ejection nozzles. He tapped Nagel's shoulder. 'How powerful is this?'

The pre-ignition sequence started, and Nagel had to shout: 'Twenty-five tonnes of thrust. The A4 propulsion unit, Walter Thiel's best work.'

The roar grew almost instantly to a scream. Despite the distance between the motor and the sandbags, everyone winced and simultaneously took a step backwards. Even with his ears protected Fischer found the assault almost unbearable, though he realized that if this were an actual launch the source of discomfort would already be far above him on its way to London's suburbs.

After thirty seconds von Braun waved to the control block and the noise dropped off a cliff, deepening and easing the pressure on their ears. Long before it had fallen silent the technicians were back at the device, leaving only Nagel and Fischer behind the sandbags, grateful for the space between them and it.

'The Director's going to be some time, Hauptmann.' Nagel had removed a pack of cigarettes from his pocket and offered one, beckoning Fischer to follow him outside.

'Actually, it's you I need, Nagel. You haven't met my colleague, Oberleutnant Holleman?'

'No. I saw you with him yesterday but didn't want to interrupt. He walks very well, I thought.'

'He's had a lot of practice. But something occurred to us. The foreign workers who were here at Peenemünde during the air raid, how are they chosen?'

'Well, for their skills, obviously. The technicians often…'

'No, forgive me. I mean the unskilled workers who were here that night, the ones who helped to recover the bodies afterwards. How is it that they *in particular* were allowed to be here after the rest returned to Trassenheide for the night? Is a trustee system operated?'

'Oh, I see. Yes, of a kind. Night workers used to be drawn from the allied nations' groups, when we had them. Now it's usually French, Czechs or Poles, the most willing and competent among them. They get certain privileges and we assign them to special duties.'

'What sort of privileges?'

'Food, obviously, and cigarettes. Sometimes even short holidays, if they're not *zivilarbeiter.*'

'And "special duties"?'

'That could be anything. Emergency repairs to water pipes. Finishing work upon which strict deadlines are imposed. Digging out damaged test sites. Just about any job that isn't capable of being dealt with before sunset.'

'And they're guarded during night hours?'

'Always, yes.'

'So there wouldn't ever be a large number here at any one time?'

'No. Typically, I doubt we'd use more than about ten or twenty on any special job, unless it was a major project. I recall we had a lot of Todt Organization workers here, day and night, to build the Settlement. But of course the site wasn't operational back then.'

'Good. Where might I find a list of these privileged workers?'

Nagel frowned. 'I've never seen one. Obviously it must exist, but as it's not my business to...'

'Whose business would it be?'

'The Army Office. They deal with all movements of non *häflinge* labour here.'

'And the officer-in-charge?'

'Zanssen's former deputy, Lieutenant Colonel Stegmaier. Though, of course, the everyday allocations are dealt with by his subordinates.'

Stegmaier the betrayer: the man who squealed on his ranking officer to the Reichsführer SS and pissed off the entire Army Ordnance Department. A man who wanted to get on, clearly.

Nagel was watching him closely. 'Be careful, Hauptmann.'

'Why? I only want to ask about the night of the raid.'

'He can be ... difficult.'

'Spit it out, Nagel.'

'He used to goad Walter Thiel. I think he regarded him as a prima donna, so he went out of his way to try to complain whenever he thought things weren't progressing as they should. Of course, this didn't help Walter's nerves, but then, few things did.'

'A personal enemy?'

'No, not that. Just the usual voice of Army Ordnance. They think we've lost sight of what we're here for, sometimes.'

Not much doubt about that. 'Who would be the

267

best man to speak to about this?'

'Other than Stegmaier himself,' said Nagel. 'Probably his second-in-command. His name is Udo Gaschler.'

Chapter Thirty-Four

Fischer found Hauptmann Gaschler at the Army Office, occupying a room with two orderlies. He knocked on the open door and collided with the warmest welcome he'd had so far.

'The Ghost! It's time we met!'

Gaschler was a big man: too big for his uniform, which popped dangerously at the midriff. He was certainly too big for his desk, which he lifted almost clear of the floor as he struggled to pull his legs from beneath it. He waved in Fischer with a ham-sized hand and loudly licked the fingers of the other; the remains of a *butterkuchen* lay mostly on a plate pinning down his paperwork, with fragments spread far wider. Neither of the orderlies seemed to regard this as a breach of office etiquette, though their own desks were regulation spotless.

'You don't mind that? The name's rather stuck since you arrived.'

Fischer had heard much worse. He shrugged.

'You see? We have nothing better to do here than make up stupid monikers, while real soldiers...' he glanced sternly at his assistants, '...keep the Bolsheviks out of our wives' beds. Tell them what

268

it's like at the Front, Hauptmann. No, don't. Let the bastards find out for themselves, when I fix their transfers. Mother of God, help us!'

One of the orderlies (he was at least sixty years old) grinned at his typewriter. The other shook his head slightly and shuffled a sheath of papers into something like a pile. Neither glanced up or otherwise reacted to what Fischer suspected was a daily routine.

Gaschler pointed Fischer at a chair. 'So, our security's shit?' Again, the hand pre-empted any response. 'No, no, don't say it isn't. I've been trying to get things fixed for months. We're like Ellis fucking Island, only instead of sending them straight on we offer premium accommodation and encourage them to wander around, getting a feel for the place. Jesus! Have a drink.'

Hastily Fischer held up his own hand to the offer. 'I'm letting one die peacefully at the moment, thanks.'

Gaschler frowned, trying to grasp the principle, but the bottle disappeared back into its drawer. 'You aren't here to inspect *this* office, I suppose?'

'Only what it does. You make arrangements for work parties?'

The big man nodded. '*Allocations*, that's the word. Who gets sent where, and when. If they're ausländer, we shove 'em around.'

'You have files on them?'

'If you can call a name, former address, age, sex, civilian occupation and reason for being here a file, yes. Otherwise, do we fuck.'

Fischer laughed. 'What about the ones you trust to do night work?'

'We don't trust *anyone*. The ones we get good results from, the ones who don't want to make trouble, go in here.'

Gaschler lifted a ledger from a shelf to his left. 'They get a chit from us for each job. It has to be returned before they go back to Trassenheide. We put their names in here every time, so we can rotate them. Can you believe that? We try to be *fair* to these bastards, give 'em all a chance for extra rations.'

'How many have you got?'

'Forty, fifty regulars, a few we've tried and then had to smack. They get lifted back out of the book.'

For the first time in days Fischer had a tiny sense of forward movement. 'So you'd be able to tell me which of them were here the night of the air raid?'

'Shouldn't be difficult.' Gaschler stuck a thick thumb into the ledger. 'Came up on the evening of the seventeenth, right? That's ... eight names. Three Poles, two Frenchies, three Slovaks. Here.'

He handed over the ledger and a pen. 'Achziger. Piece of paper for the Hauptmann.'

Carefully Fischer copied the names. 'May I see what you have on these men?'

'Certainly. What have they done, the bastards?'

'Nothing, I think. I'm just checking on how the raid was handled by crews and those who helped them.'

Gaschler shrugged and told the other orderly to fetch the paperwork on the eight men. It was produced within a minute and Fischer took it to a small desk to make notes. Details on each were basic, the product of a clerk's momentary inter-rogation on the day of the men's arrival. Three had obviously tried to make claims for skills they didn't have, perhaps hoping for better treatment. In each case the original description had been crossed out and 'labourer' inserted.

Within ten minutes all the available information had been transcribed. Gashler was flicking through a copy of *Die Wehrmacht*, finishing off his cake. He looked up as Fischer stood. 'That good enough?'

'Yes, thank you. I wonder if you or any of your men know these men personally?'

'Doubt it. Let's see.' Gaschler sniffed and took the sheet. 'Just the one. Alois Stoch, a greasy little fucker, likes to tell tales on his mates for smokes. We've had to pull him out of the camp a couple of times before he got the shit kicked out of him.'

The orderly Achziger grinned. 'Wasn't quite *before* last time, was it?'

'Hell, no, I forgot. Nice little convalescence though, eating through a straw.'

The three army men laughed fondly at the memory, and Fischer forced a grin.

'So, he'd be the one to talk to?'

Gaschler handed back the list. 'If you want a rat, he's your man.'

'May I use your telephone?'

'You can try, but whether it'll work for a *real* soldier I can't say.'

Chapter Thirty-Five

Holleman met Fischer at the entrance to the administration building. He'd spoken to the camp office at Trassenheide and was waiting to pass on the bad news.

'They say they only have five of them. The other three got sent off to Swinemünde the morning after. They went with about a thousand others, so where they are now God alone knows.'

Fischer sighed. 'Let's start with what we have.'

The five were all at Peenemünde that day: three on a work detail at Test Stand IV, the other two in the main kitchens, doing the heavy lifting for a refrigeration unit installation. Mindful of Freddie's leg, Fischer volunteered himself for the test stand. It was an easy walk, despite light rain, taking him out of the main development area to where the sea breeze swept straight in without adulteration from the site's many chemical processes and chimney ventings.

The work detail, twelve men guarded by a single middle-aged reservist, was shoring up a small section of the test stand's blast-containment ridge, which rain or poor workmanship had brought down. No one was trying to break records in the drizzle. Two men leaned on their spades while another repeatedly kicked a sod of grass up the slope in the manner of a footballer keeping leather in the air. The rest made a token effort to look as if they were raising a sweat, but there was little sign of progress.

Fischer nodded to the reservist. 'I'd like to speak to Francois D'Hont, Rémy Mullins and Janusz Budny, please.'

He got a shrug. 'Don't know their names. You'd better just shout them out. Sir.'

The last came just quickly enough not to earn him a charge. Fischer called the names. Two men dropped their spades and the footballer let the sod come to rest. They shuffled reluctantly towards him, and at that moment he wished fervently he could have borrowed someone else's face.

'We'll go there.' He pointed to the nearest observation blockhouse, which was doorless.

Inside he offered cigarettes. No one refused.

'I want to ask you a few questions. No one is in any trouble. No one will be reported for anything that's said.' He emphasized every word. 'We're just exercising your memories, no need to worry. What I'm saying, you understand, yes?'

They all nodded. A working man needed the lingua franca of the new Europe.

'When the British came the other night, you were working at Peenemünde, yes?'

Again, three very hesitant nods. The footballer in particular seemed to think he might be abetting his own hanging.

'Good. That's very good. Now, when the bombs stopped, were you ordered to help rescue – to help – the people who had been hurt? Who were in the houses still?'

A more certain, confident response this time. They weren't likely to be punished for dragging

Germans from rubble.

'Was it just houses? Did any of you help to dig up the ground? To pull bodies out of the ground?' Fischer mimed the action, heaving upwards with his good arm.

Two shrugged. The other, the footballer, nodded hesitantly. 'Dig,' he said, also miming, 'help women out.'

A Pole. Fischer nodded encouragingly. 'Janusz Budny?'

Fearfully, Budny acknowledged his identity and pocketed another two cigarettes.

'You said women. It was *just* women? No man, or children?'

A firm No. 'Five women – girls – all dead, in a ... *glowy*?'

'A trench, yes.'

Fischer, disappointed, thought for a moment. His audience watched expectantly, surer now of the rules.

'All right. After you helped dig out the people, where did you take them? Did you go with them? Did you carry them somewhere?'

The three looked at each other. Slowly they shook their heads. One of the Frenchmen held up a hand.

'I was told to sit, on the ground, to wait for someone to tell me what to do.'

'Yes.' The other Frenchman spoke for the first time. The Pole nodded. Unanimous.

'Were you guarded while you waited?'

'No, but I waited, I promise, sir.'

'Yes, I'm sure you did. For how long did you wait?'

'Long time: hour, two. Don't know.'

Fischer had a few cigarettes still and shared them out. They took them, wary but no longer anxious, and tried a half salute when he dismissed them. The guard nodded them back to work and sank into his regulation semi-stupor, holding his rifle with much the same technique as his charges held their spades.

Freddie Holleman, helping to steady a low wall outside House 4, smirked as Fischer approached.

'Only Germans...'

'Were in the schoolhouse, yes, I know.'

'Oh. Well, I suppose the odds favoured that, if only eight foreigners were here on the night.'

'But if the workers were told specifically *not* to carry the bodies there?'

Holleman pulled a face. 'Were they, though? It might just have been their place to dig. I mean, the Generalmajor had organized everyone into teams, hadn't he?'

'What about your boys?'

'The two Slovakians? Tighter than a dog's ring piece. Told me they'd worked together that night, but clearing houses, not trenches. Them and about a dozen Germans, soldiers and civilians. They'd dig, bring out the bodies, found a couple of live ones too, and then go on to the next house while another group wrapped up the mess and carried it away. They say they were kept at it until about mid-morning, then they got a hot drink and some bread with the others – I think that surprised them more than the raid – and went back to work until evening. And no, I didn't ask whether they'd seen a corpse with an extra hole.'

Fischer consulted his list. 'The three others, at Swinemünde. How do you feel about a train ride?'

'Is it going to be worth it? The chances of one of them...'

'I know, Freddie, but let's wipe them off the board. I gave you the names. Two Poles and a Slovakian – Bronislaw Michalski, Rajmund Ulatowski, Alois Stoch. Here's the bad news. There are dozens of labour camps at Swinemünde. The thousand or so from here must have been split between them and I'm betting the paperwork doesn't tell us which of our boys went where. That may be up to you.'

'*Dozens?* What the fuck are they building, pyramids?'

'They're digging fields, mainly. That and synthetic silk manufacturing – the parachutes I used to dangle from. There are more of them around the town than Germans now, I expect, all helping to build the New Order, bless them.'

Holleman rubbed his face. 'Oh, for Christ's ... all right. Von Braun organized it, didn't he? So if anyone knows it'll be your pretty boy?'

'Nagel, yes.'

Nagel knew a surprising amount. His boss, thoughtfully, had jotted down figures as he trawled the camps at Trassenheide on the morning of 18 August, trying to find bunks for Peenemünde's surplus *fremdarbeiter*. The locations that had accepted workers, and the numbers assigned to each all on a single sheet of paper. No names, of course. Von Braun hadn't cared who went where.

'Nine hundred and seventeen workers, male

and female, sent to sixty-four camps in or around Swinemünde.' Nagel shrugged. 'At the time we assumed that we'd probably want them back at some point, so it didn't seem sensible to send them further.'

From von Braun's office they telephoned the first ten camps on the list. Four took the call. All were raucously amused when Fischer suggested that someone at their end might canvass their residents for one or more of three names. All suggested that he was welcome to come himself and try.

Nagel had absented himself while this initiative dragged to its expected conclusion. He returned with a warrant.

'Your authority. Signed by the Generalmajor.'

Reluctantly Holleman took this and the list of camps and tucked them into his breast pocket.

'I've reserved a room for you at the *Graf von Luckner*. It's quite pleasant. We keep an account there so all your meals are provided, and they charge telephone usage directly to us. You'll like Swinemünde, Oberleutnant. If you have time you must see Haussmann's improvements and the old town...'

'I'm not going on holiday, son.'

'No, of course not. But it would be a shame...'

Hastily Fischer thanked Nagel for his trouble, half-wishing he'd taken on the Swinemünde task himself. Given his intimate knowledge of the town he was of course the logical choice. But the thought of his new face wandering into familiar haunts wasn't a happy one, not when it was likely to find old friends there. It was better to avoid unnecessary wear upon one's soul and others' stomachs.

He offered to walk Holleman to the Settlement station, via the guesthouse.

'Freddie, don't let yourself be put off by the camp commanders. Drop Dornberger's name as much as you need to. If that doesn't work, tell them they can explain to Reichsminister Speer why they're offering you the fuck off. Just don't waste time, because we don't have any.'

'Dornberger, Speer, fuck off. Right. What are you going to do while I'm taking the rest-cure?'

'I'm coming with you. Part of the way, at least.'

Chapter Thirty-Six

Fischer disembarked at Karlshagen, leaving Holleman to catch his connection at Zinnowitz. Trassenheide camp lay between there and the village of the same name, and he was at the main gate less than ten minutes later. It was the first time his universal badge didn't get him waved through immediately. A scowling sentry came to attention correctly but made him wait while his credentials were checked with Peenemünde. When finally the gate opened, an Oberleutnant blocked his path and baldly asked his business.

Fischer saluted pointedly. 'Your name?'

Flustered, the officer half-returned the gesture. 'Raffel, shift commander.'

'Well, Oberleutnant, you'll have spoken to the

278

Generalmajor's office, so you're aware that I needn't answer questions posed to me by a junior officer. However...' he waved down the embryonic protest, '...for courtesy's sake, let me say that if I wish to wander arse-naked around the female shower block here, I'll do so without objection or even comment from you or anyone else. Now, please show to me your detainees' list for the day *before* the air raid, and also the current one.'

He finished on a rising note for effect, and the Oberleutnant swivelled on his heel without another word. Fischer followed in the direction of a wooden office hut. Around them, damage was still clearly visible, particularly in the northern section of the camp where large areas of ground had been cleared and canvas raised as makeshift accommodation. The southern section, separated from the rest by a new wire fence, was unguarded. Here, bombed-out German families had begun to fashion something of a replacement existence for themselves. The view was a striking contrast to the one immediately over the fence. There were curtains in the hut windows, and allotments had been dug outside each block; most surreally, children played games in the dirt while their mothers hung washing on lines between the huts. Had a wire fence not encompassed this idyll it might have been mistaken for a very poorly thought-out holiday camp. Barely ten metres away the few foreign workers not actually working at that moment stood or sat around, smoking or talking quietly. There was no detainees' uniform at Trassenheide, but the shabby greyness of their clothes provided an inadvertent substitute. None of them appeared to be starving; all looked hungry, tired and hopeless. Fischer recalled the apparent good humour of a number of them at Peenemünde, chatting at the end of a day's shift; perhaps here there were just too many reminders of the reality of their condition, and the time to reflect upon them.

Oberleutnant Raffel brought a fat register out on to the office porch. It contained a series of daily tallies, the last full one for 17 August 1943, with names of detainees for each of sixty-five huts. On days since there had been a simple headcount for the camp as a whole.

'It's been difficult to arrange a proper count since the raid. Everyone's shifted around and we don't have fixed accommodation for more than about twenty percent of inmates. I *hope* we'll have a proper system again within two weeks at most.' The Oberleutnant was apologetic. Whatever he thought of Fischer, he wasn't pleased with the way standards had fallen.

At least there was an accurate record of where each of the three men had lived prior to the raid. Fischer asked for a seat in the office and excused himself. He found the names among the roll calls for huts twelve, fifty-one and fifty-nine. Copying those of their hut mates was more work than he'd expected. From the size of the units he would have assumed that each contained a maximum of twenty persons. But the tally showed a minimum of forty – and sometimes as many as fifty – detainees crammed into each hut.

About half-an-hour later he returned the

register to Raffel, who had remained in the office doing nothing other than to keep an eye on his visitor. The book was slotted into a rank of similar volumes on a long shelf: an orderly testament to the Reich's enormity-management.

Fischer offered a cigarette to the Oberleutnant. 'There are, what, two thousand or so foreign workers remaining here, after the transfers to Swinemünde?'

'From memory, one thousand nine hundred and sixteen,' Raffel smiled, just. 'My birth-date.'

'How were the transferees chosen?'

'Chosen?'

'Picked out, allocated, separated from those who were to stay?'

'Oh. The wounded we had to clear out, obviously, and many of those still walking whose huts were destroyed or uninhabitable. Then, we had word of how many homes were destroyed at the Settlement, so the necessary number of intact huts was emptied to provide for them. Many of the others remain here under canvas, for the moment.'

'There was no one specifically identified by you or anyone else to be removed to Swinemünde?'

'No. Why should there have been?'

'I'm just trying to understand how things were organized. These huts – twelve, fifty-one and fifty-nine – were they destroyed?'

'The first, I think, yes. Most of the bombs fell on low-numbered huts at the northern extremity of the camp. The others were only slightly damaged. Some windows blew out, I believe?' He said this while looking at an orderly, who nodded.

'So the occupants of these two will still be here?'

'No. All huts in the fifty series have been allocated to German families. The former inmates are at one or more of the Swinemünde camps.'

Not only the men themselves but anyone who could speak about them, lost somewhere in the maze of camps around Fischer's old hometown. Holleman was going to have to be busy.

He thanked Raffel with more enthusiasm than he felt and walked back, alone, to the main gate. A few of the detainees watched him, forlornly, and for a wretched moment he was tempted to offer some sort of acknowledgement: a nod, perhaps. How obscene that would be, he realized, just in time.

It was his very first visit to a labour camp, and it gave the Front a powerful allure. The worst that could happen there was death, or mutilation, with no contingent requirement to have a soiled anima sponged clean. You did bad things, you broke the stupid, inappropriate rules that diplomats negotiated in the name of humanity, fine: so did the fellow facing you. But here, no one could hide behind a cause, or a justification; here, there was intention, a deliberate will to occupy a lower, debased plane. He wondered if it were merely his over-acute imagination that the eyes of the detainees and their gaolers possessed the same quality of emptiness, the mark of having been removed from what even a broken mind might consider normality.

The same guard opened the gate and locked it behind him, an older man, perhaps fifty-five, sixty. A veteran of the First War, no doubt grateful to be in a place where there was reasonable food and no enemy, where an occasional kick up a Frenchman or Pole's arse – just to remind them who *should* have won, last time – wouldn't cost him. Probably a wife, and a boy in uniform, a football team, health worries, bills, a leaking roof at home and an absolute, implacable conviction that the moralities he casually assumed of all *that* did not apply to *this*. As a Bull Fischer had known that any job, if you wanted to survive it, was something you wore like a raincoat. How could a man take off *this* in the evening?

The tiny electric train that took him back to Peenemünde was otherwise empty. He tried to smoke a cigarette but his lung protested, so he watched the trees instead, pressing his face against the window and keeping his eyes fixed so that the approaching blur became a distinct form for a moment only before disappearing into the shapeless Gone. He began to number the elements of his life that could be daubed by this particular metaphor, and then tried, one by one, to dismiss them.

Chapter Thirty-Seven

She was finding it increasingly difficult to answer the question without inviting further ones, all of which required more, and more inventive, lies. In the aftermath of the raid most people had been too concerned about themselves to question the ordeals of others, but now it seemed to be a new phrase in the language of captivity: what happened to you that night?

Her answer had to be subtly different each time, shaped according to who was asking it. To those in adjacent bunks, she'd been in a friend's hut, too late to return before the curfew sounded that night. To those whom she suspected of knowing that particular friend, of knowing that the girl's hut had been almost destroyed, she claimed to have been kept late at Peenemünde, to help with an officers' dinner party. To the few bosses who were insufficiently careful of their status to ignore her attractions, who were perfectly aware that there'd been no officers' dinner, she'd said that she'd been lucky: her own hut had been untouched by the British bombs. To Élodie she had said nothing, not even when pressed about it, because it was always safest not to say anything that was capable of being used, twisted, turned or threatened with. Only one person knew the truth: the man she'd been with when the bombs began to fall – her lover, the German.

She had told herself often that he wasn't as his kind were; had convinced herself that his marriage was a form, a mistake long-regretted; had reassured herself that she was blameless and needful of the single comfort to set against the universal misery of her life. She had lain with him that night, gladly, even as hundreds of her countrymen died and her brother departed her life, probably forever. She had done what priests had always said not to do: she had forgiven herself. It had taken time, but time was what she had.

Like a schoolgirl she had built an impossible world where he had never married, where she had the ability to make a choice, where wars weren't. She lived in it sometimes, creating permutations of their life together while cleaning the guesthouse or feeding the chickens, even while Élodie talked at her, explaining a new, stupid thing she must do in order that the Struggle could struggle on, pretending to make a difference. When reality crowded out that world, she at least retained something that no strip-search or other humiliation could reveal: a final secret, a possession.

But it was an offence also, a signed pass to a concentration camp – a bullet, even, from someone in the wrong mood. She had built as much of a wall about herself as she was able, and then had willingly, wantonly, opened a door and left it ajar: this, if nothing else, she had the courage to risk willingly. If she was going to die at another's whim, it might as well be for the company of him.

While Rajmund was at Trassenheide she had been more careful; not because she feared his reaction but for the consequences of discovery, of his seeing or hearing of her punishment. She felt no shame, only regret that it had come so late, and in such circumstances. Rajmund wouldn't have understood, of course; he had the absolute certainty, like Élodie, of knowing what right was. But now he couldn't judge or be disappointed by her; he couldn't destroy their parents by telling them.

What timing, she chided herself: not to have loved any man in all the years she'd had her pick of them: the frequent, casual exercise and the slightly more memorable flirtations; the playing off, like Penelope, of earnest, would-be suitors; the constant disappointment of her hopes for someone worth having for more than a night or two. And then to find him here, in the place that fed and defined her misery – a hated enemy, a married, devoted father and, if she were honest with herself, a fool. A man, like most, who thought that time, disappointments and failing belief could be checked and reversed between an unfamiliar pair of legs. But knowing all that and not caring made it love. It was a love that didn't intensify the colour of trees and the sky, or make her hear birdsong more clearly. It didn't fill her with rapture, careless or otherwise; and certainly, it didn't make her feel younger, as it did him. But it eased the rest, and for that Zofia was grateful.

He had told her not to speak of it to anyone, as if the risks he took were comparable to hers. It was just like a man: an important man, in his world, someone who did things that very few others could. Wanting her to be impressed, he would boast about it and then smile, bashfully, as if realizing how absurd it sounded. But why shouldn't it be true? There were so many extra-ordinary things here that she didn't think not to believe him; and if it *were* true then her choice of him would seem all the less mad: just one more inexplicable thing in a place bursting with them.

The trouble – and she could see it clearly – was that small comforts quickly become big ones when others aren't available. What she could (and probably was going to) lose would hurt far more for having offered itself amid all this pain and hopelessness. It was why these hysterical thoughts of dying for him had occurred at all. Having no further prospect of happiness, she was beginning to compose herself for a final disappointment, and that should have worried her more than it did. Expecting the worst was a natural defence in her situation. But willing it was a sin, even to a non-believer like herself.

Chapter Thirty-Eight

Alone and friendless in a strange town, with a time-consuming, possibly pointless task to stretch his hours, Friedrich Holleman had expected (as someone who relished the art of seeing the worst in any situation) to be miserable. Instead, he had found a fleeting sort of paradise. Two days earlier, with a residual hangover sharpening the edges of his foul mood, he had arrived at Swinemünde and booked into *Hotel Graf von Luckner*. His low expectations of the establishment had been smoothed away almost immediately, courtesy of a sprung mattress, the best night's sleep he could recall in the twelve years since the twins arrived, and, the following morning, a semi-sumptuous breakfast – almost certainly supplied by the local black market. With that beneath his belt he had started his search, presenting himself at the gates of the first of the 'camps' (typically, two or three huts enclosed by wire, or a secured factory dormitory), where he had been refused admission. He went on to the second, and got the same. It occurred to him then that perhaps he should be acting more in the character of who he was supposed to be. At the third camp, he shouted at everyone: at the guards, the little-shit junior officer unwisely enraptured by his elevation to 'commandant', the inmates, the lot. And it had worked; after several minutes he had ticked off one of the many entries on his list, and moved on to the next.

Stupidly, he had forgotten what a piece of stamped paper did in National Socialist Germany. As far as his unwitting victims were concerned, the Army Ordnance warrant he pulled from his pocket entitled him to strut like Friedrich II across Silesia, to demand (and get) proper responses and a decent cup of coffee from the very men he had abused, to arbitrarily request lists and then to make an appropriate note in his little book while they shat themselves, and then to depart without formal goodbyes or hints as to what was going to be done thereafter.

Power, and privilege too: after five or six hours of this gentle recreation, he had the discretion to sign himself off for the day and plot a course for a shabby little bar on Swinemünde's waterfront, reconnoitred on his first evening in the town, where he could work up an appetite for his evening meal at the hotel. He had yet to discover how Baron Haussmann had improved Swinemünde, if at all; but he had given himself a brief tour of the docks, leering at the tarts, sampling fresh

Baltic mussels and gawping with other idle promenaders at the vast bulk of the *Graf Zeppelin*, Germany's first, and the world's only permanently half-completed, aircraft carrier. Though all of this was a new routine, he could conceive no alteration that would improve it. The days, he felt, could hardly be long enough to do justice to it.

His only inconveniences were an increasingly chaffed stump and the refusal of his three names to leap from the lists he'd examined so far. Eighteen camps, three thousand eight hundred inmates, of whom one hundred and seventy three were former residents of Trassenheide: nothing. All he had managed to determine to date was that the recipient camps had taken their new allocations very reluctantly, being almost embarrassed, as it were, with the riches they possessed already. Only a pioneer detachment improving the Ostbatterie defences could use almost all the hands they were given; but even there, accommodation was fully spoken for, and the commanding officer had since spent time he didn't have, trying to relocate a group of Trassenheide women he couldn't use. No one seemed to want to take more than the bare minimum of responsibility for Peenemünde's problems, and who could blame them? Not Holleman, certainly; though, as a menacing bastard from God-alone-knew-which department, he could hardly say so to any of those he now persecuted.

The much-vaunted Aryan bureaucracy had failed, naturally. The names of the new arrivals had been recorded (mostly accurately) and a headcount taken to confirm that everyone expected had arrived; but that was it. There were no further details of the workers' skills, their previous work records or any other history – all of that remained at Peenemünde and might or might not be sent on, some day. Holleman was no stickler, but it struck him that having foreigners wander around the Reich without adequate information attached of who, what or when provided opportunities for several forms of confusion, like when a Front moved forwards or backwards unexpectedly. It was on such occasions that voids opened and things got lost, or deliberately lost themselves.

So, even as he savoured the advantages of his present situation, a doubt nagged. He was tugging on a line without knowing what, if anything, was at its end, or even how long the line was. The total number of facilities in or around Swinemünde that could be termed 'labour camps' was, he had discovered, one hundred and thirty three. According to Nagel's list he could ignore half of these; but who could say whether or not some of the designated recipients of Trassenheide workers hadn't shoved them on immediately to neighbouring camps? That would be the first, most obvious recourse for a hard-pressed commandant. Several of the ones he had shouted at admitted that inter-camp transfers, or loans, occurred almost daily, and on a headcount, rather than named, basis. So perhaps he might have to visit them all. A pig of an undertaking, but it would keep him at Swinemünde for a few days more.

The largest foreign workforce in the area was based at the synthetic silk plant out at Lubin. Workers were housed on site, a camp adjoining the manufacturing area. On the third morning Holleman telephoned the works from his hotel. The civilian manager made an effort to be civil. Yes, they'd received a hundred and seven workers from Trassenheide on the afternoon of 18 August. No, they weren't all there still; four days ago the Armaments Ministry had requisitioned about a dozen men to assist with repairs at the Burmester shipyards, and these hadn't yet reported back to the works. No, he had to admit that, as his processes required skills ordinary workers didn't possess, he didn't really have much use for the new people, other than to have them help with lifting and carrying. But what was a mere manager to do when the Ministry demanded something? They were his principal, his only, customer these days and what they wanted, they got. Naturally he'd be happy to make a note of the three names and call back to let the Oberleutnant know if he'd received any or all of them.

Holleman replaced the receiver and picked up his cap from the table. He was just out of the door when the telephone rang. The *hausmeister*, whose childhood memories of the Franco Prussian War remained sharper than recollections of his breakfast, emerged arthritically from his cubicle to answer it. Fortunately, a one-and-a-half-legged Luftwaffe officer could move only slightly more precipitously, and the old man was obliged merely to shuffle to the front door and call him back.

It was Otto Fischer, eight hours premature for his daily report. Holleman had a bugger off primed and ready, but the urgency in his colleague's voice stifled it.

'It came to me in my sleep, for God's sake. The day I came to Peenemünde, the day after the transfer of workers to Swinemünde, the electric railway was still out of action.'

'Was it?'

'It re-opened about twenty-four hours after I arrived. The Trassenheide wounded and the transfers were walked or carried to Zinnowitz, the steam railway terminus.'

'So?'

'So, Freddie, how could the three workers on our list have gone with them? Did they march the three kilometres south from Peenemünde to Trassenheide in time to join the others? The five we've spoken to were busy until mid-morning at least, so it's hardly likely. In any case, who accompanied them if they did? No Germans left Peenemünde that morning for the camp – why would they? Hell, people were pouring *into* it, to help search for survivors.'

'So they went a little later that day.'

'Or they didn't go at all. Their names are on the list, and I'm betting my last bottle of Scotch that you don't find them at Swinemünde.'

'Why?'

'*Because* they're on it!'

Holleman frowned at the telephone receiver. 'I don't get that.'

'Look, there'd been a raid, the camp had been hit heavily, and the morning after they were sorting out who was to remain and who would leave to make room for the German refugees from Peenemünde, right? So, they moved the wounded and the ones who'd survived from the badly damaged huts. They brought them together, took the roll call and then shoved them out on to the road to Zinnowitz with whatever they could carry. The tally went into the book, but it must have been three names light. Now, even in the middle of all that day's confusion, I'm certain that someone was astute and dutiful enough to match names to corpses, do the arithmetic and realize that they were three short, and keen enough to remember to put them into Raffel's book when they finally turned up. If so, they'd be appended, and sticking out like a septic finger. But no, they're exactly where they should be in the order, as if they'd been gathered together with their hut mates!'

Fischer laughed aloud. 'We're being played, Freddie. Someone left a space and stuck those names carefully into the book after the event, *knowing* that we'd figure this out eventually. *Or* the names went in with the rest, even though the men weren't present. It isn't that anyone's trying to hide them. It's the opposite – they're being flagged to us.'

'Yes, but when we talk to them…'

'We won't. They aren't anywhere we're going to find them. If they were, they'd lose their value…'

'As what?'

'I … don't know.'

'They could be being marked out for the shooting.'

'I don't think so. Why complicate things? If someone, the actual perpetrators, wanted a guilty party they could have shot him while he was trying to escape. That's how it's done usually. That's the *simple* way to do it.' Fischer sighed. 'A lead, finally, and it makes no sense.'

'So what do I do? Stay here and carry on, or come back?'

'I'm telegraphing names to Swinemünde Police Headquarters, of the hundred or so workers who shared a hut with the three mystery ausländers. Pick it up, find a few of them. Get confirmation that our men didn't arrive there with the others, or follow on later that day.'

'What if they give me the wrong answer?'

'Then you're a bottle wealthier. And you don't even have to share.'

At seven o'clock that evening Fischer was waiting for Zofia to bring food and a clean shirt when the guesthouse telephone rang. It was Holleman. He was barely able to speak coherently.

'I've spent the day calling just about every camp here that's taken more than ten workers from Trassenheide. Tell Nagel the hotel bill's going to be spectacular.'

'What do you have, Freddie?'

'What *don't* I have! All those names you gave me, the ones from the three huts? Not Fucking One.'

'Eh?'

'As far as I can tell, none of the one hundred and twelve names from huts twelve, fifty-one or fifty-nine found their way on to the lists of arrivals at the camps here. And guess by how many the same lists fall short of the numbers we got from Nagel and Raffel?'

'One hundred and twelve?'

'Not yet, no. I haven't checked with the smaller camps. At the moment, it's eighty-eight. But I think we're going to find that everyone who left Trassenheide got here the same day, *except* those from the magic huts. Which means either that someone's been very precisely careless, or...'

'We're being dangled.'

'Like pheasants in a larder, waiting to smell bad. Otto, that bottle of Scotch...'

'It's yours.'

'No. We share.'

Chapter Thirty-Nine

Holleman removed his cap and wiped his forehead. Gulls swooped down almost within reach, making practice passes over his thinning hair.

'Whatever this is about, we've been written into it. It's a classic. You've got your perpetrators, your victim, your patsies and us, the stooges, the dumb kerb-pounders.'

'You read too much American detective fiction, Freddie.'

'It's very educational. They have a whole vocabulary for the stuff we do. And there's always a girl, a beautiful *dame*.'

'So, we're being pointed in a direction, or pushed, like goats. What would a Yankee investigator do now?'

'Shoot somebody. Fuck her first.'

'As in my Stettin days, the sex apart.'

'There are denouements, too. Did you have those?'

'I never saw one. They were done with, usually, by the time we were called in. The near-instinctive discovery, the lengthy recapitulation (is that the word?) and the unexpected resolution had been played out already, between the one with the knife and the one who got it. I just saw the blood, listened to the regrets, wrote out confessions and persuaded the surviving parties to agree to whatever it was we thought had happened.'

They sat upon a wooden trellis-table at the edge of the beach. Fischer had met Holleman at the Settlement station and suggested they find a discreet setting for a conversation. Sand had been an issue (*Have you seen a cripple trying to walk in the fucking stuff?*), but the location was, unquestionably, discreet. The shallow, dense zone of woodland separated the site from the Baltic so decisively that the two might have been ten kilometres apart. Even the high profile of the assembly hall had to be viewed, if at all, from the waterline. The only visible structures were the twin ruins of the War Service girls' dormitories about half a kilometre to the south, where trees had been cleared to give a view of the sea that no one had survived the raid to enjoy. The prevailing wind off the Baltic also erased any sound from the site: it might have been a moment from a decade earlier, had recent history marked its price less obviously upon the two men.

Holleman sighed. 'I don't know what to think. The effort needed to hide more than a hundred workers tells me it's a big reason, but what? Did you look at the files?'

Fischer had spent almost two days minutely examining Army Ordnance's information on its foreign workforce at Peenemünde-Wolgast-Trassenheide: two days of suffering Udo Gaschler's initially amusing but ultimately loutish monologues on the entire human condition: two days he would never re-capture and use to better purpose. He had found a mass of sloppiness and mis-information, an inexplicable disinterest in the workers whose lives they manipulated: all logged, ordered, bound and stored with impeccable efficiency. They might as well have left it at a head-count. He shook his head, saying nothing, and Holleman nodded. It wasn't as if they had been hopeful.

He took off his own cap and let the sun warm the hairless half of his scalp. 'A shooting first, that's quite straightforward. An investigation arranged, but without resources, and a deliberate effort to send us to find missing foreign workers who almost certainly know something about what happened during the raid. That isn't nearly so simple. Do we want or need to know what it is they know? We don't know, of course.'

'This is the confidential talk you wanted? To say that there isn't anything we can say?'

Fischer shrugged. 'At least we've been thrown a morsel. Look at the way it was done – the business about the workers, I mean. *That* at least tells us something.'

'Does it?'

'Why would anyone go to the trouble? If the three men – or any one of them – *had* to be removed for some reason, then it's easy. Even if there's some squeamishness about killing them, why not just arrange a transfer to, say, Courland? They'll never be heard from again. If it's a question of protecting them from us, why not remove them from the rota for that night, if it was easy enough to remove three entire huts? If anyone wants us to think that they're dead, why not find three corpses from among the many who died that evening and declare confidently, "This is N, N and N," and then box them up before we get to see them, as they did everyone except Walter Thiel? What purpose is achieved by sending them away as part of a mass evacuation, then flinging out a tease to tell us that they aren't with the rest?'

'They didn't want them dead, they don't want them alive…'

'No. Someone doesn't want us to think that they're dead, yet doesn't want us to find them alive.' Fischer frowned. 'No, not that, either. It's that someone wants us to think they're not dead.'

'So they want us to assume that the murderer is on the loose?'

'Possibly. Or that someone who has, or knows, a reason for Thiel's shooting is on the loose. But almost certainly, they don't want us to get to him, or them.'

'Why?'

'I don't know. But let's consider who's been busy.'

'Nagel, Raffel, possibly Gaschler.'

'One, two or all of them, I agree. But why not von Braun also? He decided what the *apparent* number of transferees was to be.'

'But he wasn't necessarily the one who arranged for it to be different from the number reported to the Swinemünde camps. He just needed to get rid of *X* workers.'

'Did he, though? In the early morning of 18 August there was no way of knowing just how much accommodation was going to be needed – they hadn't yet brought in all of the dead, had they? And communications were poor, so there was no way of knowing how many huts at Trassenheide had been destroyed and how many were intact. He would have needed figures for both to make any sort of calculation. It was premature, surely?'

'So why the hell was he on the telephone for two hours arranging it?'

'I don't know, Freddie, unless he had a reason for wanting to be rid of someone or something in particular. Let's assume he did, for the moment.'

'All right. So, we have four interested parties...'

'At least five. Don't forget Generalmajor Dornberger.'

Holleman groaned. 'Why make it this difficult, Otto?'

'Because one thing we *do* know is that Dornberger specifically told von Braun to undertake the arrangements. And he made it a priority in the middle of a lot of other, urgent business that morning. Besides, I'm more comfortable thinking he was involved.'

'Why, for God's sake?'

'Because he's the one who decided there should be an investigation, of a crime whose resolution is almost impossible.'

'What about the others who know of Thiel's death?'

'I don't know. I didn't get a sense of anything from them. Perhaps they rehearsed their testimony. Perhaps they don't know more than they say.'

A near-solid ridge of weed and flotsam blocked their section of the waterline; some of the birds settled on the tangle and picked at it, dragging pieces clear, washing their prizes in the water before swallowing them.

Holleman was impressed. 'Clever, aren't they? Don't they mind it salty?'

'It isn't so much. Have a taste.'

He hobbled down to the waterline and back again, frowning. 'It's a sea, isn't it?'

'The salt water lies deeper. Most of the surface layer comes from river outfalls. The two don't mix much because of the temperature difference and the lack of proper tides. It's the Baltic. Nothing about it's like anywhere else.'

'Pretty, though.'

It was: enough to discourage thinking about anything for a while. Holleman half-removed a pack of cigarettes from his tunic, sniffed the air and replaced them unopened. Fischer closed his eyes and listened to the sea's small sounds, breathed the air, felt the warmth and thought once more of the time when it was all too familiar to notice. It seemed longer ago than it actually was, however he measured it: by wrinkles, wounds, disappointments, loss. A personal stone age, set in a substratum somewhere beyond the actual lapse of years.

'We should put your girlfriend in there somewhere.' Holleman had shovelled together a pile of sand with his good leg and was making tread marks in it with the bad.

Fischer replaced his cap. 'I know, but where? If she were the killer, they'd have put her in a grave by now. If she knows something about who did it, or who might want it done, then likewise. I suppose it's just possible we've been lured to what's really a secret Polish facility, and she's in charge.'

'If it was, everything would work by now, at a fraction of the cost. You're forgetting the German genius for taking great ideas and cacking them, expensively. Come on, I need a drink.'

They returned to Peenemünde, a matter of a few steps into another world. Two guards, guarding nothing in particular, saluted smartly, and Holleman tapped the rim of his cap with a stick he'd picked up on the beach. It was something he'd seen Field Marshal Rommel do, in a newsreel. There had been sand there too, he recalled; plenty of it.

'Otto?'

Fischer slowed. 'Sorry, Freddie. Am I walking too quickly?'

'We don't quite know why we're here, do we?'

'No, we don't.'

'But we know what they've been bothered about, don't we? I mean, we know that there have been problems with things, yes?'

'We do.'

'Well, then. Forget about what happened during and after the raid. Let's imagine for a moment that it's not relevant. Or, if it *is*, that it's part of a clean-up. If that were so, we've been chasing the tail, not the snout. What about *before* Thiel's death? These are big men doing big things – I mean, fuck, the *Führer* thinks they're great fellows, doesn't he? Are they going to all this trouble over the corpse of a man who was dead anyway, one way or the other? Why don't we start thinking about what really worries them?'

'Yes, but...'

'Look at what was wrong, what we *know* was wrong. We should think about that instead.'

'And if it's a waste of time?'

'How could it be? If we find nothing, then it's one more item to scratch off a list that's so long we can't even see the end of it anyway. But if we make just one person nervous, asking all our questions about what they do, how it's done, why it still isn't done, well...'

Slowly, Fischer nodded. 'You're right. If we can't find a motive we're doomed anyway. And I know where we can make a start.'

'With whom, may I ask?'

'You may. With a disappointed man who probably yearns to tell someone why.'

Chapter Forty

Belatedly, Fischer noticed that Godomar Schubert's uniform was that of a full colonel. Both he and Holleman saluted formally.

'Please sit, gentlemen.'

Holleman obeyed, and with hardly a pause leaned forward, earnestly. 'Sorry for the interruption, Herr Oberst. We're trying to speak to everyone here about security. You'll have heard?'

'It would have been hard to avoid.' The sour expression hadn't moved a centimetre. 'I can't see how it's necessary. We have hundreds of soldiers here, devoted to keeping people in or out.'

'But it's a matter of how it's arranged. Whether or not it can be *improved*.'

'Can it?'

'Of course, sir. Things can always be improved. You are in charge of the Pilot Production Plant, I understand?'

Fischer winced. He might have tried to be gentle.

'No, I'm not. I was, until changes were made.'

'Oh?' Holleman was innocently intrigued. 'I'm sorry. May I ask what it is that you do now?'

Schubert tapped his desk with a pen, viciously. 'I'm responsible for putting Peenemünde back to work. You may have noticed that the British paid us a visit recently?'

'I did, sir, yes. A most important task, of course.

I'd imagine one would need a very organized mind to...'

'Oberleutnant, if I need a massage I'll pay a tart to do it! Do you have any pertinent questions?'

'If I may...?' Fischer raised a finger and smiled apologetically at his colleague. 'Herr Oberst, as you *were* in charge of the plant, may I ask what the approximate total of foreign workers employed in that area might be?'

'It *was* about two hundred, but of course, that was before the raid, and in the pre-production phase. I should imagine the number has declined since then, as...' he smiled for the first time, '...we are to lose that part of our operation to the SS.'

'Yes, Generalmajor Dornberger mentioned it. He seemed ... disappointed.'

'Is that what he told you?' Schubert smirked. 'I took quite a different impression.'

'Really? Well, it isn't any of our concern, of course, but I would imagine that the change is going to alter how things are structured. Won't a return to pure research...?'

'It won't just be that. Or, perhaps, not *even* that. Technical problems will continue, and the new production facilities are going to need all the help that we can provide. It's just a case of production moving elsewhere, and we must adapt to it.'

'You say problems, sir?'

Schubert sighed, and it struck Fischer that he did so in almost precisely the same way as Kaspar Nagel, Walther von Braun, Arthur Rudolph and everyone else who had expressed an opinion on anything to do with production.

'Do you have any idea how difficult it is to implement a new *field* of technology in a practical manner? We aren't building upon others' efforts here, or modifying existing models. This is the wellspring of an entirely untested applied science, which means that we're adapting dozens of related disciplines. We try to explain this...'

'Yes?'

'Never mind.'

'But of course, problems of any nature may very well have an impact upon how security protocols are applied...'

Again, the sigh. 'I was merely going to observe that it's difficult to explain to a layman why, in this case, production isn't simply a matter of numbers. Given our latest *proposed* schedule, it's obvious that technological issues will have to be resolved even as production commences. Also, the mix of technologies will itself have an impact upon the *rate* of production.'

'Why is that?'

'Which do you think is simpler to make? A wooden sword or a machine-pistol?'

'Ah.'

Schubert relaxed a little. 'Hauptmann, have you ever met a politician?'

They all grinned.

'Speaking for myself, I had met very few *real* politicians until about a year ago. Of course, Reichsminister Speer is one, if only by virtue of necessity, but he hardly qualifies as he regards the profession *per se* with a degree of distaste. No, I refer to those men who hold power as an occupation, an end, in itself. I've found that their perspectives often clash with our understanding of realities.'

'Perhaps they have a wider vision.'

'Oh, they certainly do. Or hallucination, perhaps.'

Fischer and Holleman glanced at each other. The interview had ceased to be discreet.

Schubert waved at a wall, across which were scattered a series of photographs. 'Look at that, the A4 project. In terms of manpower, resources and time, a memorable undertaking. I'd even say momentous, and I'm less prone to overstatement than some of my colleagues. But of course, I'm an Army man also, and we soldiers should think of practicalities, yes?'

Fischer and Holleman nodded knowingly.

'Don't misunderstand me. We're at war, so expectations of any project that's consumed as much time and effort as this *should* be high. But not impossibly so, not to the point at which all common sense fails. What do you think of it?'

He was waving at the wall once more.

Fischer coughed. 'A very great achievem...'

'No, I mean, as a soldier. To what *use* would you put it?'

'Well...'

'Yes, *well*. Precisely what we've come up with. The A4 carries a one thousand kilogram amatol warhead to an approximate point far more quickly than current counter-measures can anticipate. It is guided, if that's the word, by its external fins, which are trimmed before launch to achieve the necessary azimuth. For lateral stabilization in flight, there are two internal gyroscopes – we considered using radio beams, but it's probable that the British could develop effective interference measures quite quickly, and we don't want the things just falling out of the sky, or sent straight back to us, do we? An accelerometer trips engine cut-off at the required distance to objective, the missile drops to the ground and detonates on impact. What do you think?'

Fischer considered the photographs and searched for the appropriate phrasing. 'It seems to require a degree of...'

'Luck, I think, is the word you're looking for – or perhaps *enhancement*. The warhead needs to be much more powerful, or the guidance system much more accurate, to make the weapon a military resource. It is, at present, an indiscriminate device, a vengeance weapon. Gentlemen, we're going to make the British pay for Hamburg.'

Holleman shrugged. 'Still, that's worth doing.'

'Yes? Well, before I begin to list what needs to be done to make it sufficiently reliable even to do that, consider these facts, Oberleutnant. To reach England from the Low Countries we estimate that each missile will burn fuel requiring some twenty-eight to thirty tonnes of potatoes to manufacture, fuel that will not be put into more accurate weapons or, indeed, into German stomachs. Each missile's production cost – excluding labour, of course – has been estimated at approximately one hundred thousand reichsmarks. So for every two we manufacture we shall be foregoing, say, five Bf 109s or four FW 190s. And, of course, each missile will divert a thousand kilograms of precious amatol from weapons that can deliver it far, far more effectively, and on to valuable *military* targets.'

'It sounds almost as if you don't want it to succeed, if I may say so, Herr Oberst.'

'It *can't* succeed, Hauptmann. That's my point. *That* is where we have a problem with language. Do you know what the A4 really is? A test-bed. A brilliant, wondrous test-bed that will, eventually, allow us to create a new and highly deadly weapon. The A4 is *not* that weapon. Why? Because our intentions have moved too far ahead of the available technology. We wish to do what is not yet possible. Materials fail us, the physics mocks us, and our existing testing procedures are inadequate even to the task of allowing us to understand what we've managed to create. You've seen the guidance and control laboratory?'

Fischer nodded. 'An impressive display.'

'Isn't it? Unfortunately, that's almost all it is, a display. We have a radio signal system to report the rocket parameters in flight, code name *Messina*. Werhner von Braun detests it. He thinks it so unreliable that whenever we launch an A4, he just strolls outside with a pair of binoculars and watches the thing going up and coming down. He says he can derive more valuable data that way, and he's probably correct. No, gentleman. We're overstepping present capabilities by some

distance, and ambition falls into the gap between. Would you like my prediction?'

Fischer nodded.

'I will of course ask you not to repeat this but,
now that the SS have their hands upon production, and anticipating their methods with
regards to labour, I confidently expect more
people to die *making* the missiles than will die
beneath them. Of course, the principal blame for
all of this lies at our door.'

'Our?'

'All of us, here, at Peenemünde. We've allowed
ourselves to become seduced by a vision so removed from present necessities that we created,
in effect, a self-feeding paradox. To realize the
vision we require unlimited commitment. Those
who make that commitment, who supply the
means, have the greatest interest in seeing the
vision re-fashioned. Yet we persisted long after
this became apparent because seduction has a
habit of blurring vision, does it not?'

Fischer nodded, said nothing.

'It was just a matter of getting others to *see* the
vision, we thought. All our efforts were devoted
to it – the predictions, the invitations to test
launches of one or two missiles for which we'd
cannibalized the parts of a dozen others, the
lavish entertainments at which the Generalmajor
drew incredible, inaccurate vistas of a coming
military miracle. All of it to ensure the continuity
of the thing we were witlessly sabotaging.'

He fell silent, and stared at his open palms.
Holleman nudged Fischer with his knee.

'Herr Oberst, if I may be frank...?'

309

Schubert laughed sourly. 'Oh, I think you may.'

'Since we've been here, a lot has been said to us about production, but not so forthrightly. It seems to me that the fact this poisoned chalice, this thing that distracts, is being taken away by the Reichsführer should be an occasion for relief. And yet no one's rejoicing.'

'Were all things equal this would be the case, yes. But there isn't any possibility of Peenemünde being released from its obligation to see the A4 put into use. As I said, we'll be with them throughout the production process, because no one else has the relevant expertise. And, because we now have the undivided attention of those whose interest we sought so industriously, any future research carried out here will be carefully monitored. At worst, we may be reduced to little more than providing support and testing facilities for what the SS can manage to produce.'

'You've grabbed a crocodile's tail.'

Schubert smiled at Holleman. 'Succinctly put, Oberleutnant. We really should have kept our heads down and placed our faith in Army Ordnance. At least *they* didn't mind letting us play with our toys in our own way.'

Fischer stood up. 'We've taken enough of your time, Herr Oberst. I began by mentioning foreign workers. To your knowledge, approximately how many of them are employed here in a purely technical capacity?'

'Production had a few, perhaps twenty, mainly assisting in the priming of explosive charges and metalworking. In the Experimental and Development Shops another forty or so. But you'd have to speak to someone like Wehrner to get a more accurate idea of how they're employed. I suppose your biggest concern is the ausländers?'

'It was, yes, Herr Oberst. But now that the British and, perhaps, the Americans, have taken an interest also, I hardly think we can afford slack habits, whoever's at fault.'

'What did you think?'

Fischer and Holleman walked through the Experimental Works. Rain was forecast for the late afternoon, but this hadn't prevented some of the female staff from getting the most out of their summer wardrobe. Holleman tried not to stare, but his heart wasn't in it.

'Of Schubert? That he was being very honest. Irresponsibly so.'

'He wanted us to know, didn't he? Why did he suppose he could trust us with it?'

'Your amiable half-face, perhaps, or my playful charm.'

'A few days ago Dornberger told me that he was glad to be rid of production. I wonder *how* glad? I wonder how keen he was before that to actually retain it?'

'The air raid made a big difference.'

'It did. But enough to make him go entirely about-face? To cheerfully throw away a strategy that's been building for a decade now? The logic of what's going to happen – dispersal of resources after an attack, downgrading of a known target, it's all solid. I just can't see why Dornberger appears to be giving in so graciously. What does he imagine he's going to be left with once production goes underground? You heard Schubert. Who'd wish to supervise a testing range?'

'He's a general. As long as he's got someone to order about he'll be happy. Generals lacking that are called schützes.'

'I don't think the man even cares about his rank. From what I understand they throw him a new one every six months. What he cares about is what he *does*, and now he's going to be doing much less of it.'

'What's this?'

Outside the guesthouse a DKW half blocked the path. A solid looking feldwebel with a machine-pistol and blue GFP straps stood beside it, inviting comments about his parking. He watched Fischer and Holleman approach with the sort of studied neutrality that field interrogation school teaches on day one, and he didn't come to attention. The guesthouse door was wide open. Fischer was fairly certain he hadn't been careless. Not about that, at least.

Chapter Forty-One

In one sense, she felt relieved. At least she wouldn't be asked to do anything stupid, not today. But it was change, sudden change, and Zofia had learned to fear anything that wasn't part of a routine.

Élodie hadn't turned up for her shift that morning. Had they worked in an office it

312

wouldn't have signified anything, but here you didn't get to take the day off. There were no migraines, no period pains, colds didn't exist, and pneumonia was only recognized as such when they filled in the cause-of-death paperwork. So there was a Reason for it, and that made Zofia nervous. None of the other Poles would know anything, so it wasn't worth asking them. Gerhardt didn't have a smirk on his face, so it didn't seem as though Élodie had been punished for one of her many offences – at least, not publicly.

Today there was little chatter in the kitchens. At lunchtime the top men were going to be entertaining visitors from the Armaments Ministry, so everything had to be better than usual. That might have been another reason why Gerhardt didn't look happy: he had been promoted far above his abilities while the real cook (a former canteen manager) recovered from wounds inflicted by the British. Gerhardt could do dumplings, but his technique with everything else was to just throw stuff into pans and hope that it worked. Zofia could see him through the doorway, by the preparation tables, biting his nails. His assistants were useless: a local boy with a cleft palate, more shy than a field mouse, who needed to be told everything three times; a retired chicken farmer who'd never cooked a chicken in his life; and two mostly silent local women, the youngest of whom was about seventy. What they did, collectively, counted for a war atrocity. Every day Zofia watched perfectly good, fresh ingredients being brought in on the

313

truck and then reduced to pig-food by the strict application of indolence and surly haplessness. The profligacy of it so appalled her that she had sometimes been tempted to offer to help, but volunteering was the quickest route to a slap from Gerhardt. Without any sense of duty himself, he assumed that others were equally sly, or playing some game.

For a while at least he was king here, but the crown sat uneasy today. If the bosses tired of the violence he did to food he could find himself on the street, forced to eat from a ration card instead of having his pick of whatever came through the back door. And she, like all the other *zivilarbeiter* here, knew perfectly well that he took far more food than he could eat himself. He was a profiteer: a death sentence if he was caught, a kicking if he failed his customers. So today, she thought, it might work; and if it did, she could ask something in return.

'Sir?'

'What?' He half lifted a hand, but let it fall when he saw Zofia. She wasn't just one of the potato-peeling Three Fates, to be hit whenever he needed the exercise. If she turned up at the guesthouse with bruises the important Germans would ask questions, and Gerhardt – a very unimportant one – wouldn't have an answer.

'I can do ... recipes, sir. Polish food. Here...'

She waved a hand around the tables, taking in the foodstuffs that were stacked there, '...everything needed.'

The chicken farmer paused in his abuse of something involving cabbage, and screwed up his face. 'Who'd want to eat *that* shit?'

'Shut up, Wolfram.' Gerhardt looked carefully at her, trying to work out the play. 'Why? What do you want?'

'Nothing, sir.'

He considered this doubtfully. To Gerhardt, doing something for nothing wasn't a normal human activity. 'Nothing at all?'

'Just to do it, sir. I enjoyed cooking, in Poland. I wouldn't tell anyone. I wouldn't say.'

Why would she? It would gain her nothing but punishment. Gerhardt pursed his lips, but she sensed that he was interested. The chance to add to his thin repertoire was too tempting to dismiss.

'What? You'd cook what?'

She scanned the tables. 'Soup, sir. *Kapuŝniak* with sauerkraut. And *gołąbki...*'

'What the fuck's *that?*'

'Cabbage leaves with meat, minced up meat, and potato dumplings, *pyzy.*'

Gerhardt nodded approvingly. *Dumpling* was a word with which he was very comfortable. 'Pudding?'

Again, Zofia looked around. A dessert was more difficult. The kitchens had no honey and few nuts, she was sure of that. But Germans had sweet tooths, so...

'*Chałka*, sir. Sweet bread pudding.' She hoped to her Christian God that he didn't know it was a Jewish dish.

It was all too stodgy, too heavy to be balanced; Zofia would never willingly have served these dishes together, not at one meal. But heavy food

315

was Gerhardt's speciality. He nodded again, like he was doing her a kindness. 'Show us.'

It shredded her nerves, trying to give instructions to five Germans in an appropriately respectful manner. The two old women grasped everything the first time, but the boy – Kurt – had to be watched like a kettle, because whatever she told him to do he did the wrong way. At least he was only being inept. Wolfram was determined to find a better method, a German method, for each step of each recipe, to the point at which Gerhardt almost used his paring knife with intent. But slowly it began to resemble food – a novelty in this room recently. Zofia herself prepared the *chałka*, and it took her almost an hour to find the courage to ask Gerhardt if there were any raisins she might add to it. It wasn't authentic, she admitted, but the bosses might like it.

She tried to judge the moment when the real question might be least likely to offend him, but it was difficult; there had to be a context, she couldn't just blurt it out. Strangely, it was the malevolent Wolfram, suspiciously sniffing the bubbling *kapuśniak*, who gifted it to her.

'This is too much work.'

Gerhardt, his tongue protruding as he attempted to stuff the cabbage leaves, ignored him, but Zofia pounced upon it. 'Sir?'

'What?'

'Élodie could help. She knows cooking, too.'

'No, she can't.'

That wasn't helpful. Zofia couldn't think of a way to begin again, to re-frame the question.

Fortunately Gerhardt hadn't finished. He stepped back from his latest piece and glanced with satisfaction at the thirty or so that he'd done already.

'Kurt. Put more leaves in the boiling water. She's gone home.'

For a moment Zofia didn't realize that the remark was for her. 'Home, sir?'

'Home. To France, stinking wen of whores and ponces. She's finished here.' He paused and frowned. 'Wasn't her time, yet.'

Élodie couldn't have gone home. She'd have said something about it or at least tried a final grand manipulation to some great, foolish purpose, perhaps demanded that Zofia steal a missile for her to take back to France. But Gerhardt wouldn't have lied, not about that; if something bad had happened he'd have been delighted to deliver the news, and savour the details of it.

It wasn't the precise circumstance of Élodie's going that worried Zofia, but the timing. Coming so quickly after the encounter in the General-major's office and the incomprehensible behaviour of the bosses, it un-nerved her. She couldn't see how the two could be connected, but she'd learned not to believe in coincidence: everything meant something in this place. She had done a stupid thing, had been caught doing it, and now its instigator, Élodie, had been set as free as any Frenchwoman could be. If there were a price for any of this, only one person would be paying.

She felt a sudden, strong urge to get out of the

317

kitchen, to get advice.

'Sir?'

'What?'

'I have to clean the guesthouse, sir. Before the Hauptmann returns.'

Gerhardt frowned, looking around. All the portions of food they had prepared lay neatly on trays, mostly covered by cloths, ready for a final turn in the ovens before being served up. There wasn't yet enough of the soup and main course, but at least they knew how not to spoil it. He tossed his head in the direction of the door.

'Wait.' He went over to one of the bread baskets, lifted out a loaf, broke it in half and held out one of the pieces. 'Get out.'

In the rear pantry Zofia found the Three Fates, furiously peeling more potatoes for the *pyzy*. She gave the bread to Malwina, the nearest of them. Swiftly, it was broken into three and stuffed into grateful mouths. She didn't need it for herself. For the past week she'd eaten better than at any time since 1939: her lover had made sure of that. But he might have to make sure of something else if her sense of things toppling silently upon her wasn't groundless.

Chapter Forty-Two

These two weren't GFP, despite their driver. Fischer had expected the worst, but the uniforms were nondescript, without field insignia other than rank: a major and an oberleutnant. And they were far too clean and pressed – elegant, even, like they'd dropped in on their way to an expensive lunch. It almost screamed *Abwehr*.

The major smiled pleasantly, which more or less confirmed it.

'Hauptmann Fischer and Oberleutnant Holleman, I believe?'

'That's correct, sir.'

'Well, now, there are four of us, and only three seats. I think then that I shall stand, but please…'

It couldn't have been done more courteously. Inevitably, the major drew a cigarette case from his tunic and offered it. They declined, though Fischer guessed it had been a struggle for Holleman. They looked to be genuine Turkish.

'I won't insult you by playing games whose rules you know too well, Hauptmann, so I'd appreciate it if you'd return the compliment. You should know that I have the authority to enter this site without prior permission, to question anyone and to depart without offering an explanation. That would be rude, however. Let me say that I'm extremely interested in anomalies, and you appear to be one. A wounded veteran, working now as a

Luftwaffe war reporter but seconded here to examine...?'

He glanced at his subordinate, who was perfectly versed in the game the major promised he wasn't going to play.

'Security, sir.'

'That's right. Fascinating. Do you know, in my experience this sort of thing is highly unusual? The Reich is absolutely replete with agencies qualified to advise upon matters of security – my own included – yet the commander at Peenemünde lights upon a former Kriminal-kommisar whose present function is, what, dissemblance? I have to say, it doesn't strike me as a likely choice.'

'Apparently, Herr Major, I was recommended. It certainly wasn't *my* choice.'

'Yes, by Felix Linnemann. I had no idea that Herr Generalmajor Dornberger had the leisure to take an interest in football. But then a man's hobbies are *his* business, aren't they? Tell me, did you excel in your work at Stettin?'

'Not at all, sir. That's partly why I resigned.'

'And became an elite soldier. One who would follow orders far beyond the point that most men would consider prudent.'

'Prudence isn't my strongest vice. I'm here, after all.'

The major turned to his aide. 'You see, Sandi-zell? Modesty, commitment, discretion. I begin to see why the Generalmajor chose him after all.'

'Major...?'

'Schell. Air Intelligence.'

From a sitting position Fischer found it diffi-

320

cult to nod formally. 'You see more than I do, sir. To be truthful, the choice has been puzzling me since I arrived here. I'm just trying to do the job as well as I'm able.'

'Precisely what is that "job"?'

'To review security, how things are organized at this site. It's an extremely unusual facility, both in what it does and how it does it. I have no idea what criteria the Generalmajor applied in deciding that I should take it on.'

'And what are your conclusions?'

'Had I arrived at any, I should have passed them on to Generalmajor Dornberger. I certainly wouldn't discuss them with you, sir.'

For the first time Fischer glimpsed a nerve-ending. Schell frowned. 'Hauptmann, please don't misunderstand the purpose of my questions. The Reich faces hundreds of millions of enemies, all hoping for its extinction. You of all people should understand that clearly. Highly secret experiments are conducted here, and there are several thousand foreigners who may have access to information that might damage all our futures. Your feelings, your professional honour, aren't relevant here.'

'I agree, Herr Major. But the command structure certainly is, otherwise *those enemies* would be over the wire quicker than a rat through a pipe. So, please carry on with your threats, and then I can go and ask the Generalmajor why Abwehr imagines it's got pull here.'

Holleman stifled a laugh. Schell's finely shaped nostrils widened a little, but he was very good.

'Why did you go to the labour camps at Swinemünde?'

Fair enough. 'Again, sir, a matter of security. Many of the facility's workers have been transferred to the town, so it's natural that we should try to keep track of them.'

'You have suspicions? Of foreign workers who've been employed here?'

'We don't suspect anyone of anything. We're simply trying to find three men who seem to have been lost between Peenemünde and Swinemünde. *That* fact makes me interested. Otherwise, they may be as innocent as angels.'

Schell nodded. 'May I ask their names? We may be able to assist if they've absconded. Regrettably, it's something of which we and the GFP have an ever increasing amount of experience.'

'Certainly. Oberleutnant, do you have our names, please?'

Sourly, Holleman recited them from memory while Fischer watched Schell and Sandizell closely. It was there: a slight start, an effort not to glance at each other.

'Can you tell me when these men went missing?'

'On 18 August I believe, some time after the British bombers departed. They may, of course, have taken advantage of the missing perimeter fence. We can't say, as yet.'

'Is there anything else about them that you find interesting?'

Fischer shrugged. 'I've no information other than that they've been employed as labourers here. One was a volunteer – and a Judas, from what I've heard. The other two are *zivilarbeiter.* They're probably trying to get home, so perhaps something might be done at that end?'

Schell made a note. 'There *is* the possibility, of course, that these men are spies or saboteurs. Would it then be likely that they took the identities of dead men and fled? That you are, perhaps, looking for the wrong men?'

'I considered that, but it seems unlikely.'

'How so?'

'Three men are missing, not one. Three men who would need new lives. So, who would steal the identities of two Poles and a Slovakian except men of precisely those nationalities? If they got it wrong they'd be taken at the first checkpoint they attempted to cross. Are we saying then that these men, with minutes at most to affect an escape, tripped over three appropriate corpses, lifted three sets of undamaged papers and slid away? It doesn't seem likely. Nor, of course, that the features of each of the three corpses in question were sufficiently obliterated for the subterfuge to go undiscovered.'

'No, perhaps not.' Schell returned the notebook to his breast pocket. 'Well, thank you for that, Hauptmann, and forgive my abruptness earlier – one sometimes forgets the necessary courtesies. But let me say that we, also, have an interest in what happens here. The precise nature of that interest needn't concern you – we, too, have lines of command. But it would be a great pity if the ball fell because two hands couldn't agree to move in the same direction. Sandizell, please give Hauptmann Fischer our telephone number.'

It was an embossed card: Wehrkreis II Liaison Office, Stettin. The address was Fischer's old building, Police Headquarters. *Small world.*

'Of course, there's nothing I can do to make you call, but please think about what I've said. Goodbye.'

When the DKW had disappeared Fischer returned to the sitting room.

'Freddie, when did you return from Swinemünde?'

'About eight hours ago.'

'And they get someone here before it goes dark, who knows already what you've been doing? Who's been talking?'

Holleman considered this. 'Some of the little snots I knocked about?'

'Possibly. If Abwehr are working out of Military headquarters at Stettin they'd only be down the corridor from the Todt office, or whatever it's called these days. But so quickly – to put it all together, what we're doing, why we were looking at the camps? When you were given the shoulder by some of their commandants, who did you tell them to call?'

'Dornberger.'

They looked at each other. Fischer had read somewhere that American skyscrapers were fitted with elevators so fast that one momentarily imagined the floor disappearing as they descended. It was probably an exaggeration, like most things done and said by the Amis. Who, after all, would subject themselves to such an experience if they knew it was coming? But the sensation at least he understood. It was one he recalled from a dozen occasions in Belgium, Norway, Crete and the Ukraine. Different circumstances each time, but the same, sudden awareness of being somewhere at the end of a bad decision, waiting for the consequences to arrive.

Holleman was shaking his head. He seemed quite overcome. 'What game is it that he's playing?'

Game: an activity, generally providing amusement; a diversion affording entertainment; a re-creation requiring tactical decisions to achieve an end; the employment of hapless former policemen in byzantine manoeuvres designed to confound, to mislead and to demoralize, to no discernible purpose.

Fischer went to the sideboard and extracted the third, final bottle. 'Get the glasses. We'll see if we can guess the rules.'

Chapter Forty-Three

Achym, seeking to avoid trouble, found the sort he couldn't have anticipated: the entirely un-provoked, nobody's-fault-but-God's sort. And it brought him attention.

He had pushed hard for work while the brief re-building cycle lasted, trying to bribe his way on to every gang that was sent up to Peene-münde. It was dangerous: no longer having pet guards to fix it for him, he had to risk the kicks and rifle butts that came of accidentally approaching one of the rare straight *schwabs* at Trassenheide. But when his luck held, he managed to get nodded on to a truck, and most days he was helping to fix up part of what the British had knocked down.

After the raid he had been one of a gang assembled to shore up the exposed north face of the Brandenburg Tor, where all the unmarried engineers lived. It had been a rushed job, and the struts had since started to slip; so little more than a week later he found himself with another set of Poles and Russians, staring up at the familiar mess and wondering what to try next. The dolt who was guarding them stared too, yawned, and then had the thought that a couple more struts might do it.

The bachelor quarters had been cleared of residents *and* their possessions, so Achym knew that this wasn't likely to be a profitable job. A willing face usually got fed, however, so when the dolt asked for a volunteer to climb up and clear rubble from the sliver of upper hallway that now hung almost in mid-air, he raised his hand. Getting up there was easy enough: he used one of the existing struts almost like a staircase, walking like an ape, half-upright but grasping the wood as he climbed. When he reached the ledge and clambered on to it, one of the Russians threw up his spade.

The hallway retained few reminders of its former bourgeois charm. The wallpaper, a pastiche of old Viennese views, held on to a triangular patch of plaster above a corner table, which Achym's practiced thief's eye told him was too badly damaged to trade. But beneath it, and almost certainly upon it once, was a small, entirely intact, Dresden china flower-girl, the sort of bauble that the old, peacetime Achym Mazur would have regarded as symptomatic of degeneracy, or childlessness, in its owner. What, he wondered, was it doing in a bachelor apartment? The unwanted image of a pansy's boudoir, where a couple of beefy florenzers had exercised their preferences discreetly, slid to mind. He didn't care; this was gold-standard currency, perhaps forty cigarettes or more, a bribe to get him safely into a hut of his choice, perhaps even a new pet guard. All he required was a stratagem to get it out of the Settlement without one of the others staking a claim.

If only she'd held her arms demurely by her sides, she could have gone straight down his trousers. But the winsome bitch was waving to someone, or picking another flower; whichever it was, she'd stick out like a blanket-snake if he pushed her down there. So it had to be his armpit. Carefully, he clutched her there and closed his jacket, picked up the spade and very gently pushed rubble over the edge of the hallway floor on to the piles below. That was fine; one of the guards told him to fucking move himself, but without any real energy. The problem came when he had finished and needed to return to ground level. The spar he'd climbed was too steep to run down, and there was no way he could use both arms and not break or lose the little Madonna of the Pansies. So he improvised, catastrophically. He tossed down his spade, reversed and tried to back down the spar using his one free hand for support. It worked for about six seconds, and then, to the delight and applause of the other workers, he fell gracelessly onto the rubble beneath. He landed on her, of course, and as she went off to porcelain heaven she returned the favour, stabbing his chest to a depth of almost three centimetres with her *heil*'d arm.

Even the guards winced when they saw the wound, and told him to get himself back to Trassenheide. He walked, of course; no trucks were returning at that time of day, and his sort weren't allowed on the railway. By the time he reached the camp he was getting dizzy, but one of the men in his tent had been a doctor in the days before Poles discovered that they couldn't do things like that. All he could find was some industrial detergent, which he poured straight into the wound and then stood back, to let Achym get the screaming out of his system. When the patient stopped convulsing, he put in a couple of stitches with a domestic sewing needle. That night, Achym needed the rain, beating on the canvas above his head, to send him off to a more comfortable unconsciousness, and as he went he sensed that he was becoming slightly feverish. Still, he'd probably been as fortunate as any man who'd lost a golden chance to improve himself, been stabbed by a new girlfriend and hadn't eaten that day could expect.

But the wound was deep, and industrial detergent isn't meant to stem bacterial infections, so the hours that followed were considerably less comfortable. He couldn't work the following day, and by evening he was running enough of a temperature to soak his clothes and make him talk without the very necessary appreciation that he was doing so. Fortunately, there were still a few Christian souls left in the world. Two of them, tent mates, took it in turns that night to mop his head and try to get as much water into him as they could; but at dawn the general opinion was that the boy was on his way.

'He needs medicine,' said the solicitor's clerk from Krakow, who had been caught running a trade in ration coupons.

'And I need Pola Negri's tongue on my balls,' replied the blameless Lvov architect, 'so we've both got shitty luck.'

Achym rallied a little after being fed watery cabbage soup: enough to ask one of them to find Venus, as she was known generally among Trassenheide's male constituency. His nurses assumed that this was in the way of a last request: an admirable but probably doomed choice, though one that they might have made themselves had they thought of it. But he persisted as long as he had strength, and that sort of thing can be persuasive. The architect went to find her before the trucks left for Peenemünde.

She had never heard of Marcin Konopka, and so came very reluctantly, and only because the architect embellished the detail of the man's ordeal. She saw the error immediately, of course; he was just about conscious, and breathlessly asked his nurses to give them a little room. She leaned closer to catch what he was saying, so close that a healthier Achym might have had all sorts of ideas, and he whispered to her what he'd rehearsed with as many of his wits as he'd managed to retain.

He reassured her that she wasn't under any sort of obligation. What he'd done for Rajmund had been dangerous, certainly; but it was a gift to a friend, and no return was expected. He told her – and this was the most honest thing he said – that he was probably dying for want of medicine, because (at this point he shifted slightly, to give her a better view of the seeping mess beneath his armpit) he had an infected wound, and the camp had no facilities to deal with infections as the previous month's great shitting contest had proved.

He told her that he knew she had access to some areas of Peenemünde that other foreign workers never saw. He wanted her to know that he absolutely refused to allow her to put herself in any danger on his behalf; but, if it was at all possible, he'd be forever indebted to her, to the uttermost point of his ability to repay, if she could smuggle out a dose or two of any sort of sulfonamide that was available at the medical centre there. He stressed that he wouldn't be at all disappointed if she was unable to do this, as it was much preferable that she avoided trouble. But, if it *was* possible...

He considered it a very good sign that she'd taken his hand about halfway through this supplication, and on other days he would have paid cigarettes for the experience. But all he could

manage now was a slightly pained look to emphasize the embarrassment he felt at bothering
her with his troubles. She sighed, a beautiful
sound, and told him that it *wasn't* at all possible:
that she was being watched far more carefully
these days. She said that what he'd done for
Rajmund had been a wonderful, brotherly thing,
and that she'd never forget it; that, if she had
been the sort to pray, she would have knelt
without hesitation and begged God for his life.
But she knew that there wasn't a chance of her
being able to get into Peenemünde's small
medical facility, and even if some miracle allowed
her entry, she knew neither where the drugs were
kept nor which of them would help him.

To all of this, Achym nodded feebly, and tried
to return the squeeze. He told her that she'd
better go: the trucks would be departing for the
site soon, and he didn't want her to be in
trouble. He thanked her for coming, and said
that God would bless her for her kindness. As
she stood to leave he made sure that she caught
sight of him turning his face to the canvas wall:
his goodbye to life. And when he was quite sure
that she'd gone to find her truck, he turned
again and weakly asked the solicitor's clerk
whether there was any chance of a little more of
that cabbage soup; because fever or not, he was
fucking starving.

Chapter Forty-Four

'Let us ... recapitulate. That *is* the word, isn't it? Recapitulate all of what we've capitulated already.'

Holleman giggled.

'Seriously. Let's think about *him*, not a death at Peenemünde. What, at this point, would make us worry?'

They sat silently for a while, each trying to put words to their itches.

Holleman began. 'He's not telling us something.'

'He's playing games with his foreign workers.'

'He wants to lose production, but then he used to want to keep it, very much.'

'He's talking to Abwehr, who know at least something of what's going on here. But we can't say what, precisely.'

'He doesn't shoot beautiful female spies when he should.'

'He doesn't mind us knowing this. In fact, he seems to *want* us to know parts of it. So...'

Fischer and Holleman looked at each other. *So* required many more known elements before the equation began to make sense.

Zofia had brought their evening meal, a stewed concoction of potatoes, onions, carrots, barley and ... mutton, probably, though Holleman swore that he had tasted squirrel once and it was just like this, only saltier. Aware now of the arrangements he kept his leg attached in the evenings until after she returned to take away the empty dishes, and in the meantime 'eased' the chaffing by rubbing it almost constantly.

Fischer too felt an ache, and noticed that for some time he'd been flexing his bad arm and hand almost precisely to the rhythm of Holleman working his leg. As he stopped his friend grinned and did the same.

'Like dumber versions of Pavlov's dogs.'

After dinner they'd sat upon the sitting-room floor, backs to the wall, trying to ease their several private discomforts while distilling answers from confusion and not dozing off before darkness fell. Fischer watched his friend vainly trying to adjust himself into a more comfortable position.

'You should have a soak, Freddie. Try the mineral salts in the bathroom cupboard.'

Holleman grimaced. 'Thank you, no. It's Kristin's favourite therapy, and jumping into the bath after her feels like hitting a shingle beach. The only thing that helps is proper, bottled medication.' He picked up the empty glass from the floor beside him and sniffed it. 'If we're doing the invalid conversation, what about you? Does that collection of minor flesh wounds hurt any less?'

'They hurt. Some days I can live with it. Others, it's hard. If it's all getting better, it's too slowly to notice. I try ignoring it, but every time I fall into a vat of vinegar, or put on a pair of glasspaper pyjamas, I'm somehow reminded. What about

Robert Walter Dornberger?'

'He's wounded?'

'I mean, let's think about what's going on in his head, pretend for a moment that Walter Thiel doesn't – didn't – exist.'

'Then we wouldn't be here at ... all.' Holleman slid slightly down the wall, searching for numbness.

'But we know that something's wrong, and that dead engineers are only part of it.'

'Pass the bottle, then.'

About a third of it remained: a mere ninth part of the fabulous trove that Fischer had brought from Staaken airfield, for which he'd sacrificed one of his only three tokens of alleged heroism. He picked up the cork and pushed it firmly into the neck. 'No, we'll celebrate with this when they kick us back to Berlin.'

'When will that be?'

'As soon as we tell Dornberger there's not a chance of us finding the person who shot Thiel.'

'Won't he be upset?'

'Not as much as when we tell him we know what he's doing here.'

'But we don't.'

Fischer formed his finger into a pistol's barrel and pointed it at his lieutenant's heart. 'Don't be pedantic, Freddie. The Führer has told us that the German people can achieve anything. I believe it was an order in fact.'

Holleman sighed. 'All right. He brings you here, Gestapo *and* Abwehr are as puzzled by this as we are because, as that quite lovely major said, there are legions of agencies and clever people who can advise on security and most of them would be better fitted to it than us. Of course, *we* know that security isn't the issue. *We* know that it's a drastic *failure* of security that we're investigating, that Dornberger would rather keep quiet.'

'And we can understand that.'

'Of course we can. No one likes to be thought of as a stupid prick, not when he's sitting on a not-quite-secret arsenal.'

'But things are changing, thanks to the Royal Air Force.'

'Good old Tommies. Missed just about everything they were aiming for and still managed to give it to the Boches.'

'*Jerries*. It's the French who say *Boches*.'

'Is it? Well, the Generalmajor's little empire is being broken up, and he celebrates by playing hide the *fremdarbeiter*. He sends us on a pointless exercise that he's made damn sure *will* be pointless, and tips off his mates in Abwehr, so they can come and pretend they didn't know until yesterday that we were here. Which tells us...'

Holleman's eyes widened. He sat up and held out his glass. 'Put something in there and I'll make the glad day come sooner.'

After a moment's hesitation, Fischer obeyed. Freddie on form was worth it.

'He didn't tip them off for our benefit, it was for theirs. He wants them to know that we're up to something that might concern them. He's working *them*, not us.'

'Which makes our being here mean something.'

'That's right...' with difficulty, Holleman clam-

335

bered upright. 'Shit! Put Walter Thiel back on the table. He's part of it.'

'How, Freddie?'

'The day you arrived, Dornberger takes you to see the body. You're the, what, the seventh person to stare into the hole in its forehead? This is a secret, something he doesn't want anyone to know about. It's why you've been brought here, to investigate, resolve and bury quietly. But with the exception of Kaspar Nagel, who discovered it, and possibly that shy adjutant fellow, the others – von Braun, Wierer, Rudolph – were *invited* to take a look. Why would someone do that?'

'To establish a fact.'

'Yes, a fact. A secret that a *few* people need to know, rather than just one or two. Why? Is it that he wanted a number of witnesses, or *those* witnesses?'

Fischer laughed. 'You're serious? He discovers the event, has the hall cleared of everyone except Nagel, who's already seen the thing, and his adjutant Magirius. But then he tells these other three to come and see? In fact, one of them he calls over all the way from House 4. That isn't random selection, is it?'

'It's like a fucking gentleman's club.'

'Von Braun, Rudolph, Wierer – why them in particular? What connects them? One is the Technical Director: the boss, apart from Dornberger himself. But his speciality is fuel development. Rudolph is Chief Production Engineer, so he's going away soon anyway, to wherever the SS will build their slave factory. Of course, they didn't know that *then*. Wierer, he's the Projections Leader officially, but a glorified electrician in reality. Unless they all belong to the same masonic lodge, why did Dornberger share this *secret* with them?'

Holleman pondered this. 'A shared interest? They all owed Thiel for something that's been festering for years? Or they all loved him so much that the Generalmajor feels they should know?'

'I don't think a grudge would let itself be buried for so long. Von Braun, Rudolph and Thiel have worked together since Kummersdorf in 1934, but I don't know about Wierer. And what sort of grudge would it be, professional jealousy? No. They all have different disciplines, so they aren't competing, or stealing each other's ideas. As to love, well, von Braun told me that Thiel was a friend, but Rudolph doesn't strike me as the type to be too close to anyone. And Wierer, if he loved *himself* I'd be surprised. The man's a walking acid bath.'

'Disagreements about slave labour, then? Rudolph's been urging it, Thiel hated the idea and threatened to...'

'What? What the hell could he threaten? We don't live in an age in which this is considered a bad thing, so the revelation would hurt only himself. Anyway, Nagel said that Thiel was indifferent to anything that wasn't to do with engines.'

They contemplated the remaining standard motives briefly. Sex, money and power didn't seem to be apposite, because none of the gentlemen in question seemed to do the first, desire the second or lack for the third in their own fields. But Fischer sensed that Holleman was right: these weren't random choices of witness, or...

He sat up. 'Professor Wierer was appointed to collect the Peenemünde bodies and bring them to the school.'

'Yes?'

'Why? I mean, why him in particular?'

'Everyone was getting an unusual job that morning.'

'Yes, they were. But if Wierer was one of the men that Dornberger *specifically* wished to be aware of Thiel's death, wouldn't he have been summoned anyway, as were Rudolph and von Braun? What if Wierer isn't connected? What if he's the impartial witness, the man who had to know only because it was his job to know?'

'So we scratch him?'

'I'm not sure. It depends upon which moment Dornberger first became aware of Thiel's little problem. If he didn't know about it prior to making his work appointments, then no, we don't. Still, of the men I've interviewed, Wierer seems to care least about what I think. That usually indicates some quality of innocence. And he said that he hardly knew Thiel, which distinguishes him from the rest, doesn't it?'

'All right. So, we're down to just five witnesses who *might* have a common reason to know or be told about Thiel.'

'I'm beginning to think it's three, Freddie. Look at Nagel. I mean, who *is* he? A jumped-up

338

secretary, with the great fortune to have been kept out of uniform by his boss, and at best a half-informed understanding of what's being done here. If he's involved, is it because of who he is, or because he happened to be there?'

'Like Wierer?'

Fischer shrugged. 'And the shy Werner Magirius. What's his connection other than to be Dornberger's paper shuffler?'

'He won't talk to you without getting his story straight with his boss. That's guilt, isn't it?'

'Or loyalty. He doesn't want to incriminate Dornberger, even if he doesn't know how he might.'

'So you think the Generalmajor, von Braun and Rudolph?'

'I'm just saying that they have links we can't see elsewhere. They've been together a long time and they're the strategy level here, the ones who make decisions about the programme itself and where it's going. We can't say that about the others.'

Holleman nodded. 'I like that, Otto. Crap, possibly. But good, procedural crap.'

'Thank you, Freddie. So, what was the sequence that morning? The bodies are being brought into the school and laid out. Someone notices that some tags are on the wrong toes, so...'

'Who discovered that?'

Fischer thought about it. 'I don't know. I was just told by Dornberger that it happened.'

'So it may *not* have happened. If he wanted Thiel's body to be discovered, he'd need an excuse to go looking, wouldn't he?'

'You're right. And ... hell!' Fischer grinned, took the cork from the bottle and poured two more. 'What did the unpleasant but forthright Professor Wierer say? That Nagel discovered the body, *while Dornberger was stood next to him!*'

'He was led to it!'

'Like a lamb. Not only did Dornberger want certain people to witness it, he brought them to it. He knew already.'

'He did it, you mean. The bastard shot Thiel?'

'Did he?' Fischer scratched his chin. 'If he *did*, why have someone investigate the crime? A suicide impulse, a cry for help? It makes no sense. Go back to the sequence: Nagel – and Dornberger – *discover* the hole in Thiel's head. The Generalmajor has the hall cleared except for Wierer, Magirius, Nagel and Arthur Rudolph, the last of whom he calls over and points towards the evidence. He sends for von Braun...'

'How? The telephone lines were down, weren't they?'

'Except for those in House 4, yes. He sent someone?'

'Who? He'd cleared the hall, hadn't he?'

'Probably Magirius, then. Von Braun said that Nagel was at the door of the hall when he arrived.'

'What happened then?'

Fischer shrugged. 'Wierer organizes trucks – twenty or thereabouts – for the bodies. Not Thiel's, of course. Dornberger has that one wrapped and carried to one of the Experimental workshops, and the door locked. The next day, when Walter's beginning to smell badly, he's examined by eagle-eyed Otto Fischer, security advisor, former Bull and professional ... what do the Amis say?'

'Patsy.'

'Yes. Who determines that the doctor was punctured at fairly close range, but nothing more.'

'Because the body is then put swiftly into a mass grave in the woods.'

'As you say.'

'So...' Holleman perched himself on the edge of the sitting-room table, '...in effect, you were witness seven.'

'But charged with finding the man or woman who pulled the trigger.'

'No. Charged with being the man who's seen to be looking and seen to be so by ... Abwehr.'

'Again. As you say.'

The light had faded and Holleman was beginning to twitch, trying desperately not to notice that his leg was still attached. Zofia was late. The plates should have been collected by now, and Fischer was fairly sure that the workers were trucked back to Trassenheide before darkness fell. But then the door opened and she hurried in, arms full of towels. She half curtsied to them and went into the bathroom, followed every centimetre of the way by two pairs of not-disinterested eyes. There were brief but fairly frantic sounds of re-arrangement, of putting right what two grown men hadn't seen fit to consider untidiness. She emerged with the old towels and a wiping cloth, rushed back to the kitchen, swept up the tray, and was gone like a shell from a muzzle.

'That's strange,' said Holleman, who had already started to part himself from his tormenting limb, 'we had fresh towels yesterday.'

Fischer went into the bathroom. It was very neat, as fine a job as his mother would have made of the old Kaiserhof's Imperial Suite. Nothing out of place, not a hair in the bath or a surface obviously unwiped. There was little else to check. The razors were there still, as was his dress uniform, the bath salts and the tiny vial of amidon capsules that kept Holleman from climbing the wall when his missing leg became too painful. And...

'Freddie?'

'Otto.' Holleman had stretched out on the sofa, his makeshift bed, and closed his eyes.

'Your leg. It's not still prone to infection, is it?'

'Not for two years now, thank the Lord.'

'I'm glad. Then my beautiful ex-girlfriend has a problem, perhaps an embarrassing one. She's taken half my Prontosil.'

Chapter Forty-Five

The headcount was cursory, as usual: one hundred and thirty two workers had departed Trassenheide that morning in twelve trucks; the same number were counted and recorded in the camp ledger fourteen hours later, as the workers shuffled impatiently, yearning to fill their empty bellies and lose their boots. One hundred and thirty one were then dismissed: one was summoned to the camp office and told to wait.

In the middle of the room Zofia stood to attention while the evening shift lethargically moved papers around desks or chatted about inconsequential things. Her sense of time had altered drastically in the past few years; without clocks, days were measured only by the quality of light, imposed schedules, whistles, sirens and bells. But now, in this room, each moment came and went as if an ill-set metronome – her heart – marked its shortened passage. She should have been hungry and tired, but felt neither, only a very familiar sense of having been caught. The chasm between the guards' obvious boredom and her growing dread made the latter more acute, if that were possible. They had ceased even to notice her: she had been given the command, the one sent down from Peenemünde, and now she could be forgotten, like any other domestic animal.

After what seemed like hundreds of accelerated heartbeats, the office door opened, and the Horror and his one-legged familiar entered. She had been perfectly certain that it would be them. The shift commander saluted and nodded to something that the Horror whispered. A key was lifted from the wall: they needed a room for what they were going to do to her, to make her talk. The one-legged one smiled, and held out an arm invitingly. She wasn't deceived for a moment.

They made her sit down. The Horror put his

hand on her shoulder, and squeezed slightly.

'Show them to me, Zofia.'

The thought of denying it didn't occur to her. She reached under her blouse, to the small pocket in which she often hid things, and removed them. She held them out to him, palm splayed.

His finger pushed them apart, making it easier to count.

'Six. That isn't enough, not to cure something. Whatever it is will return after a few days.'

He pulled a small container from his pocket and offered it to her. 'Eight more. Put those in here, and then put them away.'

Numbly, she did as she was told.

'Two each day, for a week. If there's a problem still, then it's a *problem*, you understand?'

She nodded.

'Who did you take these for?'

She looked at the floor, saying nothing. How would they do it? She wished more than ever to be like Élodie, but that was a fantasy. She had no capacity to endure pain for abstract causes, nor for someone to whom she owed nothing. All they needed was time, and the stomach for it.

'Zofia?'

He pulled over a chair to face her and sat down. His ravaged face was close to hers, the detail of his wounds very clearly exposed. He didn't seem to care any more.

'If I wished to hurt this person, or you, would I have offered the capsules? Wouldn't I just have allowed my friend to do things until you told me anyway? You aren't going to be hurt, because nothing wrong's happened. Not even the theft...' She winced at the word: a capital offence. '...Which, if I forget about it, isn't a theft at all, is it? All I want is to speak to this person.'

He stared openly, his eyes to hers, but beneath the scars she couldn't tell honesty from lies.

'When we speak to foreigners here, we have a problem – we make them very afraid. They think they're in trouble, naturally, so then they tell us what it is they imagine we want to hear. It's hardly surprising, is it?' He smiled. 'So it would be helpful – *very* helpful – if we could have a frank discussion with someone about ... well, about things that aren't going to come back upon anyone. The person who needs these capsules must know that we give them freely, but there's a condition, that he or she speaks with us soon. If you don't want to do this, then return them to me now and you can go, without punishment.'

Why would she do that? If they wanted to hurt her, to find out who she'd stolen them for, they could do it; if she returned the capsules, Achym would die anyway; if they wanted him dead, why offer a means of living? She nodded, and pushed the container deeper into her pocket.

'Go, get some food.' He stood and placed his chair back against the wall, as if concluding a job interview.

His friend twitched his head. 'Bugger off, darling.'

Eyes on the floor, she walked quickly through the main office and out into the dusk. She

345

glanced back once only to reassure herself that no one followed. With difficulty she found the tent to which she'd been invited that morning, a nondescript piece of soiled tarpaulin among fifty others.

'I can't believe it.' Achym's voice, curiously, was a little stronger than she recalled from that morning. He took one of the capsules and asked the architect for soup, for both of them. She tried to refuse, but every man in the tent seemed keen that she shared what they had. As she ate she told him of the condition attached to his reprieve.

'Fuck! Excuse me...' He tried to rise, hopelessly.

'Achym ('*Marcin*,' he whispered urgently. 'It's *Marcin*,'), they could have made me tell them, but I don't think they want to hurt anyone.'

'They want a snitch, is what they want. Bastards.'

'For God's sake, you *needed* this! Didn't you think there'd be a price?'

Achym glanced around. The architect and the solicitor's clerk were already looking doubtfully at him. They weren't the sorts to do anything, but word would get around swiftly. He recalled what had happened to the greasy little Slovakian shit who'd swapped a few of his countrymen for cigarettes, the one who'd been terribly surprised when he found himself being kicked a lot. Squealing was a well paid and very short career, and the retirement plan stank. But at that moment he couldn't see a choice. Zofia's head was already in the noose because of him, and even if he had the guts to let her take the punishment, she'd give them a name, eventually. Every-

346

one did, eventually.

He groaned. The wound felt as if a blowtorch were playing on it, his head was pounding and his future prospects, having expanded momentarily, seemed to be contracting like a slug in a salt shower. 'Did they say what they wanted, exactly?'

Zofia shook her head, but his eyes had closed and he didn't see it. 'Just to talk. I don't know why.'

'All right. Who are they?'

She told him and he shivered involuntarily despite the heat in his side. The one that looked like the Devil's ugly brother: the lie to rumours of God's infinite mercy.

Oh, Christ. 'Tell him I'll find him as soon as I can walk.'

It was late, and she had to creep through shadows back to her hut. A couple of the women who slept closest to her watched as she took off her coat and shoes and slipped into her bunk. They probably thought she'd done what they'd been expecting her to do long before now – who wouldn't, with her looks and the chance of extra rations? So they were right, in a way. And wrong, too.

She pulled the thin blanket over her head, trying to imagine it as a turret hatch on an impossibly well-armoured tank.

Chapter Forty-Six

The assembly hall was being stripped out, reduced to a vast skeleton as its machinery – dismantled, wrapped and loaded onto or hauled by a never-ending circulation of Fords, Tatras and Schwerers – was extracted from Peenemünde. The principal route south to Zinnowitz ran immediately adjacent to the guesthouse. Fischer, dragged abruptly from a heavy, alcohol-induced semi-coma, felt a little like a Ukrainian peasant wakening ten minutes after the offensive commenced.

Counting trucks was not a useful occupation, so he rose immediately, dressed and was in the kitchen when Zofia arrived (in the bathroom, Holleman was assailing the *Threepenny Opera* so viciously that Julius Streicher couldn't have taken offence). Curtly she gave him the message and a name. He nodded, thanked her and told her that the matter was closed. Endearingly, she had made an effort once more. The bread was very fresh, the butter a reasonable oil-substitute and the almost-real fruit preserve smelled of fruit, almost. Only the coffee failed to be more than the sum of its curious constituents.

'Good morning!' Holleman roared from the doorway, almost causing two seizures. 'How *are* you?' he asked Zofia, frowning with concern.

'Leave her alone, Freddie. You can go, Zofia.'

The two men ate their breakfast in silence, glancing up occasionally when a particularly heavy load made the window frames vibrate dangerously. As soon as the last of the food was gone Holleman lit his day's first cigarette. 'Where's all that crap going?'

'I don't know. Nagel, where is it going?'

They hadn't heard him enter. He looked tired, as if he hadn't slept, and his suit looked much the same.

'For the moment, most of the production machinery's going to be stored at a depot near Chemnitz, but I'm not supposed to talk about where it goes after that.'

'Fine. Not our business.'

Nagel struggled for a few moments, but a confidence seemed like poison in his system. 'Well, it can't hurt that *you* know. It was decided yesterday. There's an underground fuel storage facility being built in a disused mine near Nordhausen. It's going to be requisitioned and converted for production of the A4.'

Holleman nodded approvingly. 'I like it. The deeper we put the SS, the fainter the smell.'

Fischer frowned. That sort of talk was all very well at the Front, or in the critical ward of a lazarett – there, everybody accepted you'd earned the right. But suits couldn't be relied upon, particularly not the sort that were about to get intimate with the Reichsführer.

Nagel didn't seem to have noticed the comment. 'The Generalmajor would like a report on your progress, perhaps at noon?'

'He's asking?'

The young man smiled. 'No, not really. He'll be done with Brigadeführer Kammler by then, and he has a further appointment at 1pm.'

'Kammler the architect: the holiday camp designer?' Holleman had a dangerously wide-eyed, innocent expression on his gnarled face, the kind that Fischer knew much too well.

The smile thinned. 'As you say.'

'I always wanted to be an architect.'

Freddie, for Christ's sake!

'Really?'

'Oh yes. I've always felt that our public lavatories are too *steif*. There's nothing about a shit-house that a Doric column wouldn't improve.'

Nagel laughed, and Fischer released his diaphragm a little.

'You should apply to Reichsminister Speer, Oberleutnant. I'm sure *Germania* will need appropriate facilities.'

Solemnly, his eyes fixed upon a distant destiny, Holleman placed a hand upon his breast. 'Friedrich Melancthon Holleman: *Reichslatrinenführer*!'

Nagel roared. Fischer sighed and considered the revelation. 'Thuringia? A little far from London, surely?'

'It's far from Allied bombers, too.' Holleman, like all true comedians impervious to his own humour, picked up the preserve pot and used a thick finger to scrape out the last of its contents. 'If I was building things that went Boom, I'd want a strong roof over my head, and gladly pay the higher train fares.'

There it was, yet another fatal weakness to add

to the others. For years the Luftwaffe had been tearing up the byways of Europe from the skies. Now the tactic would be coming home, and it would find the most highly developed rail and road transportation network in the world, laid out like pathfinder markings. Wherever they built this weapon, however they protected the factories, it had to be moved.

Holleman was looking at him, silently mouthing a word.

'Nagel, my orders were followed regarding Dr Thiel's house?'

'Of course, Hauptmann. Locked and guarded.'

'Good. Please arrange for a key. The Oberleutnant and I will examine it this morning. And tell the Generalmajor that we're pleased to accept his kind invitation.'

The approach to Hindenburg Strasse was much neater than the last time Fischer had seen it. The plots where houses had stood prior to the raid had been cleared or filled in. One might have assumed that time had reversed, that they were looking at the Settlement as it was being built, as yet awaiting the prosperous, intelligent families that would create a model German society here. Holleman gazed around, impressed.

'A pleasant place to raise kids.'

'It was. I wouldn't want to start now.'

The senior engineers' homes had been cleaned and some re-painted. The holes in the roads had disappeared and the surface had been re-metalled, which, to Fischer, seemed a little extravagant, given that car ownership here was

351

minimal. Signs had been re-erected, even if the streets they announced were now no more than memories, and many of the damaged lawns had been re-turfed. Apart from the unsightly gaps in the otherwise perfect grid, there were no needless reminders of the many dead now fertilizing woodlands a little to the south.

It was obvious that Thiel's home had remained untouched in the days since the raid. There was no sign of his wallet, but a lady's purse on the hallway table contained almost two hundred marks still, and a small jewellery box in the armoire at the top of the stairs held an un-spectacular but profitable haul for any passing burglar.

The house was a model of solid, middle-class taste, announcing its wealth very quietly. The sitting room furniture was a little outdated: too heavy and dark for the forward-looking style of the house's exterior (brought to the marriage, per-haps, by the doctor or his wife), but every ap-pliance and convenience available to the modern German family was present in the now-stinking Swedish kitchen and laundry. There were storage units with concealed handles, elegant work surfaces (crossed repeatedly by the imprint of flour-stained mice feet), an electric oven with hobs above, a refrigerator, a vortex washing machine, a Vorwerk vacuum cleaner and floor polisher. Fischer had not been given the opportunity to examine Frau Thiel's body, but he was certain she hadn't suffered the chapped hands, swollen knees or tired elbows of the traditional German *haus-frau*.

The principal bedroom had a private bathroom and wall-to-floor fitted wardrobes with sliding doors, most of them filled with ladies' clothes. A small section, enough for six suits, seemed to be all that Walter Thiel had been able to annex for his own use. Twin beds, of course, with matching covers (both thrown back untidily) and what looked to be a genuine Tiffany lamp on the table between them. Across the upper hallway and up on to the top floor, the smaller eaves bedrooms were heartbreakingly distinctive, stuffed with indispensable fripperies and mementoes of childhood. Fischer noticed that Holleman, whose opinion regarding the Thiels' taste and choices elsewhere in the house had been aired wantonly, became very quiet and efficient as he searched them.

It was all extremely comfortable, lacking in any distinctive style and bereft of clues that might have offered a prehistory to the moment at which the Thiels were expunged. Everything that an optimistic Bull might have hoped to find was missing: there were no technical papers hidden in a secret desk compartment; no two-way radio pushed under one of the beds; no signed letter from Winston Churchill congratulating Thiel on the invaluable work he'd done recently for Hawker Siddeley. When they finished searching, they knew precisely as much as they had when Fischer first turned the key in the front door lock: in the early hours of 18 August, as British bombs began to fall, Walter Thiel had taken his friend Klaus Riedel's advice and abandoned his home and possessions in a futile effort to preserve his family. They had died; their worldly imprint had survived, as intact and as perfectly unrevealing as a scholarly exhibit upon the lifestyle of the Ostrogoths.

'What did you expect?' Holleman was looking out of the rear kitchen window on to the rear garden, at the children's toys that had remained exactly where they had been dropped, probably on the warm, breezy afternoon of 17 August.

'Exactly what we found. Nothing.'

'The wife was a Russian agent. She'd been discovered by Walter, so she packed her Tokarev on the way to the trench but never returned.'

'Perfect. Of course, it would have blown his head off, even from ten metres.'

Holleman shrugged. 'I know. But I want her to be interesting.'

'There shouldn't be children here, Freddie.'

They were looking down a line of similar gardens, most of which had some evidence of *kinderspielen*. Any number of balls, a broken doll, a small goalkeeper's net, a toy dog on wheels: artefacts of domestic normality in the middle of a vast target at the water's edge, waiting for another visit from the British or Americans.

'This is total war, comrade. No point in trying to distinguish purely military targets any more, is there? Not that anyone ever made much of an effort on this fucking continent.'

'Do you notice anything, Freddie?'

'I do, yes. Who lives two doors down?'

'I don't know. Shall we introduce ourselves?'

The door opened within moments of Fischer's knuckle rapping upon it. The woman's face

354

momentarily did the usual thing, but she recovered rapidly, and then almost beamed at him.
'Herr Fischer?'

'Yes. And this is Oberleutnant Holleman,
Frau...?'

'Steinhoff, Else Steinhoff. Ernst told me
about you. He said it was the first interesting
conversation he's had at a House 4 dinner, so
I'm sure it was all about gliders! Will you come
in?'

They thanked her, refused coffee and cake, and
tried to detain her as briefly as possible, though
she seemed more than happy for even this
strange company. Twenty minutes later they were
on Hindenburg Strasse once more, strolling in
what each of them imagined was an appropriately nonchalant manner.

Holleman sighed. 'Christ! I wish we'd spoken
to more of the ladies here.'

'It was stupid of me. They have the time to take
an interest in things.'

'How do you want to do this?'

'Call Gerd Branssler. Tell him they didn't give
their names, but they promised me something,
and I want it.'

Chapter Forty-Seven

According to Nagel, Dornberger was to give Brigadeführer Kammler a personal tour of the now almost stripped assembly hall. The closest that Fischer and Holleman came to meeting the new Production boss was to catch a glimpse of his darkened profile in the back seat of the black Horch 853 that glided swiftly past the Brandenburg Tor as they emerged through it.

Holleman watched until it disappeared into the woods and sniffed dismissively. 'Wasted on an architect.' Like most pilots he coveted nice machines and begrudged anyone who had been promoted into one.

They walked – at his pace – to House 4, so they were a few minutes late for their appointment with the Generalmajor. As they entered his office he was clearly upset, swearing under his breath and slamming down papers that almost certainly hadn't offended him. It didn't seem to be upon a matter of Luftwaffe tardiness, either.

'Well?'

Fischer glanced at Holleman. 'You wished for a progress report, Herr Generalmajor.'

'Did I? Yes, of course I did. Please sit down.' Dornberger swept a few papers to one side of his desk and glanced around. 'Werner!'

Magirius popped his head around the door. 'Where are my blasted cigarettes?'

His aide walked to the desk and picked up the silver case that was sat, prominently, in front of a long, ornate pen stand. Dornberger closed his eyes, breathed in deeply and exhaled.

'Thank you. Don't go away, Werner.' Magirius stood at ease, to one side of the desk. 'So, where are we, Hauptmann?'

Fischer coughed. 'I'm sorry to say, Herr Generalmajor, that we aren't anywhere, as yet. The investigation has yet to determine either a motive or a suspect.'

'Hm.' Dornberger took a first pull on his cigarette, grimaced and stubbed it out. 'Well, you said that you wished to speak to Werner, so please continue.'

'We'd prefer, sir, to do it without your being present.'

'I don't see why. I've neither rehearsed nor told him to deny anything. Have I, Werner?'

'No, Herr Generalmajor.

'There you are, see? Werner, be very honest with your answers.'

It was going to be pointless, but Fischer asked the questions anyway. Magirius had been in the schoolhouse, but some distance from Nagel when the tarpaulin was pulled from Thiel's face. Dornberger had summoned him and told him to clear out everyone except Wierer and Rudolph. He had then fetched Doctor von Braun from House 4. He hadn't been involved in collecting the bodies, and so could offer no opinion as to who may have brought in the Thiel family. When he and the Generalmajor had first arrived at the hall (approximately thirty minutes before the discovery), about eighty bodies had been brought in already. He estimated that forty more arrived during the following hour. He knew Thiel and his family personally, of course, but not closely. He was aware that the doctor's work was quite brilliant and that he was admired and respected by his colleagues. He had no opinion on either the circumstances of the incident or the identity of a perpetrator.

Holleman, wasting ink, made a show of noting these comments. When he'd finished, he raised a hand. 'May I ask something, Herr Generalmajor?'

'Yes, Oberleutnant...?'

'Holleman, sir. It's regarding the condition of Dr Thiel's family. You told Hauptmann Fischer that there were soil traces and evidence of damage on their fingernails, presumably from an attempt to free themselves following the collapse of the trench?'

'That's my assumption, yes.'

'Were these the only corpses discovered in the trench?'

'No, I believe that there were...' he glanced at Magirius, '...five others. Three members of another family and two War Service girls.'

'And their condition? Apart from dead, that is?'

'I really don't know, Oberleutnant. I didn't examine them.'

'Could you tell us who did?'

'Professor Wierer may be able to help, or at least direct you to the correct party.'

'Thank you, Herr Generalmajor.'

Dornberger raised his eyebrows. 'Do you wish to ask anything else, Hauptmann? No? Well, let me say that the lack of progress to date is a little disappointing, though I'm sure that you've done your best. Shall we say three more days? You may have noticed that Brigadeführer Kammler has begun to press his attentions, so changes to the way we do things will be accelerating. I doubt that it will make your task any easier. I shall take another report then, after which a decision will be made on the future of this investigation. Thank you, gentlemen.'

'Cheeky bastard.' In the entrance hall of House 4, Holleman patted his pockets forlornly. 'If he's *disappointed*, whose fault is it? He fiddles his own books. Sends us all over Pomerania chasing phantoms; gets his chums to put the knuckle on us. Then he tells us we've let him down.'

Fischer rubbed his eyes, trying to ease the ache between them. 'Do you know, Freddie, I hadn't even thought to ask about other bodies in that trench?'

'We all need practice.'

'I know, but...'

'Anyway, he was lying. About the other bodies, I mean. There's no chance they wouldn't have looked at them. Not after finding Thiel with a bullet in his head. But that's not important, because it was a trick question.'

Fischer smiled. 'How did they know how many others were in the trench? The bodies weren't carried into the hall to any particular plan, Nagel told me that. They just came in as they were found. And we've been told specifically by Dornberger that they haven't been able to identify who brought in the Thiels.'

'Yet another fucking lie, then.'

'Never mind. We aren't going to find those three foreign workers. Forget them.'

'Hauptmann!'

The secretarial pool manageress waved from the door of her office. 'A message for you.' She smiled tartly and passed a piece of paper to Fischer. 'Please ask your comrades to leave their battlefield language at the Front. Our young ladies weren't raised in bordellos.'

From Kriminalkommisar Gerd Branssler: What the fuck is he talking about? The fucking thing was flown to him three days ago. Tell him to get the cork in the bottle and his finger out of his arse. The Two Graces send their love, and hope for something, soon. Gerd.

Fischer asked for a line to the Luftwaffe airfield at Peenemünde West. The station's duty officer sounded relieved. Yes, they'd received a package labelled Most Secret, for the attention of Hauptmann Otto Fischer, but they hadn't recognized the name and there was no address specified. In fact, the only other marking on the envelope was a *Geheime Staatspolizei* stamp, which had encouraged them to do nothing in the way of showing initiative, that being the safest course when in any doubt, or ignorance.

Fischer told him that Obenleutnant Friedrich Holleman would be there within the hour to sign for it.

'Straight there and back, please, Freddie. It might be all we have.'

360

Chapter Forty-Eight

For five hours, Fischer awaited Holleman's return at the guesthouse. He managed to stay angry for almost three of them before accepting, grudgingly, that there had to be a reason for it. He hadn't noticed a drone of British engines, or the concussive blast of 250 kilogram general purpose ordnance, so he assumed that his colleague wasn't lying dismembered in a crater somewhere between there and the airfield. Abduction seemed equally unlikely, though in the new Germany one could never discount the possibility entirely. Perhaps, then, he had stumbled across an inn, halfway between the East and West sites, which somehow had survived the civilian evacuations and four years' lack of any customers. The theory acquired some credibility when Holleman finally limped in, heavily scented by something stronger than aviation fuel, carrying a small bag and waving a large but empty-looking envelope.

'Where the *hell* have you been?'

Holleman grinned. 'Have I been dragging my foot? Never mind. Here's the dirt, though you shouldn't get your hopes up.'

'You've read it?'

'I assumed that you'd want me hot on the case, so yes. Have a look. It won't take long.'

Fischer withdrew a single sheet of foolscap and

read the three paragraphs.

'The concise history of a man.'

Slowly, Fischer tore the piece of paper into two. 'Well, that's it, then.'

'Not quite.' Holleman opened his bag and withdrew a bottle of Courvoisier. 'I met a mate of yours. He told me to give this to you, said you'd only to ask, you thieving bastard.'

'Douglas von Bader.'

'Funny bloke. Likes to talk, doesn't he?'

'Christ, yes. More than decent of him, though.'

Holleman couldn't stop grinning, and it wasn't entirely the fault of the liquor he'd absorbed. 'Douglas and his mates know why we're here, they think. It's a matter of some concern to the airfield staff.'

'Thiel's death? How...?'

'No, not that. They think it's about the phantoms. They think Luftwaffe have sent in a couple of their own to find out what's happening.'

Holleman had cleared the airfield's remarkably stringent security and encountered von Bader, smoking illegally at the entrance to one of the small airfield's two hangars. He asked directions to the station office, but the pilot had stubbed out his coffin nail, taken an arm, expertly prised out the fact that Holleman was formerly attached to Luftflotte 2 and then launched into his autobiography. This had required considerable investment of time. Holleman managed to sign for his package, but it was made clear to him that he wasn't going to escape without first paying a visit to the station mess. There, von Bader had done the decent, comradely thing and signed for

Holleman's drinks while recalling the Norway campaign in somewhat greater detail than the official despatches, deploring Hermann Göring's tactical error in Giving It to London in 1940 (Holleman, a part of that glorious failure, agreed entirely), graciously allowing the metal half-leg to trump his metal knee and offering Holleman, should he ever fly again, first rights to the nickname. They'd toasted Luftwaffe élan, women everywhere, confusion to the RAF and Tomorrow Never Coming, while every member of the station's staff who had wandered into the mess in the meantime had been given Holleman's abridged crash-story: an epic tale of two Hurricanes, flame-enhanced disorientation and craven relief on a cold mud-bank.

With good humour, von Bader had taken a (latest) ribbing from his mates about the recent brandy misappropriation incident at Tempelhof and the subsequent mangling of his arse for it. The further bottle, slipped to Holleman while the others watched the mess door, was unexpected, but a price had been stated. The station staff became nervous when procedures were pissed upon, particularly when reasons for it weren't forthcoming. They wanted, if it were possible, to know what the Hell was going on and seemed to think that Holleman, a stranger in the right uniform, was the man to ask. He was obliged to disappoint them, but he listened carefully to the details and promised to return for another drink if he heard anything.

'Otto, you're not a pilot, of course, unlike Douglas and me. But what would you say if I told you there was some concern at Peenemünde West about flights that hadn't occurred?'

'I should say that someone has been reading Sherlock Holmes.'

'Then let me re-phrase, for the layman. Would you imagine, during this time of somewhat heightened security, that light aircraft would be allowed to take off and land at a Luftwaffe airfield – one immediately adjacent to a secret weapons facility – without the said flights being logged in the station register?'

'I would not.'

'No, nor would I. The fellow who was supposed to log them wanted to follow procedures, but was ordered not to, both times, and told to keep quiet about it. This is the Luftwaffe, though, and every man's a radio set. When Douglas told me about it I thought, wouldn't Otto Fischer just love to know the date of these flights and who, exactly, had given the hush orders?'

Holleman opened his bag and offered another piece of paper. 'I doubt you'll want to rip up this.'

Fischer read it quickly, and looked up. 'Has it happened before?'

'Douglas says no. He asked the signals sergeant, who's been here since 1939 and never known anything like it. It's an experimental facility, after all, not just an airfield, so things like this *can't* happen. Want to hear a little more?'

'Don't tease.'

'Same aircraft, both flights, an *unmarked* Bü 181, fully fuelled on the way out. Every other light aircraft at the airfield is a Storch, so...'

'Range. Unless we're talking about modified

tanks, the Bestmann has double a Storch's range.'

'About eight hundred kilometres. Enough to reach the Low Countries, France, Sweden, Norway, hell…'

'Did you ask to look at the station logs?'

'No, but I *did* put the question to Douglas. Ninety percent of flights – the non-experimental stuff, I mean – are to Gatow, Tempelhof, Staaken or Zossen-Wünsdorf. The rest are almost all short-haul, a few to Danzig, Schwerin, Stettin – and Wolfsschanze, very occasionally, when the brass are obliged to go Führer-chasing. Nowhere that a Storch can't reach easily, and there are two of them based permanently at the airfield.'

'The 14 and 17 August, early evening and early morning. An unmarked Bestmann leaves and arrives back here in bad light, no log entries, no flight plan submitted. Do you see anything suspicious in any of this?'

'Yes, but with respect to what, I don't know.'

'No, but we know *who* did it, don't we? It's something, at least.'

'Enough to celebrate?' asked Holleman, hopefully, but he was already unsteady on his feet, or foot.

'I'm afraid not. The Bestmann returned only a few hours before the British raid. I don't have sufficient faith in the prescience of the British War Cabinet to think that the two are in any way connected.'

'All right. An assassin was being flown in to deal with Walter Thiel in case the bombs missed.'

Fischer smiled. 'Freddie, the bottle stays sealed. Find me the real reason for the flight, and I'll ask Zofia to bathe you in brandy. Speaking of whom, when she brings our food I'm going to press her a little on our poorly Pole. I think we need a gentle word about what's going on at Trassenheide.'

'Why don't you ask *her*? We've got enough to squeeze her with.'

'No, she gave us what we asked. In any case, whatever game Dornberger's playing, it keeps her out of our hands for the moment. We'll talk to the sick one before he or she recovers too much.'

Chapter Forty-Nine

'Marcin Konopka, sir.'

'And to which hut were you assigned, before the raid?'

'Hut Eleven, sir.'

The boss *schwab* looked at his aide, who checked a list and nodded.

'This isn't anything to do with you, or what you've done. We'd just like to speak to you about the camp here. And you won't be getting anyone else into trouble, I promise. Clear?'

Achym said nothing. He was laid on his sick-pallet, trying to look more ill than he felt, trusting to whatever sliver of pity his condition warranted. But he wasn't hopeful; the burned one obviously hadn't enjoyed too many of life's mercies, so he wasn't likely to be overflowing with them; the other one, the one-legged thug, well, *that* was a hard case, and no mistake.

'We'll start slowly, then. Hut Eleven was adjacent to Hut Twelve, wasn't it?'

'Yes, sir. I believe so.'

'Did you mix much with the residents of other huts? Perhaps with those from Hut Twelve?'

'Not really, sir. We don't get much chance or time to mingle.'

Achym felt perspiration trickle down his forehead, but that was good: made it seem like the fever hadn't quite gone.

'But you'd at least know a few of them by sight? You passed them every day, after all.'

'Oh yes, sir. I'd know a few of them, by sight.'

'Have you seen any of them, since the air raid?'

The patient frowned, as though the question were testing the limits of his enfeebled intellect. 'I ... don't think so. Quite a few were killed or injured, and we've been in tents since, so...'

'Yes, that's right. Your own hut, were there many casualties there?'

'A ... few, sir. I think, probably four dead and about seven or eight wounded.'

The Leg consulted the list once more. 'Eighteen and nineteen, he's one of only four uninjured from that hut.'

Oh fuck.

'Well, you can't be expected to recall things too clearly. It's a confusing experience, being under fire.' The Face smiled, and Achym recalled the fraught moment, several days earlier, when he'd first seen that twisted effort.

'You were in the work party at House 4, weren't you?'

'Where, sir?'

'The administration building. You're a brick-layer, yes?'

'All sorts of jobs, sir. A handyman.'

'Like all the rest, remarkable. Do you work at Peenemünde often?'

'It's what we're here for.'

'Yes. I meant the research site, specifically.'

'Oh. Most days, sir. The good workers tend to get chosen often. I haven't had any complaints, you can ask...'

'That won't be necessary. So, you'd talk to others who work often at the site.'

'We're not allowed to speak while working, sir.'

'No, of course not. But when you eat, and on the trucks going to and from work? You must talk then.'

'Sometimes, sir. But only about football, and girls.'

'Please tell me if you know any of these names. Oberleutnant?'

The Leg pronounced them slowly, precisely: 'Bronislaw Michalski; Rajmund Ulatowski; Alois Stoch.'

'No ... oh, yes, sir. Stoch, he's Slovakian. Bad sort, an informer, if you'll excuse me for saying so. Not popular in the camp. The *schw* ... the guards removed him for his own good a couple of times. I don't know him personally.'

'You prefer to keep your own company?'

'Best way, sir.'

'No friends in the camp?'

'None, sir.'

'I wonder then how you come to know the woman Zofia so well. Your girlfriend, is she?'

'Wish she was, sir. But I only know her vaguely, to talk to.'

'And yet she risks her life, stealing medication to help you. My *own* medication, did you know that? What a wonderful gesture to make, and for a man she hardly knows. Should I believe this, Konopka?'

Achym could feel sweat running freely now into the horsehair mattress, but the squirm had little to do with that. 'It's true, sir. She's a good Christian.'

'I'd say she was a saint, a martyr, even, because she's going to the wall for this. Am I right, Oberleutnant?'

'No doubt about it, Herr Hauptmann. The rules are very clear on thieving from Germans.'

The Face returned his attention to Achym. 'So, I hope the pills worked, because you'll need to be fit enough to see her shot. Believe me, we'll tie you to a plank, if you can't stand up.'

This was going much too quickly for Achym to think clearly. He didn't want to say anything that got her further into the shit, but he couldn't think of a single thing that wouldn't. The fact they'd now decided it *was* theft meant that she was for it, one way or the other. He might as well risk the *other*, and hope that her personal Herman really was a top guy.

'But she's ... protected.'

'In what way, protected?'

369

'She... I can't say, sir. But someone at the site wants her kept safe. A German, sir.'

'Who is this German?'

Achym didn't answer, because this was dragging his own arse to the cliff's edge. Either they, or he, wouldn't take kindly to his knowing. He wished he'd not spoken, but...

The *schwabs* looked at each other and smiled, like something could be remotely funny.

'All right, Konopka. I can see why you'd be nervous, so let me make it clear. Tell us the name, and no one ever gets to hear about where it came from. But you say it now, or you're on a truck to an *arbeitserziehungsläger* before the sun sets today. And it won't be the regulation six-week stint, I promise. I'll make sure you've found your retirement home.'

Achym closed his eyes. Every option he'd kicked around for the past ten days rubbed its arse and walked out of the tent flap, leaving a wonderfully clear view of a foreshortened future. She'd hate him, kill him probably, if she ever got the chance. Rajmund certainly would, if word got out somehow. But these were possibilities, not immutable facts like the one the *schwabs* were presenting him with. So this wasn't bad faith, or betrayal, or cheap, self-serving squealing: it was just him putting his finger in the barrel before the bullet took out his teeth. He breathed deeply, and said the name.

He'd hoped that was it. But the Face, excited as he was, wouldn't let the fucking thing go.

'For how long?'

'I don't know, sir. A few months, at least. That's

370

what I heard.'

'*Heard?* Who else knows about this?'

'Just ... me and a friend. He died in the raid. He saw them, being friendly, a while back.'

'So you *do* have a friend. I was beginning to worry for you, Konopka.'

'Did, sir. *Did.*'

They went to the other side of the tent for a whispered conference. Achym lay as still as he could, thinking of the good old days, two weeks earlier, when life was simpler and promised to be much longer; of the opportunities for small advancements that fell into his lap most days; of his lack of visibility and his expensive but malleable pet guards, helping to make his stay here bearable. He thought back further, to his parents and the hopes they'd had for him: a university education, the technical institute and the good work he'd done there, the fertile young lady he'd meet in due course and the brood of grandchildren she'd provide for them. All of it: every expectation, endeavour and half-chance, flushed down the celestial crapper by hands unseen.

They returned to his sick-pallet, and put on their officers' caps. The Face nodded. 'Thank you, Konopka. Keep the pills; when you feel better we'll see about putting you on the trustees' list.'

'You needn't bother, sir...'

'Nonsense. In fact, we'll speak to Hauptmann Gaschler, see if he can find something for you that isn't too strenuous.'

A trustee: they might as well have pinned a

large, pink sign to his back: *Rat*. He'd have to spend his entire future cigarette ration bribing guards to keep the other inmates from booting him all over Trassenheide. And a year or two from now, when the Ivans won, he'd get liberated the shit out of.

The tent flap drew back and the *schwab* Raffel entered. Achym shrank into his mattress and tried, slowly and discreetly, to cover himself entirely with the rough, soiled blanket he'd been complaining about for almost three days to anyone who'd listen.

'Hauptmann, a message from Lieutenant Colonel Stegmaier. He'd be obliged if you could spare a few moments for him?'

'Of course.' Achym's interrogators gave the prone Marcin Konopka a final glance and followed Raffel to the camp office.

Chapter Fifty

Stegmaier was a tall, pale man, slightly built, with an air of what Fischer initially took to be irritability. His manner, however, was pleasant. He introduced himself, apologized for not having spoken with Fischer earlier – he was, after all, head of Peenemünde's security, in a way – and asked if there was any assistance he could offer.

'It was my error, Herr Leutnant-Colonel. We should have made an appointment earlier. You

372

say *in a way*. Surely, you *are* head of security here?'

Stegmaier smiled ruefully. 'It's one of my briefs, yes. But the Generalmajor has kept security very much in his own hands since ... my predecessor departed.'

'This was Colonel Zanssen?'

Stegmaier almost winced. 'Leo Zanssen, yes.'

'I heard there was some difficulty involving the Colonel, some accusations regarding his conduct?'

'There were. None of them true, I assure you. The Colonel was, I believe, the victim of a concerted effort to remove him from this facility.'

Fischer glanced at Holleman, who was studying the table's surface very closely.

'Pardon me, Herr Leutnant-Colonel, but my impression – my understanding – was that you were involved...?'

This was insufferably presumptuous, but Stegmaier seemed not to mind. 'I was questioned by Herr Berger of the Reichsführer's office, at some length and at his invitation – I certainly didn't volunteer to attend. When asked, I confirmed the rumours regarding Zanssen, because they existed and I'd heard them. I offered no opinion other than to agree that he attended divine service on Sundays and some Days of Obligation, and to say that I had never seen the Colonel overcome by strong drink. Yet I seem to be regarded as the source of these filthy stories, not least because I'm seen to have benefited from them. I am, like my predecessor, stained by rumour.'

373

'A difficult situation, sir.'

'Intolerable, I would say.'

'And the Generalmajor has assumed some of the responsibilities formerly exercised by the Colonel?'

'Yes, to the extent that he controls overall security at Peenemünde. My role as Army Commander, other than to monitor technical progress, has been reduced to that of inmate management and guarding the perimeters. I supervise the arrangements at Trassenheide and Wolgast. The smaller Karishagen facility – in which *häflinge* are housed – is directly controlled by the SS, of course. Other than that, it's my job to ensure that workers are controlled adequately when outside the camps.'

'Your office keeps the trustees' register?'

'Hauptmann Gaschler does, yes. He informed me of your visit.'

'Let me ask this, sir. On the day after the air raid, many of Trassenheide's inmates were transferred to camps at Swinemünde?'

'Yes. Between nine hundred and a thousand. I can find you the precise figure, if you wish.'

'That isn't necessary. The number was determined by Dr von Braun, I think?'

'I understand that it was he who made the calculation. But I was instructed by the Generalmajor directly.'

'So, you undertook the sorting, who was to stay and go?'

'I left that to Hauptmann Gaschler and...' he turned to his subordinate, '...I believe Oberleutnant Raffel assisted him.'

Raffel nodded. 'Yes, sir.'

Fischer turned to him. 'And you supervised the transfers personally, Oberleutnant?'

'No sir. I stayed here, to direct the fire-parties and emergency demolition work. It was Hauptmann Gaschler who accompanied the transferees to Swinemünde and handed them over.'

'Thank you. I don't believe there's anything else, Herr Leutnant-Colonel. Oberleutnant, would you please arrange for the inmate Marcin Konopka to be placed upon the trustees' register? He's been very useful to us and I told him I'd try to arrange it. When he's recovered, of course.'

'Konopka, sir?'

'Yes, the convalescent we were speaking to, in the tent?'

'Oh. Yes, sir.' Rafell looked very doubtful.

'Is there something wrong?'

'Well, sir, I don't know how that man's managed to be useful, but from my experience he isn't to be trusted with anything.'

'Why do you say that?'

'Well, for one thing he's a dealer, sir. Buying and selling small stuff. Generally, we don't crack down on that sort of thing, as long as it stays sensible. It helps keep them in line, in a way. But I had suspicions that he was bribing one of the guards here.'

Stegmaier frowned. 'What action did you take about *that*?'

'I questioned the man thoroughly, sir. But he didn't admit to anything. Said he'd swapped cigarettes for the occasional nod on a work detail, but that was it. And he's one of our more reliable men, sir. Decorated in the First War.'

'Still, I'm not happy about that kind of thing, Oberleutnant.'

'No sir. Doesn't happen much, sir. Gives the lads a bit of extra money.'

Fischer coughed. 'So, if there was nothing to it, why is Konopka not trustworthy?'

'Attitude, Herr Hauptmann. He gets away with a bit too much, in my opinion. A bad example.'

'If not by dealing contraband, then how?'

'Degenerate music, sir. He plays Negro stuff on the trombone, loudly.'

Stegmaier laughed, the first hint of a sense of humour. 'Not the much disbanded Hut Twelve Big Band?'

'That's the one, Herr Leutnant-Col...'

Even with his one good leg, Holleman reached the door only just after Fischer.

Chapter Fifty-One

They found him in the male latrines. He had crawled from his pallet, out of the tent and managed to stagger almost a hundred metres before fainting for the first time. Like wounded animals do he had gone to ground in the place he'd thought them least likely to search. He was unconscious, his head lolling over the edge of the pit, fitfully breathing in the full force of the deadly miasma. Another inmate, his bare rump thrust into space, held onto the safety pole a few metres away, steadfastly minding his own business.

Fischer ordered two guards to carry the Pole gently to the camp infirmary, where the medical officer was told, over strong objections, to keep him alive for questioning. Outside, he grabbed Holleman's arm and spoke quietly.

'Freddie, stay here and watch Konopka. *Don't* let that doctor rid himself of a problem. I'm going to Peenemünde, but I'll be back as soon as I can.'

He took the electrified line to the Development Shops and from there almost ran to the Army Office. Gaschler was wedged into the same seat, looking as if he hadn't moved since Fischer's previous visit. He waved in his visitor affably.

'Achziger! Cup of coffee for a *real* soldier! What can we do for the Luftwaffe, Herr Hauptmann?'

'A few questions, if you don't mind?' Fischer took the coffee, sipped, and placed it on a small pile of chits.

'Mind? Mind a chance to forget about fucking *untermenschen* for a few minutes? Ask on, sir! Here...' Gaschler kicked a stack of box files from a chair, '...take a seat.'

'I hear that you took personal charge of the mass transfer of foreign workers on 18 August?'

'You hear correctly. In a crisis *men* are needed, not damp-arsed queers and the walking-dead (this nodding at the orderlies). I stepped forward and did my bit.'

'You counted them here and there, did you?'

Gaschler grinned. 'I did. Is there a problem?'

'No, none at all. Did the Generalmajor give you

377

any instructions?'

'What sort of instructions?'

'Anything – directly, I mean, rather than through the chain of command.

'Now why would a busy Generalmajor take time to give orders to someone he wouldn't use as a shit-scraper? I was told to take that mob to Swinemünde, hand them over, get receipts, and that was that.'

'I see. May I examine your trustees' register for a moment?'

Gaschler reached behind him, extracted the file from the rack and handed it over. The grin remained, plastered all over the lower part of his face. He was enjoying the exchange hugely and Fischer could think of only one reason for it. He was safely, snugly, under orders.

Briefly he flicked through the entries for the weeks prior to 17 August, made a note and returned the register to Gaschler. 'So, you took a certain number of inmates from Trassenheide, transported them to Swinemünde and handed over *that precise number* to the camps there?'

The big man shrugged. 'If that's what it says on the manifests, that's what I did. No one at the other end complained that they hadn't received enough extra mouths to feed, that's for sure.'

Gaschler's pet orderlies sniggered, but kept their eyes firmly on their work. Fischer nodded and made another note. It wasn't of anything in particular, but he didn't want his audience to think that there wouldn't be paper. He thanked them and stood.

'Is that all?' Gaschler sounded disappointed.

His morning's fun had been curtailed. 'What's this about, anyway?'

'Probably nothing,' said Fischer. 'Gestapo have been asking questions about some ausländers who've slipped off the table. I wanted to make sure it was nothing to do with you.'

A childish lie, easily disproved, but he had the satisfaction of watching three faces fall in formation.

He urgently wished to return to Trassenheide, but House 4 was close by and he decided to call Holleman from there. As usual there was a deal of bustle in the entrance hallway, a clatter of typewriters from the secretarial pool office and, in its doorway, the manageress, taking a batch of papers from Kaspar Nagel. Two entirely unconnected thoughts struck Fischer with such force that he could hardly separate them. He hurried forward and waved down the pair before they parted. He asked Nagel to wait a moment, and went into the pool.

The manageress wasn't certain, but she agreed to check the worksheets for the period. Fischer waited impatiently while she pored over a large, loose-leaf file and made a number of notes on a paper. He took it and thanked her effusively, adding a pointless compliment on the orderliness of her arrangements. She smiled mechanically, already dismissing him and his curious request from memory.

In the entrance hall Nagel was reading a tattered copy of the *Berliner Morgenpost*. Fischer looked at him carefully. He'd been making assumptions about the young man: an amenable object, close to power but possessing none, an innocent because he seemed to be. But it occurred now that he had conflated two states: that innocence and an absence of culpability weren't necessarily close to being the same thing. He took Nagel's arm and shepherded him towards the exit.

'What was your first reaction when you uncovered Dr Thiel's face?'

Nagel thought about it, his brow furrowed in the manner of one who wishes to convey the effort.

'I was horrified, obviously. Confused, probably a little nauseous too, because I'd never seen someone killed – I mean, not deliberately.'

'It isn't pleasant when you know the person. Why did you uncover that corpse in particular? Was it the first you'd looked at? The tenth?'

'We were told to check all of them, to confirm the name-tags. I just saw Walter's name, and I ... I hadn't even known he was dead until then, so...'

'So you had to look, naturally. You told me that the bodies were laid out in the order they came in. It seems to me likely that people who died next to each other were more or less placed together in the hall. I assume, then, that Thiel's family lay adjacent to him?'

'I ... think they did, yes.' Nagel nodded, too briskly, and Fischer felt the hair on the nape of his neck rise.

'But you're not entirely sure? Why is that? Didn't you immediately check their bodies, too?'

'No, I wasn't thinking, I was ... too upset. The

Generalmajor told me to get some fresh air, so I went outside for a few minutes.'

'When *did* you see them?'

The pause was painfully expressive, and Nagel wouldn't meet his eye. 'I don't recall, exactly. I think...'

Fischer squeezed his arm, halting him. 'Were you threatened, Nagel? Were you promised something? Perhaps it was both – a reminder that Germany needs her young men at the Front?'

Nagel's cheeks burned. 'I'm not a brave man.'

'No rational human being is. And I'm not a recruiting officer, so don't worry. Just tell me what happened.'

'I don't know. Really, I don't.'

'All right, Nagel. I think I've heard all I need to. If the Generalmajor asks, I'll say only that you've been helpful.'

'Sir...' Nagel paused. He was anxious, but there was determination too, a quality Fischer hadn't noticed before, something wanting to get out.

'I know that I'm not of much ... use. I take dictation, I organize diaries, and I can type after a fashion. I have a degree in engineering and I understand enough about what happens here to get it right for the notes I make. But all of my friends are gone, at the Front or dead, and I should have gone with them. The men here, they aren't like me, and you should respect that. They've achieved things that defeat imagination. Everywhere else, the old world's marching, committing filthy acts in the name of mad beliefs. But here, a *new* world's being made. The Generalmajor, Werhner, they're giving us the means to leave behind everything that's bad, and I'm not sorry if I've done anything – *anything* – to help them.'

Fischer patted the young man's shoulder. There are many forms of heroism, only a very few of which aren't wasted in the service of the incomprehensible.

'Stand down, Nagel. You've just done your bit.'

Chapter Fifty-Two

They returned before Achym had even begun to consider whether any options remained to him, which, he supposed, was just as well. The Face settled himself carefully on a small stand chair next to the bed while the hard case with the lonely leg cheerfully told the medical orderly to fuck off somewhere else.

'Your name, please.'

'...Achym Mazur.'

'You were assigned to Hut Twelve?'

'I was, sir.'

'You played in the band, a jazz band?'

'It was permitted.'

'Of course. I used to enjoy that sort of thing myself, a little. You must have known Rajmund Ulatowski.'

Achym was tired. He felt like shit feels after a bad night in a wet gutter, and he could think of nothing that might get him out of something similar. 'Yes, sir. He was in my hut.'

382

'A trustee?'

'No, sir.'

'No, that's right, he wasn't. He was transferred to Swinemünde, on 18 August?'

'That's what I heard.'

'You also should have been transferred. Why is it that you stayed here?'

Achym shrugged. 'Better to be where you know how things go.'

'Yes, I suppose it is. So, you took a dead man's name and card? How did you manage that? Do you have a friend among the Hermans?'

It was strange hearing a German use the term, but Achym wasn't going to be fooled by *faux* familiarity. He said nothing.

'I understand. You don't want to betray a man who can do you a lot of harm. Never mind, it's not important. Let's speak a little more about Ulatowski. You were friends?'

'We got on all right.'

'The camp office has photographs of you and him. They were taken the day you arrived, remember? If we were to show these to staff at Peenemünde, do you think that someone might identify you as close companions? As confidants, perhaps?'

They weren't going to be fooled this time. Silently, Achym made his apologies to Rajmund.

'We were ... friends, sir.'

'Good. Now, we'd like very much to speak to him, but we realize that it isn't going to be possible, so I'm afraid that you're going to have to speak for him. An ... *event* occurred, on the night of the British air raid, and we think he may have some information on it.'

'I haven't seen him since that night, sir.'

'Of course you haven't. You've been here and he's been ... elsewhere. But you may know something of what he knows.'

'What was this event, sir?'

'I can't say, other than it happened just as the British bombs began to fall. Now, we know that Ulatowski was at Peenemünde that night, and...'

'No.'

'What do you mean?'

'No, sir. He was at Peenemünde that *day*. But he came back with us on the trucks, at dusk. He was here until ... the bombs fell.'

'It's too late to try to defend your friend, Mazur. We know that he was there, and we want to know *why* he was there.'

'No, sir, I'm sorry, he wasn't. He was here, and...' Achym thought about it. Which was worse: implicating his friend in something he wasn't part of, or telling them *why* he couldn't have been where they were saying he was? And why did they think he was at Swinemünde, alive, when he'd been declared dead in the raid?

'He ... got out, sir. When the fence went down: he got out, and ran. Wouldn't you?'

The two of them stared at him, and Achym felt that he might just have shoved Rajmund out of the spotlight and taken his place.

'He *escaped?* From Trassenheide?'

'Yes, sir.'

'Then why is his name on the list of persons transferred the next day?'

'I really can't say, sir.'

They stared at each other. That was preferable, but then the Leg had a thought.

'Didn't they ask you about the fact he'd fucked off?'

'No, sir, they didn't.'

'I wonder why? Unless someone – a friend, perhaps – managed to hide the fact of it from them. I wonder how that might have happened?'

The Face smiled. 'How many people died here that night, Oberleutnant?'

'Hundreds, Herr Hauptmann. About half of them men.'

'And most of them very messily, I expect. We've all seen what high explosives do to bodies, haven't we?'

'Yes, Herr Hauptmann, a frightful sight. You wouldn't recognize your own best friend, if he'd been caught in the middle of something like that.'

'Difficult to tell one from the other.'

'Definitely.'

'One could hardly blame someone for making a mistake, in the confusion of the moment.'

'Wouldn't try, speaking personally.'

'Nor me. Hell, I've had to guess which bit belonged to which body, on days we've fought off the Ivans. It's not a science, that's for sure.'

The Face sighed, a long, contented noise. 'So, you told them he was dead.'

Achym swallowed, and nodded. 'I didn't think he'd be missed.'

'He shouldn't have been.' The *schwabs* were looking at each other again. 'So why was he identified as one of the missing workers, when he

385

wasn't? As a trustee, when he wasn't? What's so important about a handyman?'

Achym swallowed painfully. There was the faintest hint of value to this, but he hardly knew how to use it.

'If I said … something, sir. If I could tell you something that might make a difference, would that help, at all?'

The Face looked at him for what seemed like an hour. 'It might be *very* helpful. I'm sure we'd be enormously grateful for any information, wouldn't we, Oberleutnant?'

'We always are, Herr Hauptmann. We can get almost comradely about that sort of thing.'

It was vague, but they weren't going to be offering kisses, or a contract.

'Rajmund … wasn't a handyman.'

The Face laughed. 'Well, there has to be *one* Pole at Trassenheide who isn't.'

'He's a scientist. You Germans employed him as one.'

For several seconds they stared at him like he'd pissed in the holy water, and then the Leg exploded. '*Fuck!*'

The Face placed his left, human hand carefully on Achym's shoulder. 'Tell me exactly where he worked.'

Achym told him. There seemed no reason not to, now that the rest of it was out. In fact, once he started he could hardly apply the brakes. He told them about Rajmund's studies, his volatile nature and how, entirely out of character, he had volunteered as a *fremdarbeiter*, coming west to find his sister, and…

'Sweet God, look at this.'

The Face passed a piece of paper to the Leg. 'It's from the typists' work schedule. Look at the way it drops right off, about June, early July. Before that it was fairly regular, then nothing. It was him, it was Ulatowski.' He turned back to Achym. 'Your friend, he was taking papers, wasn't he? From his workplace?'

He wasn't going to admit to that. They'd shoot Rajmund as soon as look at him.

'Never mind, we know. So...'

The Leg grinned. 'They knew and didn't try to stop him!'

'Or they encouraged him. *Abwehr!*'

'No wonder he ran for it. He must have felt like the cheese in a mousetrap.'

The Face turned back to Achym. 'Ulatowski was the friend you mentioned, wasn't he? The one who knew about Zofia and the German? *How* did he know about it?'

The answer was so self-evident that Achym tried to work out what sort of trap was being set. But they were looking at him expectantly, waiting to be enlightened. And then it struck him, and before he could remind himself of his current prospects he started to laugh.

'Well, her name *might* be a clue, sir!'

Less than thirty minutes later, Fischer knocked on a newly painted door and listened carefully. It was late afternoon, a work day, but that was the thing about Peenemünde: the commute was so short, a matter of minutes at most, and then he'd be home. There should have been noises already, of course: children shouting, the clatter of domestic routines, appliances, remonstrations, laughter, anger, threats of what would happen when he returned. Anything but silence, at this time of day.

No one was going to open the door. He took out his pick and placed it in the lock. His bad hand already held the tension wrench – he'd assumed it would be needed, and he still recalled clearly the advice he'd been given at Munich by his one-armed orderly, one of life's few truly invaluable men, who'd broken more laws in his time than bones in his body. The lock wasn't too difficult for an ex-Bull, even one with a shortened right arm.

She stood at the back of the hallway, too scared to run, too defiant to hide. And once more he could see it, clear as day, what it was that would make a man throw away so much, and do it happily.

'May I wait for him please, Zofia?'

Chapter Fifty-Three

The news had reached Berlin that morning, and it needed radical manipulation. In fact, Karl Krohne was certain that this was going to be their biggest test to date, given that he couldn't, after serious reflection, see any bright side to it. He passed out the bulletins and told them all to get busy finding one. So no one took much notice of the wanderer's flying return. He had only been gone for three or four days, after all, and it wasn't as though there wouldn't be time later, in the *Silver Birch*, to savour every detail of how the girls in the north liked it.

'You're back then, Freddie?'

'Mm.'

'Not staying?'

'Not today. Back tomorrow, probably.'

Detmar Reincke had an obscene pleasantry poised, but Holleman was already out of the door. He was at his house in Rummelsburg less than an hour later. It was locked up and all the curtains were drawn, and he was obliged to go around to his neighbour, Frau Kuefer, for the spare key. That was unfortunate. Short of snatching it from her hand and punching her in the face there was little chance that he was going to be allowed to just come and go. Frau Kuefer had been resident in the street since Charlemagne was Kaiser. At least she remembered fields and a time before the district was officially part of Berlin, and she firmly believed that the day she stopped being interested in other folks' business she'd expire.

Holleman had a story ready, of course. You couldn't just improvise with Frau Kuefer. He told her that he'd been away on a training course, secret stuff, but that he'd managed to get Kristin and the children into accommodation in a nice village south of Posen. Yes, of course Franz and Ulrich were going to enrol at the local KLV there. He couldn't think where she'd got the idea that he didn't want them to go; it was just the thing to put a bit of backbone into the boys. Any-

389

way, if they didn't go to a KLV, how would they qualify for admission to a WELS and get their training for a flak emplacement, or even the Front, if they were lucky? Yes, Kristin was looking forward to getting some time to herself, once they'd gone. And how was Gerda, by the way? Still under the doctor?

He didn't allow himself any sense of loss as he moved through the rooms of his house. Kristin had packed very little, and none of the rubbish the twins almost certainly begged her to take. *Good girl.* Just enough for overnight: a family visiting a relative, what could be more usual? Hurriedly, he filled three Luftwaffe grey holdalls with clothes and the necessary bits and pieces: a first-aid kit, tinned food, two torches, a tiny kerosene camp stove, four thousand reichsmarks he'd withdrawn from his account with Deutsche Bank on 4 September 1939. The wedding photograph on the sitting room mantelpiece sang to him as he packed, but he plugged his ears. It was just the kind of thing he'd have looked for, in the old days.

As he locked up again he knew that she'd be watching – probably hadn't taken her eyes off the house all the time he was inside. She'd see the bags, but the Posen thing would explain that. There was no chance at all that she wouldn't mention it to someone – probably her familiar, Frau Brecht, or that dry goat of a daughter who lived with her. Once *she* knew, that was it: The fucking Americans would have it by Tuesday. But that was the thing, the same thing that made him feel relaxed about his absence from the Air

390

Ministry: no one would really care. It was amazing what a man gained when he lost a leg, once he stopped being of use to the regime. He became invisible, fading to an embarrassment, as palpable as a fart. And no one on the street would miss the Hollemans. Why should they, when all of Germany was moving from one place to another, trying to get out of the way of what they were beginning to understand was coming? Karl Krohne was a mate, of course; he'd probably fret for a while, make discreet enquiries. But he wasn't going to send out the *Feldgendarmerie* to chase him down. You just didn't do that, not for a cripple. Really, who would care, one way or the other?

When he'd locked up the house, he put down one of the bags and waved at her window. The curtain twitched slightly, pretending it wasn't being clutched by an inquisitive old bitch. He walked slowly down the road, heading for the u-bahn station at Lichtenberg, making it look a little more difficult than it was: just another reminder of what everyone feared for their own husbands and fathers, as common a sight these days as starlings used to be: pitiable, unmemorable and unrecalled, should anyone come asking.

The truck was waiting for him at a loading bay at Tempelhof. Gerd Branssler was owed more than a bottle of brandy for this, but Holleman and he went back further than a Berlin beat, and friends didn't let the occasional Reich get in the way of important things. The driver nodded, passed over the papers. He didn't bother checking them; they'd be good ones – a real family,

391

discreetly dead and unidentified: probably from Hamburg. There was a lot of useful stuff coming out of the city: paperwork with names but no corpses attached, histories with no inconvenient claims upon them. He lit a cigarette and handed it to the driver. That was it: no introductions, no small talk; no risks that need be taken.

Three hours at the most, and he'd be there. Then all he'd have to worry about would be teaching the little buggers to swim before they drowned.

Chapter Fifty-Four

Fischer took the offered seat and placed the folder in his lap. Dornberger signed a paper, gave it to Werner Magirius and nodded him out of the room. He was composed, serious, leaning forward slightly across the large desk

'Well, Hauptmann, here we are. Can you tell me who killed Walter Thiel?'

'I can, Herr Generalmajor, yes.'

'Please continue.'

'He was murdered by the Royal Air Force.'

'But...'

'If I may? It occurred to both my colleague and I, very early in our investigation, that there were no conceivable circumstances in which this death could have happened in its apparent manner. The harder we tried to construct a sequence of events, the more obvious this became. Walter

Thiel and his family left their house in Hinden-burg Strasse at approximately 1.20am and ran to the nearest air raid trench, about one hundred metres distant. They were seen to do so by several witnesses. I assume this to be a fact, therefore. They entered the trench and minutes later it collapsed, killing nine people besides Thiel – nine people who, almost certainly, would have departed the trench, and with some alacrity, the moment that an assassin fired a bullet into his head. So, was Thiel murdered and *then* placed into the trench? Well, if anyone can provide me with a convincing explanation of how this could occur without some resistance being offered by his wife and the other occupants of the trench, I'll consider it. That leaves one further possibility, that at almost precisely the moment the gun was fired, the trench collapsed. Was the assassin killed? No corpse was found near the trench. Did this person possess some miraculous power to deflect a large explosion and make his escape without detection? No, sir. The very obvious solution to this puzzle is that there *is* no puzzle. Dr Thiel died of suffocation, in precisely the same manner as his wife and children – about whose post-mortem condition you misled me, I believe. Their bodies were examined – briefly, no doubt – and I'm sure they were found to be in much the same condition as Thiel's. No one tried to dig their way out of the trench, no one sur-vived its collapse. The bullet was administered at some point following the discovery of their deaths.'

Dornberger had listened politely, a small smile

contradicting the frown. 'By whom, and for what possible purpose?'

'The first part of that may be answered readily, Herr Generalmajor. He was *probably* shot by Werner Magirius, and certainly upon your order. The rest is rather more complicated.'

'I have as much time as you need, Hauptmann.'

'Yes, I thought that might be the case. May I have some water, please?'

Rather than wave him to the tumbler on the sideboard, Dornberger rose and filled two glasses from it.

'Before I continue, sir, let me say something about why you chose me to conduct this investigation. Firstly, it's a matter of who I'm not. I'm not GFP, who, as you suggested, would have intruded drastically into the life of this facility and subjected your staff and their families to their habitual, intrusive routine. They would also have concluded that one of your elusive foreign workers had committed the crime and, if they couldn't locate him, would have made a rather large, unpleasant example of a number of his co-workers. Nor am I Abwehr, whom I shall discuss in a moment. For now, it's enough to say that employing them would have been *ostensibly* curious, and somewhat counter-productive. A civilian agency, such as SiPo, would have been equally invasive, and of course brought the incremental disadvantage of reporting directly to the Reichsführer SS. What you needed was someone not only without affiliations but with no possible recourse to a hinterland of support, should he stumble upon the fact that there really was no investigation.'

'I recall that I sent for you and specifically asked that you conduct one, Hauptmann. Is my memory faulty?'

'No, Herr Generalmajor. But I think that you made your choice with great care. You approached Felix Linnemann, of all people, because you wanted a deeply stupid man to recommend someone he knew to be without patronage and then to forget the conversation before his toes had peeled their next piece of fruit.'

Dornberger did little to stifle a grin.

'I think you were being entirely honest about that, sir. As you pointed out during our very first conversation, I was *not* going to be confiding in too many of my ex-colleagues. I was going to be exactly what you wanted, a very minor element in a vast and rather sophisticated game who would leave no mark of his passing.'

'When...?'

'When he had performed his set function.'

'This would be the conclusion of the non-investigation?'

'It would be whenever a party – perhaps *parties* – were persuaded of something.'

'Hm.' Dornberger opened his cigarette case and offered it to Fischer. 'Am I going to have Werner shoot you also? The poor boy might think he was being used dreadfully.'

'I doubt that you ever intended to do more harm than necessary. I'm not here to do a job and be liquidated, just to do a very precise form of job and then go, discreetly.'

'Again, the "job"?'

'To give an *appearance*, to be a cipher from

which several meanings might be drawn. One meaning, of course, might be that I was indeed investigating a murder. But I think that stands as the last, not the first, possibility. I flatter myself enough to assume you would expect me to see through the apparent facts of this case.'

Dornberger smiled again, said nothing.

'That being so, you'd want me to go further, to ask myself *why* you might want me to see this. Perhaps to ask what else could be going on here? Then again, it's possible you just didn't care, one way or the other. If so, then for whom was the message? And why was I part of that message?'

'My head's beginning to hurt, Hauptmann.'

'Not as much as mine, I assure you, Herr Generalmajor. You made an error, one so obvious that, again, I assume you intended me to discover it quite quickly. The nonsense about the three missing foreign workers, and the extraction of every one of their hut mates. Was that to lead me down a false path, or perhaps bring me closer to a truth without quite letting me get there?'

A shrug.

'May I ask what happened to the occupants of the three huts, sir?'

'Of course. The Poles were transferred to work projects within the General-Government, the Czechs and Slovaks were reassigned to duties elsewhere in the Reich, and the French were returned to France – we simply cancelled their contracts early. The Russians...' Dornberger grimaced, '...well, there's no shortage of alternative employment for those poor bastards, is there?'

'All to convince me that three – I'm sorry, *one*

of three – foreign workers remained alive, and that I should never find him. Not a murderer, of course, because you knew I should have dismissed that possibility already. No, this was a man who might be involved in something that someone wouldn't want me to discover. I was doing this, in fact, for the benefit of that *someone*.'

Fischer paused, took a sip of water. 'But I must tell you, Herr Generalmajor, that the phantom foreign worker – the one whom you persuaded me to chase, even though you knew him to be dead – was, to the contrary, in excellent health. He ran, like a hare.'

Dornberger took a long pull on his cigarette; the other hand beat out a rapid tattoo on the desktop. His eyes didn't leave Fischer's face.

'Ironic, isn't it? You used all of those transferred workers as camouflage to disguise nothing. He was alive, just as you wished me – and *someone* else – to believe. But he's no longer at Trassenheide. He went over the wire – or under it – during the air raid, probably convinced that you were about to ensure his silence. Where he is now, well, neither I nor anyone else can say. I've checked, believe me. I also know who Rajmund Ulatowski really is, *precisely* who he is, what he was doing at Peenemünde and why you want someone to think he's alive still.'

'You're certain of that?'

'Of more than that, I know who *someone* is. I believe I know more or less *all* of what this is about, but only because you and your staff have been kind enough to tell me.'

397

'Have we? That sounds very careless of us.' Dornberger leaned forward and ground the remains of his cigarette in the ashtray. 'Would you like a breakfast cognac? I think that I might.'

'Thank you, sir. May I continue?'

'Please do.'

'When I arrived here, you told me of your ambitions – may I say, your *vision?* It sounded quite fantastical to a layman, of course, but there's that about this place. It has a quality that makes a man *want* to be convinced. When I first saw the A4 I couldn't help but think of the possibilities, of where it might lead. But then, like a soldier, I went the wrong way. I thought of new weapons, the means to save our nation from the ... *exuberance* of our leaders. Your staff corrected me, though I'm sure that wasn't their intention. I think it was Dr Schilling who put it most succinctly. He told me that *you don't make weapons here: just the means of delivering them.* I didn't grasp the point at the time, but its relevance has since been impressed upon me.

'Herr Generalmajor, several of the men I've spoken to here tell me that you have often argued, enthusiastically, for the A4 as a war-winning weapon, to the point at which the Führer and most of the hierarchy have become entirely convinced of it. Kaspar Nagel mentioned, furthermore, that you've been proposed as the future commanding officer of whichever section of the Wehrmacht will be devoted to the new art of rocket warfare.'

'He shouldn't have tempted fate. But you're objecting to ambition?'

'Not at all, sir. I find it admirable, in generals. What concerns me is your sincerity. That is, the lack of it. I think you argued for the A4 project so strenuously because you knew that, once Himmler in particular could see the lie of the land, you'd lose it: that someone with even more ambition would take production of the missile entirely from you. As for this desire to be the commander of "rocket forces", I find it hardly credible, particularly as you'd be placing your – forgive me – your balls in the Reichsführer's hands, now that he's supplying the product. I suspect that you have no faith in the *military* programme here, or in its potential successors. You *know* that the missile cannot possibly affect the outcome of the war, and you allowed yourself to be put forward as the man to direct its deployment only to deflect attention from your true convictions.'

'This is quite astonishing, Hauptmann. I'm accused of having no faith in my life's work?'

'I didn't say that, sir. I'm sure you're absolutely committed to your goal. But it isn't the A4, or any variant of it. The thing's a terrible toy, a curiosity with which to frighten British housewives. And to kill them, of course, but not in such numbers as to turn the tide. We aren't, after all, most threatened by housewives. After hearing the testimony of your colleagues, the truth of it is so evident that my instincts tell me you saw it a long time ago, perhaps even before the war commenced. But you were tied to the project by the fact that only a military dimension to your dream would secure the resources to realize it. And eventually, the means suffocated the dream. You don't *want* to kill people, Herr Generalmajor, though I'm sure you don't mind, if it serves an end. Your ambition is aimed somewhere else entirely.

'What did you say to me, on the day that we met? That you *look beyond war itself*? I do you the courtesy of believing you, sir, on this point at least. Most of my generation are trapped, as it were, in a time, a series of events, of terrible circumstances. But you and certain others here are – as Americans say, I think – *just passing through*. For a time, I imagined your disengagement to be a side-product of the peculiar nature of this facility, of its seclusion and your rather comfortable, pre-war lifestyle. But I've come to see that it's the programme itself – the *real* programme – that's responsible.'

Fischer picked up his brandy and threw it back in a single gulp. 'The war – my God, the *Reich* – they're just interruptions, aren't they?'

Chapter Fifty-Five

Dornberger pursed his lips and stared into his own, untouched drink. 'Do you understand the nature of science, Hauptmann?'

'I'm sure that I could attempt a worthless definition.'

'Let me put it more precisely. Do you understand how National Socialist science works?' He waved down Fischer's reply. 'Really, it's quite remarkable. If, on the basis of wishful thinking, I wanted support and financing for an expedition to Byelorussia to, say, uncover the remains of a vast Astrogothic city that predated Rome, I could approach the Reichsführer with great hopes for a sympathetic ear. Similarly, a project to refine current thinking on the phrenological evidence for Aryan superiority would, I think, meet with great approbation, and cash enough to buy a mountain of skulls and the alleged scientists to study them. By way of contrast...'

He opened a drawer, removed an envelope and threw it across the desk.

'...it has been made clear to me that, should the war be won tomorrow and our A4 missile be the principal cause of victory, no diversion of our resources from weapons research will be considered. That is, we shall not be permitted even to *propose* potential peacetime applications for our technologies.'

'You're speaking of a space project.'

'What else would I be speaking of? No, war will be – will continue to be – our only *raison d'être*. The preposterous search for worthy German prehistories and pedigrees will continue unabated, but the first step of the greatest of all human journeys will *never* be allowed to commence, not from here. You may read that letter. It gives the Führer's personal opinion on the matter. As you'll see, it's quite unequivocal. You should be honoured, Fischer. What I'm confiding to you is something I don't even trust to my diary.'

Fischer didn't touch the envelope. 'And you've been working towards this since, what, 1934?'

'Long before that, in fact. The first vague ideas occurred to me – and to others, of course – during the First War, when the limits of contemporary science became forcibly apparent. I would say that we began our quest actively during the late Twenties. I didn't lie to you, Fischer. No one else has come close to what we've done. But all of it – *all* of it – will be for nothing more than the chance to kill a few more civilians. We've created the world's first entirely spiteful weapon, at a cost in resources that would make your eyes water.'

'Herr Schubert gave me a hint of that.'

Did he? Well, he's understandably a little bitter about how things have gone, though for reasons other than mine. His disappointment, however, has been my salvation. That detestable creature Kammler is going to reap the credit for whatever the A4 achieves in the field. Or, more likely, doesn't.'

'Shall I go on, Herr Generalmajor?'

Dornberger nodded.

'I'll leave, for the moment, the implications of what you've told me. The Pole Ulatowski was an engineer, of course, not the manual labourer suggested by the Trassenheide trustees' work register. In fact, his name had never been entered into that book before 17 August, because he was regarded almost as a member of your technical staff. He worked, I believe, as personal assistant to Walter Thiel?'

'He was a propulsion specialist, yes. As was

Walter himself.'

'He was also a patriot, anxious that Germany's secrets did not remain so. You discovered this – or rather, it became obvious to Walter Thiel that several of the notes he allowed Ulatowski to write up due to his own distaste for paperwork weren't finding their way either to the secretarial pool or to the Design Office. He told you of it, rather than confront Ulatowski. Why was that, I wonder?'

'Walter didn't like confrontations. They upset him greatly, though God knows he caused more than a few. I think he wanted me to sort things out and yet somehow let him retain his valuable little Pole. That was quite unworldly, but it suited me that he left things in my hands.'

'So, you spoke to Ulatowski. Did you threaten him into doing what he did, or did he perhaps hope to find a way to deceive you as well as Thiel?'

'I didn't, and we'll never know.'

'No. An idle thought. Yesterday, when I discovered Ulatowski's role here, I believed I could wash my hands of this investigation. Whatever the curiosities regarding the bullet in Walter Thiel, I could offer you a plausible interpretation of what had been happening here. After all, it was obvious that there'd been no murder, so whatever game you were playing with Thiel and the others could be regarded as your business, not mine. I was quite happy to fail graciously.

'But something continued to buzz in my ear. Why were Abwehr involved? Did they suspect Ulatowski of espionage? Perhaps yes, but surely they would have passed on this information to RSHA Amt III or IV, under whose jurisdiction it clearly fell? Even allowing for the ... *tensions* between the two agencies, why would the Wehrmacht's overseas intelligence service continue to take an interest, rather than wash their hands of a palpably internal matter?'

'What did you conclude?'

Fischer shrugged. 'That it *wasn't* internal. That something larger than a spy at Peenemünde was in point.'

'A leap of logic, surely?'

'A reasonable one, given that you were manipulating Abwehr as much as me. You told them, did you not, that Ulatowski had died in the air raid?'

'I did.'

'It was the truth as you saw it, of course. Still, I wondered why you would bother to do that. I concluded that it was to reassure them about something. But then you deliberately allowed them to discover, through me, that he was in fact alive – though you didn't really believe it, at the time. And why, I wondered, would you do *that?* Because, I decided, circumstances had changed, that you now required Abwehr to be anything *but* reassured. So what had altered, between the two events? That gave me some difficulty, until I heard – quite accidentally – about General Fromm's recent initiative to ensure your appointment as head of a mooted "Rocket Corps". Fromm is an old friend, I believe?'

'We're both artillerymen, we share a history. He's supported our programme wholeheartedly.'

'A friend as head of Army Ordnance would be invaluable, I expect. But the General's also a dabbler, a blusterer. He interfered in the Zanssen episode, making waves all over Berlin to get the man reinstated, because he didn't want Himmler having an excuse to worm his way into the project. Still, I don't believe the affair had anything to do with the relationship between Zanssen and Gerhardt Stegmaier. In fact, I think Major Stegmaier is probably an honourable man who's been very badly used. It was you who betrayed Zanssen, I believe?'

'That would be a very mean-spirited act.'

'Not if Zanssen was beginning to suspect ... let's say *something*, and had to be removed as Army Commander here. In that case it would be an entirely prudent move. But, as I say, General Fromm intervened, with good intentions and appalling timing, with the result that the Reichsführer had to back off and Zanssen has a very real prospect of being reinstated here. Now, once more, Fromm is blundering in, this time to preserve what he imagines is your desire to keep a hold upon the A4 programme. But that's the very last thing you want, as you've just confirmed. Why did the General do it, then? If not at your request, whose? Who else would wish to minimize the extent of SS's penetration of the secrets of Peenemünde? A difficult question, but of course, there was a certain agency already occupying my thoughts, and one thing seemed to come together with the other quite neatly.

'When you discovered their meddling, you needed to poke a stick through the bars to warn them off – hence my walk-on part in the supposed mystery of the missing foreign workers. You wanted them to know that the threat of Rajmund Ulatowski remained, that further pressures to keep you at the centre of the A4 business would rebound, and to their cost. So, what is it that has such a potential to damage Abwehr?'

'A body that deals in secrets must have some of its own.'

'I know, sir. Being in the business of deception myself, I appreciate the risks of infection. I concluded that they were running a double agent – Ulatowski, probably, or someone known to him – with a view to deceiving the enemy as to what was being done at Peenemünde. At least I hope that was their intention. One can never be sure with professional spies. I concluded also that you were complicit – obviously, since you did nothing about Thiel's revelation that the Pole was recording and removing important information from his department. Of course, such an operation, if discovered by an ill-intentioned party, might be used to great effect against its architects. It would certainly give Abwehr ample reason to fear Ulatowski's reappearance. You convinced them to end their resistance to the SS's assumption of control over A4 production, in return for your silence – and assurance, I suspect, that you would deal with Ulatowski, a man you "knew" to be dead already.'

Dornberger smiled. 'They think of me as rather a ruthless character.'

'So there it was, the mystery solved. I could now confront you with what I knew and with-

draw, my self-regard intact. Except...'
  'Except?'
'We return to the hole in Walter Thiel's head.'

Chapter Fifty-Six

Fischer took another sip of water. He hadn't babbled like this since his Kripo days, and he was feeling more than a little lightheaded. To speak to a general officer in this manner was the dream of half the Wehrmacht; but dreams don't usually have consequences.

'The shooting of Walter Thiel couldn't have been merely a device to bring me to Peenemünde, because, on the morning of 18 August, there was as yet no reason to apply pressure to your co-conspirators. At the time, neither you nor they had reason to think the Reichsführer had been given an excuse to intervene in the programme. Therefore, the bullet was for the benefit of another constituency. And this, I think, is where we return to your *vision*.

'A shooting sends a specific message. Most obviously it is a method of silencing or punishing someone. But it can also be a means to frighten a person or persons into silence, or compliance. For that to be the case, he or they would need to know of it. Yet you took considerable pains to limit the number of men who were aware that Thiel *apparently* did not die in the air raid. So, was the message intended for one, or for all of them? Arbitrarily, I dismissed Kaspar Nagel and Professor Wierer, because I could find nothing in their reactions to the discovery that hinted at other than surprise, or shock. Your adjutant I could neither dismiss nor implicate – firstly, because he didn't wish to speak to me, and more fundamentally because he *is* your adjutant and, therefore, one might expect him to be intensely loyal. This could mean something or nothing.

'Dr von Braun and Arthur Rudolph were, of course, far more problematic. I could only begin to speculate upon reasons you might have to wish to intimidate or silence these men. You've known them for years – they are, perhaps, your closest colleagues, and as we kripos know very well, most crimes of violence are directed at and within the family. However, without further knowledge of their – of *your* – pasts, whatever I might have thought was worthless. Had I been obliged to leave it there I doubt that any resolution would have been possible. I was then fortunate, however.'

'A vital clue?'

'No, sir. A frivolous error, on your part. Really, you should have appointed someone else to bring my meals. The surname isn't uncommon, but I was bound to look, if I made a connection.'

'There seemed no reason why you should. Who would be interested in a servant's circumstances?'

'That's true. But the longer I remained here the greater the chance of an accidental discovery. In any case, your curious indulgence of her behaviour was bound to excite my interest. I assume

408

you were putting in place a plausible alternative to her brother, should the wrong people discover what had been happening here? In the event, the connection was revealed by a man who *should* have been removed from Peenemünde already, had your prompt actions following the raid achieved their intended effect. The same man, in fact, whose efforts on behalf of a friend led you to believe that Rajmund Ulatowski was dead.'

'And this inconvenient fellow is...?'

'A Pole, obviously. I'm not entirely certain of his real name. He knew not only of the relationship of your pet spy to my housekeeper, but of *her* relationship to – I should say *with* – the seventh witness to your pretend murder, Klaus Riedel.

'Poor Riedel. You must have thought it a perfect strategy. The man was already distraught about his part in Thiel's actual death and, I suspect, about his own infidelities. What better way to bring him fully into line than to implicate him in an act *that he knew to be a lie?*'

'Your logic eludes me, Hauptmann.'

'Riedel is a former communist, isn't he? Gestapo have a file on him, codename *Bukharin*. Who says they have no sense of humour? They conclude that it was very probably a youthful enthusiasm – useful, should they ever need to lean upon him, but otherwise not a cause for concern, even given the sensitivity of his role here. You can imagine how disappointing this was for me, initially. The worst of it is, the information is entirely accurate. He really isn't a security risk, is he, Herr General-major? To the contrary, Riedel is the closest thing to a German patriot that I've discovered here.'

'I assume that he wouldn't follow the prescribed lead, the one that von Braun, Rudolph, Thiel and, no doubt, many others have so supinely accepted? I think he may have told you to go to hell, even when you threatened to reveal his relationship with a *zivilianbeiter* – a relationship that you may have arranged, and certainly encouraged. In fact, he admitted the sin to his wife, pre-empting any possibility of you using it against him. That's why she and their children weren't at home on the night of the air raid. They had fled several days earlier, to her parents in Kiel.'

'How do you know? Klaus would never...'

'I *suspected* something when I saw the Riedels' back garden, one bereft of any clues to a child's presence. It was confirmed to me last evening.'

Fischer paused, ordering the events in his mind. 'So, what else could you threaten him with? Well, why not the revelation of a murder, *committed with his gun*, and an entirely plausible circumstance to explain it? Let me see if I have it. Walter Thiel had discovered that his assistant Rajmund Ulatowski, abetted by a member of staff, was stealing secrets from Peenemünde and passing them on to the Allies. But who was that person, the German who could think of betraying his country in such a foul manner, and why would he do it? Of course! It was the known communist, Klaus Riedel, the besotted lover of Ulatowski's own sister! A plot fit for the most lurid novel, and our paranoid masters would believe every detail.

'Did you show the violated corpse to him as it

lay in the Development Shop, *before* it was "discovered" and carried to the schoolhouse? Or did you have Magirius shoot the body in front of him? I'd have done the latter, I think. It would add that last necessary trauma to an already breaking spirit.'

Dornberger rose and went to the window. Below, Fischer could hear the first of the early shift arriving at House 4.

'Hauptmann, Klaus is one of my very brightest. I happen also to be very fond of him. Why would I do this awful thing?'

'You did it *because* he's one of your brightest. In fact, I'd say he was probably the least dispensable man at Peenemünde. Your rockets are temperamental, aren't they, Herr Generalmajor? The science – the *art* – of keeping them from exploding as they move from storage to being armed, and then to being raised to a launch position, has a single adept: Klaus Riedel. You need him most of all, I suspect.'

'Then why have I not simply doubled his salary and arranged a holiday, to allow him and his wife to mend their differences?'

'That isn't what I meant by *need*. Three days before the air raid, a flight was authorized from the Luftwaffe experimental airfield at Peenemünde West, I believe?'

'As they are daily.'

'But this was an unusual flight. No plan was filed beforehand with the station office, nor was its departure logged. Yet it certainly *did* depart, as your own pilot confirmed to us – he was, I think, doing a little private business at the airfield, and

411

witnessed it. This was the same evening that Rajmund Ulatowski failed to appear at the truck park, to be returned with his compatriots to Trassenheide.'

'A rather bare coincidence?'

'Not really. Ulatowski was next seen here on 17 August, a matter of hours before the raid. There was a single flight *into* Peenemünde West that day, seen by several witnesses who confirm that it was the same aircraft, a Bü 181. Again, no record of this was entered in the station log, a serious breach of procedures. The person responsible insists that he intended to make the appropriate entries, both for the flights of 14 and 17 August. However, and rather curiously, orders were issued to the station officer specifically preventing this. The person issuing those orders was Major Schell, of Spionage Abwehr.'

'To what purpose?'

'To ensure that they remained non-flights. I could see why Schell might do this, if he believed himself to be operating a double agent. But you, Herr Generalmajor, you knew that there was nothing *double* about Ulatowski. So why would you have assisted someone who was attempting to harm the Reich? Why would a man, honoured with rank, privileges and even the personal apology of the Führer for having ever doubted him, risk everything to give the Allies a weapon that can have very little impact upon the course of the war? In effect, to sacrifice himself for nothing, the sort of gesture that men like Ulatowski would regard as glorious and any rational being as preposterous? I was forced to a further conclusion: that he – *you* – wouldn't.

'You weren't betraying any secrets, sir. You were simply making a proposition, about something in which our leaders have expressed no interest whatsoever. What remains to you here at Peene-münde after the A4 is taken away is nothing, an irrelevance. But what comes after *that* is everything. The papers that Ulatowski took were of minor importance, I should think, but enough to whet an interest in something: enough to explain that *thing* sufficiently to whet a vast interest.'

'In what, Hauptmann?'

'In you, sir. An interest in what you *do*. You're selling yourself, so to speak, to someone who'll do justice to the *vision*. But there is no single you. *You* is a hive mind of men who've developed their own unique talents, each of which contributes to the whole, the package. I doubt that the Allies would be interested in just a part of it. No, you need Riedel as much as you need von Braun, and Rudolph, and yourself – less would be much harder to sell. But he wasn't prepared to be a part of the proposal. In fact, he strongly opposed it, to the point at which the whole initiative might have fallen apart.

'So, Klaus Riedel's alternative options had to be made as unattractive as possible. Until the raid it couldn't have been clear how to do this, but Thiel's death – in one respect a terrible setback for your scheme – was in every other a Godsend. All you needed to do was to hang the threat of discovery over his friend's head, and I doubt that you'd ever have heard another disobliging word.'

Dornberger exhaled deeply. His usual wan

413

complexion had coloured a little, but otherwise he seemed calm. If the moment had arrived for him to call in Magirius to put a bullet either in his own head or Fischer's, he wasn't flagging it. For a few moments he considered the commemorative inkstand on his desk, as if willing its pewter Focker Scout to provide inspiration. But when he looked up his eyes were clear.

'You're quite wrong about Walter Thiel, Hauptmann. He was an innocent, a man so wholly ravished by his work that I hadn't yet found the courage to put the proposal – I simply couldn't read him. But his relationship to Riedel was of great advantage. They were like brothers. I believe Klaus actually experienced something of a mental breakdown when I shot the corpse, and I regret that deeply.

'And yes, it was me, not Werner Magirius, who used Klaus's pistol. I wouldn't put that kind of pressure upon a subordinate's sense of duty, believe me. The two workers who carried Walter's body to the hall had to go, of course, particularly as one of them was known to be entirely incapable of discretion. I had them on a truck to Rostock before breakfast, a re-assignment I have no doubt they're regretting. Naturally, I allowed you to believe that they and Ulatowski shared a fate. As for the rest, I must hold up my hands to you. You're quite correct for the most part, though I should say that my attempt to cool General Fromm's enthusiasm for my imagined ambitions may have failed. He's a little like a stung horse about it at the moment.

'So now, what do you intend to do? I notice that

Oberleutnant Holleman is no longer at Peene-münde. You've sent him away with the express purpose of concealing the noose in a safe place, I presume?'

Fischer smiled. 'It seemed prudent, Herr Generalmajor. To my surprise I find that I retain an interest in breathing. As to intentions, I have none.'

'I'm sorry?'

'Put very simply, sir, I don't care. You've committed treason, under any number of laws and conventions, and if I took out my pistol and shot you now I'd be entirely justified. But as we're speaking very freely, let me give you *my* view of things. The war, it seems to me, is all but lost. Perhaps defeat isn't yet inevitable, but to the extent that we're entirely at the mercy of an inexplicable strategy, the path can have only one destination. We've set ourselves against the World, and no one can do that. So, whatever your motives in this matter, they can't result in any harm to my country, because it will have paid the price before the Allies can use any of what you've offered them. I can threaten no sanction, because I have no hope for its purpose. All I have, Herr Generalmajor, is a demand.

'There are two files. One is a copy of this...' Fischer pushed the folder across the table, 'which is my rather damning report on the quality of security here. It's been sent to Berlin already and, I assume, is being pored over by those members of the Gestapo whom the Reichsführer has put on to *Case Peenemünde*. The other file contains my thoughts as expressed to you, today. *That* file will

415

be buried deeply and expertly, leaving – for you –
the problem of Rajmund Ulatowski, should he
ever re-surface and decide to become an orator.
With regard to that possibility, you may come to
consider my *demand* as more of a helping hand.

'It seems to me that you have, in fact, *two* problems, and they're both named Ulatowski. I think
you may have decided already to relieve yourself
of one of them. But I request – I insist – that you
don't. Zofia Ulatowski will leave here, very soon,
and we'll both ensure that she does so safely. I've
arranged with someone – from whose own disappearance you'll also benefit – that she be
removed from harm. This will, of course, earn
you a debt of gratitude from your *other* problem,
should he ever hear of it. More importantly, it
will implicate me fatally in your schemes, making
my future discretion a matter of certainty.'

Dornberger smiled. 'Her charms are very
evident, aren't they? But I hadn't thought you
susceptible.'

'She reminds me very much of someone. If I
may ask, how did you persuade her into those
pathetic attempts at espionage?'

'I didn't, of course. I persuaded a troublesome,
homesick Frenchwoman to do it on my behalf.
Still, you do me another injustice, Fischer. As you
say, Zofia was a part of this fiction, and needed to
be seen to be acting to form. But if I wished to do
her harm, I should merely advertise her liaison
with an *unnamed* German, a member of staff. I'd
be acting correctly and excising that particular
problem very effectively – *legally*, as it were. I find
that I'm squeamish, though, and I don't believe

Klaus can take more grief at present.'

They looked at each other across the desk, circling without moving, and it occurred to Fischer that what he had done here was hardly going to constitute an interruption. A man whose stratagem had been exposed like this should be angry, or worried, or considering the means to repair the damage. But he saw none of that. Dornberger coughed, scratched his nose and broke the gaze. His attention was starting to wander, perhaps back to his many other pre-occupations: the eternal bureaucracy, the over-full diary and the myriad inconveniences attendant upon constructing the means to flatten distant cities. To his would-be nemesis, he displayed no more angst than that of a man who'd been obliged to tip over his king, just as the lunch-gong sounded. Fischer recognized, suddenly, what it had been, what it had all been. *A very civilized play, with no principle at stake to make it brutal, or costly.*

He cleared his throat. 'May I hope then that our business is concluded, Herr Generalmajor?'

Chapter Fifty-Seven

He watched until the boat was lost, where the grey sky and greyer sea blended to a single memory. The uppermost slopes of Rügen's Mönchgut Hills were just visible above the haze. The island's vast holiday resorts had been abandoned, half-built, at the start of the war, but there was plenty of need there still for reliable, cheap domestic staff. Her papers were robust, the hotel a small, old establishment, and the inland town of Potbus was rarely visited by any who didn't hail from those parts. A good place to wait it out.

He had half-hoped for a sign of recognition at last, perhaps the moment before she stepped from the pier: time enough for surprise but not enough to measure *then* against *now*. But there was nothing. All he saw was resentment, almost viciousness, as she snatched at the boy's hand to steady herself. She gave him no backward glance, no farewell, no thanks or any other acknowledgement that great risks had been taken on her behalf. Fair enough. He'd offered her a chance of life, without the one thing that might make it worthwhile.

As the boat pulled away, Mazur had thrown a small bag to him, which he left on a bench at the pier's landward end. It was a nice gesture, but his damaged lung couldn't handle such a quantity of cigarettes, even if he hadn't decided to end his dependency. Still, he felt obliged to give credit where it was due, that young man could have laid his hands on contraband in Purgatory. They'd be a nice surprise for someone, if the rain held off.

Thank you for visiting fair Usedom. Come back to us when you can!

The sign – splashy, oblique red lettering on a white background – must have gone up after they gentrified the place. Yearnings for the old Koserow were only experienced from the decks of sinking trawlers, or prison. The place had changed greatly,

418

even more so than Fischer had imagined when he passed through, ten days earlier. Where there had been only clutches of rude fishermen's cottages and salting huts there was now a broad promenade, substantial red-roofed residences, a crop of misnamed *amusements* and no holidaymakers to enjoy them on a warm, early September day. A marvellous setting for regrets, for someone braced to reap a crop of them.

And yet they remained strangely elusive, and he wondered why. Nothing had changed. There was no prospect of the boat turning and returning her to him, of her at least putting a hand to his face, and smiling. There was no likelihood that the ominous news from every Front might shade into something upon which a future might be built: no sustenance that the rational mind could settle upon in the present, eviscerated age. And what of Otto Fischer himself? He saw a man without ties of affection or belonging, without a history worth recalling: half a good face, not much of one shoulder or arm, considerable pain when the weather varied too much either way, and a small hope, too fragile to speak of, that this was now the worst of it: that what was to come – the reckoning – would take no more than he yet deserved. *I wonder*, he asked himself, *whether that must be called optimism?*

For a while he was content to take in the promenade. Locals passed by, singly or in pairs, dressed as well as their ration cards allowed. A few glanced fearfully at his wounds, but more of them nodded courteously. One man, ramrod-straight despite the weight of his years, lifted his hat from across the road and bowed slightly: old Germany, hobbling on, not quite dead, not quite sure how things had turned out the way they had.

Impulsively, Fischer decided to dine here, if a restaurant survived. He would take his time, perhaps have a glass or two of wine, and then try to find his father's birthplace, or at least what *it* had become. The train to Berlin didn't leave from Swinemünde until that evening; there was time for a little indolence, at least.

'Excuse me, sir. Have you heard?'

He hadn't noticed the old gentleman cross the road.

'I'm sorry, what?'

'The Allies landed in Italy this morning. We shall be fighting on our own, I think.'

So the grand alliance of nations would soon comprise Germany, Finland, Romania, Hungary and Bulgaria – and faraway Japan, already entirely preoccupied in her existential struggle. And all that faced them was about seven hundred vengeful millions, drawing upon three quarters of the world's resources and all of its now-secured oceanic highways. A fair match, almost.

'I'm afraid the Italians haven't the heart for it, this time.'

The old man nodded, content to acknowledge a very obvious truth. 'And yet they fought so well in the last war. Why is that, do you think?'

'They had causes – their land, freedom and family. All they have now is a buffoon.'

They looked at each other, knowing what could be said, knowing that it wasn't going to be. Even so, the soldier in Fischer felt obliged to offer some reassurance to the Home Front.

'Well, Italy's hard fighting country, so we're not beaten yet. I wonder, might there be a restaurant in this village, sir?'

The old man shook his head. 'The war ... there's a hotel, the *Villa Belvedere*. They serve luncheon on some days, perhaps today. Austrian cuisine, of course.'

Fischer smiled at the little joke, took directions and thanked him. The hat lifted once more.

The hotel had a free table, of course. Few locals would squander their ration allowance on a midweek outing, and the place probably hadn't seen a tourist in months. The proprietor's wife could hardly take her eyes from his face, but she was friendly enough. He was even offered a window seat in the small dining room, a reminder to passing citizens that *Villa Belvedere* was proud of Their Boys.

Lunch was dreadful: as emphatic a riposte to the logic of conquest as might be imagined (he doubted that the inmates at Trassenheide fared worse). His suffering was mitigated slightly by the obvious shame of his hostess, who apologized when she set down the main course (a near-rancid pig's kidney stew). And against all reason and regulations they had wine still: for reichsmarks, she produced an *ahrweiler* that went far to flushing the aftertaste of unjustly butchered pork from his palate. The glass or two he promised himself became three; it might have been the entire bottle, but he caught the slight look of pleading in her eyes – for the last of their cellar, probably. He left just enough for them to toast the return of trade.

Afterwards he wandered through the village for almost half-an-hour before accepting defeat. He couldn't begin to guess at where his father's house had stood. The street plan had expanded dramatically in the previous four decades, and he suspected that the old layout had been rationalized in the process. The old church aside, little remained of the former Koserow. Time, tides and civic ambition had made it as pleasantly forgettable as any one of the smaller resorts that marched up Usedom's northern coastline: a perfect place for an assignation, rest-cure or getaway; without character or a past that it was inclined to acknowledge to more than itself. Silently, Fischer said goodbye, graciously admitting his error, and went to the railway station to catch an earlier train to Swinemünde.

At the ticket office he showed his warrant and was waved through to the eastbound platform. A total of nine people waited there, reading newspapers or staring blankly into the near-distance, irritably bearing the inconvenience of a timetable that had been a work of fiction since about 1939. The contrast between this and his experience of the transit points at the marches of the shrinking Reich was profound. There, a form of semi-organized frenzy had become the norm: mass civilian displacements gave elbow room for yet another shot at a grand strategy; war materiel and hastily-redeployed personnel flooded in to feed it; and passing by all of this, trying not to bother anyone, the sealed trains about which no one asked questions: the romance of the railways, as Fischer's Germany had refashioned it. But not here, not yet at least: here, it was still possible to convince oneself of the endurance of commonplace things, of things whose fragility he had seen proven all across a ravaged continent.

A young woman held the hand of a boy, an infant, about three years old. She sat on the platform's only bench, and Fischer placed himself carefully at its far end. The boy glanced up at him and did a comically adult double take. He turned and tugged urgently at the woman's sleeve, but she kept her face in her book and pulled him slightly closer. Finding no support at headquarters, he placed a snotty finger in his mouth and stared at the apparition, which stared back and occasionally grimaced, to make what was already remarkable even more so. Inevitably, the child began to giggle, and this continued, unwavering, until his mother and the other travellers turned to see what could be so amusing. By then, Fischer was laughing also, sharing an unexpected delight in something that life had not yet taught to fear, or despise, or turn away from in disgust. And soon, almost everyone on the platform was trying not to laugh with them.

Author's Note

This is a work of fiction, but many members of its cast were as tangible as Peenemünde itself. I have attempted to write actual persons 'in character' insofar as is possible, but I take all responsibility for errors, anachronisms and misinterpretations.

The leading protagonist, Otto Fischer, is entirely a product of my imagination, as are Friedrich Holleman, Kaspar Nagel, the named junior staff of Peenemünde East and all other named Trassenheide and Luftwaffe Berlin characters – including, regrettably, Douglas von Bader. No liaison and training office of the *Kriegsberichter der Luftwaffe* existed in Berlin or elsewhere, though field units were attached to each Luftflotte and individual Flieger divisions.

In contrast, the named hierarchy and technical staff of Peenemünde East – Dornberger, von Braun, Thiel, Schilling, Rudolph, Schubert, Stahlnecht, Steinhoff, Kurtzweg and the superabundance of Riedels – will be very familiar to students of the prehistory of space flight. Furthermore, the major events described – the British air raids of 18 and 23 August 1943, the interminable debates on A4 production quotas, the post-raid handover of production to the SS under Brigadeführer Kammler and its eventual relocation to the infamous

Mittelwerk facility in Thuringia, the Zanssen-Stegmaier affair, Klaus Riedel's communist past and the tentative, clandestine attempts by senior staff at Peenemünde to interest the Allies in their work – are all a matter of record, though for dramatic purposes I have brought forward the genesis of the latter by a full year. The initial, verifiable initiative (of both Dornberger and von Braun, via the German Embassy at Lisbon) occurred only in the latter part of 1944. However, I do not believe that my acceleration of their 'treachery' exaggerates their determination that the work of Peenemünde's engineers should survive the regime.

Walter Thiel died with his family during the raid of 17/18 August 1943, when the air raid trench in which they were sheltering collapsed. The subsequent shooting of his corpse is entirely my fiction, and on that point Generalmajor Dornberger's reputation stands entirely unsullied. Finally, there was in fact an inmates' band at Trassenheide camp, though liberties may have been taken with regard to its repertoire.

Klaus Riedel did not, to my knowledge, ever resist or even know of efforts to put out feelers to the Allies. However, he died in mysterious circumstances a year after the events portrayed here: precisely at the time those initial approaches were being made. His body was discovered in the wreckage of his car, close to the Peenumünde site; investigators found no obvious cause for the crash. Had he lived, there is no reason to suppose that he would not have joined those of his colleagues who were recruited into – some might say inaugurated – the embryonic US rocketry programme.

My premise in relocating to 1943 the future actions of Peenemünde's principals gains some credibility from a further episode. Both Riedel and Werhner von Braun were arrested by *Sicherheitsdienst* in March 1944 and held for almost two weeks in solitary confinement at Stettin. Surreally, the aristocratic von Braun was accused, like Riedel, of communist sympathies. He was told, furthermore, that informed witnesses had testified that he was wholly committed to the realization of space flight, rather than to Peenemünde's weapons programme: a rare occasion of Himmler's febrile imagination blundering into the – or *a* – truth. Von Braun and Riedel were released following Dornberger's frantic manoeuvrings via contacts in Abwehr and Reichsminister Albert Speer's representations to Adolf Hitler.

The publishers hope that this book has given you enjoyable reading. Large Print Books are especially designed to be as easy to see and hold as possible. If you wish a complete list of our books please ask at your local library or write directly to:

Magna Large Print Books
Magna House, Long Preston,
Skipton, North Yorkshire.
BD23 4ND

This Large Print Book for the partially sighted, who cannot read normal print, is published under the auspices of

THE ULVERSCROFT FOUNDATION